London 2012 'What If ?'

A ROMANTIC THRILLER

IAN C.P. IRVINE

ISBN: 1478287241
ISBN-13: 978-1478287247

DEDICATION

To my Wife and Children.

OTHER BOOKS BY IAN C.P. IRVINE

The Crown of Thorns

The Orlando File

'Marrying Slovakia'

PROLOGUE

We live. We die. With something in between that we call life. Sometimes funny, sometimes sad, a lot that's painful, but mostly, overall, wonderful. Quite wonderful.

We enter into life through a tunnel, and we leave with a simple closing of the eyes and an exhaling of our breath.

And then it is gone.

From nothing, back to nothing. And the bit in between is nothing more than memories, which are quickly lost by people who no longer have the power to remember.

Life.

Your life and mine.

Just a whisper on the wind…

PART ONE

CHAPTER 1

Monday morning
Surbiton, England

It's not that I hate my own life. Far from it. My 'life', as you may call it, is good. It's just that nowadays, I look around at other people and wonder if, out of all of the thousands of different types of lives that I could be living, am I living the right one? After all, we only have one crack at getting it right. Life, as my father used to say, isn't a practice run. This is it.

So what if I have got it wrong?

What, if instead of a Product Manager in a telecommunications firm, I should have been an Olympic athlete, an artist, a policeman, a plumber, or a musician?

So now, as I stand on the platform, waiting for the 8.12am train into London, I watch my fellow commuters jostling with each other, positioning themselves to be closest to the doors when the train comes to a stop, and wonder what they all do?

A man nudges me from behind, deliberately or accidentally, it's hard to tell. I turn slightly, casting an angry look in his direction, at the same time taking advantage of the knock forward and automatically moving closer to the edge of the platform. My neighbour looks up from reading the morning's headlines, but registering the annoyance in my eyes, he pretends not to notice that I have moved a few inches in front of him.

I wonder what he does? Perhaps he's a banker. Maybe in insurance? Hiding from my questioning look, he lifts up his paper in front of his face. The Financial Times. Probably a stockbroker. His watch catches the morning sun and glistens momentarily, a flash of expensive gold. A Rolex.

Or is it a fake? Like myself.

I look around me along Platform 1. A hundred men and women, and a few in between. Young, old, a few almost dead, some already dead for years.

A lady further down the platform catches my gaze. She is staring at me. Watching me. Observing me patiently. Her eyes meet mine before she looks away, but for a fleeting moment, it is as if she can see inside my soul.

A moment later, a door opens from the nearby waiting room, and a young woman steps out with a steaming cup of some exotic coffee which has just cost her almost an hour's wage. I wonder what she does? Marketing? PR?

I turn away, not wanting her to notice me.

Just then, an ever so polite but rather surprised voice booms across the loudspeaker, proudly announcing the 'punctual' arrival of a train. Seconds later, the train rolls into the station, and the mad rush begins. The doors open, and for a few moments there is the usual mock attempt at politeness, but then, as if in response to some invisible signal, suddenly everyone scrambles forward, and it's every man for himself and survival of the fittest. A hundred people mentally chanting the mantra of the daily commuter: 'Oh please, God, please let me get a seat today.'

Within seconds it's all over, and for a change today I am one of the winners: a seat by the window.

Resting my head against the glass, and closing my eyes, I try to block out the world and catch fifteen minutes sleep, but just as I'm about to drift off, the smell of fresh coffee assails my nostrils and I open my eyes. Opposite me, another winner - it's the woman with the expensive coffee import.

I smile at her. She smiles back then turns away from me and starts reading a book. I look at the title: 'Fifty Shades of Grey' by E.L. James. I recognise the name. It's the book all the women have been talking about in the office.

My attention now turns to the man beside her. A short haircut, brown corduroy jacket, miniscule earphones stuck deep into his ears, a flashy MP3 player clipped onto the lapel of his jacket and reading his book, 'Perfect People' by Peter James. He's probably something in IT. Beside me an older man with a balding head and a pinstripe suit elbows me gently in the side as he turns the page of another Financial Times. Definitely a stockbroker.

I turn to the window and look out at the sloping embankment, covered in the rejects and debris of suburban life tossed over the walls at the bottom of the gardens which border onto the railway lines.

So many houses. So many lives.

I wonder what they all do?

The stockbroker beside me jabs me in the ribs again, and my attention turns back to myself and I ask myself the same old question that I've asked myself a million times before: at the end of university, instead of doing the 'sensible' thing, what if I had done what I really wanted to do? What if I had ignored the advice of my parents, and what if I had sent that speculative letter to all the big London advertising firms, all those years ago. What if one of them had replied? And what if one had said yes?

But with a degree in Physics, no experience in the arts, and several offers from companies in the rapidly expanding IT industry, I took the easier, well paid option and joined an American software company in London. A steady income. A good job. The easy life.

But is it the right life?

Someone coughs, and my mind jumps back to last Friday night, and my dinner with Jane. I remember the light catching her eyes from the candle on the table in the restaurant, the touch of her fingers on my face and the taste of her lips when I kissed her against the car, and I fantasise about sleeping with her for the hundredth time.

And then I think about Sarah, my wife, and feel guilty.

CHAPTER 2
Sarah

I feel a tightness in my stomach when I think of her, and I look upwards, following the trail of a plane in the sky. The sight of the plane reminds me of the last time we flew on holiday together, and it makes me feel worse.

None of this is my wife's fault. She doesn't deserve it. She's a kind and considerate, wonderful mother, and a good partner. And she loves me, no doubt there, so in theory, our marriage should be great too. No, Sarah certainly doesn't give me any grounds to complain or be unhappy.

So, if there is a problem, then the fault must lie with me...?

I don't know why, but when we make love nowadays, I feel as if it's somebody else's body that's going through the motions, not mine. I feel detached. Mechanical. I don't feel the same old sparkle, the same lust or the excitement that I used to. And I can't help but wonder, should there not be more to it?

We've been together a long time. We got the ring, the house and the car almost eleven years ago, and statistically that's a long time for any marriage to last. I met her one lunchtime in a queue for sandwiches at the shop around the corner from work. She dropped her tuna-and-sweetcorn on the floor and I picked it up for her. We got talking, and she walked me back to my office, followed me up in the lift, and then just as I was beginning to get scared she was a stalker, she announced that she worked for the same company as me, in the department down the hall. After that I saw her every day, and a week later she asked me out. I couldn't believe my luck.

So we went out that Friday, and after a couple of pints of beer I kissed her for the first time. All my hormones were telling me that it seemed like the right thing to do , and I can remember the rest of my body seemed to agree.

After that I took the lead, and a few nights later we ended up in bed. By then I was hooked, and soon we were in love, and even sooner married. And life became good. Then, a few years later, good became wonderful with the arrival of my first baby girl. Beautiful, perfect, Keira.

But for the past few years I can't help thinking, shouldn't it be better? Where has all the excitement gone?

"*Thanks for travelling with South West Trains. We'll shortly be arriving at London Waterloo. Please remember to take all your belongings with you.*"

I wait for everyone else to get off the train, and give a couple of minutes for the crowds on the platform to thin out, before making my way into the Marks and Sparks on the main concourse of Waterloo station, where I grab an egg-mayonnaise and a tuna-and-sweetcorn sandwich. Old habits die hard.

I walk down the broken stationary escalator, one of man's best inventions, perfected by the London Underground, and fight my way through the barriers heralding the entrance to the Jubilee Line.

I get down onto the platform just as a train shoots out of the large wormhole on my left and stops behind the wall of glass protective panels and electronic safety doors that run along the edge of the platform.

The doors open, and within seconds most of us are inside. The train fills up.

I'm an old hand at riding the Jubilee Line, and I know that enough people will get off at the next station to let me sit down, and I will be able to enjoy a few minutes of reading before I have to get off at my stop further down the line at Canary Wharf. Southwark arrives and as predicted I find a seat and pull out my book, quickly losing myself in its pages.

About ten minutes and several stations later, the train begins to slow and a little alarm bell rings in my head. My subconscious, busy counting the stations as we pass them by, interrupts my reading and instructs me to get off here. This is Canary Wharf.

I emerge from the escalator into a world of sunshine, and towering, powerful skyscrapers and office blocks. In spite of the Euro crisis money is everywhere. You can see it in the arrogant, bold designs of the new buildings, the designer clothes of the people streaming into the banks, investment houses and high-tech companies all around, and in the flashy restaurants lurking at the base of the buildings, just waiting to skim their slice from the rich people who stream pass them in the evening, ready to relax and show off their wealth.

Still, I can't help but look up and admire it all. Five years of working at Canary Wharf hasn't taken away my initial reaction the very first day I stepped out of the tube and into this world, in new suit and tie, hoping to pass the job interview.

"Excuse me, sir, would you like...?" A voice interrupts my thoughts.

I shake my head, and walk swiftly past the woman in front of me, ignoring the free glossy publication full of advertisements and job vacancies that she offers me every day as soon as I step from the protection of the tube station.

At first I found it annoying, and wanted to scream 'Just leave me alone…' , but now I can't help but admire her stamina. For as long as I can remember she's been there every day, come sun, rain, or snow, always enthusiastic, smiling and polite, always determined, always hoping that people will take her wares. She must earn a pittance. And yet, she's got more loyalty and dedication to her pathetic little job than I've seen in most of the people I work with.

My office is on the tenth floor of the Russell-Hynes Building, one of the newest and most flashy buildings to be built on the wharf.

Thirty floors, all glass, silver and shiny, built within six months, and completed a month ahead of schedule, with views from my floor across the city that are just fantastic. On a good day, you can see as far as the London Eye, maybe even a little further. Which is all rather academic to me anyway, since my office doesn't have any windows and is in the middle of the building, near to the lifts and facing inwards towards the corridors and the ever busy, unisex toilets.

"Morning James," the receptionist smiles, greeting me as I step out of the lifts and walk through reception. I walk around the open-plan telesales department and almost bump into a large, man-size, furry cat, who suddenly steps out from behind one of the concrete pillars in the centre of the room, a shoulder bag full of Kitte-Kat promotional leaflets draped around its neck.

Another one of the latest marketing ideas. Pay a starving refugee from West Africa a few pounds a day to walk around Canary Wharf dressed as a big, furry, tomcat, and hand out leaflets to all the rich bankers advertising Kitte-Kat's latest high speed, low cost, special offers: "*Get 50Mb Fibre-Optic Broadband Access for the price of 8Mb. It'll make you purr with satisfaction. Meow!*"

No comment.

I stop by the coffee machine on the other side of the sales floor, nodding hello to my boss as I walk past his room on the way over to my office. Closing the door behind me, I settle down behind my computer, and sip away at my coffee as my PC takes four full minutes to boot up and log onto the network.

Opening up Outlook I find 112 new emails since Friday night, most of which are trying to convince me that my manhood is too short and that I should consider a penile extension. Spam. Which probably means our firewall crashed again over the weekend.

I delete all but six of them. The first two are from the marketing department. A few new crazy promotional ideas they want to tell us about. I read them in some disbelief, then delete them. Are these people for real?

Two of the other emails are from customers who have somehow got hold of my address and have emailed to inform me that their broadband connection only gives them 95% of the download speed they were promised. Have they got nothing better to complain about? I forward them to the support department who I know will just delete them without responding.

Saved until the end, the last two to get my attention are from Jane and Sarah. They sit right beside each other on the screen, one against the other.

I pick up my coffee again, and take a few slow drinks as I open up the email from my wife first.

"*Hi James,*

Have a great day at work today, and I'm looking forward to seeing you tonight. Going to take the kids swimming after school, but should be home about 7pm. Will you be back home in time for dinner, or are you working late again?

Sarah."

I open up the one from Jane next, a pang of guilt hitting me even before I read the first words, immediately followed by a rush of excitement and childish nervousness.

"*Hi James,*

Thanks for Friday night. It was great. Loved the meal. Loved the kiss afterwards. Maybe we can do it again sometime soon. Like tonight... What are you doing after work? Do you want to meet for a quick drink in town? Or, if you want, Mike's gone away for a few days, and you could come round here?

Jane.

P.S. No promises. If you come round here...we'll just see how it goes. Slowly does it. "

I lean forward in my seat and read both emails again, resting my elbows on the edge of the table, holding the coffee cup in both hands and biting the edge of it with my teeth. My heart is beating fast.

What the hell am I doing?

Both emails sit on the screen, side by side, screaming at me to reply to them.

I hit the reply button on the one on the right.

"*Sorry. I have a deadline to meet tonight and probably won't be able to get away from here till late. Have a great day. Speak later.*

James."

The one on the left is now alone on the screen. It demands attention. I know that I have to turn her down. I know that I have to end this madness now. To say no. Once and for all.

Slowly, I type my reply.

"I should finish early tonight. A drink sounds like a good idea. I'll be round at yours at seven.
James."

I stop for a moment. This is crazy.

Then I think of the kiss against the car, and I hit the 'send' button.

CHAPTER 3
Tuesday
Surbiton, 8.11 am

I didn't set out to have an affair. And I'm not even sure if I want to have one now. All I know is that what I am doing is wrong, and I should stop. But I can't. No matter how much I reason with myself, like the proverbial moth I can't stop myself being irresistibly drawn towards the flame.

As it turned out, I didn't see Jane last night, but that was only because Sarah had called again yesterday afternoon and announced that Nicole had fallen over and broken her tooth. If she hadn't, I know I would have gone round to Jane's last night, and we would almost definitely have ended up sleeping together.

So, perhaps it was a blessing in disguise that Sarah called and I had to go home early to take Nicole to the dentist. Luckily Jane understood and we rescheduled for Wednesday night.

As I shuffle now on to the 8.12 am train, I reach into my pocket for the nth time to check if I've got any new messages on my mobile from Jane. Nothing yet. Although I'm not really expecting anything. Just hoping…

The woman with the expensive coffee is sitting in the same carriage again, this time about three seats away. I look up and she smiles at me between all the newspapers and people trying to sleep for a few minutes. I half-smile back and look out of the window.

Am I heading towards a midlife crisis? Am I *already having* a midlife crisis?

I try to think again exactly why I spend most of my time fantasising about making love to Jane, when there's nothing wrong with my marriage.

I hate myself for the way I am behaving. And when I look at myself in the mirror or when I listen to the way I am thinking, I hardly recognise myself anymore.

As I stare out of the window at the world outside, I try to rationalise my behaviour. To find a reason, or at least an excuse, for my lying, my deceit, my self-destruction.

Perhaps it's got something to do with personal insecurity and lack of confidence. Now I'm edging towards the end of my thirties, perhaps this is all just about proving to myself one last time, that women still find me attractive? Proving to myself that I'm not yet past it.

But it's not just that. This whole preoccupation with other people, what they do, their lives? This whole fascination about the grass being greener somewhere else? Is it normal?

A thought hits me. It's something that one of my friends said to me over a drink in the pub the other day. Something that stuck in my mind. We were talking about our jobs, and whether we all enjoyed them or not, or whether we just worked for the money because we had to.

Okay, so it was probably me that started the conversation, but George had said, *'If you were to die tomorrow, would you be happy knowing that you had spent the last day of your life doing just what you did today?*'

Probably not. But the truth is, I just don't know. How can I know if another job or another life would be better than the one I have now if I haven't got anything else to compare it with? For all I know, the life I lead now is the best it gets.

The things I wanted to do when I was a kid are probably all just ridiculous ideas that would never have got me where I am today: a wife, two kids, and a house practically all paid off.

"*This is the conductor speaking. We'll shortly be arriving at Waterloo. Would all passengers please keep security risks to a minimum by ensuring they take all their possessions with them.*"

I grab my bag from the rack above and follow the others off the train.

The phone in my pocket rattles against my legs, and I dimly hear the muffled beep-beep of a message arriving.

It's Jane.

"*Hi James. Looking forward to Wednesday. Bring a bottle of white. I'll fix dinner... Then maybe you can fix me...*"

I smile. Then I think of Sarah. What will I tell her about Wednesday? Working late again to catch up for Monday? At least that sounds plausible.

I met Jane at school. I fancied her like crazy all the way through Secondary, and right through sixth-form. But when we left for university, we lost track of each other.

The closest I ever got to having anything with her before was a quick snog under the mistletoe at the Christmas school dance when I was sixteen. I can still remember it. 'Sultans of Swing' by Dire Straits playing in the background whilst we gyrated slowly against each other, round and around, our tongues probing grotesquely into each other's mouths, and my hand doing its best to make its way slowly down to her bottom without her noticing it.

Five minutes and forty-eight seconds of pure bliss. Then the lights went up and we all went home.

I spent the whole of the following year looking forward to the next Christmas party. And then she turned up with some guy from the local sixth form, and that was it.

When I finally looked her up on Facebook - after spending the past two years wondering just what it would be like to kiss her again - I half hoped that she would be fat, with five kids and spots. And then that would be that.

Unfortunately, the photos of her on Facebook were of someone slim and still very attractive. And when she replied to my first email, I soon found out that she also had no kids, and was in a very unhappy marriage. And yes, it would be great to meet up again someday. Why not soon?

That's when the excitement started again, and for the first time in two years I started to feel alive.

I actually feel nervous whenever I think of meeting her. It's the same feeling I had when I used to date Sarah, but that's all such a long time ago now.

And I can't deny it isn't nice to feel this way again. In fact it's great.

The anticipation. The wondering. The fantasising. That bit's fantastic.

The only downside is the guilt, the danger of being caught, and the knowledge that it's all wrong. After all, I have a great wife, and I'm meant to be happy.

So, just what, exactly, am I doing?

I feed my travelcard through the barrier at the end of the platform, walk through the gate, heading straight towards the underground and forgetting completely to go into M&S and pick up some sandwiches. I wander down the stationary escalator, still not fixed from yesterday and without much conscious thought, follow the crowds blindly through the ticket barriers, down two more escalators and onto the platform for the Jubilee Line.

The first train to arrive is full and I decide to wait for the next one. When it arrives, the carriages are much emptier and I get a seat straightaway, pulling out my latest book and quickly disappearing into its pages, starting off from where I left the story on the journey home last night. I've been enjoying the story, a recent Wilbur Smith, and soon I'm on a ship sailing down the east coast of Africa, a nobleman from England making his fortune overseas. Devouring the pages one by one, I can almost feel the movement of the ship beneath my feet, hear the creak of the timbers as they move with the swell of the sea, smell the salt in the air, and see the seagulls circling the ship high above.

I look up, realising I have not been paying attention and have lost track of time. The train is just pulling into a station. I quickly look at the colour of the tiles on the platform walls. Blue tiles. No, not my station.

A cannon fires, and an explosion sweeps me off my feet. Screams are all around. The ship heaves heavily to one side, and swings around to face the oncoming Arab vessel. It's coming straight for us. We're going to collide.

An automated voice booms out. "New Cross Gate North. Change here for the East London line."

I look up briefly, tearing myself away from the oncoming ship. No, it's not Canary Wharf. I return to the smoke and the smell of cordite, the screaming all around me, and pick myself up off the deck, pulling my sword free from my belt and preparing to engage in battle with any boarders.

I look up again, something pulling me back from the battle.

New Cross Gate North?

I look out onto the platform. I don't recognise it. Green tiles, new and modern, but not a station I recognise. The doors are closing, the train is accelerating away.

I look around me. A few people have got on the train and are sitting down. The rest of the carriage is now mostly empty.

New Cross Gate North? Shit. I'm on the wrong train.

I jump to my feet, closing the book and losing my place in the battle. Picking up my small rucksack from the seat beside me I move quickly down the cabin and scrutinise the map of the Jubilee Line above the double doors.

New Cross Gate North…Lewisham North… Lewisham South… Patton Street…then the last station, East Dulwich. Not a single station name that I recognise.

I check the name of the line again.

The Jubilee Line.

My heart starts beating faster, and I feel a little strange.

This is not right.

I look around the carriage. Everyone is looking at their papers, or staring at their feet. They don't see me. Everything just seems normal to them.

I stare at the map again and quickly check the stations going northwards. Alworth Street... Lambeth East. Waterloo.

Waterloo. Thank god.

Then further north, Waterloo… Charing Cross…Green Park… Charing Cross?

Where is Westminster?

I've ridden on the Jubilee Line for years now. I know every station off by heart. Southbound to Canary Wharf:- *Waterloo-Southwark-London Bridge-Bermondsey-Canada Water-Canary Wharf.* Or Northbound: *Waterloo-Westminster-Green Park-Bond Street, then upwards to Stanmore.*

So where the hell is New Cross Gate North and who swapped Westminster for Charing Cross?

I check the name of the line written in grey above the map of the network. Jubilee Line. I check it again. Jubilee Line.

The train pulls into the next station, and as it slows down I search for the name of the station on the walls of the tunnel. Please say Canada Water, or Canary Wharf…

Lewisham North. *Lewisham North? What the hell is going on?*

I jump from the train as soon as the doors open, and walk quickly along the length of the platform searching for a tube map on the walls.

My heart is beating fast now. Very fast. I feel strangely cold, my forehead is clammy, and my hands are beginning to shake. The same shakes I get when I am really hungry and I haven't eaten for ages. The sort of shakes that normally only an immediate dose of chocolate or sugar can cure.

I find a sign on the wall, and drop my bag on the floor beside it. I look at the map before me. I find the grey stripe of the Jubilee Line, and see with dread the names of the stations confirmed in little black letters beside each circle signifying the stations.

New Cross Gate North…Lewisham North… Lewisham South… Patton Street…Last station East Dulwich.

I'm in a dream. I feel lost, disorientated and dissociated from everything around me. I feel the onset of panic, and I break out into a cold sweat. My mind begins to think very slowly.

This doesn't make sense.

The train behind me has left, and I hear another one swooping into the tunnel opposite, heading back in the other direction.

I hurry along to the end of the platform and then cross over onto the northbound platform. The approaching train slows and comes to a stop, the doors part with a rush of air and I jump onboard. I go straight to the map above the next set of doors further down the carriage, and check to make sure I see the word Waterloo.

Waterloo. Fantastic.

As the train moves off I hang from the pole by the door, swaying backwards with the acceleration and looking at the other people around me. Everyone else seems oblivious to my panic. A child at the end of the carriage screams and draws a quick scowl from his large, black mother. The little boy turns away from his mother, and for a few seconds stares straight into my eyes. There are tears in his eyes. I see the quick change in his expression as he looks at me, and suddenly his own confusion is gone. I am now the object of his attention, and he is staring at my face. He alone, amongst all the people on the tube, senses that something is wrong with me.

I look away.

The train pulls into the next station, and I check the name on the blue tiles. *New Cross Gate North.* I'm back at the station I was in a few minutes ago. My eyes look quickly back up at the map, and then return to the sign. I look back at the boy, and he starts to cry, turning quickly to his mother and burying his head in her lap, his face disappearing from view into the folds of her colourful white, red and yellow dress.

New Cross Gate North. According to the strange map the next one will be Alworth Street, then Lambeth East. Then Waterloo.

As the train accelerates into the darkness once again, I feel my knees shaking beneath me. I sit down.

Is this a dream? Have I fallen asleep on my way to Canary Wharf? Am I going to wake up soon? My thoughts are slower now, and I feel as if my mind is beginning to dull over. None of this makes sense. It's all wrong.

I feel lost. And strangely, I begin to feel very alone. Everyone else seems fine, everyone else is going about their business as normal, calmly waiting for the next station to arrive, reading the papers, or talking to a friend. To them everything is normal.

Except it quite clearly isn't.

As the train moves from Alworth Street to Lambeth East I long for Waterloo. I look forward to greeting it like a long lost brother. I can't wait to see it. To jump out of the train onto the platform, for this strangeness, this weirdness all to end. For it to go away.

And then suddenly it is there. Waterloo.

The safety doors, the familiar platform I walk along every single day, the escalators up, then the connecting tunnel to the Northern line on the left, and the escalators to the train station on the right.

I take the moving stairs two at a time, and emerge a minute later, sweating, and out of breath at the ticket barriers at the top of the stairs. I move quickly towards them, reaching automatically into my pocket to pull out my red travelcard holder and to remove the ticket from within the clear plastic sleeve.

As I pull the ticket out and feed it into the barrier, the gates open before me and I move swiftly through. I swoop up the ticket as it pops out from the top of the gate, but dimly register in my slow mind that the travelcard holder is black, not red.

As I step outside onto the pavement outside the entrance to the back of Waterloo station, I stare at the travelcard holder.

Why is it not red?

I stare at the ticket in my hand. It looks different from the travelcard I normally use. I look at the date. It's today's date. The 16th of August 2012. But the photograph on the owner's card inside the other plastic sleeve is wrong. I stare at it. It's me okay… But in the photograph my brown hair is cut differently to normal. Shorter. Spiky. And there are blonde highlights on top.

My heart is beating uncontrollably fast, and I feel sick. I am scared. Very scared.

And then I throw up.

CHAPTER 4
Waterloo 9.21 am

"Are you okay, mate?" the taxi driver asks as he springs from his cab to come to my aid at the edge of the pavement.

I look up at him again briefly, then bend double once more, vomiting for a second time, the contents of my breakfast emptying itself into the gutter, joining the muesli and yoghurt so glamorously already adorning the roadside.

The cab driver puts a friendly hand on my back, and bends over towards me. He hands me a Kleenex from the front of his cab. I wipe the rest of my breakfast from the corners of my mouth and struggle a response.

"Yes." I cough a little. "Yes, thanks, I am."

"Are you sure, mate? You don't look too good to me."

"No, honestly, I'll…I'll be fine. I just had a fright that's all."

I turn away from the sadly rare gesture of human warmth from one person to another and walk back into the station.

As I walk back into the main concourse, I look around me. Everything seems normal. The vomiting has brought back a flood of senses, and the wave of panic that had swept over me seems to have subsided. In its place, as I see the familiar sights around me, I begin to feel more relaxed.

I head into Marks and Spencer's and walk around the shelves. Everything seems as it should. The sights and sounds of any normal Tuesday morning.

I walk out onto the concourse and look up at the arrivals and departures, displayed as usual on the large electronic overhead information system. I see that in five minutes there is a train to Surbiton. I consider it briefly. It's tempting. I stand in the middle of the concourse and look around.

Everything is as it should be.

I walk amongst the passengers and commuters and my calm returns. I must have dreamt it all. It wasn't real.

Breathing deeply, I decide not to go home, but to go on to work. I have had a bad dream. Something went wrong, I woke up on the train in the middle of the dream and for some reason I panicked. That's all.

So I head back towards the Jubilee Line, determined not to be stupid, and to get to work as soon as possible. I look at my watch. I'm late.

As I approach the ticket barrier, I slow down. Logically, I know that it's just all been a dream, but it doesn't stop me worrying that if I go through the barrier and down into the station beneath, the dream will come back.

I walk outside to the taxi rank. I see that the man in the first taxi is the driver who so kindly came to my assistance a few minutes before and I climb into the back of his cab.

"How y'feeling now? Are you okay, pal? You took some turn back then. Best take it easy today," he says, turning round to face me, genuine concern showing on his face.

"I'm okay. Thanks for helping me. It was kind of you. I appreciate it. Really."

"No problem, pal. Just glad to help out. So, where do you want me to take you then?" the man replies in a half cockney, half Scottish accent.

"Canary Wharf please."

"Sure thing. Sit back and rest, mate. I'll get you there as soon as I can."

I sit back in the cab and watch the thankfully very familiar scenes of London life roll by me as the taxi takes me out of Waterloo and through the streets of London. I close my eyes, and try not to think of what has just happened. Soon I begin to snooze, and it is a while before the sound of the cab driver's voice brings me back to reality.

"We're almost there, mate," he says.

I look out of the window, scanning the streets around me for some familiarity. I don't recognise anything.

"I'm sorry, I meant Canary Wharf, on the north side of the river. Are we somewhere around Greenwich?" I ask.

"No. Just like you asked pal, this is it. There is only one Canary Wharf. We're here. There's the Mountbatten Industrial Park over there, and at the end of the road beside the river is the National Asylum Centre. You don't want to go there pal. That's where they had the big riot last week. The buildings are still smouldering from the fire." The driver quips, quickly turning his head towards me as he speaks.

"What do you mean?" I ask, the strange feeling of unreality that I had on the underground beginning to surge within me again. "Where's Canary Wharf? I can't see any of the skyscrapers?"

"What skyscrapers?" the driver asks, turning round quickly to face me again, as he continues to drive. I don't answer him, but sit forward on the edge of my seat, gripping the black leather hard with my fingers. I look all around me, desperately searching for a familiar sight.

The taxi driver pulls over on to the edge of the road, his hazard lights flashing, and waves at the cars behind him to overtake.

"Are you okay, pal. You look sick again. Would you rather I take you to the hospital? There's that new one down on the other side of East India

Wharf? Mind you, it's full of them asylum seekers, but it's the closest one to here."

"East India Wharf," I say, grasping at the familiar name. I know the wharf well. It's a large old warehouse on the edge of the old harbour at the back of Canary Wharf. When Canary Wharf was built it was renovated and now it's full of yuppie restaurants and bars. We often go there for drinks after work on Thursday and Friday nights.

The taxi drives down several roads bordered by some new but run-down houses. A modern housing estate that is already showing the signs of severe neglect and urban decline. People hang around on street corners in gangs watching as we pass by. Families of all different colours and ethnic backgrounds walk along the streets, disappearing into the red-bricked houses, where young kids play in the gardens amidst rubbish and old washing machines.

Turning a corner, I immediately recognise the silhouette of the old wharf building. We are approaching it from behind, and as we come closer we swing around the edge of it and come out onto the cobbled yard in front, beside the harbour's edge.

I open the door of the taxi and step out. I stand with my back to the taxi and the East India wharf building, the water in front of me. I stare at the big empty space where there should be magnificent, towering sparkling pillars of glass and steel. Instead, I look blankly at the vacant sky. The volumes of open air. The mountains of nothingness. And I begin to shake.

I am scared. More scared than I have ever been before.

Canary Wharf, the embodiment of modern Britain, that jewel of contemporary British architecture, that glorious monument to Thatcher's Britain and all that is capitalism and wealth and greed, is nowhere to be seen.

Canary Wharf has vanished.

CHAPTER 5
East India Dock 10.00 am

I stand in silence. Not knowing what to do. For a moment or two the fear washes over me like a wave. I don't know how to stop it, so I let it roll.

What has happened to my world?

Where am I?

What is happening?

My right hand is shaking uncontrollably and I look down at it, strangely detached from my body. I see my left hand reach across and take hold of it firmly, calming it, quietening it. The shaking stops.

The taxi driver's voice again, coming to my rescue for the second time today.

"I think you should get yourself off to a doctor, pal. You don't look well…Are you upset about something? Do you want to tell me about it?" he asks, standing beside me.

"No. " I reply quietly. What should I tell him?

"No. I think I'll be okay. I'm just having a bad day. A really bad day. And on top of that I think I've just lost my job. Or maybe my job just lost me…" I turn and pat him lightly on the shoulder, trying to smile at him as I walk back to the taxi, and climb into the back of the cab.

We sit there for a while. Me not saying anything. The taxi driver giving me some space. I look back out through the open cab door, towards the Thames, and the empty grass covered island where the great tower blocks should be. Where the offices of Kitte-Kat once were. Where I used to work.

The fear slowly begins to subside, being replaced by a weird, calm, acceptance of this altered reality. I feel numb.

"I'm John," the taxi driver says, breaking the silence. "What's your name?"

"I'm James," I answer.

"Well James, I don't want to interfere, but I get the feeling that you are a bit lost? As if things are not what you expected them to be? You look confused..."

"You could say that," I reply.

Sensing that John wants to start asking lots of question I just can't answer, I pull the door closed and turn away from Canary Wharf. "John, can you take me into town?"

As he starts the engine and we move off, I thank him for his concern, and for caring.

"No problem James. I've seen it all, pal. Everything. Mine's an interesting life. I get to see lots. But a man should never lose the will to help others. After all, without our fellow man, we're nothing."

He may have seen a lot in his time, but one thing's for sure. This honest, likeable, decent man has never seen Canary Wharf. Not as I have.

"So, where do you want to go now?" he asks, as we leave the wharf area behind us.

"How about back to Waterloo. I think I'm just going to go home and see my wife."

We drive back through the estate, then skirt around the edge of what can only be described as an enormous internment camp or prison. But big. Very big. With rows and rows of brick houses and several large look-out towers inside it. Smoke is rising from the corner behind one of the walls.

"The National Asylum Centre. They almost destroyed it. Ungrateful bunch. Still, shouldn't be too harsh. 'There but for the grace of God', and all that..." the driver says, feeding me a stream of information and interspersing it with questions about why I'm not feeling well, and why I lost my job.

"New employment laws." He continues, "That's what I blame. Bloody government doesn't know what it's doing. No stability any more. Do you know, my brother-in-law turned up for work the other day, and the company he had worked for the day before was bankrupt. The company had ceased to exist overnight."

If only he knew. I look out of the window. The panic has gone. The fear has subsided, but I know it's just beneath the surface. Waiting to explode. For now though, the fear has been replaced by a feeling of numbness.

The voice of the taxi driver blends into the background, and I stare blankly at the world outside. A world I recognise, but not completely.

I notice now that it's different. But not in a way that is immediately obvious. I have the feeling that all around there are subtle differences, small changes, but even though they are there, I can't point to them straight away.

Something inside my jacket vibrates. I reach inside and pull out a mobile phone. My mobile phone. Only it's a different colour, and the ring tone is one that I would never normally choose. Too flashy by far. And, now I look closer, I notice the design is subtly different to the old one I have. I look at the display to see who is calling.

-*'Richard'*-

Who?

I answer the phone, putting it to my ear.

"James… are you there?" a high-pitched voice screams at me. "Where the fuck are you?"

"Hi. ..*Richard*? I'm in a taxi."

I don't know who Richard is. I don't recognise the voice. I have never spoken to this man before in my life. But before I can think of what more to say, the voice shouts at me again.

"James, listen, I don't know what you are playing at, but if you don't get here in the next 30 minutes, you are fired. Out on the street. Get it? We've worked on this deal for years. It's the biggest one we've ever had, and if you fuck it up, you are history. This is YOUR presentation for Pete's sake. YOUR client. We're all here, waiting for you. You're fifteen minutes late…Where are you?"

I have no clue as to what Richard is talking about. My gut reaction is to switch the phone off, and ignore whoever the hell Richard is.

On the other hand, this man at the other end of the phone seems to know me. In fact, he knows a lot about me, about where I should be, and what I am meant to be doing. Obviously something very wrong has happened to me, and if this man knows me, then perhaps he can tell me *what* is going on.

And then I hear myself saying:-

"Richard. I'm sorry…This morning has been very strange…I'm on the way to hospital just now. I was mugged on the way to work… And I've lost everything. My bag, my notes, everything...," I pause. There is silence on the other end of the phone. Then the voice again, though this time, not so loud.

"Mugged?...Are you *okay*?"

"Yes, but listen. I think I must be a little concussed. I'm having difficulty remembering some things…and I've lost the address where I'm meant to be meeting you. Where are you?" I say, hoping he will fall for my excuse.

"Shit, James. SHIT. This deal is worth ten *million* euros. Ten million euros!..." Silence. "Listen, get over here as fast as you can. I'll stall them. Can you still do the presentation? Bastard, this is a real mess. Listen, I'll text you the address now. Get the taxi driver to bring you here as fast as he can. I'll wait for you outside the building. We'll take it from there. And hurry up. Do the presentation, then you can go to the hospital afterwards if you need to. Get your priorities right man. If you want to die, you can die later. Anyway, if you don't win this deal, we're all dead."

Click. It's nice to have such a caring boss.

A few seconds later my mobile rattles again in my hand, and I open up the text message from Richard. An address in Portman Square. I know the place well. It's behind Selfridges. From where we are now, it'll take about 20 minutes to get there in this light traffic. In fact, the traffic is remarkably light for this time of day. A little strange, but a good thing for me.

I read out the address to the taxi driver and settle back into my seat.

"Is that one of them new 2G phones?" John asks, seemingly genuinely inquisitive.

"What do you mean, new 2G?" I reply. "You can hardly call 2G new. They've been out for years?"

"I mean, there's not many people who have mobile phones yet, so if you've got one, it must be one of them new fangled 2G phones?...You know, them ones with the special radiation proof technology that stops you getting brain tumours every time you call someone and zap your head with zillions of microwaves."

Before I can respond, John changes the subject and starts a running commentary about life, the universe and everything, and I sit back and start to just nod at all the right parts and tune out of the conversation. Eventually he notices I'm not responding and he shuts up.

London rolls past the taxi windows, and I consider calling Sarah. I should call her. I need to talk to her, but what will I say? How can I explain it? I decide not to. I will tell it all to her face-to-face tonight when I get back. I'm confused right now. Whatever is happening to me, or whatever has happened to me, I need to sort out before I go home. Hopefully, Richard, whoever he is, will be able to sort it out for me.

We pass through Trafalgar Square, and drive up to Piccadilly. As the taxi passes the Institute of Directors, I do a double take and turn back in my seat, staring out the back window. Outside the National Gallery at the top of the square a line of cars sit waiting patiently for a light to change; and where former mayor Ken Livingstone so proudly unveiled a new flight of stairs leading up to the front entrance of the gallery, there is still the old, continuous wall, and no new staircase. What has happened to the pedestrian precinct in front of the National Gallery?

And the pigeons. There are thousands of them, flying en masse in bliss around the heads of thousands of tourists who swarm around the feet of Lord Nelson and merrily feed them corn from little plastic punnets.

Somewhere Ken Livingstone must be livid. He hated the bloody pigeons. After waging a long personal battle against them, and finally getting rid of them by completely banning anyone from feeding them, now…well, now they're back!

It's wrong. It shouldn't be like this.

Former Mayor, dear mad, Red Ken, spent millions of taxpayer's money on improvements, but where are they all now? This is the *old* Trafalgar Square.

It is as if the redesign of the Square just never happened...

My mind is now dull, I see the mistakes. I acknowledge them, but I no longer react to them.

At Piccadilly the statue of Eros has been painted gold, and a new marble pavement covers the surrounding area. It looks beautiful. But it looks very different from the Eros I walked past only last weekend when I went shopping in Lilywhites for new trainers. Lilywhites, thankfully, looks just the same as it was last week.

Driving up Regent Street, I notice a few differences here and there. Things that appear different from what I think they should be like, but which blend effortlessly into surroundings which look just as they should.

Am I imagining this?

At Oxford Circus we turn left onto a clear street. No cars. Only buses and taxis. We pass quickly along the street without getting stuck in traffic. Something that is normally impossible to do. But obviously isn't today.

Then I notice a big change: dear old wonderful Selfridges has gone. Oh, the building, that impressive monument to the great British shopper is still there, but outside the front entrance the name 'Macy's' hangs proudly in large, tasteful, elegant golden letters. People stream in and out of the doors, oblivious to their loss, not realising how wrong it is. How can this have happened? Where has Selfridges gone?

Gone like Canary Wharf. Gone like Ken Livingstone's dreams. And perhaps gone like my sanity. I must have gone mad.

I lean forward in my seat and put my head in my hands.

Then the taxi driver's voice, "James. We're here. This is where you wanted me to take you."

I step out of the cab, swinging my little rucksack on to my back, and look at the taxi driver sitting in the front seat. I feel a surge of warmth to this anglicised jock. He's the only friend I have in this strange world, and I feel a reluctance to leave him.

"Thanks. Thanks for your help. I..."

"No problem pal. Don't mention it. Listen..." he leans forward and picks something up. "Why don't you take my card. Just in case you need a lift later on. My number's there."

A hand lands on my shoulder, and I jump with fright. A tall man, smart pinstriped Armani suit, balding, penetrating blue eyes, and a large, oversized stomach, pushes me gently to the side, reaches through the taxi window and looks at the meter. He pulls out a wad of cash, and gives the taxi driver a bundle of notes. Then without further warning he spins me around and points me towards the door of the big building in front of us.

As he speaks I guess this must be Richard. Shocked and still very, very numb, I blindly follow his lead. Behind me the taxi driver honks his horn, and just before I step through the electronic doors which slide open before us, I turn and watch with a sudden feeling of loneliness as the taxi pulls away into traffic.

I clutch the card in my hand, and slide it quickly into the breast pocket of my shirt.

CHAPTER 6

Portman Square. 10.30 am

We climb into the lift, Richard hits the 8th floor button, the doors close and there is silence. Richard looks at me, and I look at him. He goes first.

"You look fine. Are you okay?" and then without waiting for me to reply, "Listen, I've been thinking. This deal is too big for us to fuck up. Perhaps I should do your presentation for you? I've been through it a dozen times, and I know it. The last thing we need is for you to faint or forget something half way through. We can't afford to lose this deal."

Fine by me.

"Richard, I'm sorry. I didn't plan this. Any of it. But, to be honest, I'm still in shock, and the concussion is getting worse. I can't remember everything….."

"Great. Just great…"

The lifts pings, the doors open and we step outside. We've come out into what can only be described as the sumptuous boardroom of some powerful organisation. A large brown mahogany table dominates the middle of the room, about twenty people sitting around the edges, all looking directly at me.

At the far end, a large screen is embedded into the wall, and an overhead projector hanging from the ceiling is already projecting the welcoming slide of 'my' presentation. It reads,

"Cohen Advertising
presents
A new marketing brand for
Scotia Telecom's
Future Mobile Communications
By
James Quinn and Team."

I follow Richard into the room, around the expectant group, to the head of the table. I take a seat, and smile back at everyone. All eyes are on me.

One of them at the far end of the table, silver haired, expensive suit, leans forward with clasped hands on the table, and speaks.

"So, James. What have you got then? You've kept us all waiting. We've waited. Now it's your turn to impress the shit out of us. Tell us, how is Cohen Advertising going to make Scotia Telecom the No. 1. Mobile phone network in Europe?"

Mobile phones again. Does he not know how bad they are for your health?

There's an embarrassing silence. I haven't got a clue what to do. Perhaps this wasn't such a good idea after all. Slowly, very slowly, I bite the bullet and start to rise from my chair.

Then, calmly, and not a moment too soon, Richard rises to his feet beside me and puts his hand on my shoulder, pushing me firmly back into my seat.

"Gentlemen, if I may, I would like to apologise once again for keeping you all waiting. Unfortunately, as you know, James was mugged by a gang of asylum seekers this morning, just as he left Waterloo. Although he has suffered some concussion from the attack, he insisted on coming directly here to present to you personally, instead of going to the hospital, which I'm sure you will all realise is a clear sign of his dedication to this project and the importance of your custom to us, but I think it would be unfair of me to let him carry on the presentation, particularly since he is very dizzy and feeling quite faint. Naturally, I did insist he went straight to the hospital, but he steadfastly refused. So, we've come to a compromise. I'll do the presentation, and James will chip in if needed. So...without, any further delay, let's start."

There are a few loud murmurs around the table, a round of coughing, and the general sound of people settling back in their chairs, waiting and expecting to be impressed.

One person in particular fixes his eyes and every ounce of his concentration on Richard. One person in particular waits with baited breath to see what James Quinn, star of the Cohen Advertising corporation has pulled together for the future of Scotia Telecom.

Me.

I can't wait to hear what I have got to say.

As Richard starts to go through my presentation, it becomes abundantly clear that I really know what I'm talking about. I'm impressed. I'm obviously a very clever guy.

For the next ten minutes, Richard runs through an impressive summation of the mobile communications market place that supposedly exists today, reporting on the demographics, market segmentation, current trends in telephony, an overview of telecomms in today's Europe, the effects of deregulation, and a sizing up of the opportunity for future growth of the mobile industry. Who has the money to spend? How much money do they have to spend per month? What target segments should be pursued first? The teenager? The businessman? The mother at home? How much should they charge for a new phone service? Is this a profitable marketplace to be in? How soon will people start buying into the mobile market?

I sit and listen eagerly. Occasionally Richard looks over, as if verifying with me that he is saying the right things. I nod at all the right moments. But from what I can see, it seems as if Richard is doing a great job. In fact, he's doing a far better job than I would ever be able to do. Which probably isn't saying much, given my rather sudden introduction to all of this.

As I listen to his overview of the market I learn a lot. I learn that mobile phones, after they were introduced in the mid-eighties, were banned from normal public use when the government of the European Union declared that the radiation from mobile phones posed a severe risk to human health. Overnight the fledgling mobile market crashed, and most of the emerging mobile phone operators went out of business, or returned to the drawing board to find ways of making mobile phones safe for use.

It was fifteen years before a new technology was developed that was approved, tested, and granted European regulatory approval, and only now in 2012, is the 2nd wave of mobile phones being launched. Albeit by a smaller group of telecommunications companies, who just managed to cling onto the lifeboat long enough and are only now managing to climb back onboard.

Scotia Telecom, in particular, is one of those companies.

They have aggressive plans to launch the most reliable, feature rich, and price-competitive mobile phone service in Europe. And Cohen Advertising has been chosen to develop the brand and launch the new, revamped service.

"And now, if there are no questions at this point, I would like to tell you what James has come up with for the name of your new brand."

There are no questions from the floor. I have a few, but I decide to keep my mouth shut.

The Chairman of Scotia Telecom, the man with the grey hair and the money, sits forward, leaning with his elbows and clasped hands on the table, and every one follows suit. Everyone is eager to hear what I have come up with. Including me.

Richard clicks the mouse in his hand, and the next slide flashes up on the screen. A big mandarin-orange appears on the screen on a white background. A grey shadow hides beneath the base of the mandarin, adding a touch of three dimensionality to the picture. In the bottom right hand corner, superimposed on the base of the fruit, but clearly visible, is the word "Mandarin".

There is silence around the table. Richard holds his breath. I hold my breath.

I sense that my career in advertising is in the balance (which apparently has been quite good up till now...). The next few moments will determine whether I will succeed or fail. I look around the table at everyone's faces. Hoping. Praying.

No one responds. Everyone looks at the Chairman. And the Chairman looks directly at me. I sense that something is missing. That somehow the presentation has missed the mark.

I look at Richard. He looks at me. I take a second look at the screen. I know I have to say something. I know I have to do something. Time seems to slow down, and my mind goes into overdrive.

And then it hits me.

The world I now find myself is not the same as the one I woke up to this morning. In many ways it's similar, but in others it's completely different.

The mobile phone market being a case in point. In this world, the mobile phone market is only just beginning to take off. From the slides that have been presented it would seem that hardly anyone carries a phone yet, that high street phone retailers like 'The Car Phone Warehouse' and 'The Link' don't exist, and that mobile phone salesmen have not yet become as annoying as estate agents. Somehow, *somehow*, for fifteen years the world has continued to exist and prosper without mobile phone technology.

From the slide before last, it would seem that T-Mobile and O2 are still figments of someone's imagination and like a blast-from-the-past, BT Cellnet is only *now* beginning to become successful in the UK. And just like T-Mobile and O2, the Orange phone network is still waiting to be created.

In fact, unless I am very much mistaken, my presentation, this meeting that is happening just now, is the moment at which the Orange network and brand is meant to be created for the very first time, the difference being that this time around, it won't be created for Orange, but for Scotia Telecom.

I've always thought that the Orange brand was brilliant. It's clever, original, trendy, and it's no coincidence that I have an Orange phone,...or did... (I've no idea what I've got now, although I would guess that it is probably a Scotia Telecom handset.)

The problem is that I don't feel particularly comfortable with stealing other people's ideas. And I know for a fact that I didn't think of the original idea for the Orange brand. Someone, somewhere else thought of it, but that was in another world. And in this world it would appear that whoever it was that came up with the idea hasn't had those thoughts yet. And maybe they never will.

Maybe in this world, the genius who came up with that whole campaign is a train-driver, or an astronaut, or maybe he or she is working in McDonalds? Whatever. On the other hand, in this life, in this world, it might be down to me. Maybe in this life, it's my turn. Maybe it's down to me to create the *Orange* network, and *this* is the moment I am meant to do it!

And yet, I still can't quite bring myself to copy the idea exactly, even though it would appear that I have already gone quite far down the same path of thinking that the original creator of the Orange brand must have done. Even so, as I look at the blank looks on everyone's faces, and as I see the picture of the giant mandarin projected onto the screen, it's blatantly obvious that my thinking so far is a little wide of the mark. I need to do something. I need to come up with something better.

And fast.

I look around the room. Everyone is still looking at me. Waiting. No expression on their faces. I stand up.

Richard looks at me. Pleading. The figure of 'ten million Euros' being telepathically transmitted from his mind to mine. Along with the vision of a P45, a door, and a big boot.

"Gentlemen", I start, "What do you think of my idea. 'The Mandarin Network?'" And then quickly, before anyone can respond, I carry on.

"Well, it's not bad for a start. But not quite good enough. The image of an apple sure did work for the Apple Corporation…" I pause, praying that Apple still existed, then carry on regardless "...and they showed that such abstract thinking really can work in the IT industry. But what we want is something different, something better. When I first thought about 'Mandarin' I thought it was good. It's bright, it's colourful, it's different, but it's not good enough. What Scotia Telecom needs for today's world, for this world, is an image, a brand, something bright, vibrant, instantly recognisable and easily associated with Scotia Telecom, but *different.*"

"Unfortunately the rest of my presentation today was in my briefcase, and when I was mugged this morning the briefcase was stolen. So I can't show you the slides which show how the final branding will look like. So, if I may, I'll describe it to you."

"Imagine a big bold bright circle, the colour of tangerines. Inviting, tasteful, exotic, sophisticated, refreshing. And in the bottom of the circle the word 'Tangerine'.

"And that's it. Scotia Telecom's new network is 'The Tangerine Network'. It's simple, yet very effective. We build a promotional campaign based almost solely on imagery. Imagine people walking around with images of tangerine coloured circles painted on their foreheads, or on the palms of their hands. We see people talking to each other, holding up their hands, the Tangerine symbols painted on their hands. Or we see people walking down the street just talking away into thin air, a tangerine circle shown painted on their forehead..."

"The important part of the whole campaign is that although we are advertising mobile phones and the network they use, we will never ever see a person actually holding, carrying, or speaking into a phone in any one of our adverts. It will all only ever be just implied..."

I go on, creating imagery and pictures and painting the brand in the minds of those sitting around the table. I waffle on, creating the best bullshit I have ever done, and really, even as I listen, I find that I'm impressing myself, let alone anyone else. Where it's all coming from I don't know. All I do know is that it's good. *Very* good. I go off into freestyle, describing newspaper adverts, television and cinema campaigns, posters, and flyers, a whole campaign, an imaginative campaign, a *fantastic* campaign...and then suggest that in order to promote and support the expected demand, Scotia Telecom should build a new network of Tangerine Shops across all of Europe, selling a new range of Tangerine branded mobile phones. And then I invent a couple of strap-lines, like *'Tangerine. Have you picked yours yet?'*

The last part wasn't so good, but I know that it can be worked on. Just so long as they buy the rest of it. I turn to Richard and hand over to him. Richard is expressionless. This has all caught him by surprise. It's not exactly gone according to the script.

I turn to look at the Chairman of Scotia Telecom.

He is studying a long, fat cigar. He pulls out something silver from his pocket and snips off the end of the cigar. The man on the right of him, immediately produces a box of matches, lighting one and handing it to his boss, who slowly turns the cigar in the flame, puffing clouds of blue smoke into the air as he does so. Eventually, satisfied with the even burn of the tobacco, he sits back in his chair and looks at me.

He smiles.

Almost as one, the rest of the people in the room smile too and there is an audible exhaling of breath.

"I like it James. I like it very much. For a while I was a little concerned there, but boy, did you swing it around. I think we can do some business together. I like it. *Tangerine.* ...Hmm. I like it a lot. I think we should drink a toast to the future of Scotia Telecom, and *The Tangerine Network.*"

A door opens at the back of the room and a tray of champagne glasses and several bottles of champagne appear as if from nowhere. Within minutes corks are flying and the tension in the room evaporates. The deal is done.

Scotia Telecom are happy. So is Richard. And from what I can gather, my first presentation as a high flying advertising executive has been a roaring success.

CHAPTER 7
Seven Dials 2 pm

A few bottles later, and Richard isn't fit to drive anywhere, so we call a taxi and leave his car in the garage underneath Scotia Telecom's headquarters.

Now the ten million euro deal is in the bag, and there is the better part of two bottles of champagne in his stomach, Richard couldn't be more concerned about my health if he tried. If I was a cynic, I could be forgiven for thinking that since I'm the man who came up with the 'Tangerine' idea, Richard is just scared that if I were to die from my concussion, then the ten million deal would go with me.

Deciding to reserve judgement on that for now, I bundle an almost incoherent Richard into the taxi, and head off towards Covent Garden.

Now the excitement of the presentation is behind me, I'm back to facing facts. I've got a problem. As the taxi takes us out along Oxford Street towards Tottenham Court Road, and before turning down to Seven Dials in Covent Garden, where, apparently, the Cohen Advertising suite of offices is, I start to wrestle with the reality that now surrounds me.

London is different. At first glance, most things seem to be the same. But on closer inspection, a lot of shops, the buildings, the traffic, the signs, even the way the people dress, a lot of it *is* different. Some of it is a *lot* different, but other things, just *slightly*. It's strange, even though life does *seem* the *same*, overall it's just *not* right.

Suddenly I want desperately to talk to my wife. I pull out my mobile, and ignore Richard who has just leaned back on the leather seats of the taxi, and started to snore very loudly. I dial my home number and put the phone to my ear.

There is no dial tone.

I dial the number again.

Still no dial tone. The number is not recognised.

I dial my wife's mobile.

There is no connection. Number not recognised.

It's then that I realise that the O2 network which Sarah uses was not mentioned on the list of mobile operators that I had shown in my presentation to Scotia Telecom. Which means that I can't call her O2 number, because the O2 network doesn't yet exist.

Shit. How do I contact her?

And why isn't my home number being recognised?

I throw the mobile into my small rucksack shouting "Useless pile of shit" loudly in frustration. I begin to shake again. I've had enough of this dream. I want to wake up.

EAAUUUGGGHHHHH…

A sudden stream of projectile vomit explodes on the floor, covering my trousers, my suit jacket, and most of the taxi. Richard has just thrown up.

The taxi driver turns around, sees the scene and pulls over. Jumping out of the front, he takes about two seconds to open the rear door, grab Richard and drag him out onto the pavement, …just in time for him to vomit for a second time. This time catching the taxi-driver's feet.

The driver shouts something at us both, in some language I have never heard before, but which I guess is probably Eastern European, maybe Albanian. Richard is by now sitting on the pavement, looking up at me with a very childish look on his face, white bubbling champagne oozing out of the corners of his mouth, along with some half-eaten cornflakes.

Eugh.

"You give me 35 euros. You give me now!" the taxi-driver demands from me.

"Sorry, what?…euros…no, sorry, I've only got pounds." I reply, reaching into my pocket and pulling out my wallet. I reach inside and pull out some notes. "Why do you want euros?" I reply, getting a little annoyed, preparing to pay him in the Queen's own money. This is Britain . Bloody taxi-driver should take pounds. But when I look at the notes in my hand, I don't recognise them. They're strange, like foreign money, the wrong colours, the wrong sizes…

As I look up at the taxi-driver, one massive question mark on my face, the Albanian reaches out and snatches all the paper from my clenched fist. He spits on the ground, swears, at least I think he is swearing, and turns and jumps back into his cab, driving off and leaving us to fend for ourselves.

A small crowd has gathered around us, admiring the spectacle of Richard throwing up into his lap and over his own trousers, with me, standing there, covered in puke, trying to work out whether I should laugh, cry, or jump in front of the next car, and simply end it all…

And then a policeman appears, as if from nowhere.

"Hello gentlemen, celebrating a little too much are we?"

I look up at the policeman, almost speechless.

"Can I see your ID cards, please?" he asks me.

The crowd is all around us now, as if we are a couple of buskers about to start juggling or swallowing fire. Which would be a miracle in itself, as right now, I don't think Richard could swallow anything and keep it down for more than a few seconds.

"My ID card?" I ask. What is he talking about?...

Richard throws up again, this time on the feet of the policeman, who, not surprisingly, does not seem very amused.

He bends over Richard to say something to him, and at this point, the pressure just all gets too much: I don't have any idea what is going on; I don't have an ID card; I can't explain anything to myself, let alone a policeman. Fear surges within me. I'm scared, I'm lost, I cannot cope. So...so I do the most logical thing I can think of ...and I leg it. I run away.

I push my way through the crowd that opens up hurriedly before me, and run like the proverbial clappers. I run for two blocks, disappearing down the side streets off Oxford Street, towards Dean Street. People stare at me as I dodge past them , and I realise that not only do I look a sight, but that I smell terrible too.

What am I going to do? I can't go home like this.

I get to the end of the street and stand on the corner, gasping for breath, beside the Prince Edward Theatre, where, to my great relief, 'Mary Poppins' is still playing. A welcome and familiar sight.

I stop to think. I need to change my clothes, but I haven't got any money. I don't carry any credit cards, so I can't just walk into a shop and buy some. I decide to go an ATM and use my switch card to withdraw some money. I find one on the corner beside the Palace Theatre where 'Singin' In The Rain' is still playing, another welcome sight from the London I know. Unfortunately, the green bank card I pull from my wallet, is a different colour from the blue Barclays card I started the day with, and when I insert it in the machine and type in my pin number, the machine keeps it. Shit. What the hell am I meant to do now?

I turn around, and look about me. Suddenly London does not look so friendly. People are staring at me, and I know I must look an odd sight. A sweating business man, covered in puke. And then, just when I think it can't get any worse, I realise that I've left my small rucksack in the cab. With my mobile phone in it. My last contact with those who know me.

What do I do? I have no money, and I desperately need a change of clothes. I can't go home like this.

As I look across the road at All Bar One, another friendly sight, I realise I am very close to Seven Dials in Covent Garden. Which is where the offices of Cohen Advertising are meant to be. *My offices.*

I hurry across the road, past the All Bar One, one of my favourite pubs where I have spent many a happy evening with Sarah, ...and a few with Jane.

I cut through the cars waiting at the traffic lights, ignoring the disgusted stares of some of the drivers, and scuttle off down towards the Seven Dials roundabout before turning into Monmouth Street.

Cohen Advertising should be around here somewhere. I had briefly seen the address of the office on the front of one of the packs given out at the Scotia Telecom presentation, and I'm angry now that I didn't take better note of the street number.

I hurry up the road, past a hotel on the left, and a row of very expensive shops on the right hand side. Not the sort of place I could ever afford to shop. I'm about three quarters of the way down the street, when I see two policeman come out of one of the doorways in front of me, each of them helping to support a very drunk Richard. I dive off the pavement, ducking through the doorway of the nearest shop, finding myself in a very upmarket erotic shop.

Red walls, rails full of expensive silk night-gowns, large, very large vibrators with diamonds, yes, *diamonds*, on the end of them, padded cufflinks, and cushions with very tasteful but incredibly rude pictures on the front. And two very famous beautiful models whom I instantly recognise from TV and the covers of a thousand different magazines, but that doesn't stop me from stumbling into them and knocking one of them flying as she is examining a crotch-less silk teddy.

She looks up at me from the floor, where she is now sprawling in an undignified, non-supermodel like pose, and is just about to shout, when she sees the puke covering my suit and trousers. Instead, she gags and looks away, covering her mouth with her hands. Her friend pushes me from behind, and goes to her aid, both of them by now covering their noses. I reach out to help her up from the floor and in spite of myself can't stop staring at her face as she lies on the wooden floor beneath me. A perfect face, which has adorned the cover of Marie-Claire and Vogue. I hesitate. Would it be the wrong time to ask for her autograph?

Just then a large, burly bodyguard grabs my biceps and removes me from the shop, the manageress screaming from behind, advising me to take a bath.

Thankfully, by now Richard and the two policemen are turning the corner at the end of the street, where I can just make out the back of a police car parked on the edge of the main road. A few seconds later I see it drive away, and I relax a little.

I walk to the doorway from where the boys in blue emerged, check the writing on the brass nameplate, and then walk in.

The hall emerges into a large yellow reception area with parquet flooring, from which an impressive wooden staircase sweeps upwards. The scent of flowers fills the air, coming from several large bouquets which overflow from a number of large vases dotted around the room and positioned carefully on top of two glass coffee tables, in front of white leather couches. Several large pieces of modern art adorn the walls. Colourful, yet discreet, they look expensive, and that's exactly the point.

The room exudes quiet sophistication. It says, "Hey, We're creative, we're clever. We're tasteful. Now give us your money."

A gorgeous, curvy blonde, wearing a tight, low-cut black top and a string of pearls stands up from behind a hotel-style reception desk, and smiles at me. I can't help but smile back at her.

"Not another one…James, what on earth have you two been up to? The cops just dragged Richard in off the street and asked me to identify him and corroborate his story that he is the owner of one of London's top advertising agencies, and not a drunken bum. They've arrested him for being drunk and disorderly. What am I meant to tell his wife?"

I sink down into one of the large leather couches, exhausted and at the end of my tether. The receptionist immediately rushes forward, and leans over towards me, grabbing my arms gently and imploring me to stand up again.

"Get up James. You'll ruin the furniture. You're covered in puke and you smell awful. Come on, let's get you up to your office before the others get back from lunch. You don't want them to see you like this, do you?"

Ah. So I have an office. My *own* office?

I stand, and let her guide me up two flights of stairs, and through a large open plan area to a suite of offices at the back of the building. She directs me to a door and pushes me gently through.

"Sit down, and I'll get you a cup of coffee. You need to sober up."

"Actually, I'm not drunk. I haven't been drinking…" I protest, but she's already gone and I collapse in a chair.

She returns a few minutes later, closing the door behind her, and coming over to me.

"I've closed up downstairs for a few minutes. Everyone else is out at lunch. Richard called the office immediately after the presentation to give the good news, and everyone went straight down to the Crown to celebrate. They'll be just as drunk as you when they get back."

"I'm NOT drunk!"

"Of course, you are. How did this happen then?" she asks, waving at me to stand up again, and immediately pulling at my jacket and slipping it off my shoulders.

"Richard puked on me." I reply, looking around the office.

I stare at my desk. Beside my green brass lamp is a large, glass paperweight. I recognise it immediately. It was my grandmother's. Since I inherited it, it has followed me from one desk to another, wherever I work. And the last time I saw it, it was on my desk in my office, my other office, in Canary Wharf.

"Listen, I have a problem," I turn to her, putting on my best pleading voice. "A big problem. I need your help, but I have to ask you NOT to tell anyone else. Will you promise me to keep it secret?"

"Yes." She says, holding my smelly jacket at arm's length from her body. "What problem? Do you want to tell me that you are an alcoholic?"

"No. I'm NOT drunk! It's just that I can't remember much. I'm sorry but I don't know your name. It's a miracle I even know my own name..." I blurt out, pretending to rub my head. "I was mugged this morning, and I was hit pretty hard over the head. I think I must have some sort of concussion..."

"Mugged?...What?...You're not telling me that Richard made you do the presentation anyway?"

"Well, yes... But to be fair, he did do most of it. Anyway, the thing is, I haven't got any money. Everything was stolen...and I can't walk around like this...Can you go out and get me some new clothes...*Please?* Some jeans, a shirt and a jumper and jacket? Anything...just something for me to change into?...Please?" I ask, sounding as pathetic as I can. Which, right now, isn't too hard.

"Sure. Okay. You mean, *now*?" she replies, looking at the jacket, and turning up her nose.

"Yes, now would be a good time. Please. I want to go home. I need a bath, and I need to talk to my wife. Today has been one hell of a day."

"Oh, I meant to tell you. Your wife called. She wanted to wish you luck again for the presentation. She said she couldn't get through to you on your mobile. She'll see you tonight."

The receptionist, who still hasn't told me her name, turns and hangs my jacket on the coat-stand by the door. Then without more than a second's warning she steps back towards me and pushes me into the chair behind the desk. Before I can protest, she kneels on the floor in front of me, and slips my shoes off each foot. She reaches up with both hands and starts to unbuckle my belt, and with a practiced familiarity which catches me unawares, reaches behind my back, grabs hold of the top of my trousers, and then yanks them down to my ankles, and off my legs altogether.

Then, just as I begin to think my day may be getting a little better after all, she stands up, walks back to the door, picks my jacket off the stand and leaves me sitting alone in the office in my boxer shorts. My tartan boxer shorts.

For a few seconds I am lost for words, but quickly recovering my senses I jump to my feet and chase after her across the open-plan office.

"What are you doing? Where are you going?" I shout.

"You can't sit in those trousers. They're covered in sick. I'm taking them straight to the 4 -hour dry cleaner, and I'll pick up a pair of trousers, and some clothes in the shop down the street. I'll be back in a minute. Don't worry, the others won't be back from lunch for another hour."

She disappears down the stairs, and I am left standing in the middle of the office in my shirtsleeves and boxers, and a pair of socks that has a big hole in one toe. I look about me, at the empty desks, and flashing PC screens. Thank god no one else is around.

Alone for the first time today, I walk back to my office, sit down and start to examine my new surroundings.

Apart from the paperweight, nothing else is familiar to me. The room is totally enclosed, with large glass windows and some blinds that can seemingly roll down and block out the main office outside whenever I may want some privacy. My desk is large. I have two phones, one white, and one red, just like the Prime Minister. I think it's designed to make me feel important. There are some large wooden filing cabinets along one side of the office, and behind me there is a window, not too large, that looks onto some mews in the street below. It's not a bad office, in fact it's much better than my one in Kitte-Kat, wherever that is now. On the wall, there are a couple of posters, and photographs of what looks like advertising campaigns from the past. But whose past? Surely not mine?

For the first time today I come face to face with my situation.

I have gone mad.

There is simply no other explanation. How can this all be happening to me? Where is Canary Wharf? Where is my job as a Product Manager? What am I doing here? Who is Richard, and the friendly receptionist? And how come I have an office in an advertising agency?

Just *what the hell* is going on?

Since throwing up in the gutter outside Waterloo train station this morning, which now seems like a lifetime away, I have been on pure autopilot. It's like I'm living in someone else's body, watching everything through someone else's eyes. I'm going through the motions, coasting along, taking it all in, trying to understand it all, but underneath, there is no emotion. Okay, occasionally, there is a twinge of pure and utter fear, but by and large, I seem to be managing to hold it together. For now, I think I am in control. But as soon as the receptionist returns with some clothes, I'm going straight home to Sarah. She will be able to tell me what to do, and what is happening to me.

And then I think of Jane. I'm meant to be having dinner with her tomorrow night. What will she think of all this?

I hear voices. Laughing. Footsteps thundering up the stairs.

Shit. The office staff are coming back from lunch.

I pull myself as close to my desk as possible, making sure my legs are tucked under the top and no one can see my cheap, tartan, boxer shorts.

Just in time. The people see me through the large glass window of my office and start singing, en masse.

"For he's a jolly good fellow, for he's a jolly good fellow..." Before I can stop them, they're pouring into my office and standing in front of my desk. "...a jolly good felllllloooooooowwwwww, and so say all of us. Hoorrrrraaaaaayyyyyy!"

Who are these nutters?

"James", one of the prettiest girls shouts, coming around to pat me on the shoulder,

"Well done! You pulled it off. Fantastic."

"Yes, and what happened to Richard then?" a spotty young man with spiky hair and a pink shirt asks from the back. "Is it true the Big Dick got nicked and banged up for being drunk and disorderly?"

I think for a minute. Then I get it.

"You mean Richard? ...Yes, unfortunately, I'm afraid it is." I reply, incredibly conscious that I am sitting in my boxers, and that the girl beside me may be able to see them.

I want these people out of my office, and now.

"...Anyway, I can see you have all had a few beers, and that this deal is important to you all..." I start, not knowing exactly what I should say to these people. Strangers. I'm almost naked in front of them, and I hardly know them.

"A few?" Someone giggles, "We only came back because they ran out of alcohol in the pub."

"Well, why don't you all take the rest of the day off, I'm sure Richard won't mind. He can hardly complain now can he?"

There is another cheer, and they all start to sing again.

"But if I were you, I'd go now, whilst the going is good. If he gets let out of the police station and comes back here, well, it won't be a pretty sight, will it?"

The singing doesn't subside, but they all turn to go. One of the girls at the front, her eyes quite red and swaying slightly, sits on the edge of my desk, and leans across to me.

"You know, James, this means that you'll probably be made a partner now won't you?. Congratulations."

She drunkenly leans across to shake my hand, but at that moment, her bottom nudges my grandmother's paperweight and it rolls towards the edge of the table.

I see it going and I jump up and dive across my desk, managing to catch it just in time, just as it reaches the edge.

Suddenly there is silence, and the singing stops. The girl on my desk looks at me in disbelief, and then spontaneously bursts into laughter. The rest join in.

It's then that I realise that I'm standing up and in full view of everyone, practically exposing myself to a room full of drunken advertising executives who have nothing better to do than stare at me and laugh their heads off.

It's at moments like these that your mother's advice to always wear your best underwear, just in case you get hit by a bus, doesn't seem so daft after all. If only I'd paid more attention, I would have worn Ralph Lauren or Polo Sport, instead of Marks 'n Sparks.

Suddenly the receptionist appears, pushing her way through the team. A new pair of trousers and shirt in one hand. A camera in the other.

Big white flash.

Embarrassing photo duly taken. The moment is captured forever, and destined to become a picture on Big Dick's wall, a memento of the day we won the Scotia Telecom deal, and a source of constant and unending office mirth. The day I was caught with my trousers down. Funny ha ha.

CHAPTER 8
Trafalgar Square 4 pm

I walk out of the office clutching a bundle of British euros, one hundred to be exact, all new in blues and greens, bearing the Queen's head on one side, and the map of Europe on the reverse. Courtesy of the receptionist, my new best friend, who as it turns out, is better known as Alice.

Euros. So when did Britain lose the pound?

So many changes. So many questions.

I have to get home now. I have to see Sarah, I have to hold her in my arms, close my eyes and let her kiss me on my eyelids. Like she used to do when we first met. She will make me feel good again. She will make it all go away, and when we fall asleep together, when we wake up in the morning, it will all be back to normal. I know it will.

After all, none of this can be true. Can it?

I decide to walk to Waterloo. I can't quite face the underground yet. Something happened there this morning, something that caused all of this.

Just the mere thought of travelling on the tube again brings back the memories of this morning, and the fear surges, and rushes through me. I manage to bottle it all up. To control it. But only just.

No, I'll walk.

I head down Monmouth Street, then towards Leicester Square, and down to Trafalgar Square. Again, I'm struck by just how little traffic there is. Tall thin, old fashioned Routemaster red buses stream past me, unimpeded, frequent, and full. Another difference. And as I watch them pass me by, it strikes me how few modern red buses there are on the streets today.

At Trafalgar Square I stand underneath Nelson's Column and watch little children squealing with pleasure as they feed the pigeons from their hands. A Japanese mother stops me and asks me to take a picture of her and her husband and their two little girls surrounded by the birds. I smile. The first time I've smiled today. I remember the first time I came into London with my parents, and I remember just how exciting I found it all. I loved the pigeons. I was always against Ken Livingstone's idea to get rid of them from the Square, and now they're back, I'm glad.

It takes me five minutes to walk down to Embankment and when I get to the Thames I climb the steps up to the Jubilee Bridge crossing to the south side of the river. I cross to the middle and stop to look out across the skyline of London.

I love this view. It's better than the Seine in Paris, or the Vltava in Prague, or the Danube in Budapest. This river beats them all.

But then I spoil it all. I look past St Paul's Cathedral into the distance and immediately spot two big mistakes in my reality. My heart skips a few beats, and I grip the rails in front of me, white showing across my knuckles.

Since I left Trafalgar Square I hadn't noticed any other changes to the streets. Everything seemed normal. For a while I was even hoping that things were back to usual, hoping that maybe I was beginning to wake up from the dream. When I got to the river, the Jubilee Bridge was there, just as it should be, as was the London Eye. Majestic as ever.

But when I open my eyes again and look towards where Canary Wharf should stand, just visible in the distance, I see nothing. No tall buildings. No modern skyscrapers. None. Not a single one.

And then I spot mistake number two. The new Swiss Re tower is not there either, its' absence conspicuous by the patch of blue sky that fills the space where the cigar shaped tower should be.

I close my eyes again and pray. A silent prayer. Please God, make it all go away. Make this dream end.

But when I open my eyes again, the dream is still running. I look to my right and there is no sign of London's latest and greatest skyscraper: the Shard does not exist either.

Feeling a little nauseous, I turn and walk to Waterloo. I can feel myself starting to unravel. At most I can probably hold it all together for an another hour. But after that, I think it's going to be too much. I need to see Sarah. Soon. Only she can give me the strength I need to make sense of all of this.

I walk to the end of the bridge, down the steps, past the Queen Elizabeth Concert hall, and the statue of Nelson Mandela, down underneath the railway bridge taking trains across the river, and eventually into the arrivals hall at Waterloo.

A shiver runs down my spine as I remember throwing up outside the station earlier this morning. It seems such a long time ago now.

I look at the overhead signs announcing the arrivals and departures, but this time as I look more closely, I notice that the signs themselves seem different in size and design to those being used the last time I was in the station, which would have been only last night. They are hanging in rows, individual plasma screens suspended from special roof supports, announcing the latest trains scheduled to arrive or depart from each platform. They appear to be hanging in the same place as yesterday, but the plasma screens look different, as if they were from different manufacturers. And they look slightly more advanced. Anyway, they seem different. Just another one of the growing list of differences that I have noticed today.

The next train to Surbiton is in two minutes from Platform One. I run quickly, and I make it just as the doors are closing.

It's a brand new train. I haven't been on one like this before. It must be one of the much-heralded new rolling stock that South West Trains had ordered for the Olympics but was delivered over budget and too late. It's swish, comfortable, and as I find out, incredibly punctual. The train leaves at 4.28 pm exactly. On the dot. Just like in Germany.

Another change. Another error in my reality. Trains are never this punctual.

As the train pulls out of the station, I close my eyes, scared to keep them open just in case I spot more and more mistakes in the scenery around me. Things that are wrong. Things that shouldn't be there, or things that are missing.

I keep my eyes shut for the rest of the journey, dozing a little between stations, until after what can only have been about twelve minutes, we arrive at Surbiton train station. I am almost home.

The electronic doors swoosh open in front of me, and I alight onto the platform. The station looks exactly the same as when I left it in the morning, and I begin to pray that it IS exactly the same.

I walk out of the back of the station, pulling the key to my Ford Mondeo out of my pocket. My trusty reliable Mondeo. I walk to the back of the car park to the corner where I have parked my car every day for the past three years.

I am tired. Very tired. I can't wait to sit down, close the door and switch on my CD player. And relax.

I look up as I get closer, but can't see the last few cars in the corner, because of a large black Four-by-Four parked in front of them. My pace hastens slightly. I'm almost at the Four-by-Four now,...almost...

I stop dead. My parking space is empty. My Ford Mondeo is gone. Nowhere to be seen.

I stand in the space where by rights my car should be, remembering in my mind how I locked and checked the doors this morning, before I caught the train into London. I can distinctly remember parking it here. It's only then that I look at the key in the palm of my hand and realise that it is not the key to a Ford Mondeo. It's not the key to my car. At the least, not the one that I drove to the station this morning.

My hand begins to shake again, just like it did at Canary Wharf. Except this time it doesn't stop when my other hand grabs it and tries to reassure it. No, this time, both hands are shaking, And my legs soon join in.

I look around me. My car is nowhere to be seen, and even when I am finished walking around the whole car park, I am still not able to find it.

Sweating and feeling a little faint, I walk back to the steps leading up and over the railway line, and sit down. I need to calm down. *'Hold it together man. Hold on.'* I whisper to myself. *'You're almost home. Everything will be all right soon.'*

As I sit on the steps, my head in my hands, a terrifying thought hits me.

What happens, if when I get home, Sarah isn't there either?

Shaking my head, refusing to ponder this absurd idea further, and desperate to prove it wrong, I jump to my feet and hurry up the steps and over the railway tracks to the front of the station to find a taxi.

As I do, I recognise my first face. The flower seller who stands in the concrete hallway above the platforms. He has been there every day for as long as I can remember. I see him every day when I come home from work and walk to the car park. I've never actually said hello to him before, but when I recognise his face, I can't help but feel good. Perhaps things are going to be okay after all. From here on, things are going to be normal again...

I stop and talk to him for a few moments, and eventually buy the biggest bunch of flowers he has. I can't wait to surprise Sarah. It's been ages since I bought her some, in fact the last flowers I bought were for Jane. Jane...what am I going to tell her tomorrow night?

For the first time today, I feel the sexual urge which I normally have whenever I think of Jane, and it takes an effort to block her out of my mind. My main priority for now is to get home, and find Sarah. My wife. I curse myself for thinking of Jane. *What am I thinking of?* Sex should be the last thing on my mind. Right now, what I need more than anything else in the entire world, is to look at my wife, and for her to tell me that I am not mad, and that everything is going to be okay. And only she can do that.

Walking out I find the normal queue of taxis lining up for business. Since it's early, there are only another two people waiting, and it's only a few minutes before my taxi lines up in front of me.

"Hinchley Wood, Hillside Avenue please."

The driver whisks me out of the station and down Victoria Road. I don't look out the window as we drive down Surbiton's high street, keeping my eyes on the flowers. I have to think quickly. What am I going to say to Sarah? How do I explain that I'm home early?

What do I tell her about why I'm wearing a different set of clothes?

I can't pretend that everything is okay. How can I? My job is gone, Canary Wharf is gone, a sizeable portion of London is gone, and replaced by God knows what...and when I left this morning I was a Product Manager in a telecomms company who spent all of his time wondering what it would be like to be doing something else...Well, now I'm coming home a Senior

Advertising Executive in a top London firm, and this morning I just won a deal worth ten million euros.

I look out of the window just as we turn into my street. Truth is, as soon as I get through the doors, as soon as she comes up to kiss me hello, as she does every night when I get home from work, ... I think I'm just going to break down in tears. There'll be no holding back. No lies. It'll all just come out. The whole ridiculous, unbelievable truth.

The taxi pulls up in front of my house and I lean forward and pay the meter. Six euros. How much is that in real money?

Getting out of the cab, I press the large bouquet of flowers against my chest, then open the gate and walk up the path. I pull out my keys and put the key in the lock, just noticing for the first time that the flowers in the front garden are much more colourful than normal. If fact, they look much better than they ever have.

The key doesn't turn.

I try it again. It sticks in the lock.

I force it a little, pull it out, and then push it back in.

Suddenly the front door opens in front of me, and I am pulled off balance, falling forward and slightly inwards into the house. A woman inside steps back and screams. Raising my hand quickly I manage to catch myself in the doorway before I fall on top of her. I look up and stare at the woman in front of me.

The woman screams again and tries to push me out and close the door. I push my foot forward through the doorway, a stupid thing to do, and I curse as the pain surges through my ankle and up my leg.

"Get out! Leave me alone....I'll call the police..." she threatens from the other side of the door.

I pull my foot out and the door slams shut. Shaking, and just as scared as the woman, I stand with my nose a few inches in front of the green door, staring at the wood only centimetres from my face.

I try to control my breathing. It's coming in short bursts, and my heart is pounding. Slowly, I step backwards and walk back towards the gate, and then out onto the road.

The woman is at the window, pulling the curtains open slightly, and I see a phone in her hand. What is she doing in my home? I look up and down the street. Am I at the wrong house? No, this is it. Definitely. *No. 33.* No mistakes. This is the house where I have lived for the past ten years. This is the house where both of my children were conceived, and where I carried Sarah across the threshold. This is *my* home.

I gesture to the woman, waving and pleading with my eyes for her to come to the door. The curtain closes, and I walk back up the path. I ring the bell. I ring the doorbell of my own home. Why?

The door opens, and the woman appears in front of me again. She looks scared.

"Why are you trying to get in? I'm warning you, I have called the police. They're already on the way..."

"I am sorry. I am looking for someone... I have the wrong key...May I ask who lives here?"

"I do. We do...my husband and I. He'll be back from work soon. I called him too...please leave me alone..." she begs.

"It's okay, I promise", I say, "I have no intention of hurting you...I'm just looking for someone...a Mrs Quinn? Wife of James Quinn?"

"Sorry, I don't know her. Never heard of her..."

I step back from the doorway, and look up and down the street again. I am very confused. Very scared. What is happening here? When I turn around again, there are tears in my eyes, and I cannot stop them from streaming down my cheeks.

The look on the woman's face changes and the sternness leaves, her features immediately softening, blue eyes now questioning me from behind the face of a fifty year old lady.

"Are you okay? What is the matter?...Are you lost?"

"Yes." I reply. "I am very lost...You see, I was mugged this morning, and I received a bad blow to my head... I have forgotten everything...including where I live." The tears are still pouring from my eyes.

The woman is silent. As I try to stem my sudden outpouring of emotion, wiping my cheeks and swallowing hard, I look deeply into her eyes. I can see her struggling with a decision. And then I see her make up her mind.

"Would you like a cup of tea?" she asks kindly.

I hesitate. Looking past her at the interior of my house, I see now that there is floral wallpaper, and a bright red carpet. My house, the house I left this morning, has pine floors, and white walls. Two years ago it took me a month to strip the floors, to sandpaper and varnish them, and a week to give the walls two coats of paint.

"No thank you." I hear myself replying. I don't think I could cope with walking inside and being surrounded and encaged by the dream. I would prefer to stand outside in the sunlight. "But thank you for offering. It's very kind of you. I'm sorry for scaring you a minute ago. I was probably just as scared as you were."

We both laugh. I don't know why I do. I have nothing to laugh about.

"May I ask your name, and how long you have been living here?" I say nervously. Scared of the reply.

"Certainly. I'm Mrs Henderson. Jenny Henderson, and my husband is Paul. We've lived here for eight years now."

"Do you know who lived here before you?" I ask her.

"It was a young family. A Canadian couple, I think. They left and went back to Canada. Does that help you at all?" she asks, a touch of real concern in her voice.

"A little. Thanks." I reply, handing her the bouquet of flowers. "Thank you very much, Mrs Henderson."

I turn and walk away. I don't look back. I don't live at No. 33 anymore. And from what Mrs Henderson just said, it seems that I never have.

CHAPTER 9

The Angel, Thames Ditton.

It's a four minute car ride to the Angel Pub on the edge of Giggs Hill Green in Thames Ditton. My favourite pub, my local, where I have spent many an evening sitting with Sarah. It's the place we go to be together to relax on evenings when the kids are at friends, and we can't be bothered going out and making a big night of it.

It took me half an hour to walk here after discovering that Mrs Henderson was living in my house. I couldn't think of anywhere else to go.

After I left my house, I cried for ten minutes, ignoring the strange looks from people as I passed them in the street. The tears only dried up when an old lady stopped me, and asked if there was anything wrong. What could I tell her?

I think I have moved beyond the panic stage now. I don't feel anything anymore. What else can happen to me? If someone were to stub a cigarette out on the back of my hand, I would probably just look them in the eyes as they did it, without flinching.

Yet, although I don't feel any pain, I have an overwhelming feeling of longing. I long for my wife, Sarah.

Like Canary Wharf, my job, the Swiss Re tower, and a thousand other things, I have now also lost my wife. The only reason I am not stepping out in front of a passing car to end it all, is because I know my wife has not disappeared completely. I know she is out there somewhere. I know she called me at the office this afternoon and left me a message, and I know that I am meant to call her back.

The only problem is, I don't know where to find her, or how. And I can't call her, because her number doesn't exist, and our home, where we lived for ten years, is no longer our home, and is inhabited by someone I have never ever seen before.

The Angel is an island of calm and reassurance. It looks exactly the same as when I last saw it two days ago, and probably exactly the same as it did twenty years ago. Nothing has changed. The low ceilings with dark, wooden beams and the dingy lighting giving it a genuine oldie-world feeling, orange walls that have faded into a light brown with a continual coating of nicotine and wood smoke from the fire, the dank, musty smell from the old carpet and the pewter jars and copper pots hanging above the open fireplace, where a continuous log fire has burned for the past two hundred years. The only thing that changes is the bar-staff, who seem to come and go every couple of months.

How can I find my wife?

I need to talk to someone. I need help. But who can I talk to? Who else can I tell this whole stupid, unbelievable story to, who won't laugh at me?

Of course. *My mum.*

I get some change from the bar, some strange looking shiny silver and bronze euros, and close the door of the old-fashioned telephone box in the back of the pub. I dial the number, praying that my mum will pick up. Suddenly a voice, a voice belonging to someone I have known longer than any other human being in my life. A voice that I have heard from before I was born, when she carried me in her womb and sang to me as we walked around the house, her heavy with child, and me desperate to get out into the world.

"Mum." the tears flood down my cheeks again. I don't even try to stop them.

"*Jamie?* Is that you son?" my mum, sixty years old, my rock, my salvation.

"Yes..."

"Where are you Jamie?" She interrupts me. "The party's already started. You're late. Don't tell me you're working late again. Not tonight. Not tonight of all nights. Jamie...*please*... make an effort...the girls are already here, ...*oh, it's the door bell...*When will you be here? You are still coming, aren't you?"

A party? My little girls are there? Sarah?

"Yes...I'll be there in half an hour..."

"See you Jamie...but make it quick...you have to get here before ten past six...Don't be a second later...."

Click. The line is dead.

I leave my pint of beer, half finished, by the phone, and walk straight out the back door. My heart is beating fast again, and adrenaline shoots through my body. Walking faster and faster, I eventually break into a run, hope surges afresh, and a picture of Sarah and the two girls fills my mind. It's been less than ten hours since I saw them last, but it seems like a lifetime ago.

It takes me twenty minutes to run to Kingston, through the pedestrian precinct, between the Bentall Centre and John Lewis and then around and down underneath the railway tracks.

I run fast, the crisp autumn air cooling my forehead, but by the time I get to the river and turn right into the river road running from the Thames to the main Richmond road, I am exhausted and soaked through with sweat.

I slow down as I approach my mother's house, and I stop across the street from it, bending over and resting on my knees, catching my breath. Still bent over, I look up at the house where I was born and where I grew up.

I smile. The house looks the same as I've always known it. The green windows and paintwork, the large rose bushes in the front garden. The path running down the sides of the detached house on either side. My parents weren't exactly the greatest DIY experts in the world. The house has been kept in good condition, but it is probably the same now as it was fifteen years ago. Nothing has changed since we all left home.

I hear music and the sound of voices coming from the front room, and I notice now that the road is full of cars. A party? Why? My mother hasn't felt like having a party in years. Not since....

The door opens and my mum steps out.

"Jamie, Come on, Come on...There isn't much time." she cries, waving at me to hurry.

As I cross the road towards her, the smile on her face disappears. She looks me up and down, at the strange clothes I am wearing, ...not exactly my normal choice.

"Jamie, oh Jamie, you could have made an effort. And you're soaked through...You go right up stairs to the bathroom, my boy, and I'll bring you in some of your dad's clothes to wear."

I open my mouth to argue, but then think better of it. For the first time in years, it's just nice to be treated like a little boy again. She steps aside as I walk up the garden path, ushering me indoors. I stop in the doorway, and look at her.

"It's good to see you mum. It really is."

"Get yourself inside lad. I'll run you a quick hot bath."

A kiss on the cheek, then I'm running up the stairs to the bathroom, just as if I were a kid covered in mud, who'd just come back from playing football in the park.

The bathroom is like I have always known it. It's never changed since my first memory of it, which is probably when I was about six years old. The green tiles on the wall, the green bath and basin, the plastic tray across the middle of the bath for the soaps and nail brush, and a large, squashy brown sponge, a souvenir of a Greek holiday long ago. And the smell.

My mother's bathroom has this scent, this ever present smell. Perhaps it's the soap, or something in the toilet, or maybe it's perfume. It smells of lemongrass, or the wind or the sea. Something which I can never quite place, but which is incredibly refreshing and reassuring.

I lie back in the bath, and close my eyes. The steam from the warm bath rises around me, the mirror mists over, and I relax.

I know this place. It is my home. Where I was brought up, where I learned to live, where I did my home work every night, and where I lived with my mum and my dad. For a moment, I am where I belong. Surrounded by the world as I know it. My life as it was, and is, and should be. Everything is going to be fine.

There is a loud bang on the door, and the sound of children's voices, two little girls squealing at each other at the top of the stairs. I open my eyes, and I hear my mother outside the door, speaking sternly to the children, and telling them to go back downstairs. I start to think of Nicole and Keira, and can't wait to hug them. Are they really only just downstairs?

My mother's voice.

"James, I've brought you a cup of tea and I've put some of your father's clothes on your bed. Please hurry up. The guest of honour will be here in fifteen minutes."

She opens the door slightly and slides the tea just inside. I climb out of the bath, leaving the security of the warm water behind. Wrapping a towel around my waist, I pick up the tea, and sip it, whilst I wipe the mirror clear of condensation.

A face stares back at me from the behind the mist, and I drop the cup on the floor, hot tea splashing over my foot. I jump backwards and swear loudly, the edge of the bath catching the back of my knees, and tipping me back over into the water again, towel and all.

Splash.

Footsteps.

"Are you okay James? What's happened?"

My mother again.

Still sitting in the water, I reply. "Fine. I'm sorry, I just dropped the cup."

"Oh…, are you sure you're alright?"

"Yes," I reply. Lying.

Footsteps going downstairs.

I climb back out of the bath, and prepare myself for meeting the stranger in the mirror. I approach cautiously, heart racing, knees trembling, either from the fall, or from the shock of meeting the new me, I don't really know.

The man is thinner than I am. His hair is dark and short at the sides, with blonde highlights on top, like the photo that I found in my travelcard earlier this morning. Stepping closer to the mirror I study the person who I guess is meant to be me. There are wrinkles around my eyes where I cannot remember them before, but overall I still manage to look more healthy than normal. There are no big black bags under my eyes, my hairline has not receded as much ….at least, in comparison with where it was this morning after my shower.

It's not a bad me. In fact, the man I am introducing myself to is perhaps a bit more like the image of the man I have always wanted to be, but being self conscious I have always been too scared to try anything different. Too scared to cut my hair shorter at the sides. Too scared to go for the subtle blonde highlights.

My nose almost touches the man in the mirror, and as I breathe out, the mirror steams up again, and the mystery man disappears. I quickly wipe it clean, and the man is back.

Actually, truth be told, he is better looking than I am. More style. Probably more self-confident. In fact, I wouldn't mind looking like him at all. Which is good, because I have a feeling that he will probably be following me around for a while. Either until I can figure this all out, or until the doctors eventually catch up with me, and some sort of enforced medication takes hold.

The doorbell goes downstairs, and I am quickly brought back to my new reality, if that is what it is. I unfasten the wet towel, and hang it on the electric towel rail, one of my mother's few modern appliances, if fifteen years old can be called modern. I reach up and pull down a fresh towel, drying myself quickly and wrapping it around my waist.

Stepping out of bathroom I shoot across the landing and into the front bedroom, my bedroom, the room where I grew up, studied, fought through puberty and crowned my youth by making love to Annabel Crawford one Tuesday morning in 6th Form, the prettiest girl in the school.

I sit down on the edge of my bed, and look up at the Airfix aeroplanes hanging from the roof on thin see-through fishing coil. I made them all one summer, while I listened to Pink Floyd and fought the onset of acne. A Spitfire, a Hurricane, and a camouflaged German Stuka Dive Bomber. Dusty, dirty, twenty years on, they still keep the skies of my old bedroom free from any modern invaders.

I look at the curious collection of posters on the wall. Bon Jovi, Duran Duran, Madonna and the crowning glory on the back of my bedroom door, a large picture of Neil Armstrong on the moon, which I swapped for two Mars Bars with my friend's big brother.

Standing there, staring at my youth, I forget about everything. I forget about the disappearing skyscrapers, the ten million euros advertising deal I've just won, about losing my job, my house and my wife, and once again I am young, loved, and secure.

The door to the bedroom suddenly swings open, and two young screaming girls burst in. They run past me and around the edge of the bed, and climb onto the mattress, where they proceed to jump up and down, each trying to scream louder than the other.

I watch them in amazement. Neither seems the slightest bit interested in the fact that a strange, half naked man is sitting in the bedroom, clothed only in a towel. It's then that I notice that they are jumping up and down on my father's clothes, the ones that my mother has just laid out for me.

Stressed, I shout at the kids, and grab one by the arms and legs, pulling her gently but firmly off the bed and depositing her on the floor, shouting at her to be quiet, perhaps just a little too loudly. She looks up, staring at me in silence, then quickly bursts into tears. The other one, younger and most probably her sister, takes only microseconds to burst into tears too, and suddenly she is scrambling off the bed and following her elder sister out of the door and down the stairs, both howling like banshees.

Little monsters. Where are their parents? No respect for adults, and where on earth did they learn to behave like that? Thank God that Sarah and I have both been blessed with two beautiful, good natured little girls. I can't wait to see them.

Closing the bedroom door again, I stand up and let the towel drop to the floor. I pick up my father's blue denim shirt and brown corduroy trousers. Underneath is a pair of socks and a pair of fresh blue cotton Y-fronts. Putting the trousers down I lift one leg and with my back to the door, I bend down a little bit and lift one leg up, managing to put my foot through one side of the pants.

Magically, a hand appears from nowhere, coiling itself around my front and down into my crotch, grasping my penis in its palm and holding on tightly. The bedroom door closes. Another hand on my shoulder, and hot breath on the side of my face. I stand up straight, smiling, but not turning around.

Sarah?

Familiar words whispered in my ear.

"Hello darling. Why are you hiding from me?"

A voice which is not Sarah's...Familiar words, but spoken by a voice that does not belong to my wife.

I turn with a shock, stepping away quickly. As I do, my feet trip on the insides of the pants, and I stumble, losing my balance and falling backwards against the wall, my penis stretching quickly inside her clenched palm, and then mercifully whipping itself free.

As I go down, my skull cracks hard against the plaster, a resounding thud which resonates down through my head.

"Ouch!" I scream momentarily, but almost as quickly forget it, as I look up at the sight of Jane kneeling down towards me.

Jane! ?

I quickly control my shout, and it becomes a whisper, my hand rubbing the back of my head.

"Jane…," I try to speak, but am prevented from doing so, first by a flood of kisses, and then a woman falling on top of me, laughing uncontrollably.

" Did I give you a fright?…Oh, James, I'm sorry, but I can't help it…" She blurts out in between giggles, "You look so funny…all tangled up…so vulnerable…"

And then she's kissing me again. Smothering me with affection, her hand wandering downwards, starting once more where it just left off.

"Jane…what are you doing here? What if…?"

"What if what? What if your mother walks in…?" she laughs…

And just then, the door opens and she does.

"What's that banging?" my mum asks, as she comes into the room. "Are you all right?"

For a second she stares at us both, lying on the floor, her face blank. My mind races. Oh my God. To be caught in bed with your lover by your wife is one thing, but to be caught with your pants down, red-handed, by your MOTHER, is another thing completely.

"Mum…I can explain…" I shout, jumping to my feet, and quickly pulling up my pants and snatching the trousers from the bed.

"Don't bother, son. Don't bother. I thought I'd seen it all. But this takes the biscuit!"

As I struggle with the trouser legs, and whipping up the zip, my mother turns to the door.

"Mind you, what you young folks get up to in private is none of my affair."

"But it's not an affair mum. Honest. This is the first time…" I cry out in my defence.

She stops in the doorway, and turns back towards me.

Laughing. Howls of laughter.

"Listen son, I was young once too, and your Dad and I got up to …well, how do you think you came about?" Her face alight with the memory. "Anyway, maybe I'm just jealous, " she laughs again.

"Jealous?" I stare at her. I look back across at Jane, still sitting on the floor. Still laughing too. "What on earth have you got to be jealous about?"

"That, after so many years you're still so in love with each other and still fooling around. You're lucky son, not everyone has that."

And with that she closes the door and walks away.

I turn and face Jane. I am speechless. Thoughts race through my head. Not only has my mum gone crazy, but it will only be a matter of seconds before

Sarah will be racing up the stairs, and my marriage will disappear just like my job, my house and almost every other part of my life.

Quick, … I have to get Jane out of the room. Suddenly the bedroom door opens again, and the two screaming children return, rushing past me on either side, and jumping on Jane, joining her on the heap on the floor.

"Mummy. Mummy." They both scream. "Did Daddy shout at you too? Was he nasty to you as well?"

Jane looks up at me, her big, bright, beautiful eyes, smiling at me.

"No. Daddy and I were just playing…It's okay."

And then it dawns on me.

Sarah won't be rushing up the stairs. And my marriage won't be coming to an end after all.

For the simple reason, that it seems I'm no longer married to Sarah.

As far as I can tell, I'm now married to Jane.

CHAPTER 10
The Party

This new part of my reality strikes me dumb. I sit down on the side of the bed, and then lie down on my back, facing the ceiling.

The Spitfire chases the Stuka Dive Bomber, and my head begins to throb.

"James, are you okay? Sorry I'm laughing, but you should have seen yourself. It was hilarious."

The two girls jump up on the side of the bed, and one rolls onto my stomach.

"Daddy, daddy, are you still cross with us?" the older girl screams, her words almost immediately echoed by the smaller girl, albeit in a slightly more childish, higher pitch. "Addy, Addy, are you sill cos with us?"

With my hand still cradling the back of my cranium I look down at them, both now preparing to do somersaults on my midriff.

"Girls, leave daddy and mummy alone for a moment. We have to get Daddy dressed for the party. Go down to Nana and we'll be down soon." Jane shoos the two girls out, and kneels down beside me on the mattress. She lifts up my head, and bends forward to look at my scalp, separating the hair away from the area of the bang, and inspecting it closely.

"Ouch! It's bleeding. We'd better wash it and put a plaster on that. Are you alright?" she says, genuine concern now showing in her voice.

"I feel a little sick," I say. Actually, physically I feel fine. Mentally though, it feels as if someone has just removed my brain through my nose. And my heart is beating so fast that I think it is most probably going to burst at any second, or just stop.

Then all of a sudden, thoughts start to pour into my mind. A flood, too many at once to make any sense of, and I struggle to control them. By now I am sweating, and I genuinely do want to vomit.

Jane is bending over me, looking into my eyes, I think probably checking to see if my pupils are dilated, or maybe just to see if I am still alive.

I need Sarah. Where is Sarah. Where is my wife?

"Come on, let's get you into the bathroom. I hope you don't have concussion. We'll put some cold water on your neck and head, and get you dressed. If you feel ill at all, we'll get you off to the doctors. But the guest of honour should be arriving in a few minutes, so let's welcome him first and see how you feel then? Okay, honey?"

Honey?

She kisses me on the forehead, and then once, long and slow on the mouth. Another sudden flurry of thoughts. And feelings. Sarah? Jane? Sarah? Jane?

The kiss, in spite of the bad timing, and incredibly poor surroundings and circumstances, is, I must admit, rather nice. At the same time I am conscious of the weight of her large breasts on my chest. It occurs to me then, just how mixed up I am. One second, I am missing my wife and am dumb with a mixture of worry and fear, and the next second, my penis has taken control of my whole body, and a sexual impulse is dominating all normal, realistic, mental processes. Confusion wracks me, and I close my eyes.

Jane stands up and pulls my hands upwards. Before I know it she has led me into the bathroom, washed me, and helped me to put on my clothes.

Ouch. She puts TCP on my cut scalp, and then applies a plaster. She looks me in the face once more, checks my eyes for any more signs of my pupils exploding, and then kisses me again.

"Sorry, honey. I didn't mean for you to fall over and smack your head. But I think you'll live..." I utter something incoherent back, but it doesn't matter, as Jane has turned away and is already leading me down the stairs. At the bottom, we turn and go straight into the kitchen. The two monsters are sitting at the table, scoffing their little round faces with crisps and peanuts, and don't take any notice as we walk in.

The door to the dining room opens and the sound of lots of people laughing and joking bursts through. My mother pops her head round the side of the cooker, switching off the light on the wall.

"He's parking the car. Quick, come on in. Girls, you too."

Who is parking his car? What is this party for?

I walk into the dining room, and immediately can't help but notice that the wall between the dining room and the front room has disappeared. What used to be two separate rooms, only two days ago when I last stopped by to drop off my mother's shopping, has now become one large comfortable, tasteful open living area, straight out of the TV property program *'Location, Location, Location.'* And in the centre is a large banner, announcing "*Happy Retirement!*"

'Happy Retirement' to whom?

The room is full of people and the front curtains are drawn closed. On the other side, I notice my uncle, and some distant cousins who I never really knew, their wives and husbands in tow, but before I recognise the faces of the other people, someone switches off the lights. Suddenly we are engulfed in darkness.

Someone else goes "*Shuuuuuush!*" very loudly, and everyone stops speaking. All eyes are now on the door to the hallway. Jane steps up behind me, wrapping her arms around my waist, her chin on my shoulder, and her two little monsters…my two little monsters ?…stand beside me, pulling on my trouser legs.

We all hear the sound of the front door opening, and a few seconds later, the bang as it is shut firmly from within.

A ripple of excitement runs around the room, and all the people, some more of whom I have now recognised as a relatives whom I haven't seen in years, prepare to cheer and pull their party poppers. I join in, my attention now focusing as much as anyone else's on the handle of the door leading to the hallway.

Who is the mystery guest going to be? It can't be anyone I know…

The door handle turns, the door opens, and a hand reaches inside and searches for the light switch on the wall.

A flash of light. The sound of shouting, the sound of cheering. Poppers going bang all around. Everyone goes wild. The light is bright. Too bright. I blink to adjust my eyes. I see the person standing in the doorway, his jaw dropping and the surprise registering in his eyes. Stunned, he looks around the room for a moment or two before it dawns on him just what is going on. A second or two which rips open my heart, and impales me deeper and faster and more sharply than any spear or blade could ever do. A second or two, which tips me over the edge and into the darkness.

I see but I do not believe.

I hear his voice, laughing, but I do not dare to believe that it is him, and when he turns and sees me across the room and then winks in my direction, my knees give way and I crash to the ground.

But as I close my eyes and my mind shuts down, I realise that it is him. There is no mistake.

It is my father.

Who died of a heart attack five years ago.

But who now lives once again.

PART TWO

CHAPTER 11
Kingston Hospital

I blink a few times, the bright light shining in my eyes startles me, and I wake up rudely.

I am in a sterile and uninviting hospital room, a doctor standing above me, waving a small pencil torch back and forth into my left eye.

The doctor smiles.

"Welcome back, Mr Quinn. How are you feeling?" he asks.

"I don't know yet." I reply. "It depends on what the matter with me is." (I'm still a hypochondriac then.)

"You're in hospital…"

"I can see that…which one? How did I get here?"

"You're in Kingston Hospital. Your wife brought you in earlier this evening. Do you want to see her?"

Sarah. My heart skips a beat at the mention of her name. It seems like years since I saw her last.

"Yes," I reply quickly. "But can I ask you some questions first?"

"Sure", he says, sitting down on the side of my bed, resting his hands on his knees and looking simultaneously concerned, friendly and paternal, just like a doctor in a hospital drama on TV. Except this is real.

"What is the matter with me? And please tell me the truth. A lot of strange stuff has been happening to me recently, and I need to know why."

"Well, we've given you a complete going over, checked everything there is to check, and the only thing we can find wrong with you is that it looks as if you might be suffering from a little concussion. There's nothing else. You suffered a small bump on your head, and your blood pressure was perhaps a little too high. But the concussion, if there was one, seems to have gone now and we have brought your blood pressure down. We would like to keep you in for observation overnight, but if everything stays the same, there's no reason not to let you go home in the morning."

Concussion. I understand it all now. Everything that has happened today has just been one big dream. I've been lying in this hospital bed all the time, whilst my subconscious has been working overtime creating a whole new world for me to live in.

But now it's over. In a few minutes I'll be with Sarah, and I will be going home to hug Keira and Nicole. Relief floods through me, and I relax back onto the big white fluffy pillow.

"Thanks Doctor. I suppose that could explain it all…Can I see my wife now please?"

The doctor turns and walks out. I turn and look out of the window. Outside it's dark, and I can just see the lights on the top of the Bentall Centre in Kingston, not too far away. Then I hear footsteps and the door opens again.

Sarah…

Only, as I turn to greet my wife, Jane walks in.

There is a moment of pure confusion. My mind races. Am I back in the dream, or is everything back to normal, but Jane has come to visit me? If so, I have to get rid of her quick, before Sarah comes in.

"Jane…"

"James. Bloody hell, you gave us all a scare. The girls haven't stopped crying. And I've been so worried…"

She comes across to my bed, and wraps her arms around me, kissing me passionately. There are tears pouring down her cheeks. "I'm sorry, James, this is all my fault…I didn't realise that you'd hurt yourself so badly."

Not knowing how to respond I wrap my arm around her head, and hold her close to me. I hold her there for a long time and as she sobs against my chest, I stare blankly into space behind her. My head races. I am still in the dream. I haven't woken up yet.

Or have I?

A bizarre and extremely frightening thought occurs to me. It comes at me from out of nowhere, and it refuses to leave, burrowing itself deep inside my consciousness and going round and round in circles, until suddenly it doesn't seem so daft after all.

What if this is not a dream? What if this is all real? I mean, everything I can touch, and feel and see is real. At least it seems to be… What if my memories of Sarah and Keira and Nicole, and Kitte-Kat, what if *that* is the dream, and *this* is the reality? And what if the reason I cannot remember anything about my new life, I mean, this real life, is because I *do* have concussion and I have lost my memory? Perhaps there is a perfectly rational explanation for all of this?

What is it that they say...I think they call it *Occam's Razor?* …basically it goes, 'that which at first sight seems to be the obvious answer, generally turns out to be the answer'. So, if that is the case Jane and her two little monsters, and the rest of this world…*this* is my reality. Not Sarah. Sarah and the rest are just a figment of my imagination.

Is that possible? Should I ask the doctor? No. The absurdity of the suggestion hits me straight away. If I ask that they'll put me on drugs and lock me up in some mental institution. No, I have to figure this all out for myself.

So what shall I tell Jane? The *truth*? And what if it's not the truth, and I am in fact just mad?

No, I can't tell Jane either. If she's the only wife I have, I don't want to scare her with such wild thoughts ...at least not until I have had some more time to think it all out.

So do I really have concussion? Did I maybe really get mugged this morning, and if so, did I actually really have concussion all along? Perhaps I didn't make it all up this morning after all. Maybe it was true. Then, maybe, when I banged my head at my mum's for the second time it just made it worse?

Shit. This is too confusing.

On the other hand, if I do have concussion, or did, or might have had, if at all, or even if I don't and never did have, they...the doctors and my wife and everyone else, they now think that I do, and that now gives me a totally legitimate excuse for not remembering what on earth is happening in my life now. For example: *how long have I been married to Jane?* I don't know. *What are our children called?* I don't know. *How long have I been in advertising?* I don't know. *Where do I live?* I don't know.

And if none of this is actually real, and it *is* all a dream, then by *pretending* to have concussion I can at least excuse myself from a lot of embarrassing moments, while I try to figure out where the exit door from this particularly bad reality is, an excuse I can use while I learn all about my life again.

"Jane, let's talk" I say, pulling her gently up and off my chest.

I lift up her chin, and dab the edges of her face with the edge of the white hospital blanket. She stops crying and looks into my eyes. The good news is that it looks like she genuinely does love me. (Which is not to say that Sarah doesn't. Although maybe that isn't relative anymore, particularly if Sarah is just a dream and Jane isn't).

"Jane. The doctor says I've got concussion. I don't want to scare you, but I don't really know what's going on. I can't remember much..."

"What do you mean? Have you got amnesia? How bad is it?"

"I don't know... it's too early to tell."

"But you know who I am, don't you?" she says, wrapping my face in both her hands and staring at me with her big, beautiful eyes.

"Yes, but..."

"But what James, but what?"

"I can't remember much else. I can't remember when we got married, the names of our children, where we live...nothing...it's all patchy...blurry..."

"Oh no..." she cries out again collapsing on my chest.

I stroke her hair, soothingly, wondering what to do next and where we go from here. A moment passes.

"Is it permanent?" she eventually asks, pulling herself up and starting to pace the room.

Good question.

"I don't know. The doctors say that my memory might come back, a bit at a time. Until then we just have to take it day by day, and to start learning a lot of it from scratch again." I got that bit out of a film. Which, if you think about it, proves that I don't have complete amnesia, doesn't it?

"James?" Another person has just walked into the bedroom. It is my father.

"Dad..."

Now this bit is really strange. Either this is real, and I am talking to my real live father, who in my dream died five years ago, or this is a dream, and he is still dead, and somehow I am getting a chance to talk to him again in my new, imagined world, or, and this is the weirdest one of them all: maybe he was dead, and is now alive again. Which, of course, is ridiculous.

"Jane, the kids are waiting outside with Mary. Tell them their father is okay, but I think it's best if they don't come in just yet. Why not take them home, and bring them back tomorrow? I would like to talk to James alone for a while, if that's all right with you," my father says, holding open the door for Jane.

She kisses me once more on the lips, and strokes the side of my face, smiling. As she walks out of the door, I can taste her salty tears on my lips.

Suddenly I am left alone with my father. There is so much I want to say to him. So much that I never ever got the chance to say before he died.

I was away on business, in Germany, when I got the phone call in the middle of the night from my mum, telling me that he had been taken into hospital. I got a cab straight to the airport, and waited for three hours in the departure lounge, and caught the first flight home. When I got to the hospital the next day it was too late. The whole family was there. Everyone, apart from me. As he lay in the bed that night, nearing the end of his life, the rest of my family had managed to say something to him and make their peace with him before his heart eventually packed in. Everyone except me. I never got to tell him how much I loved him, how much I loved all the toys he used to make for us as children, how much I loved going fishing with him when I was a teenager, and how sorry I was that we had shouted at each other after the Christmas Dinner the year before. And now I have a second chance to say all the things I never did before.

Perhaps that is what this is all about.

A tear rolls out of the corner of my eye, and I immediately wipe it away. I am not a man for showing emotion, and normally I force myself to bottle it all up inside. Never in my life...this one, or any other, have I cried in front of my father, and I'm not about to start now.

My father sits down on the side of my bed, and smiles at me.

It is three hours before he finally leaves, asked by the nurse to give me some rest, and when he goes I feel happier than I have done for years. We've had a good old father-to-son and man-to-man discussion. And in spite of myself, the old eyes do leak, and I cry again, only this time I do nothing to stop them flowing. Nothing at all.

CHAPTER 12
Effingham Road, Surbiton

The taxi pulls up at a house in Effingham Road in Surbiton. It is a large house, one which I recognise and have driven past many times before. Detached, spread over four floors, with its own driveway and wrought iron gates, it is impressive. Only someone who had money could buy this house and it's the sort of house that I have always aspired to owning myself one day. So it is hard to believe Jane when she insists that I have already owned this particular house for almost six years.

As I pay the taxi driver in the blue euros, the front door opens and two screaming children, my children, coming running down the path and jump up at me demanding my attention.

They say that when you go for an interview the person asking the question and conducting the interrogation makes up their mind about you in the first few moments after you walk through the door. The rest of the interview is just a formality. I would never have thought that the same maxim could have been applied to your own children, but truth be told, I disliked them the first moment I saw them. Of course, how was I to know that they were *my* children: that these were the kids I had fathered and whom I was meant to love unconditionally, to protect and nurture for all their years?

Yes, I must love them, and that love must start now.

I reach down and pick them up in my arms, and smile, kissing them both on their little foreheads and squeezing them, before putting them down again.

"Go inside, and help your mother with the bag..." I start to say, but thankfully they have already gone, to find something more exciting to do.

"Son, are you okay?" my mother asks, engulfing me in her arms before I can reply. My mother. From what I can see, she is the only true point of continuity so far in my personal life.

As I approach the front door of my house, my new house, I make a decision. One of those gut instinct decisions that I have only made a couple of times. Like the day I decided to marry Sarah...no, bad example..., like the day I decided to study Physics at University (did I?). Perhaps that's a bad example too. Maybe in *this* life there are no good examples to compare with... But that is exactly the point. I make a decision, that from now on I will assume that this is indeed my real life.

Lying in hospital all night with the doctors checking me over every few hours was a pretty sobering experience. It changes a person's perspective and it has become apparent that there is probably nothing wrong with me at all, apart from concussion. So I must assume that everything which I remember as being true can really only be a dream. It will be hard, but I can see no other way. I cannot keep second guessing everything, and confusing myself as to what *is* real, and what *was* real.

If I can physically touch the door, and I can touch Jane, and the two children, whom I *will* love, *must* love, and if I can breathe the air, the same air as they breathe, and if I can feel the pain on the back of my head, then this has to be real, and this is real. Yes, from now on, this *is* my life, and I must learn to live again.

I turn to Jane, who is behind me, carrying my overnight bag. I smile at her, swooping her up in my arms before she can say anything, and carry her over the threshold of my new life. Our new life. For a few seconds there is a momentary vision of me doing the same thing with Sarah ten years ago, but I blink hard and mentally erase the picture. It goes slowly, the last thing I remember being the smell of the perfume she wore, and the sound of her laughter. But then it is gone, and I am inside the hallway of my new house with Jane in my arms, and the smell of her perfume and her laughter.

My house is large. Very large. We enter through a large hallway with a chequer board floor of white and black tiles. A large wooden staircase leads up to a landing with a small hallway leading off it, before the staircase turns and disappears further upstairs to the first floor proper. Bright light floods down into the stairwell from above, presumably from a large window or cupola in the roof. A small table sits on the first landing, a large bowl of yellow flowers looking impressive and inviting.

On the ground floor there are three large reception areas. And I mean large. The room at the front of the house has a large bay window and a white baby grand piano in the window alcove. More flowers sit on top of the piano filling the room with beautiful fresh scent. One whole wall is lined with bookshelves, the other dominated by a white marble fireplace, and in front of it, two large white leather sofas sit in the middle of the room upon a white, deep, shag-pile carpet. It's a fantastic room, and I fall in love with it immediately. Either Jane or I have excellent taste.

The next room is a sizeable dining room, centred around a huge mahogany table. This leads onto an impressive music room cum TV room. If you can call it a TV. It's like a small cinema, with one wall covered by a massive LED TV, and surround-sound speakers in every corner.

I walk out of the cinema into the kitchen. A gorgeous kitchen. Large windows overlook a forest of a garden, the four walls covered in expensive cupboards, kitchen appliances, washing machines, two floor-to-ceiling American style freezers, and a massive red Aga cooker. The focal point is a central podium, encircled by six high stools, with what seem like fifty shining copper pots hung from ceiling hooks above it. All the surfaces in the kitchen are either shining steel, or expensive polished black granite. The floor is made up of large red kitchen tiles. It looks… it looks just great.

A side door takes me into a large conservatory, and then out through a door into the garden, full of flowers, and equally as impressive as the rest of the house. It's amazing.

Jane is following me around, hanging onto my arm. She smiles as she can see the pleasure on my face at seeing the house, as if for the first time, not fully grasping yet that for me this is the first time.

My mother follows us out into the garden. A taxi has arrived to take her home and she has to get back to cook dinner for my father. I thank her for babysitting, and kiss her goodbye. She goes, leaving Jane and I alone again.

"So, where do we sleep?" I turn and ask her.

"You honestly can't remember?…How can you forget that?" she winks at me. "Come..." she says, grabbing my hand and leading the way. "Come with me…".

She leads me upstairs, past the landing on which there is a large playroom for the children and a bathroom, then up more stairs to the first floor. Three bedrooms, and another bathroom. She takes me into the largest of them all, the one at the back of the house, and closes the door behind me.

A plush white carpet, a large bed with the biggest down pillows I have ever seen, and massive windows overlooking the gardens, with sumptuous white curtains. One wall is covered in mirrored wardrobes, and there is a half-open door leading to an en-suite. And on the large dresser a white orchid.

Like all the rooms I have seen so far, this one is immaculate. Clean. Ordered. Not a thing out of place.

I sit down on the bed and look around. Jane stands in front of me, running her hands through my hair.

"Welcome home, James…" she kisses me, then pauses, and sits down beside me. "James, can you honestly not remember anything about us? Not even…well, …" and she looks suggestively at the pillows and the bed behind us.

"No". I say truthfully. How can I tell her that in my dream I have spent the past ten years making love to another woman?

I can see in her eyes that Jane is trying her best. She is trying to be as positive as possible, but I know that inside she is confused, worried and full of questions. But what can I say to her?

"Just think," I whisper, holding her hand. "When we make love, it will be like making love for the first time again." And for me, it will be.

She smiles.

"Jane, can we go and talk to the children? Maybe I should talk to them and explain what has happened to Daddy…?"

As we get up to go and find the children I notice a framed photograph on the dressing table. It's a wedding photograph of two young people, both of whom I recognise immediately.

One is Jane, and the other is me.

I pick it up and stare at it, scared by what I see. In my hands I am holding the proof that I really am not dreaming this. I can see with my own eyes that I married Jane, and even more, I can see that on the day of our wedding we both looked incredibly happy. Very happy. And yet, even as I look at it, I see another photo superimposed on top of it in my mind. One of me wearing a kilt, and holding the hand of Sarah, on the steps of a church in the East End of Edinburgh.

I put the picture back and leave the room, closing the door behind me as if I were in somebody else's house.

Following the sound of the children's voices upstairs to the second floor, I find them both sitting with Jane on a bed in one of the rooms at the front of the house. A big sign on the door of the room proudly announces, "*Keep Out. Allison's Room.*"

So what is the other one called? And which one is Allison?

As I walk into the room, both of the kids look up at me, and I see that the older one has tears in her eyes. She begins to cry. The younger one stares at her sister for a second, and then immediately copies her. Jane looks over at me.

"I've just told them that you are not very well, and that the doctor says we should let you rest for a few days…and that, for a while, you might not remember some things…"

"…but Mummy says that you'll soon be better, and that it was only because you were feeling ill that you shouted at me", the large one immediately says in-between her tears.

"..and me," repeats the little one.

"Mummy's right." I lie, kneeling down in front of them both. I don't know how long it will take for me learn about my new life, and to forget the dreams of the other one. As I look at the two girls, I think immediately of my own two daughters,… at least, I think of Keira and Nicole, and I miss them. How can I miss a dream? How can my memories of them be so strong if they're not real? What is real? *I remember everything about Keira and Nicole…their births, their christenings, their first words and their first steps, their first teeth, their first days at school, times they were ill,…how can all of that be a dream?*

"…Mummy's right", I continue, "...but Daddy might behave a little strangely for a while, until I get better…I might forget things that we did in the past together. I might do strange things or say silly things…but don't worry and don't be scared. It's not that Daddy doesn't love you both very much …"-or at all-"it's just that daddy banged his head and everything inside got all shook up, and now it'll just take a while for all the thoughts and memories to find their way back into the correct boxes in my head. I'm hoping that you can help me remember everything. Daddy would love that."

What else can I say?

"I know..." Jane exclaims to the girls aloud, coming to the rescue. "Why not go and get your birthday and christening books, and your favourite photo albums, and we'll all go downstairs and have a cup of orange juice. Then you can play a little game with Daddy and show him all your photographs. And first one downstairs gets an extra chocolate biscuit."

The two girls both jump up, and the little one runs out the room. The larger one, obviously Allison, runs across to the other side of the room and starts looking through her shelves. I look over at Jane. Tears are running down her cheeks and she is wiping them away with a clean, white handkerchief. She smiles, then looks away. "I'd better go and help Elspeth," she says, "She can't reach the shelves…"

I am instantly alone. In my head I hear the voices of Sarah and Keira and Nicole, and in my heart I can feel a longing for them like I have never felt before. But then it is gone, and Allison is pulling on my hand.

"Daddy, here. Can you carry these?"

So together we go down the stairs to look at photographs and find out who I have become, and to learn about a life lived without memories, a life spent growing up in another world. A life lived and yet not lived at all.

My life.

CHAPTER 13
Memory Lane

Jane was a June bride, married on the 4th June 2000, a long silk dress which trailed gracefully around her feet, holding a posy of beautiful rare red orchids, with four of the cutest bridesmaids I've ever seen. Standing beside her on the steps of a church which I cannot place, is a young man, spotty, dressed in a green Gordon Highlander kilt, but looking immensely proud, and actually, if I may say so, damned good looking.

It's me.

I smile in spite of myself, and Elspeth giggles. She reaches forward to the photograph and points to Jane's stomach, and says, "That's me. In mummy's tummy."

"Yes darling, that's where you lived until mummy and daddy decided to have you, but that wasn't until a few years later. I wasn't pregnant when I married daddy."

Elspeth laughs, jumping up and down on the spot with her thumb in her mouth and from the way they anticipate the photographs as we turn the pages, it's not hard to tell that we've all looked together at the photographs a hundred times before.

Although most of the people in the photographs are complete strangers, I do recognise a few faces at the wedding reception, which appears to have been held in the grounds of some large stately home. My oldest friends in the world are there, Alex, and his brother Iain, with whom I played football when I was six, my parents, my gran, some aunts and uncles and a bunch of friends from University.

In a few of the photos there is someone who appears to have been my best man, but whom I have never seen before. Sadly I recognise none of Jane's family, apart from her brother, whose face rings a bell. As I try to place him, I suddenly remember that he was a Prefect in the year above me at school.

Over a hundred people must have come to the evening do, and some of the photographs were hilarious. Especially the one of my friend Alex lying in a small fountain, his legs kicking in the air, the surprised look on his face just typical of him.

"He got very drunk…fell in, then his brother climbed in to get him out, and he slipped…"

And sure enough, the photograph on the next page was of Alex and Iain both sitting in the fountain together, laughing and hugging each other, a water lily dangling from the top of Iain's head. It looks like it was a wonderful day. I almost wish that I had been there.

We look at two whole albums of wedding photographs, and just when I thought I was done, Allison reappears from upstairs with four new, large ones.

"All right, darling. But Daddy and I will look at them ourselves. It's off to bed with you both. You've got school in the morning."

Quite unexpectedly, a very attractive blonde woman suddenly appears at the door to the room and starts speaking to Jane in broken English.

"Shall I take babies in bed, now, Mrs Quinn?"

"Yes, thank you Margareta. That would be nice."

Margareta rounds up the children, ignoring the protests of Elspeth who tries to hide behind one of the large white leather chairs, and only volunteers to cooperate when a lollipop appears magically out of Margareta's jeans.

"Who's she?" I ask as the door closes and silence returns to the room.

"Our Polish Au Pair girl. We've had her almost a whole year now…It was your idea darling. You chose her…" then quietly. "Since they're out, do you want to look at our honeymoon pictures?"

I look at the daunting pile of albums that Allison has dropped on the floor in front of us.

"So many photographs from on honeymoon?" I ask.

"Well, it was more than just a honeymoon. When we got married we gave up work darling. We both wanted to take time off and see the world before we settled down to our careers and had children." Jane explains. "…Look, there we are at the Oktoberfest in Munich, and here, look, that's you in Florence, pretending to be the statue of David. Not quite so big, but much more beautiful…"

So for the next hour, as we go through the albums one by one, we trace the path of a two-year around-the-world trek that took us to every continent of the world and back, including six months spent working for Saatchi and Saatchi in Hong Kong, and six months spent working for Australia's top advertising agency in Sydney, not far from the Opera House.

We are curled up on the floor in front of the crackling fire with her lying between my legs, head resting against my chest, my arms wrapped around her, holding the album pages as she turns them over, pointing and reminiscing.

Occasionally I lift the book close to my eyes, and stare. Looking at the images recorded in the album is both amusing and scary at the same time. I see myself doing all these things, standing in front of famous monuments in far distant countries I have only ever dreamed of visiting, and yes, it is me, definitely me. Yet I have no memory of it, and no memories of the woman who is constantly by my side. Constantly my companion.

"Tell me about us," I ask her gently.

She turns and looks up at me. Tears well up in her eyes again. I can see she wants to ask me if I really can't remember, to question me, not willing to simply accept that I can so easily have forgotten a lifetime's memories.

I wipe the tears away and stroke her hair.

"Please tell me," I say again, the hidden plea surfacing just enough for Jane to realise I am asking her for help. Help to get my life back again.

"We were married in 2000," she starts. "We'd been living together for four years by then. I moved in with you just after you got your first job with Saatchi's in London..." And so I learn about myself. About my first job in advertising, when I won my first account, how when after we had toured the world we came back to London in 2002 to have our first baby, all prepared to live in a garret somewhere and starve, a small, tightly knit family, but spoiling it all by finding a fantastic job within two weeks with 'Peters, Hall and Irvine', and then ending up buying a terraced cottage in Teddington, with no garret, but a very large garden.

That was fine for a while, but then Elspeth came along in 2005 and we ran out of space. So in 2006 I left PHI, moved to a bigger salary with Cohen Advertising and bought the relative mansion we live in now.

It would seem that I have done a lot in my life. Yet I remember so little of it. Though that which I have done, almost all of it I have done with Jane, whom I met again at an inter-varsity rugby dance during university and kissed for the second time underneath the mistletoe.

One kiss, that led to a lifetime of memories.

None of them mine.

CHAPTER 14
Candlelight

It is late that night when Jane leads me into the bedroom, and I close the door behind me.

We had climbed the stairs together, hand-in-hand, like lovers going to bed for the first time. Downstairs, the warmth of the fire, the wine, the smell of her perfume, the smell of her skin, the touch of her lips when we kissed, the intimacy, and my need…together it began to make it all seem so right.

I knew it would come, that it would be inevitable, and I could see the need in Jane's eyes. Not a physical need. No. Rather, the need that I must give her the assurance that I would love her now, as I had done before; that I had not woken up from my dream a different man from who I was before my concussion. Jane needed me to show her that our union was still strong, and as we climbed the stairs together, turning at the landing and then on and upwards, our bedroom coming closer, both of us could feel that what would happen on the other side of the door this night, what would happen on the marital bed, would mean as much to one as it meant to the other.

So I close the door to the bedroom, and Jane kisses me softly on the lips.

"I'll be with you in a minute darling…" she says squeezing my hand and disappearing into the en-suite. I stand alone by the door, not moving. I am nervous. Very nervous. What should I do? I feel like an intruder in someone else's house. This room is strange to me. There is nothing that I can associate with, nothing that is familiar. I feel as if I shouldn't be here at all. Like a teenager about to be seduced for the first time by a more experienced woman he barely knows.

I switch off the light hoping that everything may seem more manageable in the dark.

As my eyes adjust, I notice a glow from underneath the bathroom door which slowly begins to diffuse throughout the room, until I can see once again.

By now, things are not so clear cut. The edges of my reality have begun to blur, and I know that I need this as much as Jane: I am desperate to reach out, to touch another person's soul, to seek salvation from the abyss that has threatened me for the past two days. I need saving. I need Sarah.

It slips out faster than I can control. It sneaks under my guard and envelopes me. Sarah. I need Sarah.

I bite my lip and step forwards, spinning around, my hands flying upwards to grab my senses and pull the hair from my head.

My spinning takes me to the end of the bed, and I sit down on the mattress, looking across the room at my reflection in the dresser mirror, a threatening image which peers back dimly through the darkness and the murkiness which is engulfing me.

Sarah is a dream. This is real. THIS is real. *THIS.*

The door opens to the bathroom and Jane steps out. She is carrying a small candle in her hand, the light from the yellow flame casting a warm glow around her. She stands in the doorway, a long, black silk nightdress flowing down and around her body, contouring and complimenting her beautiful natural curves, the swell of her breasts accentuated by the flickering of the flame.

She steps forward, one of her long naked legs limbs protruding through a split in the nightgown. My eyes journey down, turning at the end of her toes, and following her curves back up, until I meet her eyes. I linger there, the moment and the feeling that it invokes within my loins casting me back twenty three years to the first time I danced with her at the school Christmas dance, to the first time our eyes met and something deep within us connected. Something that has somehow lasted all this time, and taken until now to come to fruition. Something that has reached out through the passage of the years, and brought us to this moment now.

I rise, and move towards her. Slowly. Lifting one of my hands, searching, clasping hers, now outstretched and inviting me, needing me, urging me.

There are moments in everyone's lives which define us, that shape us and tell us who we are, moments of which we dream, and for which we lust. For some it is a moment of fame, for others, a moment of glory, or sudden wealth. More commonly, at least amongst men, such thoughts, are almost entirely sexual in nature. I am no different from most men. In that I am perfectly normal.

I have fantasised about this moment for the past twenty years. It has never left me. There have been times where it has driven me to distraction, and where the sense has gone from my head. There have been times where I have treated Sarah terribly, because she has not been the sexual woman of my dreams, because she was not Jane. I have, I know and admit, made love to Sarah many times, and wished, hoped for, and imagined that it was Jane.

For the past two years this fantasy has driven me to the edge of reason, taking over all my senses, squeezing out my sanity, engulfing me, swallowing me, until it had to be fulfilled.

Now it is here. The moment. The time. All that I have wished for.

Jane steps past me and places the candle on the dresser in front of the mirror, beside our wedding photograph. Her back is to me as she reaches up with both hands and slips the straps of her nightdress over the edges of her shoulders.

The black silk falls silently to the floor, the orange glow from the candle bouncing off the mirror and revealing in reflection one of the most perfect bodies I have ever seen. Large, full breasts, perfect nipples, a fantastic waistline, a firm stomach.

I step up behind her, and wrap my arms around her waist, nestling my head between her face and her shoulders. She looks at me in the mirror, and I stare back at her reflection, feasting my eyes on the perfection, capturing every single part of this vision, recording it and storing it. Memorising every, single, minute detail. This, I believe now, is the moment that will define me. When I am old and sitting in a wheelchair and wondering about life, and questioning what it was all about, this will be that single instant in time which I will remember more than any other. This is my moment. This is my dream. And it is everything I have expected.

Perfection.

My response is no secret. It presses against Jane, bursting to escape the confines of my trousers, striving to unite us both, to melt our bodies into a single, fused one. To release, and let flow. To seal the moment for ever.

She turns, her eyes looking up at me, thanking me for my approval. Her cheek slides along my face, the warm skin electric, tingling, alive. Her lips kiss my left ear, her hands reaching down, finding me, welcoming me.

"Please James, I need you...*just* you..."

The words are whispered, but they echo in my head, and they shake me to the core. For suddenly it is not Jane speaking but Sarah, the same phrase, the same sexy low husky whisper, the same glancing kiss on my ear lobe. The same gesture of intimacy that Sarah has shared with me a thousand times over the past twelve years, the same phrase that only she and I have held secret between us. Suddenly Sarah is speaking in my mind. I hear her voice, I hear her say the words, and I feel her touch. Suddenly Sarah is alive, and it is Sarah that is beside me. Not Jane.

I step back, shocked and scared.

What am I doing? What is happening? Where am I?

Jane looks up at me, reaching out to me, pulling me back.

"Darling, darling…what is the matter? Are you okay? I'm sorry…have I done something wrong?"

I blink and look around me. Like a bell reverberating in an empty church, Sarah's voice echoes in my head. I hear her speak, I feel her words, and yet…

"James…?"

I look at Jane. I see her there, I know she is real. My senses cannot lie? Can they?

I shake my head and turn away. I reach the bed, lie down and curl into a ball, my hands tightly clenched fists pressing urgently against my forehead. I close my eyes and begin to shake, sobbing, Jane curls up beside me, lifting a blanket to cover us both. Stroking my head, whispering softly, rocking me gently.

I keep my eyes closed, and when I open them I am alone. The room is full of sunlight and Jane is gone.

CHAPTER 15
Gone Fishing

Throwing on a dressing-gown, a male's, which I suppose must be mine, I take the steps two at a time down to the kitchen. No one is there. I walk quickly around the ground floor and find it empty. Back in the kitchen I notice a piece of yellow paper stuck to the kettle.

"James, sorry to leave you alone. Hope you are feeling better today. Your car is in the garage. I've taken the Volvo. Gone to work. Call me."

How can I call her? I don't know where she works.

In the bathroom I find everything I need to shave, and I run myself a big hot bath. The house is very quiet without the screaming of the children, and I lie soaking in the still water. Thinking.

Reaching no conclusions, I dry myself down in a large red towel, and wrap it around my waist. One of the mirrored wardrobes in the bedroom I find is full of men's clothing. All my size. Taking down a fresh pair of blue jeans, an expensive looking black cotton shirt, and a lambswool jumper, I look at the designer labels and realise that this is just another indication of how much more the advertising world pays in comparison to…in comparison to what? To a Product Manager? I have to stop making these unhelpful comparisons.

The doorbell rings, and I answer it, signing for a large bouquet of extravagant flowers. An expensive bouquet of flowers. Not the sort you often buy for your wife, more the sort that comes with a note from your boss wishing you a good, and speedy, recovery. The sort of bouquet that comes when your boss realises that his best ad man really did have a bad concussion after all and that maybe he should have insisted he went to hospital immediately instead of presenting to clients.

The front room is full of natural light, and I sit at the piano for a while, playing some music, something I learned long, long ago. It's been a long time since I played. I don't have a piano at home, and even if we did, I would never have the time.

Margareta appears from nowhere and comes into the room, sitting on one of the sofas, and listening to me play the beginning of one of Beethoven's pieces, although I can't remember which one it is.

"I didn't know you could play, James?" she says, genuinely surprised.

I look across at her and see that she is studying my face. Her lips are open, almost as if she is about to say something. But she doesn't. I look down and focus on the black and white keys, trying to prevent my fingers from tying themselves in knots, and turning a Fugue into Chopsticks.

A soft hand rests on my shoulder, and Margareta is beside me. I can feel the heat from her chest against the side of my right cheek.

"James, you play... excellently. How is it that you have never told no one this about. You always surprise me, my James."

The hand and the word 'my' are a gesture of intimacy that catch me by surprise. Stupidly I feel my face flush, and realise that I must be blushing. Why?

"I...." She starts to say something.

"Yes?"

"I...James, I am worried about you. Are you okay?" she asks, her hand not moving, the intimacy continuing.

"Yes, Margareta, I am fine. The doctor says..." I try to reply, but am quickly interrupted.

"Margareta? What for you call me Margareta? Do you not like to remember to call me Gretka? Like you normally do?"

I stop playing for a moment and turn towards her. For a brief moment I begin to wonder if there is something that I am missing. Something that I should know. But then she laughs, shyly, and walks out of the room, saying, "The children are happy you played with them last evening. You make them glad."

A few minutes later I hear the front door close and I am alone in the house again.

Bored with the piano, and not able to remember anything else, I get up and examine the book collection on the shelves. An eclectic mix, but I'm pleased to find that I still love Wilbur Smith. There are about ten of his books on the shelf, and I take one down. "*The Green Nile*". It's not one that I have ever read before. I look at the others on the shelf and see: "*The Lion Feeds*", "*Rage*", "*Elephant Song*", "*Zambezi*", "*Desert Sands*". At least three titles that I haven't read yet. Taking them down and looking through the introductory pages I find that they were all published in the late nineteen-nineties. Strange, I was sure I had read all of his novels.

The clock chimes on the mantelpiece, breaking the spell. It's twelve o'clock. My stomach begins to rumble. I wander back to the kitchen, and stand in the doorway, leaning against the doorframe. The kitchen is spotless, and there are hundreds of cupboards. All the pots and pans hang motionlessly from the ceiling, and the cooker looks like it has never been used at all. The size of the kitchen makes me feel uncomfortable. I just wouldn't know where to start if I was to attempt to cook myself lunch. Not here.

As I hover indecisively in the doorway, I notice a set of small hooks on the wall underneath one of the cupboards, from one of which hangs what looks like a key fob with an electronic pad. I pick it off its hook and walk through to the garage.

Inside I find an Audi…an Audi '*Something*'… that's as best I can describe it. I have never seen this model before, although it looks very expensive and it reminds me a little of the Audi TT that I have always wanted to drive, but could never afford. Since it's a double garage, and there is only one car parked inside it now, according to Jane's note on the kettle, this must be my car.

Fantastic.

Inside a walk-in cupboard under the stairs I find some shoes that fit my size, and a leather jacket which also fits me very comfortably. I'm getting used to this and I take them, not worrying anymore that I am stealing from anyone apart from myself.

A button on the wall opens the garage door, and another one beside it sets the metal gates in motion, gliding slowly inward and onto our gravel driveway. The key fits neatly into the door of the Audi, and I slide into the front seat, which is already adjusted perfectly to my height and leg length. A turn of the key sets off a loud alarm, and it takes a moment or two of rapid fumbling with the electronic pad, pressing the button several times, before there is an electronic *'beep beep'* and the alarm shuts off. Thank god.

A low growl, a little like a TVR but not quite so gutsy, and the Audi springs into life. Brilliant. Driving out of the garage and into the street, another press of a button on my keypad and the garage and the gate close automatically behind me. As I turn the corner at the end of the street, I feel the edges of my mouth turn upwards into a broad smile. Boys toys, and all that. But it's a BIG boy's toy. The biggest I've ever had.

I can understand how concussion may have made me forget my job, my wife, my children and my life, but there's no way that I'd ever have forgotten this.

No way.

If anything, this must be the dream. Not the other way round.

My father is sitting at the back of the pub, in the corner by a window. From there he gets a good view of the boats passing by on the Thames, and he can keep an eye on his fishing tackle resting on the side of the river, which is just ten steps away from the back entrance to the pub. It's his favourite spot, either sitting on the river bank alone with his thoughts, or sitting in that same spot, keeping a pint of London Pride company, and enjoying the atmosphere of the best kept secret in Sunbury-on-Thames. Few people come to the Riverside Inn, and most people don't even know it's there. The locals keep it to themselves, and the bar owner, a retired banker from the city, likes to keep it that way. It wasn't hard to guess he would be here, on his second day of retirement. When he was alive...before..., he used to talk all the time about when, once the 'bloodsuckers' had got their last drop of blood from him and he'd clocked off for the last time, how he was going to spend the whole summer down here, just fishing. Not a care in the world. Just him, his pipe, and the river.

"Hi dad," I say, sitting down beside him with two fresh pints of Pride. "Are they biting today?"

He smiles at me, shifting the pipe in his mouth with his left hand.

"Hi son. How are you feeling?"

He lifts his right hand and pats me on the shoulder. My father was,...is..., never one for great shows of affection, but this simple pat on the shoulder is quite a large gesture for him. A warm feeling floods through me, and a million memories of my father are rekindled. I realise then just how much I have missed him, and how incredible it is now, just to be able to sit with him and have his company once again.

"Have you eaten, Dad? I'm starving. Jane went to work, and I just didn't feel like cooking anything by myself."

"No, I haven't. I'd forgotten all about eating. Actually, I was just thinking about going back outside and trying to catch Old Ralph."

Old Ralph. After all this time, dad's still chasing Old Ralph. Which means that the battle between him and the legendary catfish has been raging for over twenty years. Twenty years. Do catfish even live that long? Of course, when the battle started, it was just plain old "*the biggest catfish you've ever seen*", but over the years, and several close calls in which it could have gone either way - my dad in the river, or Old Ralph out in the net - my dad has come to respect the fish a lot. "That big catfish" became "*Ralph*", and then ten years later "Old *Ralph*." It's been "*Old Ralph*" ever since. They've become friends, and have grown old together. I often wonder if he ever did manage to catch it, would he be lonely afterwards? Sometimes, dad would just come down and stare at the river, sitting for hours on the edge of the water, smoking his pipe and planning his strategy, without ever casting a line. It was almost as if they were psyching each other out, or were they just enjoying each other's company? I wouldn't be surprised if the whole time my dad was down there, *Old Ralph* was lying on his back just under the edge of the river bank, in the cool shadow, just blowing bubbles, catching flies, with one fin behind his gills, and the other lying on his stomach. I could so easily picture him just lying there, catching the cool current, and looking up at my dad through the surface of the river. Two adversaries. Neither in a hurry. Neither going anywhere fast.

So we take our baskets of fish and chips out into the warm autumn sunshine and sit on the green tarpaulin already laid out on the bank of the river. My father baits the hook, and casts the line back out into the river, into a shaded pool underneath some trees on the other side of the river. He fits it into the tripod, and sits back down. We eat in silence, the fish tasting excellent, and the chips crisp and salty, but soft in the middle. Just right.

"How bad is it son?" he eventually asks, licking a piece of batter off his fingers.

"What?" I reply, knowing full well what he's asking.

"Listen, I'm not Jane, and I'm not your mother. I know you, son. You wouldn't tell them everything, in case they go off the deep end and panic. Just how bad is it? How much can you remember, and how much have you forgotten?"

It's a fair question, but to be honest, I haven't been hiding anything. It's been in my interest to tell them the truth on this one.

"It's just like I said, no worse, although, actually, it probably couldn't get any worse. It's like the past ten, maybe even twelve years, have been wiped clean from my memory. Just like they never happened. In fact, to tell you the truth Dad, I don't really know how much I have forgotten."

"And what did the doctors say? Will it come back…your memory?"

"They don't know. Although, they think there's a fair chance that it will."

He's silent for a moment. He looks across at his rod, then back at me.

"And Jane, son. What can you remember about her? Can you remember how much you love her? Can you remember the wedding?"

"Dad…"

"Listen son, I'm just asking. Jane's a wonderful lass, but if you can't remember marrying her…can you remember falling in love with her?"

It's a big question. A good question. One I don't know how to answer, except truthfully.

"Between you and me, dad, I don't know. It's like…it's like I've just started dating her again…except, I've already got two kids, I haven't had the honeymoon, or…"

"Or the other stuff?"

"No."

"Well, the way I see it son, you're either a lucky man, and you've got the opportunity now to fall in love all over again, and to have all the excitement, and lust, that goes with that… or…"

"Or what?"

"Or you're in big trouble."

There's a tug on the line, and my dad jumps up, dropping the by now empty basket on the ground, and grabbing the pole from the tripod.

The line goes slack, before he can even start to play the fish. He reels it in, and the bait is gone.

"That's Old Ralph" he smiles. "That's him."

"How do you know?" I ask before he says anything, already knowing the answer. I've heard it a thousand times before.

"Because only he knows how to get the bait off the line, without getting snagged. He's a wily bugger, is Old Ralph."

He bends down, opening up his box of bait, and threading a new large maggot on his hook. It's covered in a concoction of gook, a special mixture that my dad has mixed up over the years and swears to. "My secret weapon...*He loves it.*" I hear him say in my mind, recalling this moment from a thousand times in the past.

"...I'll just give him some more of this... My secret weapon.... He loves it..." he says aloud a fraction of a second later, almost as if he had heard me.

"Listen son, just promise me, that if things get difficult, if things get strange, you'll tell me. Whatever it is. No matter how weird it is...I promise I won't tell your mother, and I can only imagine what must be going on in your mind."

He looks across at me, and as he casts the line back over his shoulder and lets it fly back onto the river, he smiles. For a second there is a look in his eye, and it's almost as if he knows exactly what's going on. It's almost as if he knows the secret, and for one moment I wonder if he knows the answer. Should I tell him?

Perhaps not. At least, not just yet.

"Thanks dad." I reply. "I promise."

"Here, you take this, and I'll go and get us both another pint." He hands me the rod, and pats me on the shoulder as he goes past, stopping for a brief second. "Remember son, we love you. And we're here for you."

It may sound soppy, but it's one of those Walton family moments. A moment in time that I never ever thought I would experience again, and a moment that I will never forget as long as I live.

My dad.

CHAPTER 16
Back to Work

Alice gets up from behind the reception desk and comes running round to greet me, enveloping me in a warm, tight hug.

"James…" She says, squeezing me so hard I struggle to reply. "What are you doing back so soon?"

"I couldn't stand being alone in the house. I got bored." I lied. The truth is, I don't feel at home in my own home, and I got fed up of being alone with my own repetitive thoughts.

"Who sent me the flowers? Was that your idea or Richard's?"

"Richard's. Honestly. He was really worried about you…"

"About me not coming back, about me forgetting all about the Scotia Telecom deal, about him not getting the ten million euros deal after all…"

"Don't be so cynical James. Anyway, it's not just about 'him' getting the ten million euros deal. It's your deal.."

"And he knows it. That's exactly what Richard's worried about. Where is the old man anyway?"

"He's in his office. He's got Mather and Sons with him just now, but they'll be leaving soon. I think he will want to see you then. You never know,…maybe today's the day."

"What do you mean?"

"You know, '*the*' day. '"

"What day?"

"The big 'P' day!"

The phone rings on reception, and she answers it. She makes a sign in the air, and a face, turns to the computer screen and reaches for her mouse. I take the hint, and leave her to it, climbing the stairs to the first floor. I walk into the open plan area and head towards my office at the back of the floor.

A chorus of "Hey James…", "How are you James?" and ""Remember me, James?", and "Don't forget, you borrowed fifty euros from me last week!" from everyone around the office, followed by a round of laughter. As I approach my office, the floor goes quiet, and I can feel all eyes drilling into the back of my head.

Opening the door, I find a large, framed, one-meter-by-one-meter square photograph hanging on the wall behind my desk. Underneath the picture are the words, *'James Quinn, Calvin Klein Model of the Year 2012 '*. And above, looking surprised and shocked, is me, captured for all the world to see, plain as day, in my wonderful Marks and Spencer tartan boxer shorts, and very little else.

Everyone bursts into laughter. Including me. I look totally ridiculous.

"Hi James, do you want me to come now or later?" a voice asks from behind. It turns out to belong to a red headed woman, probably about twenty-three, called Claire. My PA. Apparently.

"How about in ten minutes? Give me time to get myself a cup of tea, and get my coat off."

"...and what about the rest of your clothes? Keeping them on today are we?" someone else says loudly from somewhere behind her.

"Funny guy." I say loudly in reply.

"Don't worry, I'll get your tea. You just take it easy." Claire offers and walks away quickly.

Admiring the photograph of myself again, it strikes me then that the people at Cohen Advertising are a friendly, tightly knit bunch who know how to have fun. I decide not to take down the photograph but to leave it hanging there. It'll remind me of the first day of my new life, and that it's best not to take yourself too seriously.

Closing the door, and blocking off the chatter coming from the lively office outside, I sit in my chair behind my large desk, grasping the armrest firmly and surveying my new world. The office of an advertising executive in the heart of London.

I like my office. It has a good feel to it. The décor and the woodwork is sophisticated, yet not over the top. Simple, but smart. Rising, I cross over to the filing cabinets and look through each of the drawers, familiarising myself with the contents, mentally making a map of my new territory, learning the new landscape.

Returning to my desk, I go through the drawers one by one. Diaries, pens, paper, two rulers, a calculator, calendars, an empty stapler, useful office stuff, and a photograph of Jane and the children turned face down and under a pile of papers in the second drawer up. I pull it out and look at the smiling faces of the girls, but feel nothing. There is no familiarity, no paternal instinct, no smile that creeps on to my lips as I look at my supposed offspring. Instead the children are strangers. Pretty strangers, but strangers none the less. Jane smiles back at me, attractive as ever, and I look closely at her face, following the contours of her cheeks, the sparkle in her eyes, the curl of her lips, and the dimple on the left of her face. I see the resemblance between her and the girls, but I don't recognise anything of me in either of them. They are their mother's daughters.

The third drawer is locked, and doesn't respond to any coaxing or pulling. Strange. Then I remember the small black key on the end of my keychain with my car keys, and I pull it out from my jacket pocket, trying it in the lock. It turns.

The drawer opens, revealing another diary, a digital camera, and at the back of the drawer, a box of computer disks. I pull out the disks, and open them, wondering if I should take the time to look through what they contain now or later. Taking out a few and looking at the titles, I notice that at the back of the box, behind the disks, there is a small bag of white powder.

For a second or two I stare at the bag.

I look up. Can the others outside see me?

Quickly crossing to the windows of my office, I turn the toggle on the blinds and instantly the world outside disappears. I lock the office door, trying the handle once, then return to my seat.

The bag is still there. Small. Probably about 3 grams worth.

I close my eyes. My forehead is clammy, the memories quickly flooding back, my pulse already racing.

It has been almost seven years since I became clean. Since I realised how close I had come to destroying myself, and since I was fired from my first job.

I hadn't taken much, and I was not an addict that couldn't live without it, but I had come uncomfortably close to the edge.

I had only started because it had helped me through a bad patch. It helped me gloss over bad memories, to deal with the pictures in my mind that I needed to forget. To cope with the grief. And since I couldn't turn to Sarah, to tell her how I felt about it all, Charlie had become my friend. My confidante.

Though not all friends are good.

In hindsight, being caught snorting a line in the bathroom with another member of the marketing team at one of the office parties had been a blessing in the disguise. Fired on the spot, the wake-up call had come just in time.

It had been a good company, and an interesting job that I had lost, and I had been a fool.

But never again.

I pick up the sachet, and walk quickly to the bathroom, where I lock myself in one of the cubicles. For a second, I stare at the packet. The stress, the confusion and the fear of the past weeks hits me like a wall, and my blood pulses.

I could be happy. In a minute I know it could all go away. I could feel great. I open the packet with my fingernail.

When I return to my office a few minutes later, there is a smile on my face. And I do feel great.

High.

But not because of the cocaine. High because I did the right thing and flushed it down the toilet. Because the last thing I need right now is to go backwards, to start chemically altering the world around me. It's already weird enough.

High, because for the first time in days, I am in control.

"So, Claire..." I say to my new PA as she brings in the tea a few minutes later,- I've never had a PA before, this is a bit of a novelty to me, "Tell me about the rest of my week. What have I got on?"

She looks up at me, a bit surprised.

"...oh, Sorry, Claire, I don't know if you've found out yet, but..."

"About your concussion? Yes, I know. Richard told me, and anyway, it's my job to know."

"Good. So you'll understand if I ask you to please be patient with me. I've got temporary amnesia...I honestly can't remember a lot of things. The doctors say it'll come back, but for now, I'm hoping that you'll help me get through the next few weeks. I'm going to rely on you."

She smiles then, and sits up straighter in her chair, clasping her notebook to her chest, and opening a large green diary on her knee.

"Well, this afternoon, if you feel up to it, you've got your meeting with the Board of the Millennium Dome to discuss Cohen's creating the new advertising and marketing campaign for the "Pleasure Dome", or whatever else we suggest they call it. Then tomorrow at 11am, you've got your inaugural kick-off meeting with the Scotia Telecom marketing team. That's scheduled to last over lunch until 4 pm. Which will allow time to get back to the office for the team meeting with Richard at 5 pm. Then in the evening, you're meant to be taking your wife to the opera. I've got the tickets as you requested last week, but they were expensive."

I nod a few times, wondering what on earth I'm meant to be doing at each of these meetings. And the Millennium Dome? What does this mean? Does it still exist?

"And what am I going to see at the opera?"

I hate the opera.

"Tosca."

What?

"Thank you Claire. And will you be coming with me to these meetings?" I ask, hoping she will. I think I'll need a little guidance.

Her lips break into a large smile, and she beams.

"Yes, James. If you would like."

"I would like that. In the meantime, can you get me all the files we have on both Scotia Telecom and the Millennium Dome. I want to read over them again tonight."

"Certainly. Although, the meeting with the Board of the Millennium Dome is only the first meeting with the full board. There's actually not much on file yet. Richard is really looking to you to develop this one pretty much from scratch, from Cohen's perspective. The deal is ours, on the face of the campaign you did for the Tate Modern last year and your previous history with the Dome project, but at Cohen's you really haven't done anything on it yet."

Great. Which means that I can't learn anything from any of the work I've may already have done. I'm really am going to have to do this from scratch. I hope I'm actually quite good at this.

I look across at Claire. She's quite pretty. Slim, her red hair in a bob, blue eyes, a nice figure, and when she smiles, two small dimples appear in her cheeks.

"Claire, concussion is a really funny thing. There's a possibility that I may act a little weird in the next couple of weeks, and since you're my PA you'll probably get the brunt of it, so I want to apologise in advance."

She nods.

"Some of the questions I may ask might appear a little silly, but please bear with me. Humour me for a while. Can you do that?"

She nods again.

"Okay, so let's start. Can you get me the files, and then after I've seen Richard, we'll go to the pub for a quick lunch and a case review, and then we'll head off to the Dome? Okay?"

Just as she gets up to leave, Richard appears in the doorway. He winks at me as Claire walks past him.

"So, you're back then, are you? Can't keep a good man down, that's what I say," he says, closing the door behind him. He walks across to one of my cabinets, slides it open and reaches inside, taking out a small bottle of whisky and two glasses. He pours us both one, and then sits down in the chair opposite me where Claire was sitting only two minutes before.

"I just wanted to pop down and say, well, sorry about the other day."

"For what?"

"You know,…for the thing in the taxi,…and for not sending you to the quack's straight away. I didn't realise it was so serious," he says, going bright red, and looking down at his shoes. Richard is embarrassed.

"At least not as serious as winning the ten million euro deal with Scotia Telecom?"

"Exactly…" he blurts out immediately, then realises it was a mistake. "No, I mean…"

"It's fine Richard, I know 'exactly' what you mean."

A moment's silence. Richards gets up and walks to the front of the office, resting one hand against the glass partition and looking out between the slats of the blinds onto the floor beyond.

"How long have you been with us now James?" Richard asks. Putting me on the spot. It's a question I really can't answer.

"Oh...long enough."

"Long enough for what?" Richard spins around. "You're not thinking of doing anything silly are you?"

It's really quite amusing, I think Richard thinks I'm considering leaving. On the contrary, I've only just joined.

"Listen James, it's time you and I had a chat. Time you and I thought of the bigger picture. Time you and I thought of the future."

This is getting interesting. Richard is looking down at his glass, cupping the glass in his palm and swirling the whisky around and around.

"You know, this Scotia deal is the icing on the cake of a really successful career with us so far. When you joined us in 2006, after you left Peters Hall and Irvine, I knew that you'd deliver the goods. I could feel it in my bones, you know what I mean? I could tell, I could tell you had it in you. And you've not let me down. I think the time has come James."

"And what time is that Richard?" genuinely interested. What is he talking about?

"Oh, don't play games with me James? You know exactly what I'm talking about. You've been gunning for this for years...you've been biting at my ankles almost every day, eager, pushing, chasing me in my footsteps, and now the time is here...Hang on a second, have those Saatchi boys been talking to you? You wouldn't think about going to them now would you?"

"Calm down Richard. Firstly, no I haven't been talking to 'those Saatchi boys' and no, I'm not playing games with you. Just tell me what it is you're getting at?"

"Stop it James. I'm not a fool. I know what you're up to. Now you've got the Scotia deal, you can write your own ticket wherever you go. And you and I both know that where you go, the Scotia deal will follow. So stop playing games man. What is it that you want...?"

I open my mouth to protest once again, that I honestly don't know what he's talking about, but am silenced before I can say a word.

"Okay, you win. I mean, I should have done it last year when you got the Body Shop deal, but I didn't and perhaps it was a mistake. A mistake that I'm admitting now, okay?"

"Listen Richard..."

"Bloody hell James. You drive a hard bargain. Okay, okay, you win, *okay*? You get a 40% rise in your base, the office opposite mine, a new car, and the big P. There it's done. It's yours."

"The big P?" It's that letter again.

"Are you trying to screw me? " Richard shouts. "Okay, 60% rise in base, and I'll backdate it all to when you won the Body Shop deal. And you're a Partner as from today!"

I smile. So that's what this is all about. I've just been made a partner. The Big 'P'.

For ten years I've believed that I've been a Product Manager. Quite a good salary, but nothing special. Then one day I wake up and find out that I've got a new career. Then on my first day on the job, I win a ten million euro deal, and on the second day in the office I get a 60% pay rise and get made Partner.

On the face of it, I seem to be doing quite well for myself.

"Done." I click my glass against Richard's. "I'll drink to that."

"So are you staying?" he asks, still a little nervous.

"Yes, Richard. I'm staying."

"Good." He says, knocking his glass back, and walking towards the door. "Now just make sure you do a good job on the Dome project. That one's worth another €5m, and in spite of what's been said, it's not a done deal yet. The Saatchi boys are still sniffing around it. It's up to you to tie that one down. That's €5m, not just for me, James. It's €5m for us. Partner. "

And with that, Richard is gone.

We're sitting at the back of the "All Bar One" opposite the Palace Theatre where 'Singing in the Rain' is still playing. I feel at home here, a rare piece of continuity in my otherwise fractured world. We've just finished eating, and now I have the contents of the Millennium Dome file spread out over the table top. Claire is reading aloud to me from the notes of the first exploratory meeting we had with them, before they gave us the contract.

Occasionally she reads a line to me, a line which the minutes insist that I am meant to have said at the first meeting. It's a strange feeling, hearing her saying words that apparently came out of my mouth, but which I cannot remember ever saying. Even more interesting though, is just the whole thing about the Millennium Dome. The background notes make compulsive reading in their own right, and as I scan through the pages, I am lost in the history of the project.

The Millennium Dome was first conceived by the Conservative party when they were formerly in power. Then, when Labour took over the reins of government, Tony Blair decided it was the only good thing the Tories had ever come up with, and pledged to build the Dome for the people of Great Britain. Something that would act as a flagship of British know-how and engineering, something that the world would marvel at, a landmark building that would mark the start of the new millennium, and which the British people could be proud of. And something that would bring in billions of pounds of foreign cash as the tourists flocked to London to see it.

So they built it. And it was a great success.

My heart starts to beat faster as I read the rest of the third page of my notes.

In the fourth paragraph, towards the bottom of the page I have scribbled on the side that one of the contributory factors towards its success, was the decision to build it in Hyde Park.

Hyde Park?

Or to be more specific, the top of Hyde Park, near to Speaker's Corner. In the centre of London, with easy access to everywhere, and smack bang in the tourist heartland of the city.

"James?" Claire interrupts me, destroying my train of thought.

"Have you been listening to a word I've been saying?" she asks, a little nervously.

"Sorry," I say, putting my finger on the page marking where I was and looking up. "What did you say?"

"Obviously not then. I just wanted to ask... well, I just wanted to know, honestly, where I stand just now?"

Her face has flushed, and the paper in her hand has begun to shake a little.

"What do you mean? I think you're doing a fine job. I'm very pleased by what you're doing. What exactly do you want to know?" I ask.

"It's just that, ...well, when you say you can't remember anything. I was wondering...I mean, the other night, and last week, ...the past six months...? Have you forgotten all that too? Have you really forgotten 'us'?"

"Forgotten 'us'?" I close the file on the Millennium Dome, and put it on the table. She has my attention now, my undivided attention.

"Yes...I mean, James, it meant something to me, even if it didn't to you..."

"What did?" I have a funny feeling about this.

"WHAT? So it's true then...you genuinely can't remember anything? Oh dear..." She looks away for a second, staring out of the window on to the street. She swallows, and in a second her whole demeanour changes. When she turns around she is a very different person.

"Forget it. I'm sorry I mentioned it." She looks quickly at her watch. "Oh no, it's late. We've got to be at the Dome in fifteen minutes. We'd better hurry."

The journey over to the Dome is a little awkward. We sit in silence. Whereas on the one hand I want to ask her what on earth she was referring to, on the other I have a strong feeling that it's best left well alone. I'm slow, but not totally stupid.

For the second time in two days, I'm left wondering if there is more to my new life than meets the eye.

CHAPTER 17
The Millennium Dome

"Come in, come in." the President of the Millennium Dome committee welcomes us to the boardroom, situated in a suite of penthouse offices near Marble Arch, with an impressive view over Hyde Park and a structure that I can only describe as an identical copy of the Millennium Dome, the same Millennium Dome that I last saw in North Greenwich.

It's huge and it dominates the north of Hyde Park: Londoners and tourists are thronging around the awesome marvel that is now one of London's top attractions, and shop-workers and office-workers taking a break are lounging around outside in the cafes that form part of the complex.

From the eighth floor of our office building we are about eye level with the upper quarter of the mesh of wires and pylons that thrust outwards and upwards from the centre of the Dome, supporting its roof and dancing on the London skyline.

And from where we are, I have to say, it just seems so right. The green of the trees, the grass, the open space around, its location so close to the centre of London, and the accessibility that this location easily provides to the attraction. In hindsight, Hyde Park is such an obvious choice. No wonder it's such a success.

"Twelve years, and still going strong," the chairman of the committee comments as we drink coffee and stare out at it, from the large, panoramic windows that frame the object of their achievement. "Twelve years, and no sign of letting up."

"How on earth did you get permission to build it in Hyde Park?" I ask, the words tripping out my mouth before I could stop them. "And I thought the Dome was only a temporary construction?"

"It was. And still is." He replies, patting me on the right shoulder as he turns to sit down at the head of the boardroom table. "A five year licence from the Queen to build and operate the Dome from 1998 to 2003. But due to its unparalleled success, and its undoubted role in bringing in over five billion euros worth of additional tourist revenue in the first two years of operation, coupled with the fact that the Dome rapidly became part of the London skyline, an image that is now synonymous with the new prosperous

Britain, and is known by children and adults around the world from the slums of Bangladesh to the richest mansions in China or California, we were given an extended licence first for another ten years in its initial form, and then more recently for another five years to convert the Dome into an international arts centre. A venue for classical, and rock concerts to rival Madison Square Gardens, or the Hollywood Bowl. Or an exhibition hall, or a theatre. Whatever we want. And that's it really. Why you're here. We want you guys to help us with the ideas, then to help brand it, promote it, and market it. Make sure we become the Number One and most sought after entertainment venue in the world." He smiles, nodding at the rest of the board members as they file into the room and take their places around the large, glass table.

"It's exciting." I reply. "...And a big challenge. But one which myself and my partners are eager to get started on, and one which we know and feel extremely confident that we can deliver on." I bluff, seamlessly.

"Tell me, Mr Wessex." I leave the window, and sit down opposite the Chairman of the board, Claire taking a place beside me. "What do you think are the contributory factors to your success so far? In your words, why do you think the Dome is so successful?" I would really like to know. A memory, unfortunately a very clear one, of another Dome, in another place, haunts me, floating in front of my mind's eye. I can see it clearly. A vision of another Dome that was a monumental flop.

"Of course, I wasn't chairman of the board at the beginning and I didn't take over till 2001. But it's clear to me that the answer is made up of a combination of things. Marketing. Location. Good layout. The brilliant show, and the fantastic themed attractions, easy accessibility, government sponsorship. The fact that David Miliband promoted it so much when he became Prime Minister after Blair, cannot be overlooked. Everywhere he goes in the world, he takes one of our marketing team with him. And in practically every speech he makes in front of the cameras, he continues to extol the virtues of the regularly updated themed exhibitions inside the Dome, and how they continue to represent the best of British ingenuity, technology, achievements, knowledge, science."

"So what was so special about the marketing?"

"Simply the fact that everybody was clearly informed on how to get to the Dome, where it was, and how much it would cost to get in. We set their expectations correctly and then delivered. No one was disappointed when they eventually saw it all. But I think the master stroke of the whole thing was the way Peters Hall and Irvine promoted it. It was their idea, and the Dome Board accepted it. They suggested that when we presented the package to the public and talked about the pricing structure for entrance, we shouldn't say that we were charging for entrance to the themed attractions like 'The Body' for example, but rather, that we should really promote the spectacular show that was put on in the centre of the Dome as being the *main* attraction, and that we should charge fifteen euros a head for that, and five euros a head for access to the cinema to see the 'Mr Bean' film. Doing that, we could then say that entrance to the Body and the other themed areas was all free... All thrown in, once you paid for your entrance to the show. Peters Hall and Irvine knew that people wouldn't object to paying for entrance to another show in the heart of London, especially such a fantastic one, and that by then offering 'free' entrance to the other also well advertised attractions of the Dome, it would just all seem like so much better value for money than our original idea of charging entrance to the themed areas, and giving the show for free. It was a good idea. And every day it brought tourists to the heart of London, who, after leaving the Dome's attractions, would pour into the shops and restaurants on Oxford Street and the West End in their thousands and spend, spend, spend. And that part was a *great* idea. The economy thrived, and everyone loved it. Hang on a moment...You were with Peters Hall and Irvine then, weren't you? In fact, correct me if I'm wrong, but weren't you one of the people who worked on the team that proposed this in the first place?"

A bald-headed bespectacled gentleman at the far end of the table interrupts him.

"Yes, Mr Wessex. Mr Quinn was at Peters Hall and Irvine until 2006. He was a key member of the team, and in fact it was his idea to propose the strategy you have just so highly praised. That's one of the many reasons why we are so keen to give the contract to Cohen's. We wanted Mr Quinn back on board again."

Ouch. Suddenly Richard's keenness to make me Partner makes even more sense. It's a double whammy. He needs me for both the Scotia Telecom deal, and now also this. Clever Bastard.

At the same time, I can't help but be impressed. By myself.

What the Chairman of the Dome committee has just explained makes so much sense...the idea that 'I' had had to promote the Dome was really straightforward. So simple. Yet, so effective. That combined with the excellent location in the middle of the city. No wonder the Dome has been so successful. The Dome in North Greenwich, the one that I know...the one that I have dreamt of...the reasons for its failure are all so clear to me now.

Firstly, no one knew how to get there, or how or where to buy tickets for it. There was so much confusion about that. And on top of that, the tickets were far too expensive. It took people away from the centre of London, getting there was awkward, and that deterred lots of people from going. What's more, when you got there, you were surprised to find the stage-show going on in the middle of the Dome, in the arena. No one had ever publicized the entertainment, no one even knew it was there.

I only went to the Dome once, at the end of its run, but when I eventually did, I saw the show four times in one day, *and* I bought the CD of the music by Peter Gabriel. Music which he composed especially for the show.

The show was great. Perhaps I may have felt a little bad about paying £20 to see the themed areas of the Dome, but I wouldn't have had any problem buying a ticket to see the stage show itself. Which is exactly the point that I was apparently getting at. Pay for the show, and get into the Dome for free. *Brilliant.*

I mentally pat myself on the back. Who would have thought that the person behind the success of the Dome was me?

Good job, Mr Quinn.

"So, Mr Quinn. Since you've done it once before, we can't wait to see what you are going to come up with next. We're all very excited about it. Of course, there's no pressure, but we were hoping that Cohen's could give us a first draft in two months time. Then a final version a month later. ...Just before Christmas."

Like the man said, no pressure.

No pressure at all.

CHAPTER 18
A Warm Welcome Home

The meeting with the Dome committee breaks up shortly after 5 pm, and I find myself sitting on the train back to Surbiton in a rather relaxed mood. The most relaxed since the nightmare began, or since I woke up from the concussion, depending which view I'm meant to be taking nowadays.

Today's been a good day. Actually, I rather enjoyed it. I find that when put in a position where I have to start acting or talking like an advertising executive, I actually seem to be quite good at it. It would seem that I definitely have a latent talent for this sort of thing. Take this afternoon's meeting for example. After we'd got over the preliminaries, and Mr Wessex had dropped his bombshell about the expected timescales, I found that I almost instinctively knew what questions to ask and what to do. When I ran a few ideas by the team, which just came to me on the spur of the moment, there were smiles all around the table. They liked them. I even liked them. And when we left the meeting, Claire and I had established a bond with the Board that I'm sure is going to develop into a sound working partnership.

Should I be so surprised? Maybe I'm being too critical of myself. Why shouldn't I be good at this? After all, before I talked myself out of a career in advertising just after I left university, that's all I had ever wanted to do. I loved advertising. I was always coming up with dummy campaigns in my mind, which I often thought of writing up and sending to the big companies. Not because I wanted to get any money for the ideas. Just because I had them, and I thought they were good, and I wanted to share them with the people who might benefit from them.

If I hadn't grown up and become so bloody serious, perhaps I would have ended up in advertising, ended up doing well, ended up succeeding. Just like I am now…!?

Whilst slowly demolishing some sandwiches which I bought at Waterloo, I reach across and pick up a spare newspaper that someone has just left behind when they got off at Wimbledon. An Evening Standard.

It occurs to me now that in the past couple of days, since my concussion day…my 'C' day, as I think I'll call it from now on, I have not seen or read the news. Perhaps because I am scared of finding out more about the life which I am now leading. Scared to read about a world where everything is so different and yet so similar.

The headline on the front page grabs my attention.

"*Prime Minister Miliband launches new campaign to arrest all illegal immigrants at U.K. borders. New National Border Security Police being introduced in January 2013 with enhanced legal powers.*"

Prime Minister Miliband?

What was it that Mr Wessex had said at the start of the meeting?…Mr Miliband had personally championed the Dome project after Blair? In this world, how long did Blair manage to hang on to power? And has Labour been in power continuously since then?

I realise it's about time I got up to speed with the world that I now live in.

A few minutes later, just as I'm finishing the article about the asylum seekers, the train pulls into Surbiton station. I walk along the platform and climb the stairs, stopping to say 'Hi' to the flower seller, and buy a bunch of flowers for Jane, then make my way down and out to the newspaper shop on the corner.

Inside, I scoop up a copy of every newspaper I can find, and gather up about ten different glossy magazines, ranging from 'Time', 'News Week', and 'New Scientist' through to 'Mary Claire' and 'Vogue'. Not bothering to wait for a taxi, I walk down Surbiton high street, my arms full up and overflowing, brimming with information about my new world. I look around me closely as I go, noticing the changes, absorbing everything, swallowing everything, remembering everything the way it is now, and not the way it was only four days ago. A life-time away.

The plan is simple: open up a good bottle of Shiraz, lock myself in my bedroom, and read everything I can get my hands on. By tomorrow morning I'm going to know more about this world, about what's going on today and why, than any other person I meet.

For better or for worse, this is my world now, and it's about time I discovered a little about it.

When I get home the children are misbehaving, running around, screaming and shouting. Margareta is chasing them from room to room, trying to encourage them to settle down and go through to the dining room where their dinner is getting cold.

Jane is upstairs, lying down on her bed, trying to recover from a migraine, which is no doubt being helped by the ruckus downstairs.

"Daddy, daddy..." Allison runs at me as soon as I open the front door, jumping up into my arms and knocking my magazines and newspapers everywhere.

" 'addy, 'addy." Elspeth follows immediately behind her, charging at my legs and going into a headlock around my knees.

I fall back against the door, pinned there by both my new offspring.

"Let Daddy in the door please? …That's better, now let go…please Elspeth, no don't drag along the ground like that, you'll hurt your knees. Elspeth please stand up, and let go of my ankle. You'll hurt yourself,.. oh no…Look, I told you you'd hurt yourself. Stop crying. Here, let me look at that…Okay, I'll kiss it better. But only if you'll eat your dinner?"

I kiss her on the knees, then carry her through to the kitchen and deposit her in the big children's chair.

As usual the kitchen is spotless. Nothing is out of place, and the children's dinners are arranged nicely on the centre island. Fish, peas, and chips.

I feed them both a few mouthfuls, and smile back at Margareta who is looking at me rather strangely, as if she still looks like she wants to say something but is holding back. Then I leave the screaming girls alone with her, closing the kitchen door behind me.

The bedroom light is switched off, and Jane is lying on the bed. I fumble in the dark for a few moments before managing to find the light switch on the dresser.

"Thank god you're home James. I need you to rub my neck and shoulders. I'm dying. I can hardly see for the pain..."

"Another migraine?"

"Yes!"

"But you had one last night too? How often do you get them?"

"Too often. Once or twice a week. It depends upon the weather."

"But the weather's fine…"

"Don't argue James. Just be a dear and massage me please."

"I wasn't arguing Jane. Just trying to understand. What sort of weather sets them off?"

"James, please, not now."

"What?"

"James, how was your day, darling?"

"Fine. Good. In fact, it was a great day. I have some really exciting news for you. Something to celebrate."

"What? Another deal? Another big bonus? More work? More late nights away? When do I ever see you? And when I do, you don't even remember me!"

"Jane, that's not fair. Come on, what's wrong? What's going on?"

"What do you mean? Nothing's going on. I'm just tired and have a headache."

"Okay, I'm sorry. I'll keep my news for another time. Show me where to rub your neck."

I walk across to the bed, taking my trousers and shirt off, and putting them on the chair beside the bed.

"What are you doing James? Why don't you put them in the wardrobe. Please hang them up."

"I will in a minute, I just want to rescue you first."

"James, you know how I prefer it if you hang everything up first. You know how hard it is for me to keep this house tidy if everyone just treats it as a waste dump."

"Jane, this house is spotless. It's the most tidy house I've ever seen."

"So don't mess it up. Please put your clothes away."

I hold my tongue, and hang my trousers, and throw the shirt into the basket in the bathroom. Sitting down beside Jane on the bed, I stroke her face, kissing her gently on the forehead.

"What's wrong baby? Are you all right?"

She's silent.

"I'm okay. It's just a headache. Here, please rub my neck, just here. Like you used to…"

She rolls over onto her stomach, and flicks the hair off her back with her hands. In spite of the welcome home, I still feel in a good mood, and perhaps a little playful. I run my hands down her neck, and along her shoulders. She feels wonderful. Her skin is soft and warm. I lean forward and kiss her neck. Pausing, waiting for a reaction, before kissing her again.

Jane moans slightly, wriggling her shoulders, and readjusting her hands in front of her face.

She is wearing a long black one piece dress. Very businesslike, but also very attractive. It only takes one movement to slide the zip down her back, and gently tug the dress over her shoulders. Her back is tanned, and graceful, her soft curves rolling gently around her body, drawing me towards her.

My kisses seem to hit the mark, and soon Jane turns over towards me, a smile appearing on the edges of her lips, a sparkle shining in her eyes.

"James, you know how that turns me on. You shouldn't…not now, the children aren't in bed yet."

"They're downstairs. Margareta is looking after them. They're fine...it's you that needs the attention. Here, let's see...what happens if I do this?"

She squirms, her body undulating in front of me.

"Don't be silly James, you know exactly what happens when you do that…And so what happens if I do this?" she reciprocates, her hands reaching downwards.

It's been a good day so far. A very good day, and things only seem to be getting better.

We kiss passionately, fumbling quickly with each other's clothes, our need for each other driving us on, taking us over. As I slip her bra off, her breasts fall free. They are beautiful, soft, tender. I kiss them, stroking them with my hands, licking them slowly, pushing my eyes against them, and feeling the nipples against my closed eyelids, squeezing them around my face.

This is my dream. This is the moment I have fantasised about for years. It's exactly how I imagined it would be, exactly as sweet and wonderful as I had dreamt of.

Jane says something, but I don't hear her.

I feel her tug at my boxer shorts, I feel them slide down my legs, her hands reaching for me again.

And then all my thoughts stop. Instinct, desire, loneliness, desperation, lust, and all the repressed pent up emotions from the past week surface at the same time. I raise myself up on top of Jane. I enter her. I lose myself in Jane, and she in me, and I am lost in the moment, a glorious, wonderful moment that I will never forget for the rest of my life, in this life or any other life that I will lead, and for this one incredible moment that surpasses all meaning and understanding, ...for one moment, Jane and I are one.

And in that moment, there is clarity.

A single moment of awareness where all my questions are answered, where I see and understand, where I can touch the truth, and I have the knowledge and the insight of the why and the where and the how.

And then, in a flash, it is gone.

Instead, in its place, there is exhaustion. An honest tiredness. Relaxed, untroubled, worry-free.

I awake sometime later, lying on my back, with Jane resting her head on my chest, fast asleep, my arm wrapped protectively around her shoulders.

As I open my eyes, my heart begins to pump faster, a sickening sense of guilt descending upon me from above.

It has happened. I have done it. I have been unfaithful to Sarah. I have slept with another woman.

Suddenly the euphoria of the act of I have just committed is swept away by a feeling of such self-disgust and self-loathing, that I lie there in the dark, in shock.

What have I done?

Jane stirs on my chest and I quickly move away from her, turning on my side and distancing myself from her in the bed.

I lie there on my side, staring into the dark and thinking of Sarah, tears welling in my eyes, until sleep mercifully overtakes me once more and anaesthetises the pain.

My eyes open slowly, my mind dimly becoming aware of a new sensation beneath my waist. I open my eyes and look down. It's Elspeth and Allison jumping up and down on top of my legs.

"Daddy, mummy. Greta is crying. Greta is crying."

Jane surfaces from beside me, covering her nakedness with a quick tug of the bedclothes.

"James, you go. She likes you. I can't face her just now. I'll read the girls a story."

Slipping from the bed, I pull on my big dressing gown and wrap the belt tight around my waist. I find Margareta in the front room sitting on the piano stool, her head and shoulders slumped forward, tears running down her cheeks and dripping on to the black and white piano keys.

Closing the door behind me, I walk over and stand behind her, placing my hands on her shoulders.

"What's the matter, Margareta? Why are you crying?"

She sniffles loudly.

"What is the matter?" I ask again.

She lifts one of her hands from her lap and places it over mine on her shoulder.

"James, you do not talk to me no more. You have forgotten me? Do you not remember?"

"Remember what?"

"Everything… Why you not talk me no-more?"

What should I say? What does she mean? I understand that she is a long way from home, probably very lonely. Probably very vulnerable. But how am I treating her badly?

I kneel down beside her, resting on my haunches so that my face is level with hers. I smooth away some hair from her face so that I can see her eyes and I am about to ask her how I can help, when, slowly, she turns to look at me, and then, without a word, she leans forwards and kisses me full on my lips.

It's not unpleasant, but it's also not expected. I'm so surprised, that I rock backwards and fall over onto the carpet. In a flash, Margareta is on top of me, smothering me, her hands everywhere.

"James, James, you say please you still love me. Say it for me please."

I hear footsteps coming down the stairs, and in a second I am out from under her, diving for the sofa. The door opens a second later, and Jane walks in. Margareta is alone on the carpet, crying again, and I am sitting on the sofa, pretending as if nothing has happened.

"Margareta, please don't cry," Jane starts. "I know I have not been treating you well lately. I have not helped you enough with the children, and I am sorry. Allison just said that you told them that you wanted to go home. *Please* don't. I will try to help you more, and Elspeth and Allison have promised to be tidy, and well-behaved. Why don't you go to bed, get a good sleep and then we can talk about this later?"

Margareta gets up, looks at me, then bursts out crying again. She squeezes past Jane and disappears through the doorway and up the stairs.

CHAPTER 19
Bedtime Stories

At 2 am, unable to sleep, or halt the endless stream of thoughts which flood through my mind, I realise that I'm not going to get back to sleep, so I slip out of the bedroom and go to make myself a cup of hot milk in the kitchen. This in itself, proves to be too difficult a task, and I give up after ten minutes. I can hardly even spell 'Aga', let alone figure out how to make it work, and finding the fridge, where I guessed the milk would probably be, took several attempts in its own right. First I opened the door to what turned out to be the very latest in washing machines. Then, I ended up opening two large freezer doors with racks and racks of frozen meat and pre-cooked meals. Only on my third attempt did I find the milk in what I can only describe as the biggest fridge in the world. It looks more like a walk-in cupboard with snow in it.

After putting the milk back in the fridge, and leaving the kitchen, vowing never to return, I pick up my newspapers and magazines from where I left them on the hall table, and make myself a very large whisky in the lounge.

Choosing some relaxing late night Jazz music, I settle down into the big white leather sofa and pick up one of the papers. Apart from the Evening Standard which I scanned on the train, it's the first time I've read one since my big 'C' day, and I find that my hand is shaking a little. I'm both anxious, nervous and intrigued. What am I going to find out? What will I learn about the world I'm in? Will it be just the same?

My first choice is the Daily Mail. No particular reason, just that it was on the top of the pile. It proves to be an interesting choice. The headline leaps of the page and grabs my attention.

"*President Colin Powell issues Syria and Iran with final warning*".

President Colin Powell? Last I remember, President Obama was on the American throne. I read on.

'President Colin Powell today issued Syria and Iran with an ultimatum, warning both countries that they had until 12 pm on Saturday 24th September to declare an end to hostilities with Israel. In his strongest rhetoric yet, since being re-elected for a second term,

President Powell warned that failure to comply would be viewed as a declaration of war on the United States and its allies, and that on Sunday morning, America would take whatever steps it considered necessary to end the month-old conflict. America already has 650,000 troops stationed in Iraq and Saudi Arabia, and it is expected..."

Skipping a few paragraphs, I go to a photograph of Colin Powell standing beside Saddam Hussein. Underneath, the words; "General Colin Powell taking the unconditional surrender from President Hussein at the end of Desert Storm-Revisited, the code name for the second Gulf War in 1996."

What?

I abandon the article and look at the next page.

"*Scottish Pound reaches new high against the English euro. Concerns grow over Scottish-English trade deficit.*"

I pick up another paper, and open it randomly on the fifth page, finding a big photograph of Princess Diana sunbathing on a boat somewhere in the Med, alongside a smaller photograph showing the burnt out, and torn and twisted metal remnants of what used to be the same boat, poking out of the water on the edge of a beach. Dominating the whole page, is the title. "*Jury retires to consider verdict in the Diana Boat-Tragedy Enquiry.*" Underneath, "*After an exhaustive enquiry which has taken five years to complete, the Government Select committee in the public enquiry into the death of Princess Diana has finally retired to consider its verdict and prepare its report. The deliberations are expected to take a further three months, before the final report is compiled and presented by the Government select committee, which was appointed to investigate the death of Princess Diana in 1993.*"

"*It is hoped that the report will finally explain the mysterious circumstances which lead to the death of the "People's Princess", and is expected to confirm the circumstances leading to the unexplained explosion on board the boat on which Princess Diana was celebrating her engagement to Dodi El Fayed, son of the Harrods owner, Mohamed Al-Fayed ...*"

I look up. My mind is racing.

On the third page of the Times there is a small article that catches my attention. "*Scotia Telecom appoint Cohen Advertising to lead development of a new mobile telecommunications brand.*" Underneath there is a photograph, a particularly ugly one, of Richard shaking hands with the Chairman of Scotia Telecom. There is a quote from Richard underneath in which he almost single-handedly takes credit for the whole deal by himself. Nowhere does he mention the team at Cohen Advertising, and my name isn't mentioned at all.

An article in the Guardian shows the latest photographs from America's second manned mission to Mars. I read this with great interest. When I was younger I always fancied being an astronaut, until the day I went to the science museum in London and saw the inside of the space suits, and how an astronaut had to go to the toilet into a bag that was wrapped around his leg. One bag for what came out the front, and another for what came out the back.

So we've been to Mars already, have we?

As the whisky goes down, and one glass become two, which then becomes three, I learn from the broadsheets about the new world I live in. A lot which I never believed possible. Yet, at the same time, I discover that my new world has a lot of problems. The Aids epidemic in the UK has reached epic proportions. One in a thousand people in the UK are now estimated to be HIV positive, one in ten thousand people have Hepatitis C, and cancer is now killing two out of every five adults over the age of fifty. The newly privatised Health system is on the verge of collapse, and because of the increased popularity of improved public transport, and the inexcusable mismanagement of funds and resources, the privatised motorways are falling into such a poor state of disrepair that several will have to be renationalised, or else face closure.

Without doubt, the biggest problem in the UK at the moment would seem to be the Asylum situation. In 1996 Britain joined the European Monetary Union, and adopted the euro. Not long after that most of the Eastern European countries such as Slovakia, Poland and the Czech Republic also became member states, and their citizens were allowed to travel freely all around Europe. Britain, the only country in Europe to do so, immediately agreed to allow any of these new European citizens the right to work in the UK and the right to claim full benefits when they did so. The British Government was warned that there was an ethnic minority of gypsies in Eastern Europe that may immediately take advantage of the situation and travel en masse to the UK. The Government estimated that this would be in the order of 5000 people. The result was rather different. In 1997 alone, in the first year after membership for these countries was agreed, an estimated 150 000 gypsies arrived in the UK. Each year since then, another 125 000 arrived. A continuous stream of poverty, underprivileged, uneducated and unskilled workers, many with criminal records. All of them claiming benefit, few of them working, all of them demanding to be housed. Coupled with the increasing stream of non-European economic migrants, almost all of whom claimed asylum, the immigration system became overwhelmed and began to fall apart. And then when the situation deteriorated in the Middle East and West Africa a whole new tide of immigrants began to find their way onto British shores. No one could tell a genuine asylum seeker from a bogus one, and the meaning of the word 'asylum' got lost.

Diseases which had not been around in the UK for many years, many sexual, suddenly started to sweep through the population. The support services were overwhelmed, a housing crisis ensued, and the National Health Service collapsed. The labour government, struggling to repair it, was forced into accepting a radical programme of privatisation, which was completely unable to care for so many poor people. The taxpayer had to subsidise all of their treatment, as the immigrants couldn't pay for it themselves.

The school system made an attempt to cope with all the immigrant children, the majority of whom couldn't speak English, but soon found the bigger problem was not getting them a place, but rather keeping them in the school at all. Most of the immigrant children were not used to going to school, and they ran away at the first opportunity. Truancy levels went sky high, and petty crime shot through the roof in the areas where the children, who should have been at school, were roaming the streets, stealing both out of necessity for their families, and frustration with the new world they found themselves in. A world where the majority of children couldn't understand their new language, and where they felt isolated and unwanted.

Which was true. In the neighbourhoods and areas where the new immigrants were housed, social unrest grew, caused both by the frustrations of the immigrants and the anger from the locals towards their new neighbours, who they perceived as unwanted spongers that abused the system and took as much as possible, giving nothing in return.

Bigotry - perhaps in some cases understandable, hatred, ethnic tensions, misunderstanding and mistrust, all grew to such a level that the summer of 2005 found frequent riots on the streets of Britain, which lead to the deaths of many people, and the destruction of hundreds of millions of euros worth of property.

Britain had never experienced such riots before, and although they wanted to, they were powerless to stop the influx of even more asylum seekers: under the European Constitution Britain had to accept anyone from any other member state, who wanted to come to this country.

At the beginning of 2006, exhausted by public criticism, and bleeding from the internal haemorrhaging of the party, from disillusioned MPs going over to the opposition, the government were finally forced into taking radical action. It started to build very large, institutionalised *'National Asylum Centres'* on the outskirts of major cities. Immigrants arriving in the UK were only allowed to live within the confines of these walls, where whole mini-cities were created with their own churches and mosques, shops, entertainment centres and parks.

In this way, the government met its European obligations, but protected its own society from further erosion. Existing immigrants who failed to meet the new 'Nationality Laws' ...(which decreed that everyone learn to speak fluent English, as well as a number of new governances which defined what 'English' meant, and how people had to behave in order to become 'anglicised'...), were rounded up and interned in the camps, or offered the right to return back to their own country of origin.

Conditions in the glorified concentration camps deteriorated, and soon people were voluntarily asking for repatriation in their thousands. Only in the past year has the immigration problem begun to lighten, and according to the press reports, three of the many National Asylum Centres were even able to close their doors, hopefully for the last time. Although the problem is still acute, it is now not expected to worsen. The aim is to control the situation and prevent further rioting and civil unrest, as more of the immigrants voluntarily decide to return home, and the situation slowly dissolves.

As I read, I think about what I saw in the area I used to think of as 'Canary Wharf' and what the taxi-driver told me that day as he drove from there to Scotia Telecom.

It is hard to imagine how bad things must have been in the UK in the past few years, and then I think of the Britain I know and have dreamt of, and how this problem is only just beginning to emerge there. Wherever that dream-world is.

Satiated with knowledge for now, I turn to the sports columns for some light relief. What is happening in the world of football? Who does David Beckham play for now, if at all?

Although I look in all the papers, his name does not crop up once. He is nowhere to be seen.

It's almost as if he had never played football at all.

I'm tired now. I have learned enough about my new surroundings for one night. Perhaps for a lifetime.

In this world there is as much hatred and disillusionment as the one I know. While so much seems to be different, in reality, nothing much has changed at all.

The flames in the fireplace flicker and I lean forward, picking up the metal poker, and pushing back a lump of wood into the centre of the flames.

Settling back onto the sofa, I watch the edges of the wood glowing red in the centre of the fire, and return to my thoughts.

There was, is, a scar on Sarah's left cheek. A pretty reminder of her eleventh birthday when her parents bought her first bicycle. She couldn't ride yet, but that didn't stop her carrying the bicycle out of the house when her parents weren't watching, setting it down on the side of the road, and climbing aboard.

She managed to go three yards before the edge of the pavement came up to meet her smooth cheekbone, but thankfully there wasn't any real need for stitches.

I used to lie in bed beside her at night, gently tracing the discoloured skin with my forefinger, following the tiny contour back and forward. It always made me smile.

Sometimes she would wake from whatever dreams she was having, and she would smile at me, look into my eyes for a moment or two, then go back to sleep, my finger still following the same soft sensuous path, back and forward.

Perhaps other people actually didn't find Sarah as pretty as I did, and maybe, there were even some that perhaps found her rather plain. But for me, there was never a single moment since we first met in the sandwich shop that I didn't find myself drawn to her.

Which makes me ask myself the question for the first time, but properly, just why it was that I started to look elsewhere? What madness was it that drove me to the Facebook website, and started me on the path to my own self-destruction?

A good question, but one which I should have asked myself long ago. Not sitting here, now, in Jane's house. For a while I ponder the answer, then get up, putting the fireguard around the dying flames, and go to bed.

Somewhere within me I must already know the answer.

But as I start to think about it, like so many times before, I find that it is still too painful to remember.

CHAPTER 20
Déjà Vu

Surbiton has always been the busiest suburb of London. The people who live here are a curious breed. We are city dwellers who need the buzz of the city, but cannot stand to live there. So we live on the fringes of the countryside and the outskirts of the noisy metropolis. One toe in one world, and another in the other.

I'm no stranger to the London commute. I've done it for years. Every day the same routine: hurry to station - train delayed or cancelled - fight for place on platform - fight for place on train - try to sleep if you have a seat, or spend thirty minutes staring at people's faces if you have to stand all the way into London - arrive late at Waterloo - rush for tube…etc.

So, today, when I'm standing on the platform waiting for my next train, why is there so much space around me? I look up at the electronic departure board. There are already six trains showing in the next thirty minutes. One direct train to the centre every nine minutes, non-stop all the way.

What?

Where are the delays? Where are the cancellations?

The first non-stop train arrives. Twelve spotless, fresh blue painted shiny carriages, that look like something straight from the 22nd Century. The electronic doors open beside white markers on the platform that indicate where the entrances to the train will be, and the waiting passengers calmly walk on and take a seat. There are enough spaces for everyone. There is no fuss, no commotion, no one fighting for a place.

I sit down by the window. The bright red seat is comfortable, rather plush, and I relax. No one is standing. I look around at the faces of my fellow passengers. Some people are talking to each other. One is laughing. A few people are smiling. The latent stress and tension that usually fills the air, is simply not there.

Unheard of.

Just before the doors close a young woman rushes out from the coffee shop on the platform and jumps aboard. She walks in, looks around her, sees me, smiles, and sits down opposite.

She is an attractive girl, nice make-up which compliments her features, and a smart suit. She's clutching a cardboard cup of expensive Columbian coffee. As she lifts off the lid from her coffee, and takes a sip, she smiles at me again.

Her face is so familiar, so…Yes, I recognise her now. The woman who sometimes sits on the 8.12am opposite me in my dream, the woman with the caffeine addiction, who I last saw last Monday morning when I caught the train…

I shake my head slightly and turn to look out of the window, wiping the memory from my mind and starting to think of today's work.

"James, hi, ignoring me today or what?" she says, leaning forward in her chair, a twinge of laughter on the edge of her words.

"Sorry," I say, turning to her, a little embarrassed. "No, I wasn't, how are you?"

I hadn't thought about this. I will obviously know lots of people who I will have forgotten. I'm going to meet people in the street who I may have known for years, but who will be like complete strangers to me. I will walk past people, not knowing that they are a good friend, or even an ex-girlfriend or lover.

What do I say to these people, when they stop me and ask me why I'm ignoring them?

"Oh, I'm fine." She says, sitting forwards a little. "Did you hear about Samantha?"

Samantha?

"No?"

"She was fired. Last Friday. Can you believe that? She has an affair with the boss, and when she ends it, he fires her! It happened just like you said it would..."

Frankly, I don't even know the girl, but it doesn't surprise me at all.

"So…what are you doing about Jane, then?" she asks, a little quieter.

"What do you mean?" My heart beats a little faster.

"Have you told her yet?"

"Told her what?" I ask.

"About…," she hesitates. "No…no, you asked me not to mention it. You were drunk when you told me, and maybe it's best if I just forget it." She pauses again. "...But if you want any more advice, just ask me, all right?"

She leans forward and touches me on the knee at the same time as she says 'okay?', exaggerating her smile as she speaks.

How do I know this woman? What does she know about me? And moreover, it's only been a few seconds of absolutely riveting conversation, but already I find myself asking the question, "Do I really *want* to know this woman?"

Probably not. In fact, by the time we arrive at Waterloo, the problem of trying to figure out what I should say to her, hasn't really occurred again, mainly because she has talked non-stop all the way. I'm not a religious man, but I find myself praying that this woman is not a really close friend of mine. I couldn't stand it. Thankfully, when we get off the train, she has to catch a tube, and I decide to walk.

She 'bugs' me though. And what she said to me won't go away. I ask myself how well I must know this woman, for me to be telling her stuff about myself and Jane that even 'I' don't know. In spite of the fact that spending a second more with her is probably the last thing I want to do, it occurs to me that perhaps I should grab her the next time I see her and arrange to take her out for a drink after work. A few glasses of wine, and maybe I can get her to tell me exactly what I told her.

It's a bit annoying that complete strangers know more about me than I do.

Walking down the steps from the bridge towards the Embankment, the irony of the whole situation dawns on me. For the past couple of months I have travelled to work every day, looking at everyone else, guessing at their lives, wondering if I was leading the right life, doing the right job, or earning the right salary. And now when I'm travelling to work, I *have* a different life, a new job, and a new salary, but I know nothing about any of it. It's not other people's lives that I am wondering about. It's my own.

Who am I? Who do I know? Am I enjoying my life? And then a big question hits me.

Am I a nice person?

When I get to the office, I walk up to Alice, who looks up at me whilst answering an incoming call. I smile at her, and give her a bunch of flowers that I have just bought at the flower seller on the corner. My questions have got me worried. Alice appears to be a friend of mine, and from now on, I'm going to be super-duper nice to everyone, especially those that are close to me. Maybe I am a nice person and maybe everyone does like me, but just in case, I'm not taking any chances.

"Can I have a word?" I whisper to Claire as I pass her desk upstairs. "And can you bring in two cups of tea? And do you have any paracetamol? I have a headache, and it's killing me."

She takes a seat in front of my desk, my diary open at today, ready to take notes, or to help guide me through today's appointments. Scotia Telecom at 11 am, the partners team meeting…my team meeting…at 4 pm, Tisca or was it Tosca?, at 7pm. I take two paracetamol and wash them down with some tea.

"Put the book away, Claire. I want to ask you something personal. I want to ask you what you think of me? Am I a nice person?"

Claire turns a little red. Whether from anger, or embarrassment it's hard to tell.

"What do you mean, James? What sort of question is that?"

"It's an honest question," I pause, picking up my cup, and tapping the handle with my finger. "You know that I've lost my memory, that I can't remember things, and that there are..., well, shall we say, that I have forgotten things that are important to me..."

She looks down at her lap, and the colour rises still further in her cheeks. She coughs once, raising her hand to her mouth. A movement that I find both polite and attractive.

"...The thing is Claire, I get the feeling from you that previously, I mean now, that we are good friends. And that perhaps in the past we were quite close."

She shifts uncomfortably in her seat, and looks up at me. There is a question in her eyes, a question that I cannot give her an answer to.

"Claire, I need to ask you a question. The thing is Claire, the concussion wiped a lot of my memory clean. I've forgotten who some of my friends are...no, literally...I can't remember who they are at all. I can walk past them in the street and not know that last month we were the best buddies in the world. But I've not just forgotten about other people. I've forgotten about myself. I don't know *who* I am... I was hoping that maybe you could tell me a little about myself. About who I am? And whether or not I am a nice person? Do people like me? And about my wife? Do you like her? Does she like me?"

Sometimes I am fool. A big, stupid fool. As soon as I ask the question I regret it. It would seem that not only do I have a big foot, but I have an incredible ability to jam it down my own throat.

Claire stands up, tears running down her cheeks, words starting to flow, her emotions brimming over.

"James, I'm truly sorry about the problems you are having just now. I would like to help you, I really would...but, all things considered, *am I the right person to ask any of this?* ...And as for asking me about your wife? Do you not think that I am the last person in the world that you should be asking about her?"

She closes the door behind her, walking across the open plan floor and down the stairs into reception. A few people look up from their desks as she goes past, casting a quick glance over at me.

From now on, perhaps it's better if I don't ask other people for their opinions of me.

The impending Scotia Telecom meeting takes over my concentration, and soon I am lost in my thoughts, and my own notes, which Claire brought to me yesterday morning. My notes are thorough, and the file contains references to the various Word and PowerPoint documents that I easily find on the PC in my office. By the time 10.30 am comes along, I'm ready for the meeting.

Gathering my stuff together, I walk past the photocopier, taking out a card from a new leather wallet that I took from one of my cupboards at home. I copy the card, and hand the details to Alice at reception.

"Alice, whenever I need a taxi in future, can you try and get hold of this guy? He's the man that looked after me when I got mugged and got the concussion. A good guy. Encourage everyone else to use him too. He deserves the business."

I found the card this morning, in a pile of things that had come out of my pockets when I went into the hospital. When I picked it up, the face of the friendly taxi driver flashed into my mind, and I put the card carefully aside. John McRae. He helped me, and I owe him one.

The meeting with Scotia Telecom passes without incident. Thankfully Richard doesn't come along, I'm a big boy now, and he leaves it all up to me. This time around there are only two people from the Scotia marketing team. It turns out that the meeting is mostly about them opening up to Cohen Advertising and detailing a lot of their strategy that they hadn't told us about before. Now we're their best friends, they drop their pants and show us everything. Warts and all. It means that we'll have to change some of our strategy, which I was going to have to do anyway, since a lot of what we presented to them last week were ideas that I just made up on the spot. Of course, that is one small detail that I keep to myself, and do not share with them.

Afterwards, a couple of the team offer to take me around to a pub in a little lane behind the Square, called the "*Four Tuns*". I join them for a while but my mind is elsewhere. Luckily, I don't have to stay too long, as I have a genuine excuse. Richard's team meeting. Which I actually have no intention of going to. Before I left the office, Alice gave me the low down on what happens at these things.

Nothing much.

Just a company bullshit session, where Richard gets up and tells everyone how wonderfully we are all doing, and how much harder everyone has to work to keep us all doing so wonderfully. I don't know what it is about him, but the way people laugh when they talk about him, it really seems as if no one seems to like the guy. The title "*Big Dick*" probably is not an anatomical description of any sort, more likely just a plain honest description of the type of person he really is.

The worrying thing is, if I have been there for so many years, and if I have now just been promoted to partner, how much like him am I? Am I a Big Dick too?

I walk slowly along Oxford Street, feeling a little guilty that I am skiving off the first meeting that I should be attending as a full blown partner. The guilt grows as I get towards Oxford Circus. Unfortunately, my headache is back, so I take another two paracetamol, washed down with some coffee from Starbucks.

As I walk out of the coffee-shop, I look at my watch. 4.45pm. Perhaps I should go to the meeting after all? Show up, say a few words…take a little credit away from Richard?

I like the last thought, so I wave my hand in the air, and a big, black cab pulls up beside me. Fortunately, I get back to the office in the last few minutes after all the serious stuff has taken place, and as I walk into the open plan area upstairs, I arrive just in time for everyone to cheer at me, and for Richard to pop open a few bottles of champagne and officially announce my promotion. Good timing.

More alcohol comes my way. It's my second drink of the day, and it's not even 5pm.

I get up and go stand beside Richard, and make an impromptu speech. "Sorry, I'm late, just over at Scotia Telecom, etc etc."…." The big ten million euro deal, that I and my team won…not Richard." etc etc.

Richard pours himself another glass of champagne, and says a few more words. While he is speaking I deliberately edge away from him. Frankly, I feel a little uncomfortable about standing beside him whenever he is drinking. Once is enough, and that isn't something I want to repeat.

By the time I leave the office at 5.30pm and meet Jane on the corner of the street outside the entrance to The Ivy, I have had another drink. Or maybe two.

I smile as I see her standing waiting for me.

"Wow! You'ıe looching great this evenıng." I greet her, my words a little slurred for some reason.

"James, tell me you've not been drinking already?" Jane replies. "You'll ruin this evening."

Why should she think I'm drunk?

"Drunk? Me? No, I'm not. I've only had one, or maybe two…But you are looking fantastic, darrling."

And she is. Really. Underneath her evening coat, she's wearing some sort of designer label, figure hugging black dress. And what a figure that it is. I move towards her to hug her figure myself, attempting to kiss her at the same time.

"James, you're drunk!" she says, side stepping me, and letting me walk straight into the wall behind her.

I manage to avoid the wall, being quick of foot, and agile as I am. However, turning to look back at Jane, I find that the turn is slightly more difficult to master than I had expected and I stumble a little, taking two, quick, rather unsteady and comical steps to the right.

"James… You're plastered!" Jane shouts at me.

Unfortunately, I think she might be right.

I find this rather surprising, and quite unexpected. I have only drunk drinks three, sorry, three drinks. Maybe four. But I can hold my drink well. I hardly ever get drink. Sorry, Drunk.

So why am I drunk now? What's going on?

"Jane…I'm sorry. I didn't mean to get drink. Sorry, drunk. I don't know what's happening. I didn't drunk very much at all." …"Sorry, drink very much at all... Just a few quick glasses of champagne to celebrate my promotion..."

"What promotion? What are you talking about?" Jane asks, genuinely surprised.

I move towards Jane, reaching out to her arm for support.

"Oohhh…I'm sorry. I wanted you to tell me about my promotion last night."

"What?"

"I mean, you wanted to tell me about my promotion last night. I tried, but you had a headache."

"You're not making sense James. I don't know anything about your promotion." She glances over at the entrance to The Ivy where the doorman is standing and looking over at us. "James, this is so embarrassing!"

The doorman of The Ivy is coming towards us now.

"Mrs Quinn, is everything ok? Can I help at all? Is there a problem?"

Mrs Quinn? How often does she come here then? My wife is a bloody regular at The Ivy, one of the most exclusive restaurants in London.

I turn towards the doorman, wanting to explain things. Wanting to tell him about my promotion, but somehow as soon as I see him, my feelings change.

"Problem, no. Thanks. She's not having a problem. I'm just a little drink, sorry drunk. Don't know why. Now go away."

The doorman stops in mid-step, and looks at Jane. He's wearing a black top hat, and a long, black coat, split at the back, like the ones concert pianists wear. I take an instant dislike to this pompous little man, and the feeling of warmth and love that I have towards all humanity is suddenly replaced by an upswell of anger and aggression.

"Go away, I say!" I say.

In fact I say it again.

"Go away, you stupid little black penguin. Fuck off. Just fuck off!"

I'm quite surprised by what I just said. So is the doorman.

Jane shouts something at me and walks off.

I stumble after her.

She turns at the corner of the next street, and stares at me. She looks lovely. Oh no. She is crying. When I catch up with her, she turns her back on me.

"Jane, please, doanwory, I'm not drunk. I'll be better in a minute. We can still go and see Tisca."

"It's *Tosca*. And I've been looking forward to this for months. James, how can you do this to me? Have you any idea why we're going to Tosca tonight? Have you any idea what day today is? *Any idea at all?*"

"Friday?" I reply, unsuccessfully fighting the overpowering urge to giggle, and letting a ripple of childish laughter slip out.

"James. It's my birthday? My birthday! I know you've forgotten a lot, but how could you forget my birthday?"

Uhoh.

She has a point.

I think. But unfortunately, although she has a point, I never actually knew it was her birthday, so technically how could I forget it in the first place…?

I open my mouth to say something. Then the logic of this hits me and I stop in mid sentence, before realising that I have forgotten what I was going to say. I make one of those stupid faces that you sometimes see drunk clowns making on television, lifting my finger up in the air as if to emphasise my own point. Whatever point that was.

"James,…I'm sorry," Jane says, taking a small step towards me. "I mean, maybe I shouldn't be so hard on you, because of the amnesia…It probably wasn't your fault you forgot it was my birthday…but I'm finding this all so difficult and I'm trying so hard to cope with it all. And I'd really hoped that this was going to mean a new beginning for us. That you would try harder. Care more for me. Give up your old ways…" She pauses, starting to cry, and reaching for a handkerchief to wipe away her tears. "But you're just the same aren't you…you haven't changed at all, have you?"

I'm struggling a little to keep up with what this is all about now. Is she angry about me forgetting her birthday, or being drunk…or not changing…?

"No, I have changed, Jane. Honestly…I'm a very different person now…" I try to protest..

"Oh, are you James? So, tell me then, who did you get drunk with? Who were with you with?"

I know the answer to this one. Good. "The usual crowd…people from work…" But now it gets hard. I don't actually know the names of that many people at work. At least, not yet. "Well, there was Alice…and of course, Claire…" I start, going for the easy ones.

Jane looks at me in disbelief.

"Claire? You were drinking with Claire? On my birthday? James, how could you…?" She immediately bursts into tears, turns and walks away, hailing the first taxi she sees.

I try to follow after her, but the sudden movement makes me dizzy and I have to rest against the wall, which slides away from me, leaving me lying on the pavement.

I'm tired. Very tired.

I close my eyes and sleep.

Something wet and cold lands on my nose and runs down my face.

I open my eyes slowly, still drunk, but sobering up quickly. It's raining. The raindrops are coming down fast and heavy, large, fat and very, very wet.

I groan. My head hurts.

It's dark, the streets are not so busy now, and it's late. Very late. I look at my watch. 12.15 pm.

What happened?

This time when I reach for the wall, I find it gives me the support I need, and I stagger to my feet.

Coffee. I need a coffee.

Opposite the Hippodrome on the corner of Leicester Square, I find a café still open and serving food and drinks. Thankfully already the fog is beginning to clear, and I am sobering up fast.

Bizarre. Very bizarre. One minute I'm pretty sober, then I'm really drunk, and then a few hours later, I'm okay again. I've never experienced anything like that before. How come I got so drunk so quickly?

My head throbs again, and I raise my hand to my skull, stroking the hangover that surely is soon to come. Shit... That's it! I took four paracetamol today to kill my headache, two just before I started to drink champagne. The alcohol must have reacted with the painkillers, making me very drunk very quickly. Far more drunk than I would normally ever get. What a screw up. What was I thinking? I ruined Jane's birthday, all for no reason whatsoever. Will she believe me that it wasn't intentional?

What am I going to tell her?

A couple on one of the other tables looks across at me and whispers to each other. I must look pretty crap. Disheveled, unkempt, a right tramp. I stir the coffee, and notice how the white of the milk forms thin white lines that swirl round and around, before disappearing into the vortex in the middle of the cup.

After my first coffee, I order another, and sit staring out through the window, watching the rain run down the glass, and looking after the people as they hurry past in the street outside.

The minutes pass, the coffee kicks in, and I start to feel a lot better. For a moment I consider taking another paracetamol, but think better of it. I've had enough for today.

I return to people watching. I'm in no hurry. I've missed my last train, and I've got no particular reason to hurry home now. I'm in the doghouse anyway.

A woman hurries around the corner on the opposite side of the road, and runs past down towards Trafalgar Square.

Sarah?

It's Sarah!

I jump up, and dive around the edge of the table, knocking over the cup of coffee on the table, spilling it everywhere, the cup rolling over the edge and smashing on the floor.

The manager looks up from behind the counter at the front of the shop, sees me rushing for the door, and heads me off.

"Oi…Mister! Have you paid yet?" he shouts, raising his hand to stop me.

"Here…" I say coming to a temporary halt and plunging my hand into my pocket, pulling out a 10 euro note. "Keep the change."

I'm out the door, and around the corner as fast as I can, frantically scanning the street ahead, searching for Sarah. A big hand lands on my shoulder, pulling me brusquely around.

"Mister, It's sixteen euros. You only gave me ten."

"What?" I ask, looking briefly at the spotty teenager in his white overall, and then quickly back down the road to where Sarah must now be getting away.

"You owe me six euros…"

"Sorry, listen…take this?" I find a twenty in my pocket and thrust it at him, breaking free and running down the road. The rain is falling hard now, and its freezing. It's difficult to see properly, trying to run and keep the water out of my eyes at the same time.

I run faster, a surge of adrenaline coursing through my much abused body.

There! There she is… She's just crossing the road in front of South Africa House, dodging around a taxi coming up from Charing Cross. I put on a quick spurt, and catch her just as she turns the corner towards the train station.

"Sarah! Sarah!" I shout wildly through the downpour, reaching out and grabbing her elbow roughly as I draw up beside her.

She spins around, takes a look at me and screams, shaking my hand free and hitting out at me.

"What do you want? Leave me alone!" she shouts.

It's not Sarah.

She's got the same blonde hair, and the same haircut. She's the same height, and build, even wears the same coat as Sarah has. *But it's not Sarah.*

"I'm sorry. The wrong person…" I try to blurt out, but the woman is already running away, shouting loudly for help as she runs across the road, ducking in and out of the traffic.

I look around and realise that a few people are staring at me. I ignore them, and for a few minutes I remain standing where I am, the cold rain running down my face and dripping off my nose, and drenching my clothes from head to toe.

It's a few minutes before I catch my breath, and realise that I am shaking. The sense of disappointment I have is overpowering. I cannot believe it. In an incredible rush of emotion that leaves me feeling very, very lonely, it dawns on me then, just how much I have really missed Sarah.

For a few moments, Sarah had been there. She was real, and I had seen her with my own eyes. The reaction I felt when I saw her was not something out of any dream. It was a gut reaction, a *real* reaction that came from my very core, spontaneous and automatic… When I first saw the woman through the café window, my reaction was immediate, instant...no thinking was involved. No dream, whether dreamt whilst unconscious or in a coma, or high on drugs, could ever grab you like that.

Which means just one thing. One thing that I have known for a while now, a conclusion that I cannot fight anymore or pretend that I can explain away by some bullshit about having a concussion or amnesia, or a split personality or anything else like that.

The fact is, Sarah must be a real person. A real person that I have known, whom I have loved, whom I married and lived with, and who is the mother of our two very beautiful children.

Shit, …I miss them all so much. *So much…*

I want my babies! I want my wife! *I want my life back!!!*

The rain is coming down in torrents now, a river of water streaming over the pavement around me, flooding the gutters and rushing down the road. Everyone else has dived for cover in the doorways, and the streets around me are strangely empty.

As I come face-to-face with my emotions, I sink to my knees, look up at the sky and start to cry.

My tears are lost in this world of water.

And in this moment, I am more alone that I have ever been before in all my life.

This life, and the one before.

CHAPTER 21
Home Truths

Sneaking back into your own home after an evening out without being discovered is one of those skills that I have always lacked. Not for me, the quiet opening of the door, and the tip-toeing into the kitchen, hoping that 'her upstairs' hasn't heard me.

No.

As I fumble with my key in the lock, I remember a joke I once heard being told in a comedy club.

"...A man comes home from the pub, very drunk. Wife, well, she's been waiting up all night, lying in bed, just waiting for the sound of the door clicking open downstairs, frying pan underneath the pillow. She's just waiting to give him an earful, to give him hell, and to ruin the end of the evening for him.

Of course, we all know that this is obviously the wrong approach for any man to adopt.

No, the best thing to do is to open the door as loudly as possible. Make no pretence of the fact that he is drunk. Then go to the bottom of the staircase and shout up the stairs, "I'm home petal, just going to the bathroom, then I'll be straight up for a kiss and a cuddle, and a bit of you-know-what, and how's-yer-father. Best warn you, darrrllllinnnnggg,... I'm feeling quite frisky!"

And if he does this, when the guy then goes up the stairs, taking each stair as loudly as he can, by the time he gets to the bedroom, the wife will be pretending to be sound asleep, and he won't be able to wake her up for love nor money."

I always think of that whenever I get home late, but apart from having a little laugh to myself as I open the door, things are never really that bad for me to have to follow such wise words of wisdom.

Except maybe this time.

Probably best if I just sleep downstairs on the sofa.

The other difference between myself and the man in the joke is that by now I'm completely sober.

As I walk into the house, my clothes are wet through and I am shivering with the cold. So I head straight to the shower room attached to the kitchen and the laundry room, where thankfully I can also get some fresh clothes without having to go upstairs.

The water is warm, and incredibly refreshing. I stand in the jet for ages, savouring the warmth, and letting it penetrate through to my bones until the water begins to turn cold. I emerge from the water invigorated and alive. And very much awake.

I find the kettle and heat myself some water, this time managing to navigate around the kitchen enough to find a tea bag and the milk.

At the bottom of the stairs I listen for a while, but hear no sounds from upstairs. The automatic timed lighting in the front room has gone off, so I switch on the light on the wall, and sit down, relaxing into the soft leather of the sofa.

There is but one thought in my mind.

Sarah and the children.

I have thought of nothing else since the moment I saw the woman through the window of the café. Nothing else. It's like a curtain has been raised from my mind, and for the first time in a week I can think again. The answers to the riddle still lie tantalisingly beyond my mental grasp, but there is one thing that I do know now. Beyond doubt.

Sarah and the children are real.

They are not a figment of my imagination, or a product of any dream. They are not something that my mind created while I was in a coma, or because of the concussion.

The concussion? What the fuck was that all about? How on earth can I have been wandering around for the past week, believing that I am suffering from amnesia, thinking that the reason I cannot remember anything about this world is because I have forgotten about it all. Shit. All this bullshit about me getting concussion was the excuse I dreamt up to explain to everyone else why I didn't know who they were or why I had seemingly forgotten everything.

Then, wallop, I fall over and bang my head for real, and suddenly my own explanation is being thrust down my throat by the quacks in the hospital, the same reason that I knew was rubbish, but which by this time, my subconscious was desperate to accept because it was the only thing that made sense.

And I would probably have accepted it, except for one thing.

The power of human emotion.

I love Sarah. I love my kids. I miss them. Terribly. After deluding myself for the past seven days that they were not real, the veil has been lifted from my eyes, and I can suddenly see.

I can see everything.

My so-called imagined past *is* real.

Which, in itself, presents me with a bigger and larger problem.

Where am I now?

And where are Sarah and my children?

The phone rings four times at the other end before it is picked up. A croaky voice, full of sleep, and struggling to wake up.

"Hello?"

""Hi Dad, it's me, James."

Instantly alert, "James, are you okay? What's the matter son? Is Jane okay? The girls?" concern immediately showing in his voice.

"Don't worry. Everything's fine. I just need to talk to you?"

"James, what time is it? It's still the middle of the night...", then to my mother, whose voice I can hear in the background. "It's James...I don't know. Go back to sleep dear, I'll wake you up if there's anything wrong...James, what time is it?"

"It's five past four. Can I come round?"

"Sure son, why not? It's not like I've got to go to work tomorrow or anything. Come round now and we can talk. But drive carefully, James."

The door opens before I even knock, and I step inside to be greeted by a smile, and a pat on the shoulder. My dad is already dressed, wearing one of his typical tartan shirts and brazes, Mark n' Sparks blue slippers, and his empty pipe in his mouth. It's only been a week but already he has become the typical grandfather figure in retirement.

"I've made us both some hot chocolate, son. Let's sit in the front room and have a chat, shall we? Your mother wanted to get up and come down and join us, but I told her to let the two boys have a talk alone. She's upstairs, but she told me to say she's there too, if you need her."

We sit in the front room, a fake-wood gas fire burning in the hearth, its golden glow relaxing and calming, photos of me, Jane, and our children sitting in frames on the sideboards, and covering the wall. Including one of myself and Jane on our wedding day. Pushing myself up and out of the chair, I walk across and pick it up, staring at the image of me with a woman in a white dress, who I know that I never married.

My father says nothing. He sits there, playing with the pipe in his mouth, looking at me patiently. He is waiting for me to speak. Wise enough to let it come from me in my own time.

"Dad, you told me that if I wanted to talk to you about anything, no matter how weird it was, that I could?"

"Sure son. And I meant it. No matter how weird."

I put the photograph back where I got it from, and sit back down opposite my dad, picking up the hot chocolate and sipping it.

"Hmm. The chocolate's good." I say to kill time. What am I going to tell him? How can I tell it to him, without him thinking I'm mad. How can I tell him that he's meant to be dead?

"Dad,…I don't know where to begin. The thing is, I'm very confused just now. I don't know what's going on any more, and I need to speak to someone else apart from myself. I need a second opinion. Some advice. And you're the only one that I can think of who might be able to help."

"Does Jane know that you are here?"

"No." I shake my head. "No she doesn't."

He accepts that. He doesn't ask any more questions.

"I know this may sound like a daft question, and it's the sort of thing that I should know, at least you'd expect me to know. I mean, I do know, but, what I think is the answer, it's just not what you might think the answer should be…"

"So, what's this question then?" he asks.

"Dad, …am I in love with Jane?"

I watch his face, waiting for a reaction. I expect surprise, shock, something. But instead there is just understanding, and patience, and love and concern.

"You want me to tell you honestly, son?"

"Please…"

"Then I think the answer is no. We actually talked about this just three months ago. You and I. Down by the river. But before you got that bump on your head…The thing is son, it's difficult for me to tell you everything, because I was hoping that this memory loss might give you a second chance. For you and for Jane. So I didn't want to tell you what you told me before, because in a way, I'm hoping that if you've forgotten the things you were unhappy about before, then maybe you won't rediscover them. Maybe you can both fall in love again, get over the things that were upsetting you? Forget…."

"Forget what?"

"That's for you to tell me son."

Quiet.

The clock ticks on the sideboard, and the fire crackles.

"Dad, am I having an affair with someone?"

Silence.

"Dad… please?"

"Yes, son. You are. "

"Who with?"

"I don't know them all. Just one."

"Them *all*? How many are there?"

"I don't know son, but your mother and I know about Margareta. We guessed long before you told me about it yourself."

"Does Jane know?"

A pause.

"I think so."

"And what happened when she found out?"

"I don't know. But I don't think she's confronted you yet. But yes, I think she knows."

I am silent for a while.

"Dad, that's not really what I want to talk about. It's connected, I suppose, but ..." My voice trails off and we sit in silence for a few moments more. I sip my hot chocolate again. The fire flickers and jumps. Almost as if it were real.

"Son, just start at the beginning. That's almost always the best place."

And so I begin. I tell the story of a man who wakes up one day in one world, who is married to a woman he loves but doesn't appreciate enough, a patient, kind woman, mother of two children he adores, in a house he loves. The story of a man who looks up from his book on the tube on the way to work, and realises that he doesn't recognise the station the tube is stopping at, or even any of the other stations on the tube-map. How he steps off the train and onto the platform, and finds himself in a new world, a world different to the one he lives in.

A world where he has a new job, a new wife, new children he has never seen before, and a house he needs a map to find his way around. A new life. But with no memories of this new life, and only memories of the old one. Incredible, detailed memories of the old life. Not because they are made up, but because they are real.

Yet, with no explanation for it, the man knows that the new world is very real too. In every sense. The people are real, his surroundings are real, everything he can see, touch or feel is real.

My father listens patiently. My father, who created me and gave me life. Who helped me grow up, who told me about the facts of life and shared with me at every possibility the wisdom of his years, yet always, always, first giving me the chance to learn and experience things for myself. Never lecturing, never preaching, only advising. My friend, as much as a father. My father, who died five years ago.

"And your friend, this man,...he still loves his wife, and his children?"

"Yes. Very much..."

"So, what does he feel for his *new* wife?"

"I don't know. Something. Maybe a little. But nothing in comparison... She's a stranger... No, he fancies her. He's attracted to her physically, but he doesn't love her."

My father is silent for a while. I can see that he is thinking, taking seriously what I have said, and carefully considering his reply.

I wait patiently, for what seems like an age. Then finally he sits forward in his chair, taking his pipe out of his mouth and grasping it tightly in the palm of his hands.

"Then given what you've just told me, son, wherever he is now, I would just tell your friend this: tell him to find this woman. If she exists. Tell him to find her, wherever she is. To find out if the love he has for her is *real*, and if she, in return, has love for him...But be prepared that if she doesn't exist, to accept the new life he has *now*. Tell him to embrace this new life and live it to the full. No,... *not* to forget the old life. But to realise that it has passed and that it no longer exists. The past is gone, and only the present and the future is important now, and by that I mean, the present that he can see, touch and feel all around him wherever he is now."

He turns to me, looking me straight in the eyes.

"You see son, a man, a true man, deals with whatever life throws at him at any point in time. A man cannot control his life, he cannot plan it, only a fool really thinks he can. No, the true mark of a man, is someone who accepts that life always changes, and that the most he can do, is to accept the changes that life thrusts upon him and endeavour to learn to live with them, in the best way he can. To accept the life he has, *whatever life that may be.*"

He leans forward and touches me on my knee.

"Son, only you know what is real. Only you. What is real to me, is not the same as what is real to others. What we perceive as reality is forged by the experiences we have had. The experiences that make you who you are, are different to the ones that have made me who I am."

"You are asking me for my advice son. Man to man, father to son. Don't get me wrong. I love Jane, I always have. And your mother and I love the children. But we know that for a few years now you have not been happy. Something, I don't know what, isn't right between you both."

He pauses for a moment, rising to his feet and moving over to the drinks cabinet in the corner. He takes out a bottle of malt and pours two large glasses, handing one to me as he returns to his seat.

"Put down that cocoa rubbish and take this. You'll need it. Son, I'm going to tell you something now, something that no man should ever tell a son, but something which I think you should hear, because I want you to know that I understand what you are thinking. Something that you must never ever repeat to anyone else, either tomorrow or at any time in the future when I'm dead and gone. And something which after tonight we will never ever refer to or mention again."

He looks at me now, his eyes suddenly alive with emotion, but his voice ice calm and steady, urging me to confirm the pact.

"I promise." I reply, already nervous of what he wants to tell me and wondering if I am ready for it.

Holding the glass in both hands, he looks deep into the orange liquid, his eyes searching the depths of his mind, reliving something from long ago.

"Son, I know what it is to dream of someone else. I know what it is to yearn for something that you can't have. I know all of that, and I can never forget the feeling. You see, about thirty years ago, I had an affair..."

My jaw drops open. What? My father…, my dad, an *affair*? In a second, the perfect image of my father that I have always treasured in my mind is shattered. In an instant everything that I thought my father stood for is gone, …*changed.* My father…an affair? How? Why? My parents have always had one of the strongest relationships I have ever known. They practically define marriage. Or at least, I thought they did…

Dad stops for a second and looks over at me, seeing the shock in my eyes.

"I didn't ask for it to happen son. It's not something I'm proud of, and it's something I can never forgive myself for. And there are no excuses. But, I was young, stupid, and a fool."

"Did mum ever know?" I hear myself asking, not wanting to believe a word of what I am hearing.

"Your mother? God no! If she did, she would have left me immediately. No, I made sure she never found out."

"How long did it last for?" I ask.

He gets up from his chair and stands in front of the fire, looking deep into the flames.

"A year," he replies slowly.

"A…a year?" I stutter back, raising my voice.

"*Shsssh!*" my dad says, turning and waving his hand at me. "You'll wake your mother."

"But, I thought you and mum were always in love…I thought you were the perfect couple…"

"And we were, and still are. But things are never that simple. Just like what you're going through now, things happen, life gets complicated. But it's up to us to manage and take responsibility for everything we do." He says, coming back over to his chair and putting his hand on my shoulder. "The fact is James, I loved this woman. Don't worry, I loved your mother too, and I knew that I would never leave her, but it took a long time for me to end it. And when I did, I did it because I had to, because I knew I must."

I look over at my father, and realise with a shock, that I have never really truly understood who my dad was. I have never *really* known him. And there is still so much about him that I have to learn. It suddenly dawns on me that I have only ever seen him from one point of view: him being my dad, and not someone who was also a man. A man with feelings and needs and emotions, just like myself. *Me.* James Quinn.

And then I understand that my dad and myself are more alike than I had ever realised before.

"James, the thing is..." he continues, not waiting for me to fully recover from the shock, " ...the relationship you have with Jane is not the same as what your mother and I have. I love your mother, but you don't love Jane. When I stopped seeing the other woman, I never stopped loving her, but I knew I didn't want to lose your mother either, and at the end of the day, your mother, and my children, were more important to me than anything the other woman could ever give me. I had too much to lose. But you don't. The love is already gone. And I would hate for you to spend the rest of your life longing for something else that you can't have. James, you only get one life to live. Life, as they say, isn't a practice run..."

I sit in silence, just staring at the man before me, trying to take it all in, trying to understand.

"Son, I would never have believed that it was possible to love two women at the same time, but unfortunately it is. But, ...I learned that it is not possible to simultaneously have *relationships* with two women. You have to choose. I know you are married to Jane, and I know that I have always drummed into you how important it is to work at keeping a marriage together, ...but what I would say to you now is that since we only have one life, I would never want you to stay together just for the sake of it,...to spend your one life in a loveless sham, like living a prison sentence from day to day. Love is the most powerful force in the world, and we have to work with it, not against it."

"You want my advice, son? Fine, I'll give it to you. It doesn't matter whether I believe your story or not. In your mind, you love another woman. Another woman who is as real to you as I am to you now, right? Then son, the way I see it, you only have one option. If you believe all of what you told me, then you have to find out if what you think you feel is true. And to do that ... you have to find this woman."

"No matter what it takes son. If she's real, and she exists, ...wherever she is or may be...you *have* to find her."

PART THREE

CHAPTER 22

It's hard to take it all in, … almost too much to digest.

Getting back into my car, I drive around the corner from my parents' house, park in a neighbouring street and switch the engine off. I sit there in the silence and the dark, trying to organise my thoughts and to accept the revelations my dad has just unleashed on me. I am angry.

I think of my mother, and the pain she would have felt if she had found out about the other woman. And I wonder if perhaps she knew, after all, but put up with it, letting the affair run its course. Or perhaps she never knew. All those months of lying, all those months of deceit.

Yet, it worked itself out in the end, and in spite of what happened, my childhood was only full of good memories. For all the years I can remember, my parents succeeded in bringing me up in a happy home. A *loving* home.

For the first time ever, I think of my parents as two people, people who have feelings, and emotions, and their own lives to lead,… just like myself or Sarah. I see them in a new light, as *people* and not parents, and I realise that there is still so much I have to learn about them, and from them.

Eventually, I smile, and the initial anger I felt fades and goes away.

Although I am shocked by what my dad has just told me, I also feel strangely honoured by the fact that in my time of need, he trusted me enough to tell me a secret he had kept quiet all his life. A secret that will remain with me, and one which I will never speak of or mention again. He has trusted me and I will honour that trust.

Anyway, what right do I have to be angry that he had an affair? Wasn't I lusting after Jane when I was with Sarah?

Switching on the engine and starting on the journey home, my thoughts turn back to myself, and to the self-revelation of my own hypocrisy.

What is it in the make-up of a man that creates in him the ability to stray from a loving home and wife? Why did I ever start to look away from Sarah?

I find myself starting to ask myself some searching questions about my relationship with Sarah and why on earth I should feel unhappy with her.

Which, let's face it, MUST be the case, *somehow*, even if I can't see it myself just now.

What is wrong with our relationship? Have I been running away from something? And if so, what?

Now I am angry with myself for not having asked these questions long, long ago, and I know that I have to understand the answers before I find Sarah again.

A fox runs across the road in front of me, distracting my attention and breaking my chain of thought as I watch it disappear through the crack in a fence into someone's garden.

Coming to the end of the road and turning slowly into a new street, my thoughts turn back to the advice my dad has given me about Sarah.

'Find her', he said.

So where do I start?

London is one of the largest cities in the world. It takes an airplane ten minutes just to fly over it, it covers hundreds, maybe thousands of square miles, and is home to over seven million people. And that's assuming she even lives in London.

As I drive back to my house in Effingham Road I consider the task my father has just set me, and am resolved to accept it.

I find myself in a rather strange predicament. One that has no explanation, that makes no sense, but is, nevertheless, real.

The past I know and the past I am meant to have are not the same. The wife I married is not the same person that I sleep with every night, and the children whom I do my best to tolerate, are not the ones I fathered. And yet, they are.

A sane man would not be able to resolve this puzzle, but I realise that I can no longer consider myself a sane man. There is probably no other single person on the planet who would claim that which I do, or insist that their past and their present are in no way connected by any single strand of continuity. There is no doctor of the mind who would understand me, and no physicist who would be able to make sense of what I know to be true.

By all definitions of the word, I must be insane.

Yet, I know now, with more certainty than I have ever had about anything before, that Sarah and my children are real. The problem is, paradoxically, that Jane and my new family are real too.

So, if Sarah and Keira and Nicole are real, where are they now? And how can I find them?

As I turn into the drive and open the door to my house, I am confronted by the fact that, for the moment, I have more pressing problems.

"Where have you been? I've been worried sick!" Jane shouts at me, as soon as I close the door. "The children have been asking for you, and I didn't know what to tell them." She is standing at the bottom of the stairs, in her dressing gown and slippers. It doesn't look like she slept at all.

She begins to cry, then turns her back to me, as if to walk away towards the kitchen. With one foot raised, as if she were about to take a step, she hesitates, her hand resting on the banister of the stairs. Then slowly she turns and walks back towards me, stopping a few inches away, her eyes looking up at me questioningly, sad and confused.

"James, what's going on? Where have you been?" she says in between sobs.

Before I can speak, she wraps her arms around me, and starts sobbing onto my shoulders. Her body shakes against mine, and I can feel the emotional release within her. Looking over her shoulder, I see little Allison is standing on the stair landing, looking down at us, and above, little Elspeth is gingerly walking slowly and carefully down the stairs to join her. Allison has her thumb in her mouth, silent tears rolling down her cheek.

"Come here, all of you," I say. "Don't be worried. Daddy just spent the night at Granny and Grandad's. I didn't call you because I didn't want to wake you up. Now, let's go and make some breakfast? Pancakes anyone?"

"Me daddy. Me," shouts Allison, her tears drying up instantly, and jumping down the stairs and running into the kitchen.

"'ee, Addy. 'ee Addy," mimics Elspeth behind her, and following just as fast as her little legs will carry her.

Jane looks up at me and looks into my eyes. I reach out and wipe away her tears.

"James,..." she starts to speak. Then the light in her pupils changes, as if a decision has been made. She swallows hard, wipes away the rest of her tears, and pulls herself up straight. "Your parents? Okay... Okay, fine. As long as you are okay. As long as everything is alright." She pauses. "Come on, let's get breakfast."

She turns and walks away.

Is that it?

What about the interrogation? What about the endless questions and the anger? Where is the angry confrontation?

As I bend down to undo my shoes, I hear Jane shout after me.

"And James, hang up your coat please, and put away your things. When you came home last night - before you went to your parents - you left your clothes in the shower-room. You know how I hate a mess."

In that moment I understand Jane a lot more.

She suppresses problems and avoids confrontation. Last night I upset her. I ruined her evening, but now she's just brushing it away, forgetting it happened. Better that than confront me over it. Like my affairs with

Margareta and Claire, which she no doubt knows all about, but just pretends aren't happening. She creates her own reality about the marriage and doesn't face its problems.

Instead of facing me and her worries and emotions, and probably because she knows she won't be able to control me, her outlet is to channel all her unhappiness and anger into controlling the state of cleanliness and order in the house. Nothing is allowed to be out of place. Dirt, or mess, or disorder of any sort is not tolerated. The only real control mechanism she has over me is to nag me constantly about hanging up my trousers, putting away my shoes, not leaving a book on the table in the front room, making sure the pictures are straight on the wall, the books on the shelves are in a perfect line. There are never any dirty dishes in the kitchen, never any old newspapers lying on the sofa. Even kitchen waste seems to be itemised and recycled according to strict guidelines.

I live in a museum. Not a house.

We do not live. We exist.

We are visitors in our own lives.

As I sit in the kitchen and talk to the girls, helping Elspeth with her pancakes, I make up my mind that things are going to change.

CHAPTER 23
Where to start?
Monday

I feel guilty about Jane.

I sense the pain, the anger, the distrust that she carries around within her, and I know that I am the cause, at least, I was the cause. The more I learn about myself the more I realise that I must have treated her badly in the past. The man she has known as me has been deceitful to her, …and in spite of myself, the man she knows now is in danger of deceiving her again. But what can I do?

As the weekend passes, I do try hard, but in truth I find that I am only going through the motions of spending time with Jane and the children. My mind is elsewhere, my thoughts a one-track process, trying to figure out how I can go about finding Sarah. Yet, no matter how hard I think, my mind draws a blank. It seems a hopeless task.

The chances of bumping into her in the street are millions to one. In all that time I've lived in London, I have only ever accidentally bumped into about five people I know, none of whom were really close friends. So what chance do I have now of accidentally coming across Sarah, my wife?

None.

By Monday morning, I am beginning to feel the enormity of the task, and a mild depression is descending upon me. What hope do I have?

As I sit on the train into Waterloo, it hits me just how completely ironic this all is. Instead of looking at other people and wondering at what lives they lead and what jobs they do, I am sitting wishing for my old life back, and wondering if I'll ever get to be me again. Nothing fancy this time. Just me. Plain, old, boring me.

I close my eyes and try to make the thoughts stop. The carriage is warm, and the gentle rocking of the train soon begins to soothe my troubled mind, and I fall asleep.

I awake with a start, my arms folded across my chest, and my head hanging forward at an awkward angle, a trail of glistening saliva dribbling out of the corner of my mouth. A guard is banging on the window from the outside of the train, and looking up I quickly see that the train is empty apart from me.

I jump to my feet and move to the electronic doors, which the guard is just opening for me.

"Lucky I spotted you mate, otherwise you may have ended up back in Portsmouth." he smiles and laughs at me.

"Thanks." I say sheepishly, before disappearing fast along the platform.

Something is troubling me now. Something is prodding at the corners of my mind. Something which I was dreaming about on the train, and which is now trying to fight its way into consciousness. But what? What is it?

Needing the fresh air, I walk across the Thames and up the Embankment to work, still troubled by my dream, whatever it was.

By the time I get to the Strand, I realise it has something to do with Jane although just what I can't get yet, no matter how much I focus on it.

"Morning Alice," I say as I walk past reception and up the stairs to my office, not stopping to pick up my mail. I'll let Claire get it later.

It's got something to do with Jane? But what's that got to do with finding Sarah? How can that help…?

As I reach the door to my office it hits me like a hammer between the eyes.

So how did I originally find Jane then? How, when stupidly I started to dream of Jane instead of Sarah, how did I go about tracking her down?

Facebook. That's how!

Swinging the office door closed behind me, I drop down into my seat and switch on the computer, waiting forever for it to boot up. Logging onto the company network, I hit the 'Search' button on the toolbar. I type in Google, wondering while I wait, if Google is one of the things that has successfully made the cross-over from my world to this, mentally crossing my fingers that it still exists.

Fantastic, …it does.

I type in 'Facebook', hit the return key and hold my breath.

Website not found.

I type in the title again, just in case I had typed it wrong the first time around.

Website not found.

Blast...

Maybe it's called something else in this world? I remember that before Facebook there was Friends Reunited, so I try this, also with no luck.

I pull myself closer to the keyboard, and rattle off a sequence of names into the search engine.

"School & friends", then "School Reunion" and "Old School friends"

Blank. Blank. Blank.

I try a hundred different combinations. All blank. *Website not found.* Try again.

Just then Claire walks into the room, carrying my mail and a cup of tea.

"Good morning James…"

"Claire, If I have a student friend who I've lost contact with, but now want to find, can you think of any way to find them on the internet?" I interrupt her, speaking but continuing to type on the keyboard.

She puts down my tea on my desk and comes round to stand behind me, peering over my shoulder.

"You mean, like, if you wanted to track down someone you knew long ago, maybe your best friend at school, or someone you fancied, and whom you want to get in contact with again now?" She says, leaning forward, so that I can feel the heat from her chest against my cheek.

"Yes. Exactly. Do you know of any website that can help me track an old friend down?"

"No." she replies. "No, I don't . But it's a bloody good idea though. You could make a fortune doing that…" She steps back, and walks around to the front of my desk, sitting down in the seat opposite me.

"I mean, *really*. That's a fantastic idea James. Brilliant! How come nobody else has ever thought of it? You could make a million doing a website like that. You could call it "Find-a-friend" or something like that…wow…When did you think of that?"

"I didn't," I reply, without looking up. "I'm just looking for someone, that's all…"

She utters something back, but I don't hear her. I'm still typing at the keyboard, refusing to give up. I ignore her and she eventually gets up and walks out of the office, now thinking in a world of her own.

Shit. What am I going to do now? What can I do if Facebook and Friends Reunited or Myspace or anything like that don't exist?

After an hour of trying the most obscure combinations of different words, I give up. The Friends Reunited website obviously hasn't been invented yet, and there's nothing else that comes close to doing what I need. Claire eventually returns, bringing in my diary, and we sit down to organise the rest of my day. Still wrapped up in my own thoughts, I postpone my appointments for the rest of the morning, freeing up some time to think.

I've got to take a structured approach to this. *Think man, think.* What do I know about Sarah that can help me find her?

Pulling out a blank piece of paper, I start to write down as much as I can about her early life, about the things she did before I met her. Anything that might give me a lead to go on, that might provide some continuity from her past to her present, wherever that may be now and anything that might be able to give me some clues to help track her down.

Closing my eyes, I bring up a mental picture of Sarah, trying to remember everything she ever told me about herself.

In the picture that immediately pops into my head, Sarah is laughing, running slowly away from me down the garden path towards the swing at the bottom of the back garden where Keira is calling for mummy to push her. I have a camera in my hand, and as I call her name to get her attention for the photograph, she turns and smiles, looking so beautiful, her eyes flashing in the sunlight, her skin rosy and fresh. As she comes round to face me I can see that she is heavily pregnant, and I start to smile at the thought, although the feeling is quickly replaced by something new,...an odd feeling, something which quickly becomes unpleasant. I begin to feel uncomfortable. Suddenly, Sarah doesn't look so beautiful anymore. Puzzled, I open my eyes and let the light wipe the memory clean. That was odd…

Breathing deeply and closing my eyes again, other memories begin to flow, and I begin to write down bits of information, facts about her life, pieces of the jigsaw that I may be able to put together.

She was born in 1975. 15th February. Went to Rosedean Secondary Modern. I can't remember what primary school she went to. Maybe she never told me. Her parents, George and Martha, were both English. They divorced when she was young, about twelve I think, and she went to live with her father. Grumpy old bastard. Never liked me. In fact, I think he hated me. George Turnstone had a hang-up about life, and was always blaming his crap existence on other people. Fact was, that was why his wife packed up and left him. She'd had enough of his negativity, and had to escape. She moved to Spain and died about five years ago. Her body was shipped back to the UK, and buried in a graveyard near Richmond, where she was born and brought up. Sarah used to go and visit her grave every year on the anniversary of her death. Without fail. A bunch of tall Irises, her mother's favourite flowers, and a freshly lit candle always adorned the grave when she left. Every year…without fail…Unfortunately, that was every year on the 6th of July, almost ten months away until her next visit. No, I can't wait that long.

As soon as Sarah was old enough she escaped from her father and moved to London, where she started to study History at King's College, then to Teacher training college in Mitcham. She always wanted to be a teacher and help people learn what made us what we are today.

"History..." she used to say, "... is alive. It never dies, it reaches out to us from the past and influences every single thing we do each day. If we don't understand our past, we'll never find our way into the future…"

Her words seem strangely prophetic now.

Dedicated as she was, after leaving college she strove for two years to get a job in London teaching history, but couldn't. There just weren't any jobs. So she started working as a PA in a Law firm, then moved from one company to another, moving up the food chain. I met her whilst she was working at the same firm I was, a fledgling Telecoms company that never really went anywhere.

Her best friend was Mary, a girl she met at college, one of the few girls on the course who got a job in teaching. Last I heard she was Head Teacher in Chemistry at some school somewhere north of Birmingham… *Ironbridge.* That was it...birthplace of the industrial revolution and location of the world's first iron bridge. I remember Sarah telling me all about it once when we went to visit Mary.

A plan of attack slowly materialises on the paper in front of me.

1: Find father and visit him. Get contact address from him for where Sarah is now.

2: Visit graveyard where mother is buried. Try to see if I can get contact address from curator of graveyard.

3: Contact Rosedean Secondary Modern. Maybe they have some alumni scheme?

4: Likewise for King's College.

5: Ditto for Teacher training college.

6: Try finding her best friend in Telford. Maybe she's still working at the same old school?

7: Check to see if Centric Telecom still exists. If it does, maybe they have a record of Sarah working there.

The last one on the list is a long shot and I know it. Centric Telecom is the company where we first met, but it went bust two years later. In this world, maybe it still exists, but even if it does, who's to say that Sarah ever worked there, and that even if she did, ten years later what chance is there that the HR department would still remember her and be prepared to pass over her contact details to me.

Suddenly a thought hits me, and I turn to the keyboard.

Why not just type in her name into the search field and see if it comes back with anything? Maybe if she became a history teacher in this world, she might have authored some paper or other, or appear in some article where her name might be picked up?

Entering her name into the search field on Google, I hit return and hold my breath. For a few seconds I do not breathe. Could it be this simple?

Five entries found.

My hands are suddenly shaking, and I click on the first entry.

"*Cooking Made Simple*" by Sarah Turnstone.

A big picture appears on the screen of a fat woman dressed in a white apron and a big white hat. She obviously loves to cook. But unless something has gone horribly wrong with Sarah's metabolism and hair colour, it's definitely not her.

"*Cooking for the Blind*" by Sarah Turnstone.

Nope.

"*Cooking for…*"

Sadly I realise that none of them offer any hope. It's not going to be that simple after all.

CHAPTER 24
Tuesday

The drive up to Norwich brings back a lot of memories. Good memories, although at the time I just didn't realise how good they were. I never dreamed that I would look back so fondly on the times I used to make the journey with Sarah, with Nicole and Keira screaming and crying in the back seats, complaining how boring it was and asking incessantly, "Daddy, are we there yet?"

Once, to try and liven up the trip, I taught the girls how to sing "Stop the Car I need a Wee-Wee", one of the songs we all used to sing as kids when we went on the Sunday school picnic to the countryside. Keira and Nicole loved it, and sang it over and over again. And I mean over and over again. They wouldn't stop. After an hour, it was driving Sarah and me up the wall, and we had to bribe them with sweeties just to shut them up.

Fond memories. Memories which I would give everything to have back now.

Sarah's father lived in the centre of town, in a private road of listed terraced cottages. Each one had a painted front, blue, white or a dark red, ...dating back to the start of the eighteenth century. The effect wasn't as bad as it sounded, and in fact the houses and location were considered 'very desirable'.

Not too sure what I was going to say to him, and not even sure that he would be living there, I knocked on the door. A minute or two passed before there were any sounds of life from inside the house but eventually I was greeted by a deep voice shouting "Who's there?"

This was the difficult part. What should I say? In this world, Sarah has never met me, and I have never met her father. He doesn't know me from Adam.

"Mr Turnstone? Hi, I'm a friend of Sarah's from university. I was wondering if we could chat for a minute?"

The sound of a chain rattling, and a lock being unbolted. The door is ajar on the end of a chain, and a wizened old face pokes through the gap, eyes squinting at me from the darkness of the hallway.

"I don't know you. What do you want?" he croaks in a deeper voice than I can ever remember him having before.

"Mr Turnstone, I'm sorry for disturbing you, but I am a friend of Sarah's from university, and we've lost contact. I'm trying to track her down. I was wondering…I was hoping you might be able to help put me back in contact with her again…"

"Sarah?" he cuts me short.

There is a pregnant pause, and for a few seconds I am scared stiff that he will confirm my ultimate fears by saying that he has never heard of her. That in this world, Sarah does not exist.

"Sarah?" He repeats.

The door closes and the sound of the chain being unhooked. A second later the door opens again.

Mr Turnstone steps into the doorway, eyeing me up and down. He looks older than when I last saw him, and he appears unkempt, three days of white stubble poking out of the end of his chin and around his jaw. A smell of dampness, an unclean smell, assaults me as a draught carries it out from the hallway. My spirits sink. The house is in a bad way, and it looks like Mr Turnstone hasn't washed in a long time. He looks awful. There's no way that Sarah would let him get into this state if she were alive.

"Sarah?" He repeats for the third time, almost absent-mindedly. "Can't help you lad. Sarah and I don't talk any more. Haven't seen her for years."

My heart leaps.

"So she's alive then?"

"Alive? Of course she is. Look, what do you want?"

"I just want to find her, that's all… I haven't seen her for ages…" I try to explain.

"Well, neither have I. I can't help you. I'm sorry." He turns in the doorway, slowly, as if he is struggling with the onset of the years. Resting a hand on the doorframe he steps back into the darkness, before turning again cautiously to close the door behind him.

Refusing to accept defeat so easily, I step forward, and put a hand on the door.

"Mr Turnstone? Can I just ask where she lives? …and if she's married?" The question slips out before I can stop it, catching even me unawares.

His tired mournful eyes examine me for a second. But then with a surprising show of strength which catches me by surprise, he swiftly closes the door in my face, leaving me standing on the doorstep staring at the tarnished, brass doorknocker which almost scratches my nose.

"Married?" he mutters from the other side of the door, just loud enough for me to hear. "Not any more she isn't. Not any more…"

Flicking open the letter box with my fingers, I bend down and speak through it, hope surging anew.

"Where does she live? Where can I find her?"

"Blowed if I know. Haven't spoken to her in years," he replies. "Last I heard she lived in London. Now bugger off and leave an old man in peace. 'Else I'll call the police."

London?

As I walk down the street back to the NCP where I parked my car, I realise I'm not much further forward.

On the other hand I do know two things I didn't know before.

She does exist.

And she's not married.

As well as the fact that Sarah's father is even more of a grumpy bastard now than he ever was before. And he still doesn't like me.

CHAPTER 25
Wednesday

Driving to the station in the morning on the way to work, I feel strangely elated. Almost excited. The confirmation yesterday that Sarah does exist, the likelihood that she is not married, both fill me with hope.

For a moment though, the excitement is tinged with a feeling of dread, as I think briefly about something that happened on Monday: the moment when I was trying to picture Sarah in my mind, and I saw her walking away from me down the garden path... At first I had been so happy at the memory, but when she turned towards me, and I saw that she was pregnant, I had suddenly felt so uneasy? Why?

Parking the car, I replay the picture again in my mind, and the feeling of dread occurs on cue. Like the last time, the smile on my lips swiftly disappears as the initial warmth is replaced by a curious uncomfortable feeling. So much so that I cannot continue with it, and I mentally have to clear the picture from my mind's eye to make it go away.

What is it about the picture? Why do I react so emotionally towards it? I don't understand.

Sitting on the train into London the excitement eventually returns, and the curious incident in the car park is forgotten. I look forward to the rest of the day, which consists mainly of an early morning meeting with Scotia Telecom's creative team, allowing me to free up the afternoon to search for Sarah.

One of the new found joys of being a Partner, as opposed to an 'employee' is that I am completely in charge of my own time. No one tells me what to do. Even Richard. He can only 'suggest'. Which means that I'm free, in theory, to dedicate as much time as I want to finding my family.

In reality, - a term I am learning to use lightly-, it is not so simple. I have clients and responsibilities that I would be foolish to neglect, and which given that I actually enjoy my new career, is also something I do not want to do. Somehow I will have to shuffle the two. I have to find a balance and mix the search activities in between my work schedule.

The meeting in the morning goes well, and I introduce the Scotia marketing department to a few of the team from Cohen's that I have selected to work together to define messaging, imagery, and strategy, and to thrash out the branding. In the coming weeks there's a lot to do. Once we get these components right, we will start to plan media and advertising, putting the finer detail to a pan-European campaign for radio, television and cinema. In the coming weeks we'll be picking some famous name actors to sponsor the brand, and promote it on a two year contract; granted the small print gives us an out if we change our mind, or the fickle public change their mind about the popularity of the big name we sign.

There's a real temptation to work late, and avoid going home. The office offers me a secure environment where I can control what goes on around me. When I jump on the train and head back to Surbiton it becomes painfully clear that I am in control of nothing. At home I have a wife desperate for me to love her, two children who look up at me with tearful eyes, and for whom I still feel nothing, ...except guilt and sympathy, and a house that remains cleaner than an operating theatre, no matter how much of my mess I leave lying around.

The problem is that I just don't feel 'at home' at home.

And I know that I have started to avoid it.

Perhaps, if Jane just stopped trying so hard to get me to love her, maybe I might start to feel something for her. I am attracted to her…it's hard not to be. But…now I've got to know her, I don't think it will ever go beyond the lust and desire stage. The more time I spend with her, the more I notice that she lacks qualities that Sarah had and the more I see little things that annoy me and make us incompatible. In fact, the more time we spend together, the more I realise that she is not Sarah.

Which focuses my attention even more on finding her.

After the meeting with Scotia Telecom I leave Oxford Street and catch the Jubilee Line down to Waterloo. As I sit on the tube I think about what should I say to the Admissions Officer at the teacher training college in Mitcham where Sarah went, or where at least I think she may have gone. It is a long shot, and I know that even if she is a former student and they still have contact details for her, they are unlikely to give them to me. But I have to try. If you don't try you don't get. Simple as that.

As the tube pulls out of Green Park, I look out at the blackness of the walls as we shoot through the tunnel. In my mind's eye I anticipate the moment we should pull out into the next station, and vividly remember what it used to be like arriving at Westminster Station. Sleek, modern, clean and by far the most amazing station on the underground network. Or at least it used to be. Instead, the train arrives at Charing Cross. The wall tiles are old, green, and dirty. The first time that I have ever been in this section of Charing Cross, or on this platform.

My heart skips a beat as I read the title on the wall...Charing Cross, and for a second I remember the confusion I felt the first time I rode the Jubilee Line, and ended up in this new world.

I am surprised to see that the station looks so old. From first appearances it would seem that this is one of the oldest stations in the network. Interesting. For some reason I would have thought that it would be new, like Westminster. Does this mean that in the other world, *my* world, somewhere beneath Charing Cross station there is a section of dormant line and platform that no one knows about any longer?

The doors on the tube open, and people get off and are replaced by another random selection of tourists, businesspeople, women and children.

The doors begin to close, my eyes casually jumping from the faces of my new fellow passengers back to the name of the station which silently calls out its identity from the old tiles of the curved tunnel walls.

Charing Cross. Charing Cross.

The doors are almost closed now. A woman passenger is moving just across my field of view, but stops in her tracks, poised motionless between me and the sign on the wall. I suddenly have the weirdest sensation that time is seeming to slow down, as if I was looking at the second hand of a clock and noticing that it seems to hesitate for a moment before it continues onwards towards the next second: '*Tick*'..., a pause, and then the '*Tock*'. An instant that stretches out into an age.

The lady in front of me remains clearly defined, but behind the woman's head the sign on the wall seems to shimmer oddly...the letters of the words Charing Cross shake and wobble, then fade away and for an instant are replaced by new letters, a new name...the colour of the old green tiles changing to a modern blue. Looking from the sign to the platform around me, I notice that the whole station beyond the tube doors momentarily changes appearance...a wobble, a distortion in what I see that lasts for only the slightest moment of time...*Westminster*...It registers in my mind, but as I subconsciously blink to adjust to the visual aberration, it distorts and reforms again, solidifying back to the way it was. My eyelids complete the action of blinking and open, and all is as it was. The doors of the tube complete the action of closing, and the woman in front of me continues moving past my field of view. Outside, the station is once more the way it was.

Charing Cross

What?

Did I just see that?

I blink again, and look around me. No one else noticed anything.

Did that really just happen, or did I imagine it?

My heart starts to race again, faster and faster, and sweat breaks out on my forehead, a surge of energy coursing through my arms and legs. I close my eyes and try to replay the moment in my mind, trying to re-see what I just saw.

Over and over again I replay the moment. And each time, it is the same.

For a second, no, it can't have been anything like that…it could only have been a moment, a fraction of a second…half the time it takes for the electronic doors to close…*whatever*…the point is that for a microsecond, the sign on the wall changed and reformed to say *Westminster*…and the whole station followed suit. For a microsecond the station outside the doors was Westminster.

And then it was gone.

The train pulls into Waterloo, and I jump off, crossing the platform quickly, and jumping on the next tube to head back towards Charing Cross.

I am shaking. Not out of fear. But out of excitement.

A smile has begun to creep on to my lips. My heart is still racing, but this time from anticipation and hope.

'Did I just imagine that or was it real?' I ask myself for the hundredth time.

The tube pulls out of the dark tunnel, my pulse probably about 120 beats a minute.

Charing Cross.

I watch as the doors open and the people move in and out. I step up close to the doors, standing transfixed with my eyes glued to the sign outside.

The doors begin to close.

Please God. Please….

Charing Cross…Charing Cross…Charing Cross…

The doors are almost closed now…

Charing Cross...

The doors close.

Charing Cross…

The walls outside become dark, and we are in the tunnel again.

I look around me. A woman sitting on one of the seats against the opposite side of the tube looks up at me, and quickly looks away. I turn around, and we arrive at the next station.

Green Park.

There is already a train on the opposite platform heading back to Waterloo and I jump through the doors and race the ten metres through the adjoining tunnel, squeezing through the doors of the other train just in time.

I must have imagined it…it can't have been real… I didn't see it after all…Shit…shit…*SHIT*.

The carriage jostles a little, and the train pulls forward and gathers momentum through the black tunnel ahead. Suddenly there is light again.

Charing Cross.

I'm back in Charing Cross…..

CHARIIIINGGGG FUCCCKKKKINGGG CRRROOOOSSSSSS!

The doors open and I jump off and walk back and forward along the platform looking all about me, examining the station, reassuring myself that it is Charing Cross, and there's no way that I could have seen something written on the walls that looked like the words 'Westminster'. A myriad of emotions race through me. I am not thinking clearly, but what should I be thinking?

The hope and the anticipation quickly mutates to anger, and then the most immense sense of disappointment. A wave of depression that surges towards me, towering above me in a wall that crashes all around me, leaving me close to tears.

Sitting down on one of the plastic bucket seats lining the wall I ride the rollercoaster of feelings, letting six trains go past. Slowly my heart begins to slow, calm returns and I begin to stabilise. Around me people get on and off the tube trains as they arrive and depart from the platform, oblivious to my predicament. No one pays me any attention. Perhaps I am invisible?

So what did I see? Either I imagined it or it was real, but whatever I saw, it's gone now. I'm back in Charing Cross, a very real station within a very real underground tube network.

But, if I didn't imagine it,… if it was real… then the implications are staggering…

If I did see Westminster, even if only for the tiniest moment of time, then it means that I am not mad. That Westminster exists. That I never had concussion. And that somewhere, someplace, in my 'other' real world, wherever that is, Sarah, Keira and Nicole are waiting for me to come home.

CHAPTER 26
Wednesday
Teacher Training College

"So, Mr Quinn? How can I help you?" the bursar of the teacher training college in Mitcham asks me as she waves me to a chair in her office and invites me to sit down. "I hear you are trying to track down an old friend?"

"Yes, that's correct. Well not completely. You see, I am trying to track down a friend of my friend, who now lives in South Africa. He's coming back to the UK soon, and I'm trying to organise a get together of his old friends. I know that one of his close female friends went to teacher training college in London and I have about a month to try and locate her so that we can invite her to the party. I was hoping that you may be able to help me find her." I lie through my teeth, before smiling at her as sweetly as I possibly can.

The bursar, a rather jolly and large lady in her mid-fifties adjusts herself in her seat, and leans forward on the desk, clasping both her hands together under her chin as if she is just about to pray.

"Well, you see, Mr Quinn. Unfortunately, that may be difficult for me to do, because, as I am *sure* you can understand, it is a policy of the college not to give out addresses or contact details of its alumni. It's not really something that we normally do..." She smiles, a broad smile that can't help but elicit the twinges of another smile on my lips in return.

"I know, but this is very important. You see, my friend is coming home,...I don't know how to say this....you see, my friend is coming home to die...he has terminal cancer. We're trying to get everyone together for a last reunion...before...," I break off my eye contact, and looking distantly out of the window, blinking, as if to hold back an embarrassing tear. And all without an Equity card, or any previous acting experience.

There is a moment's silence. I swallow, cough a little, and then struggle to say.

"I'm sorry..."

Another silence.

"Mr Quinn, I don't know what to say...it's difficult...you see..."

"I understand." I reply. "Hopefully I may have luck elsewhere then, it's just that I haven't got much time...and neither has my friend."

The last part was a bit over the top, but lo and behold...it works.

"Okay, Okay, Mr Quinn. Let me see what I can do…" she says, sitting up straight and turning towards the computer. She moves the mouse on the pad, and the screen jumps into life.

"What did you say the name of your friend was?" she says, putting on a pair of glasses, and blinking a few times at the computer screen.

"Sarah Quinn…I mean Sarah Turnstone. Turnstone." Correcting myself quickly.

I sit quietly while the woman in front of me fights with the latest in modern technology. I watch her typing quickly on the keyboard, and clicking with her mouse on various icons on the screen. Eventually she speaks, excitement in her voice.

"Yes,..yes, here she is. Sarah Turnstone…"

My heart surges and I lean forward.

"Sarah Turnstone…and here…oh,…oh dear…" the woman suddenly exclaims, lifting the glasses from the bridge of her nose, blinking and leaning forward, staring at the screen ominously.

"Oh, I'm sorry, Mr Quinn, but Sarah hasn't filled out an alumni form or provided us with a forwarding address. I'm sorry. Even if I wanted to, I couldn't help you. It seems we ourselves are not able to communicate with her either." she apologises, turning to face me.

"What about Mary? Do you have a Mary in that year? She was her best friend, and she might be able to help me?"

"Mary who?" she asks, tilting her head to one side and smiling at me.

"I don't know her last name…"

"Then, unfortunately, there is nothing I can do. There are a hundred people in each year. That's probably about four Marys and I can't give you any of their details, even if we knew exactly which one it was."

"Is there no way we can do anything to track Sarah down? It's really important…I have to see her…"

The look on the bursar's face changes and becomes a lot more serious. She lays her glasses on the table in front of her and sits back in her chair, scrutinising me intensely.

"Mr Quinn…I sense that perhaps you are not being entirely honest with me? I feel that perhaps there is something you are not telling me…? Eh, what say you Mr Quinn?"

I suddenly feel like a little child being told off by the headmistress in school, caught out at doing something naughty. I struggle to find a way to respond, but am cut off before I can react.

"Mr Quinn, would I be correct in thinking that this 'friend' of yours, is in fact yourself? That it is you that need to see Miss Turnstone again, and not a colleague of yours…?"

I look down at my shoes, and bite my lip.

"I am sorry, Mr Quinn. I am sorry I cannot help you. But, if I may, can I offer you a suggestion?"

"Yes," I reply, looking up at her smiling brown eyes.

"Why don't you try the Electoral Register?" she replies.

By five o'clock I am back sitting in my office, searching the internet for details of the electoral register. Why did I not think of that before?

Within seconds Google has returned a whole selection of online companies that provide a search and tracing service, for a price. It turns out that they are much the same as each other, and all offering almost identical packages, which enable the user to locate the address of almost everyone currently registered as living in the UK.

The blurb promises that they contain the details of over 35 million people in the UK, at over 27 million addresses. But they warn that almost 20% of the population have opted out from the electoral register.

All I need to provide is a first name, surname, and a middle initial, and typically in return for €5 a go, the websites will give out blocks of addresses, fifty names at a time, including their dates of birth, and listed telephone numbers, along with the dates they were first registered at that address.

Thankfully, when I put in *Sarah Turnstone*, with *D* for *Dinah* as the middle name, there are only twenty-five respondents in the whole of the UK.

Just in case I miss anyone I pay for the list through three different sites, and print off all the results.

Then I settle down with a fresh cup of coffee and start to go through the addresses, line by line.

After thirty minutes I have narrowed the choice down to the only three names that live in London.

Unfortunately, when I look at the date of births I find that one is an eighteen year old girl, and the other two are both over fifty.

Shit.

I make another fresh cup of coffee and start again, this time widening my search through the results to anywhere within a sixty mile commuting radius of London. This provides me with another four names, none of whom are Sarah's age and born in 1971.

The phone rings and I pick it up.

"James, are you still at work?"

It's Jane.

"Yes…Sorry, I had to work late…"

"When will you be home?" she asks. I can hear the plea in her voice, and I don't know how to fight it.

"Soon. I'm just finishing up here, I'm not really getting anywhere now. I'll probably be home in an hour."

When I hang up, the guilt returns.

As I turn off the PC, and flick the light switch on the wall on the way out, I realise the paradox. Before I was with Sarah and felt guilty about chasing after Jane. Now I am with Jane and I feel guilty for chasing after Sarah.

The train ride back to Surbiton is quiet, I've missed the rush hour home, but am too early for those coming home from a night out on the town.

A lot has happened today. I am exhausted, both physically, mentally and emotionally and am not looking forward to an evening of intense conversation with Jane. I just want something to eat, a bath, and to go to bed.

I need time to think.

Although the teacher training college has her down as a former pupil, according to the Electoral Register, Sarah Turnstone does not exist.

It's only as the train pulls into Surbiton train station I remember the words of her father ringing in my ears.

"Married?" he had muttered from the other side of the closed door. *"Not any more she isn't. Not any more..."*

Two steps forward and one step back. In this case, a big step back.

The explanation for her not being on the electoral register is simple.

She was married, and she is probably still using her married name. And without knowing what that is, the chances of tracking her down are even less now than they were before.

CHAPTER 27
Thursday

Jane and I are sitting in the kitchen, two cups of coffee cooling on the worktop between us. We sit opposite each other on either sides of the island in the middle of the kitchen. The coffee is untouched. The house is silent.

Margareta has taken the children to play school and we are alone.

We are having a serious chat.

"Jane" I continue. "I *know* you are unhappy. It's not something you can hide any more. And there's no point. Why do you want to continue living a lie from day to day. We have to admit that there are some serious problems with our relationship that need to be sorted out..."

There is silence.

"Come on, we need to talk about this. I know that you were really upset about me getting banged on the head and getting amnesia, but I know that you were also hoping that this would give us both a fresh start?"

I pause, looking for a reaction. There is none. "Maybe you were hoping that I would have forgotten all about the problems we were having before, and that I would wake up a new man, and that we would be able to start afresh, and maybe fall in love again?"

She looks up at me, reaching out and cupping her hands around the coffee, as if she was seeking some sort of solace from its warmth. She looks away and out into the garden, into the distance.

"I know about you and Margareta," she says simply.

A tear runs down her eye, and I want so much to reach out and wipe it away, but I don't.

"You've changed." Her eyes are mournful, and dull. There is none of the usual sparkle, no spark of attraction from her to me. "I don't know who you are anymore."

More silence.

"Jane. I can't explain it, but I'm a very different person now. You're right. I'm not the same person that you knew a few weeks ago." I get up from my stool and walk around to her side, sitting on the stool beside her. "I know you know about Margareta. And it's not something I am proud of. It's almost as if I woke up in the hospital and found out that I am a different person to the one I thought that I was. When we got back from the hospital, I couldn't remember anything about Margareta. I didn't know who she was, let alone that I had slept with her. Every day to me is like a new voyage of discovery. I'm finding out things about my past that I don't like, things about me that I can't believe that I have done. Things about me that I know I have to change, because I don't want to live like that. I don't know who I am anymore."

"And I know about Claire too." She turns and looks at me, her blank face, empty and soulless.

How can I have done this to her?

"How many others are there James? How many other woman have you been screwing behind my back? How many?"

She says it very calmly. A simple question. As if she was asking me what time I was coming home from work tonight, or what I wanted to do at the weekend.

"I don't know. Hopefully none." I reach out to her, resting my hand on hers. "But at the same time I don't know exactly why I would want to have an affair with them in the first place. There must be something seriously wrong with our relationship for me to want to do that." Her eyes squint and narrow and I can see a flash of pain shooting through her. "Jane, I'm sorry. I'm not implying that *you* are doing anything wrong, or that it's your fault. It may be all my fault. But the point is that there *is* something wrong, and we both have to address it. Together. We can't just keep going around pretending as if there is nothing wrong. And you have to realise that it doesn't matter how clean and tidy the house is, it's me, …us…that needs to be cleaned up, not the house. Stop wasting your time trying to sweep everything under the carpet and imagining that it's all going to be all right. It won't…"

"What do you mean it *won't*?" she says, looking up at me. I can see a sudden anxiousness in her eyes.

"Wrong word. I mean. It won't get better unless we do something about it…" I stroke a hair away from one of her eyes, and follow the contour of her face with my index finger. She lifts her hand from her lap and grasps mine, holding on tightly. "We need to work on our relationship Jane, but I think we both know that it's not guaranteed that we can get things back to the way they were. I don't know what went wrong, or how we got to where we are today…and there is always the possibility that we…can't…fix things…But there's no point in living a lie. We have to do something. And we have to start now…"

"How?"

"The first thing we have to do is to ask Margareta to leave. She can't live here anymore. I was hoping that maybe you could talk to her today or tomorrow, the sooner the better. Tell her that we are going to try and look after the children ourselves, and that we won't need her here anymore."

"Why me? Why do I have to tell her?"

"Because if I do, she'll just think it's about me rejecting her, and I don't want to hurt her."

"Oh, so that's great. You don't want to hurt Margareta, but you don't care about how much you've hurt me!"

"Jane, that's not true. That's why we're having this conversation now. I do care that I've been hurting you, and I'm fed up with it. I'm fed up with living a lie, with hurting people all around me. I just want it all to stop. For us all to face up to where we are, and how we got here, and to put an end to all the deliberate lies and hurting."

Jane lets go of my hands, and gets up, going over to the kettle and flicking the switch to boil the water again.

"Okay, okay. I'll do it."

"Maybe you could talk to the Au Pair agency. If we give her a good reference perhaps we can help arrange for her to get another family…"

"I know what to do James. Just leave it with me." A moment's silence. "And us? How do we fix us?"

"Step by step, Jane. Step by step. One day at a time." I get up and walk over to her, wrapping her into my arms and hugging her close.

We stand like that for a long time, holding each other tight, and worrying about the future and what it holds.

When I eventually make it into the office, it's late. 1 pm. Just enough time to eat a few sandwiches and prepare for the afternoon ahead.

The first thing on the agenda is a meeting with the Dome Committee. Things are progressing. I've put together a small team of creatives to start to develop the proposition, and it's important to start going over some of the basics with the Dome team. To make sure we both understand where we are coming from and where we are going to.

I've appointed a manager to oversee the project and he has already drawn up a schedule of contact meetings between ourselves and the client. The good news is that to a certain extent I can sit back and let them get on with it. From now on I plan only to spend an hour or two a day checking what is happening, making sure I agree with the work flow being developed, and ensuring that it is on track.

Likewise with the Scotia Telecom deal. Which means that both projects should start to run pretty much without me, enabling me to concentrate on finding Sarah and my children.

The meeting with the Dome Committee takes place in their offices at 2.30 pm and it only lasts an hour. Outside on the street afterwards I make my excuses to Claire and the rest of the team, and catch a taxi by myself down to Covent Garden.

Since my experience on the tube yesterday afternoon a question has been working its way around my brain, popping up periodically, and demanding an answer. And the place most likely able to provide me the answer is situated in the corner of Covent Garden. The London Transport Museum.

After forking out the five euro entry fee, I spend fifteen minutes wandering around the exhibits, an interesting collection of old buses and trains, some of which I may have been on myself when I was a kid. But nothing which helps me find the answer that I'm looking for.

Eventually, I approach one of the guides who has just managed to free himself from a group of Japanese tourists all wanting photographs to be taken with their own cameras standing together beside an old horse-drawn bus. As the guide hands back the last of the cameras to its owner, I ask him.

"Excuse me. I was wondering if you could maybe help me with an enquiry about the design of the tube network. I'm interested in trying to find out more about the Jubilee Line, when it was built, who designed it, that sort of thing?"

"The Jubilee Line? No problem. I'm sure I can help you, but if you don't mind, could you come with me over to my office? I'm just going on my tea-break, and besides, I can help you better there..."

I follow him over to an office in the corner, which is actually the inside of a very old red Routemaster London bus. We step inside, and the guard takes off his bus-conductor-style cap, and puts it on his desk beside a computer.

"Draw up a pew," he invites me. "And take a look at this," he says, handing me down a large, blue book from one of the shelves running along one side of the bus, and flicking it open to where a small piece of protruding blue plastic marked 'Jubilee' is stuck to the corner of one of the pages.

"'*The London Tube Network*" by Adrian Richards. ' he says."The best book there is on the London Tube network. You'll probably find most of what you want to know in that section. Anyway, since I'm making one, do you fancy a cup of tea while you read it?"

While the friendly assistant makes us both a cup of tea, I start to quickly skim through the chapter on the Jubilee Line. I only get to half way down the first page and my heart almost stops.

"....*The Jubilee Line was inaugurated on the 1st May 1979, operating between Stanmore and Charing Cross. Since then it has been expanded several times, and the line now serves 21 stations, some of which were originally opened over 100 years ago. In fact, the northern end of the line between Wembley Park and Stanmore was originally opened in 1932 as a branch of the then Metropolitan Railway. Later, the local services from Finchley Road to Wembley Park and the Stanmore branch became part of the Bakerloo Line in 1939, when the London Passenger Transport Board opened a new section of twin tube tunnels between Baker Street and Finchley Road with stations at St John's Wood and Swiss Cottage.*

The first decision to build new extensions to the above and create a whole new underground line was made in 1969, when the requirement to build a new line to relieve the over-pressed Bakerloo line in the West End was finally recognised. The first stage of the plan came in the form of a new Line to link up the four km (2½ miles) of twin tunnels between Baker Street and Charing Cross - with the former Bakerloo Line branch between Baker Street and Stanmore.

Originally called the Fleet Line, following the successful opening of the new line, further plans were made to extend it along the line of Fleet Street (hence its original name) through the City of London and then south-east to Lewisham. However, although the extension was finally authorised in 1972, political developments in 1990 prevented commencement of the planned development.

During the early nineties, talk of development of the Canary Wharf region of East London, coupled with a proposed plan to build a large "Great Exhibition" style centre to promote British achievement and to celebrate the new millennium, led to revised plans being drawn up. Objections to the location of the proposed "Millennium Dome" being situated in Greenwich, led eventually to two alternate plans being drawn up. Although both new routes now took the newly named Jubilee Line extension south of the Thames via Waterloo, one now ended up back north of the river at Stratford, whereas the other one took it south down to East Dulwich, via South Lewisham.

The first of these projected routes passed through Waterloo, and then onwards to new stations at Southwark, London Bridge, Bermondsey, Canada Water, Canary Wharf, North Greenwich (proposed site of the Millennium Dome), Canning Town, West Ham and Stratford.

When the transport committee's report into the proposals highlighted the fact that the proposed sight for the construction of the Millennium Dome in Greenwich was an area of reclaimed land, which contained buried poisonous industrial waste, effectively making the site unsuitable for construction of a public project, the first plan lost popularity and was later completely abandoned when it was subsequently agreed to build the Millennium Dome at the north end of Hyde Park.

The plan that was finally adopted in 1993 was to add a new section from Green Park, starting with a new station at Westminster, before diving beneath the Thames to Waterloo, and then running on to stations at Lambeth East, Alworth Street, New Cross Gate North, Lewisham North, Lewisham South, Patton Street, and then finally on to the last station at East Dulwich.

Unfortunately, as soon as work started at Waterloo to extend the line northwards towards Westminster, the project ran into trouble. It quickly became apparent that sinking a new deep level underground station and tunnelling so close to Westminster and Big Ben and the Houses of Parliament could pose unexpected risks to the structure of these world heritage buildings. After a much publicised and heated debate, in which the decision to redirect the line was decided by only one vote (22-20) of the committee set-up to oversee the line's construction, this part of the plan was abandoned. Consequently, it was decided to continue to run the northern section of the line through the existing Charing Cross station, and then onwards and northward to Green Park.

After several more delays, and a greatly increased budget, the extended Jubilee Line was finally joined to the existing line on 28th December 1999...."

I look up from the book, the museum guide standing in front of me, offering a steaming mug of tea towards me.

"You look like you've just seen a ghost. Are you alright?" he asks, handing me the cup.

"Ghost?" I reply, absentmindedly, my mind not quite with him yet. "Almost..."

I leave the museum desperate for some fresh air. I walk around the square, listening to the buskers singing songs and watching the jugglers trying to impress the crowds and con as much money out of their pockets as possible.

In my mind's eye, the edges of a jigsaw puzzle are slowly beginning to come together.

A large, complex, jigsaw puzzle that has many pieces and forms a picture I simply do not understand. Yet...

Tiny strands connect the existing world to my previous world. Little strands of continuity that point to the two worlds being interconnected after all.

From what I have just read, including the world I grew up in, it would seem that Charing Cross has always been a station on the Jubilee Line. In my world, in the 1990's when the Jubilee Line was extended, the station was mothballed and Westminster was built. But in this 'current' world, the Charing Cross Jubilee Line branch was never abandoned, and is still being used. It seems that back in the early nineteen-nineties there were two plans to extend the Jubilee Line. The first of these plans was the one that was adopted and built in my previous world, and the other plan was the one that was built in my current world. Two different worlds, with two different Jubilee Lines. But both coming from a common past. *My* past.

My mind flashes back quickly to the incident on the tube yesterday, when for the briefest moment of time I could have sworn that the station outside the tube carriage switched from being Charing Cross to Westminster...and then back again.

It was real. It did happen; I am convinced of it.

How, I don't know.

But for a split second in time the world I am now in, toggled or flipped back to the old world that I used to live in. For a split second in time, the world outside of the carriage doors was the world where Sarah and Keira and Nicole still live and breathe, and now miss and probably mourn me.

It hits me then, for the first time.

Sarah and Nicole and Keira probably think that I am dead… Or maybe worse, maybe they think that I have abandoned them?

The thoughts alarm and sadden me, and the excitement I just felt is quickly replaced by sadness and a feeling of intense desperation.

Another thought hits me between the eyes, a sudden realisation that both lifts my spirits but also raises a whole new string of questions that I cannot possibly answer. A possibility that both confuses and frustrates me, but which gives me a gift that I seize hold of with a passion I have not felt in some time.

For suddenly I have been given the gift of 'hope'.

If, even it was for the *briefest* moment of time, a link was opened from this reality into my previous existence, a doorway from this world to the other, then maybe one day it will happen again.

A doorway that I can step through.

From one world to the other.

CHAPTER 28
King's College

I look at my Rolex. It's 4.32 pm. My appointment with the admissions officer of King's College is at 5 pm, which means I'll have to hurry.

Hailing a taxi, I sit in silence on the way down the Strand and along towards the Law Courts.

If I am right in my thinking I now have three possibilities for my future.

The first of these is that I accept the status quo…a term which probably really doesn't apply here… but leastways this means that I accept the circumstance I am now in. I learn to live my new life with Jane and our children, and do my best to enjoy it and move forward positively. I fix my relationship with Jane and I learn to love my children. For better or for worse.

The second option is that I continue to search for Sarah.

And lastly, I can pray and hope for the possibility that someplace, sometime, another opportunity will present itself for me to step from this world back to my own.

A woman further ahead of us, probably a tourist and looking the wrong way, steps abruptly off the pavement and into the path of my taxi. The taxi driver hits the horn, and slams on the brakes. The woman steps backwards quickly, the look on her face a mixture of embarrassment and shock. The driver mumbles something and drives on.

Behind the startled tourist in the window of a travel agency, a large poster of a desert island and blue tropical seas beckons the passer-by. I suddenly think of Robinson Crusoe and realise, abstractly, just how much in common we have with each other.

Unexpectedly cast ashore on a desert island from a sinking ship, Mr Crusoe realises that he can sit on the beach all day long and wait and pray for a passing ship to come to his rescue. Or he can move from the beach back into the countryside on the island and learn to live as best a life as he can in the new world he finds himself in. In fact, after an initial period of hardship, and with the right attitude and approach, Crusoe could find himself in Paradise. A paradise of his own making.

In truth, the best approach for Crusoe to adopt is to realise that the passing ship may never ever come. And that, in the meantime the best thing he can do, is to accept that eventuality and learn to live each day as it comes in the best way he can.

Realising his options, he should throw himself into his new existence, finding joy and pleasure from wherever he can. At the same time, being a sensible man, he should make preparations for the possibility that one day a ship may appear on the horizon. A day which may never come. But might.

Thinking about Mr Crusoe, I realise there is a lot I can learn from the old guy. Yes, I can live in hope from day to day that someplace, sometime, a magical door will open up back to my old world. And yes, when the time comes I can step through back to my real life. But, realistically, like the ship on the horizon, that day may never, ever come.

The realisation depresses me, but sobers me up. It helps me firm my resolve to continue with my search for Sarah. Wherever she is in this world.

What happens when I find Sarah, is something I should best leave for the day it happens. I can only cross that bridge when I come to it.

"Mr Quinn? Hello. So how may I help you?" the Admissions Officer asks me from behind a large post-office style counter as I introduce myself, looking quickly at her watch and frowning ever so slightly. I think I have just been told off. It's ten minutes past five, and my appointment was at five. Best apologise.

"I'm sorry I'm a little late, I couldn't get a taxi."

"No problem, Mr Quinn." She smiles. The woman is a curious blend of academic and a hippie, mother figure. She is wearing a large, home knitted red jumper, with brown horn-rimmed glasses dangling around her neck on the end of a long piece of black cord. Her cheeks are red, her brown hair beginning to show the first signs of grey flecks. I wouldn't be surprised if she has been working here, doing the same job, for the past twenty years. Maybe she even knew Sarah…

"I'm looking for an old student from here. She studied History and graduated some time in 1992 or 1993. I was hoping you could help me find her?"

"Are you a friend or relative?" she asks me, picking up a pen and starting to make a few notes on a pad in front of her.

An interesting question.

"A friend."

"You realise of course, that if we do have a forwarding or contact address for her, that I cannot give it out to you?" she says, smiling at me, but ruffling up her forehead at the same time, a set of parallel lines appearing and making her looking both stern and incredibly authoritative.

"I was hoping that…" I start, unsuccessfully.

"What we normally suggest, Mr Quinn, is that if we *do* have a forwarding address, *then* you should write a letter to your friend care of this address, and we will forward it on to her. It's up to her if she replies or not."

"Okay. Thank you." I stand corrected. Why is that all these academic types are able to make me feel like a naughty little boy?

"Fine. Now we understand the rules, let's see what we can do for you then, shall we?"

She lifts up the glasses from around her neck and puts them on.

"What did you say the name of your friend was?" she asks.

"I didn't, yet, but her name is Sarah Turnstone", I reply hopefully.

"Ok, then. Can you wait here a moment please?" She says, as she walks away to a computer on a desk in a room behind the counter.

I look around the room, catching the eyes of another student who is busy copying a telephone number down from a poster on one of the walls. Apart from me and the other student the room is empty. A couple of black padded seats line the wall, like those you might find in a doctor's waiting room. I take a seat, and twiddle my thumbs, looking expectantly back towards the counter and the door through which the lady just disappeared.

"Here we are, here we are." She suddenly announces, as she walks briskly back in and takes up her position behind the counter again. "We've got her on file, forwarding address and everything. Sarah Turnstone. Graduated 1993. History. 2.1. With Honours." She says, looking up and smiling at me.

"Does she live in London? Can you tell me that?" I ask.

"Mr Quinn… I am sorry. I can't."

"Please?"

She hesitates. I can tell this woman goes by the book on everything. Never breaks a rule.

She looks at the piece of computer printout in her hand, and frowns again.

"Okay, Mr Quinn. I'll tell you one thing and one thing only. According to our records she lives in Norwich."

How wrong can I be. She did break the rules.

"Norwich?" That familiar sinking sensation hits me. "Would it be Potterbank, number 42, by any chance?"

"I can't really say, Mr Quinn… you see, that *really* would be breaking the rules…"

"Look, I already have that address. If that's the same address you have down on your files, it means that the file is out of date, and she hasn't given you a recent forwarding address. That's her father's address, and she doesn't live there anymore. I went up to see him a few days ago."

"Her father? And he doesn't have her forwarding address?"

"No. He hasn't spoken to her for years. Look," I say honestly, fed up with not getting anywhere. "...the fact of the matter is that I'm desperate to find Sarah. It's really important I find her. And I'll do anything I can to track her down. But if the address you have in your hands is her old home address, then there's no point in leaving a letter for her with you, because her father doesn't know where she is either."

She takes her glasses off and looks at me straight, letting them dangle against her chest on the end of the cord. She looks at me, then glances at a tall charity box sitting on the counter. For a moment I am confused, but then I wise up. I take a 10 euro note out of my pocket and pop it in the "RNIB: Give to the Blind" canister.

"Ah. That's very generous of you Mr Quinn." She smiles. "I suppose there is no real harm done if I confirm that the address I have in my hand is the same as the one you just mentioned. And apart from that we have no further records..."

As I walk out of the door and catch the lift back down to the street I wish things could just be a little more simple. Why is it that people never keep their details up to date with their old colleges and universities?

I decide that I can do with a good stiff drink, and am just about to walk through the door of the nearest pub, when my phone rings.

CHAPTER 29
The Phone Call

"Hello?", I answer, hesitating in the doorway of the Golden Oak opposite Kings College.

"*James!* Just what the fuck do you think you are playing at?"

An angry voice. A woman's. A voice I don't immediately recognise. An accent, probably Australian or Kiwi.

"I'm sorry, what did you just say?" I reply, taken aback.

"I asked you what the fuck you think you're playing at? Have you gone deaf as well as mad?" the voice continues. "We had a deal. A good deal. What the hell do you think you're playing at?"

I hesitate before I answer. The voice at the other end is silent.

"Do I know you?" I ask, playing for time. Obviously, she knows me. And it's not a wrong number. She knows my name is James.

"Don't you think you can play games with me James. I haven't got time for this. I just want to know what's going on. I went out on a limb for you. I stuck my neck right on the block, and now you're making me look stupid. What's going on?"

Oh no. Another person that I seem to have pissed off. Another person that hates me.

"Listen, I'm sorry..." I start.

"Don't you tell me to 'listen' James. Don't get smart with me. It's a fucking phone. I'm holding it against my head. What else am I going to do but 'listen'?" she interrupts me again.

"Who..."

"*Right.* I'll tell you what we're doing. After all I did for you, you owe me an explanation. You're meeting me in thirty minutes time. The Pitcher and Piano behind St Martin's in Charing Cross. Thirty minutes. If you're not there, I'll make sure you regret it for the rest of your life. Nobody crosses me and gets away with it James. No one."

Click.

She hung up.

But who was it? For the life of me, I couldn't recognise the voice.

Whoever it was, I have no choice but to meet her. I look at my watch. 5.55 pm. Whatever I have done, it sounds serious. Suddenly my new existence is taking on a new dimension. It never occurred to me that the new me might have serious enemies, or serious problems. Problems which I may find difficult to deal with, and which are not of my making.

A number 26 bus passes me, and I make a dash for it, managing to cross the road between the traffic and jump onto the open back. I climb the stairs and take a seat at the top of the bus, hiding in the corner.

Who was it? Who am I going to meet? And why? What have I done?

I search the mobile phone for the call register. Dialling the last number back I prepare myself to hang up if she picks up. I'm hoping that she will have left by now, and that I will get an answering machine, with her name on it.

Even better. It goes through to a reception.

"*Peters Hall and Irvine*, can I help you?"

Ah.

Curiouser and curiouser, as they say...

I arrive at the Piano and Pitcher in good time. Ten minutes early.

Taking a seat in the corner near the window, I start to savour the malt whisky in my glass. A double.

I don't have long to wait.

A couple of minutes later, a taxi draws up outside, a middle-aged woman in a business suit jumps out, and hurries towards the door.

She walks in, immediately scanning everyone in the bar, looks in my direction, and makes a beeline for me.

"Start explaining James, and it better be good. If it's not I'm going to fucking kill you, then feed you to the birds."

"Hi", I say, getting up from my comfortable seat like a true gentleman and offering her my hand to shake. Whoever she is.

She stares at me, looks at my hand in disgust, and drops down opposite me on one of the large soft sofas. A low lying drinks table is the only protection I have between myself and her.

There is something very odd about her that reminds me of someone I know. Her face is vaguely familiar. I strive to place it, to remember who she is or where I know her from. Somewhere… *something to do with work?? To do with Kitte-Kat?*

"Listen, I'm really sorry you are so pissed off with me, but I'm afraid I haven't got the faintest idea what I have done to upset you so much. Perhaps a really good place to start would be for you to tell me what I am so guilty of doing, and why you want to kill me?" *...and who you are? And how you have my number? And what's this all about?*

The woman sighs, closing her eyes and doing what looks incredibly like counting to ten. Trying to calm down.

"James", she says again confirming again that she definitely knows my name. Except when she says it, it sounds like 'Jaiiimmmees'. An Aussie. Definitely an Aussie. "I'm going to try *really hard*, okay, really hard, not to kill you. But don't push it, mate. Don't push it. We've known each other for a long time. And we're friends...at least I thought we were...so, I'm going to give you the benefit of the doubt. For another hour....*then* you're dead. When you first contacted me, I didn't want anything to do with it. There was *no* possibility of it happening. But no, you wouldn't take 'no' for an answer, and you just pushed me and harassed me until eventually I succumbed. Next thing you know I'm out there going to bat for you."

I lean forward in my chair. Are we talking about playing cricket, or something just a little bit more important?

"So, bloody muggins here goes to the rest of the partners and persuades them that we need you, that it would actually make sense to get you back on board. But when, after two months of persuasion, and weeks of hard work they *do* come round to the idea and *agree*..., you bloody go ahead with the Scotia deal yourself! And then yesterday, to top it all, I hear that you've taken the deal for the Dome, and you're now staying at Cohen Advertising!"

Aha...So that's what this is all about. PHI want the Scotia Telecom and the Dome deal. Fifteen million euros worth of business. And I'm the ticket.

"It sounds like I owe you and PHI an apology. So, if I've done wrong, I will apologise. Whole heartedly. The last thing I want to do is hurt my friends. But I have a very good explanation..."

"Come on James, it's not like you have thousands of friends any more. You can't afford to piss off the few of us that still like you. This explanation you have, it had better be a good one. A right stonker, because if it's not, I'm going to tell Richard all about our little deal, and he'll kick you out on your ear."

"Actually, he probably won't. I'm a Partner now."

She looks at me for a few seconds, her mouth half open, as if she had been frozen in mid sentence. Then suddenly she laughs, and flops back into the chair, as if the tension that was gripping her had suddenly evaporated.

"A Partner at Cohen Advertising? Richard made you a Partner?" She laughs again, and I am a little insulted. Why shouldn't Richard make me a Partner?

When she laughs for the third time, I recognise the smile, and suddenly I remember where I know her from... She's the girl who used to hand out the free magazines outside the tube station at Canary Wharf. The girl who I used to pass every day on my way to work at Kitte-Kat, and who impressed me so much with her enthusiasm, loyalty and politeness. It's her. It *really* is her.

Another life, ...another career. I always knew she could go far, given the opportunity...but a Partner at PHI? From what she's saying, this woman may even have been my boss when I worked for them.

"Okay. Okay. I owe you a full explanation, and I'm going to give you one. But I have to warn you that you may not believe me. First of all though, I think that we should both get a drink. A stiff one..."

I go to the bar and return with two large malt whiskies. She's taken her jacket off by now, and she's started to unwind. As I walk back towards her, I realise for the first time that she is actually a very attractive woman. Her long dark black hair, her brown eyes, a curvy figure... not at all bad.

Passing her a drink, I settle down opposite, and take a sip of my Glenmorangie.

"If you're sitting comfortably...I'll begin." I say, trying to inject a little humour into the situation. She frowns. "The thing is...I've got amnesia. I've forgotten all of our conversations. Our arrangement. About moving to PHI. Everything."

The look in her eyes, lets me known instantaneously that I've just been a little too blunt. She reaches for her coat, puts down the whisky and starts to get up from the sofa. Her face is turning slightly red, and I guess that I have only a few seconds before steam starts pouring out of her ears, or her head blows up.

I jump to my feet and reach for her arm.

"No, honestly. I have... I'm not joking. I'm telling you the truth!" I exclaim. "Honestly... listen, I'll get my wife to back me up. You can hear it from her...she'll tell you the truth." I pull out my Scotia phone, and dial my home number. Margareta picks up the phone.

"Hi...it's James, is Jane there?"

"James? You bastard...I hate you! I never want see you again...." And Margareta burst into tears.

The voice is loud enough for the woman from PHI to hear too---whatever her name is---and she stops, and turns to me, questioningly.

"Margareta?" I ask.

Shit. She's crying really loudly now. "James...*you ruin my life.* You bastard!!!" Then suddenly the line goes dead. She's hung up.

"Em..sorry about that," I mutter to the woman in front of me. "I'll call Jane on her mobile. Hang on a second." I quickly look up Jane's mobile number in the memory. Jane's got a new mobile phone, a perk of the Scotia deal, and I haven't memorized the number yet. It rings three times and then it's picked up.

"Jane?"

"James...listen it's not a good time. Elspeth and Allison are in hysterics and Margareta is just walking out of the door as we speak...I just told her, and she didn't take it well..."

"Listen Jane, this is important. I need you to talk to a colleague of mine, and tell her about the concussion you gave me?" I interrupt her.

"I gave you? *You're blaming me now*? So suddenly this is all my fault?..."

"Listen, I didn't mean that. Can we talk about this another time...but right now, *please*, please just tell my colleague what happened, and why I've got amnesia."

"What's her name then?"

I look up at the woman now standing in front of me. She can hear Jane's loud voice too, and she heard the question as well.

There's nothing for it, but the truth.

"I don't know. I don't know her name..."

The woman from PHI gives me a look that could kill, shrugs off my hand, which is still gripping her arm, and turns to leave again.

"No please don't go." I shout at her.

"Who are you shouting at?" Jane bellows down the phone to me. "James, if you think that I'm going to speak to another one of your bloody women, and sort out another one of your messes, you've got another think coming. It's obvious you've got so many women on the go that you can't even remember their names. You got yourself in this mess, now get yourself out. And don't come home until you've done it."

She hangs up.

I pull the phone away from my ear and stare at it.

When I look up, the woman from PHI is walking out of the door. A second later and she is gone.

I catch a taxi back from Surbiton to my house. Nowadays I've taken to walking to the station in the mornings: it's healthy and pleasant and anyway, there's nowhere to park an €80 000 Audi at the station. From my new house in Effingham Road, it's only a ten minute walk, across a large open park, and down the high street. No problem.

But tonight, "I just can't be arsed.", as one of my friends at Kitte-Kat used to say. I hear her voice saying the words in my ears, and I realise that it's only the first time I've really thought about my old work since I left it. Is that a good or bad thing?

Perhaps it just shows how much more I am enjoying advertising than the world of telecoms, broadband, and techno-mumbo-jumbo.

I want to get back as soon as possible to sort things out with Jane. With such an unstable life all around me, I need to make sure that things at home start to find an even keel.

It's only 6.45 pm when I finally pay the taxi-driver and walk through the door to my little castle, but already the girls are up in bed, and Jane is sitting in the music room at the back of the house, a large glass of white wine in her hand, and " The Very Best Classic Chill-Out Album -Ever ", playing in the background. Jane's perfect anti-stress solution. Wine and song.

She looks up at me as I walk into the room, and then looks away.

"I knew it was too good to last," she says.

"What?"

"I was beginning to relax, to unwind. To enjoy the music…but now you're home!"

"Thanks a bundle. Where's the wine?" I ask.

"In the fridge."

"Where's the fridge?"

She looks at me as if I'm stupid, so I venture into the kitchen on another voyage of discovery, and manage to re-find the fridge. I'm getting the hang of it now.

"What happened to your date then?" Jane asks rather directly, which is actually a good sign. Perhaps she's taken seriously everything I said about not sweeping things under the carpet.

"It wasn't a date, and you going off on one didn't help. But I suppose I can't complain." I flop down opposite her in another one of the comfy chairs. "She was a Partner from Peters Hall and Irvine. She arranged to see me,…I didn't know what it was about until I met her…and she was furious with me for having forgotten something important which she apparently told me once, a while back. I was just trying to be straight with her, so I told her about the amnesia. You were my alibi. So thanks."

"Okay, sorry. I just overreacted, but I was mad with you. Call it pent-up emotion, latent anger, whatever. There's probably more to come, so get used to it."

"Fine. Thanks for the warning. So how did it go with Margareta? You've told her?"

"This afternoon. Were you not listening to a word I said? I told you earlier, she's gone."

"What, 'gone' as in, 'left and never coming back?'…Already?"

"Yes. Too soon? Do you miss her? Want her back?"

"Jane, it was my idea for her to go. I want her out of the house, so that we can spend time together sorting out the mess we're in. I'm glad she's gone. It's just a little soon, that's all."

"What? Hoping to get in one last shag before she left?" Jane turns to me. I look at her and say nothing. A minute later, she says "No. That was unfair. I'm sorry."

"So how did she take it?" I ask.

"You really want to know?" she asks.

I think about it for a second, and decide what's done is done.

"No. But where's she gone? Home?"

"No. Don't worry about it. I gave her a 1000 euros and a reference letter. She's rich. The agency picked her up, and took her to another house. It was all arranged. She's going to be fine. I wish I could say the same for us..."

The conversation dies for a minute, and we listen to the music. I recognise the track. I don't know who wrote it, or what movement it comes from, if it does come from some sort of 'movement', but it's one of the theme tunes from the film 'The Hunger' with James Bowie. One of the best vampire films ever made. Catherine Deneuve and Susan Sarandon. The first time I ever saw two women kissing each other. Although that's not the reason I liked the film.

"So, what happened with the woman from PHI?" Jane asks.

"She left. Walked out of the pub whilst I was on the phone to you just before you hung up." I look at my glass, and swirl the wine around a little. "Did I ever talk to you about going back to work for PHI?"

"No."

"Oh...Well, it looks like the possibility has come up. Whoever the woman from PHI was, I think she'll be calling Richard tomorrow, and even though I am a Partner, I don't think he's going to be very pleased to hear what she has to say."

She comes back into the room, having changed the CD to another laid-back dinner Jazz album, and sits down on the same sofa as me, tucking her legs up underneath her, shaking her head and pulling the hairband from her hair, so that it falls down free over her shoulders.

"The woman from PHI is called Helen." Jane announces. "She called once before, ...a while ago. Sorry, ...I forgot to mention it. Her number's on a piece of paper in the kitchen. She seems keen to get hold of you again. And she's called again twice in the past hour. I told her the truth, so don't worry. She knows all about your loss of memory now. Anyway, she said she's going to call you again first thing in the morning just to confirm that you'll meet her for lunch at 12 pm."

I look at her in disbelief. Then I see the twinkle in her eye.

That's one-up for Jane.

"Thanks!" I say with a smile.

"Thanks nothing. You're going to give me the best orgasm tonight that I've ever had, and if you don't, I'll call up Richard and tell him about the whole PHI thing myself."

CHAPTER 30
Drowning

I could hear the screaming.

The corridor on the lower deck of the ship was pitch black, the lights out, but as I felt my way along the walls, trying to find a door, the sound of their bloodcurdling cries drew me on and on. Nicole and Keira. Ahead of me somewhere, locked in one of the ship's cabins.

Something pulls on my feet, and I fall forward, tripping up and sprawling headlong. As I go down I bang my head, and I wake with a start.

I look around the room, gently acclimatising, becoming conscious of the rhythmic breathing of a woman beside me.

Jane.

Lying back on the pillow, I close my eyes, and try to relax.

Soon the blackness is around me again, engulfing me, and drawing me back to the dream. This time I am on the deck, it is night-time and a terrible storm is raging about the ship. I am shaking with cold and I am afraid. Very afraid.

And then I hear it. "James...over here....James..." again and again. Sarah is calling to me.

"James..." Her voice is coming from somewhere towards the stern. The sea is getting rougher now, and I fight hard to stand up and make my way forwards. I grab hold of the railing and pull myself along towards the back of the ship, the cold wind pushing me back and whipping the waves over the side of the ship and making progress impossible.

"James....quickly...*please....*"

Then suddenly, out of one of the side doors, a group of people carrying wine glasses and blowing party poppers, dressed in tuxedos and ball gowns, spill out onto the deck beside me. Laughing, shouting, arms wrapped round each other's waists.

They don't see me. They are not affected by the storm, and walk past me, upright, without a care in the world. I stare at them in disbelief, calling to them for help. They start to dance, music from an orchestra being piped over loudspeakers I cannot see.

I hear Sarah calling to me again, and make another effort to move forward, searching for her, trying to see her in the tumultuous world around me.

Suddenly she is there, ahead of me, almost within reach.

She is crying, reaching out to me, hanging on to the other side of the rail, dangling from the ship, the water beneath her surging up in waves, and threatening to sweep her away.

I cry out to her and she turns and sees me, the horror and fear in her eyes piercing through the void between us and ripping into my heart.

The ship rises violently beneath me and a wave hits the side of the ship broadside. A wall of freezing water sweeps me off my feet, and I struggle to hold onto to the rail. The wave passes and I pull myself up again, the salt stinging my eyes and making it almost impossible to see.

"James…quick…I cannot hold on much longer…be quick…"

I find her again, this time only one hand gripping the rail, the other nowhere in sight.

Quick, I must be quick.

"Daddy…daddy." the voices of Nicole and Keira call to me from behind. Petrified by the storm raging around them, they are standing near the door to the deck where the party-goers just emerged from below, holding hands and wearing their best party dresses, looking at me, *imploring* me, Nicole hugging what looks like a large teddy bear to her chest.

I turn to look at them, shouting "Get back inside, please,…*go back inside*! "

The ship falls down, down, ever downward into another trough which opens up, threatening to swallow us whole.

I glance first at Sarah, and see her only remaining hand beginning to slip, and then back again at the girls. I see the wall of water heading towards them both, and I freeze.

Who do I save?

Sarah or my beautiful daughters? Who?

Who do I love more?

The wall of water catches me in my back, catapulting me across the deck, and driving me against the bulkhead. I fight against the water, sprawling, reaching out, trying to grip anything I can touch…

A piece of metal…

Quick…my fingers curl around it and close, clenching tightly, refusing to let go.

The water passes by and I open my eyes.

I struggle to my feet, gasping for breath.

But Keira and Nicole are gone.

And when I look at the rail only metres away, so is Sarah.

Washed away. Drowned.

I start to scream Sarah's name. Loudly, please hear me Sarah….*where are you?* Please…

A hand grips me from the side, and gently shakes me.

"James…wake up…wake up!"

I open my eyes with a start, the world of water and the ship beneath my feet vanishing in an instant. Instead, Jane is by my side, kissing my forehead, calming me, reassuring me. Cooing to me like a child.

I blink and breathe, and relax, the nightmare quickly dissolving before my eyes.

A few minutes pass, Jane helping me back to normality, loving me, hugging me.

And she asks me, one question.

"Who is Sarah?"

The thing about a dream is that if you are woken from it suddenly, when the dream is not allowed to finish itself properly, it's like someone has just pushed the 'pause' button on a film, and for the whole day until you fall sleep again you are trapped in exactly the same emotional state you were in the moment you were woken up. Your mind is waiting for the dream to finish, for the sign saying "The End" to roll across the little cinema screen in your head.

I cannot describe the feeling that the dream has evoked within my body. I can only try to ignore it. For to try to quantify it, would be to look at it, to examine it, and then I would be engulfed once more.

But the sound of my family calling out to me from the sinking ship stays with me, and I cannot shake off their voices, or drown them out, no matter how loud I play the music in my car.

My first meeting of the day is not till 10.30 am. By 8.30 am I am parked outside a cemetery in Richmond, waiting for the gates to open. I've come to see if Sarah's mother is still here. With my other options quickly running out, this is becoming one of my last hopes.

Strange, that I should be trying to find hope in a graveyard.

Perhaps I should have come before, but I hate graveyards. I still can't face them, and I haven't stepped foot in one in years, not since…

A car pulls up beside me and a council workman in a blue overall gets out, thankfully interrupting my train of thought. "'Allo mate. Wow you're keen. I thought that this is the last place I'd find a queue of people waiting to get in. I mean, most people aren't dying to get in…they're already dead."

I smile. A laugh is out of the question. I hide the emotion that is just about to wash over me like a wave, swallow hard, and steel myself. I have to do this…

Sarah's mother's plot should be near the middle of the cemetery, underneath a weeping willow with a large, black polished headstone and a bowl of dead flowers at the top of the grave, the flowers that Sarah puts there year after year. No one else comes to the grave, so the old flowers are still there when she makes her annual pilgrimage with fresh ones, a whole year later.

Except this time, they are not. No flowers, no headstone, no grave.

I walk around for a while, looking everywhere, hoping to see her name visibly etched on one of the other stones. Several times I stoop down at a grave, pulling aside the overgrown grass and peering at the weathered letters on the headstone, fighting the emotion that threatens to overwhelm me, and struggling to stop the pictures from forming in my head...

I try to focus on the job in hand, but no matter how hard I look, I have no luck.

Realising that it's not possible to look around the whole graveyard, and a little glad of the excuse to leave, I drive over to the little curator's house near the entrance, and catch the workman who is just emerging from the door with a cup of tea and a spade.

"Can I help you mate?" he asks as I wind down the window.

"I'm looking for a grave…my mother-in-law's. I think it's in here somewhere. Is there anywhere I can check to see if it is?"

"Sure, give me a few minutes and I'll check on the computer inside. It's all computerised now. I know the name of everybody…hang on a second, I like that…I know the name of *every body* that is in the graveyard. Not bad that, just made it up? What do you reckon….new material…?

"Keep the day job pal. Don't give it up…. The woman I'm looking for is called Martha Turnstone?"

"Turnstone, rather appropriate. Almost like Headstone….?"

I raise my eyebrows, and stare at him. He gets the message, and disappears inside.

Five minutes later he's back.

"Sorry mate. She ain't here."

"Are you sure?"

"Listen, it's like I said. If she ain't in the computer, she's ain't in the ground." He smiles, closes the door to the house behind him and walks over to the car. "Sorry mate. I hate to be the bearer of bad tidings, but maybe your mother-in-law is still alive!"

I smile back at him. Not because he's finally cracked a 'dead'-funny mother-in-law joke, far from it, but because he might have just struck gold.

If Martha Turnstone *'ain't in the ground'* then maybe she is alive. In her house in Spain. Just one phone call away.

"Richard wants to see you, when you get a chance?" Alice informs me as I walk through the door.

"Any idea what about?" I ask.

"Yes. I think he just wants to see if you are happy. He mentioned something to me about checking your diary and setting a regular catch-up with you. And also to remind you that the Partner's meeting is this afternoon, just before the all-hands meeting at five."

"I know. I'm meeting someone for lunch, but will be back in plenty of time. Thanks."

Which means that I am going to be pretty busy for the rest of the day. I want to spend an hour on the Dome Deal before lunch, and then meet quickly with the project manager for Scotia Telecom who should have a few new ideas to show me.

The phone on my desk goes for the first time about five minutes after I have managed to settle behind my desk. The Red Phone. I'm still not too sure why I have a red phone as well as a normal one. There must be a reason?

The voice at the other end is immediately familiar to me. It casts me back to my university days, the college bar, drinking and trying to ask out as many women as possible.

"James? *Where have you been?*"

"*Stu? Stu Roberts?* Bloody hell, it's you isn't it?" I blurt out in complete surprise.

"None other. Why do you sound so surprised? You knew I'd be chasing you up. You never turned up for the meeting yesterday."

Oops. Another angry caller. Except Stu is an old friend. A good friend. Someone I haven't seen for years,...probably about four, not since we last got drunk together at the wedding of one of our mutual university friends. Stu Roberts? Who would have thought it? He is certainly one person that I have no intention of mistreating.

"Listen Stu, if I'm meant to have met with you yesterday, I am really sorry...but before we go any further I think there's something I have to tell you...apart from the fact that it's fantastic to hear your voice, and that it would be great to see you again."

"What do you mean? We only spoke a couple of weeks ago, and we met just last month..."

"Shit, sorry... Stu, listen, I won't bullshit you with any excuses. I was in hospital. Fact is I fell over, banged my head. Got concussion and amnesia.

Can't remember much from the past couple of months. Including you, our meeting and anything else I've promised you."

"Ouch. Are you alright? Are you back at work?"

"Yep. In fact, I've just been promoted to Partner and I've won another major deal. Listen, honestly, please forgive me, but what were we talking about? And what are you doing nowadays? The last time I can remember us speaking was in the college bar the day we finished our last exams?"

I say, playing it safe, prompting him for some clue as to when I really did see him last in this world.

"Bloody hell. You *have* got amnesia! Have you forgotten everything?"

"Yes…I mean, I can remember that when you left college you went into banking, but that's about it?" I say.

In my world the last time I saw Stu Roberts he was working as a sports reporter for the BBC, but after leaving university he did have a short stint in the bank, working part-time around a busy training schedule preparing for the Commonwealth Games. Since childhood Stu had always been an excellent athlete, his slim but powerful build helping to make him a brilliant runner. Until one day in the run-up to the games an unlucky sports injury had brought a promising career to an untimely end.

"Banking? You mean you can't remember anything about me winning the Gold Medal for the 400m at the Olympics?"

"Which Olympics?"

"1996…Australia."

"You're kidding!"

"No, I'm not. Listen, …are you really okay? "

"Absolutely. Don't worry about me. The amnesia's only temporary. The Docs say it'll all come back eventually, but that I have to be patient since it might be a while before I remember everything."

"Good, but for now it's obvious that I've got a lot to refresh you about. What are you doing tonight?"

"Can't. Wife problems. Going to the Opera. What about Monday?"

"Monday's good. 8 pm. Usual place?"

"Where's that?"

"Waxy's. Upstairs at the entrance."

"You mean, Waxy O'Connor's? Okay, sounds good. Listen, can you tell me what it's about? Anything I should prepare for?"

"A quick summary then? Fine..., I work for the British Olympic Committee now. Actually, when I say that I work for them, maybe I should say that I'm the Chairman. You and I were talking about the advertising and promotional campaign for the British Olympics in London in four years time. It's worth fourteen million euros to whoever gets it. And you're the front runner."

The Olympics in London 2016? Not again! It hadn't even really occurred to me that the Olympics might not have taken place in this version of the world...I've just been through seven years of build up to the 2012 Olympic Games in London, put up with months of not being able to get a seat on a bus or a train because of the millions of tourists, all of whom had tickets to see the Games, whereas as I never got a single one!...and now I've got to do it all over again!?

"Wow. ...How on earth can I forget something like that? It sounds mega."

"It is. But since you've forgotten everything about it, I think I should let you know that this is a hush-hush deal. I'm not putting it out to tender. Political reasons. The business is yours if you can deal with it."

"Who else know about it? Anyone else here at Cohen's?"

"No. Not unless you've told them about it. Maybe your PA. No one else."

"Good. Let's keep it that way."

"Funny, I thought you'd say that. Eight o'clock then?"

"It's a date. Have a good weekend…and sorry mate."

"No probs. Listen, take it easy. But if you still want the deal, you've got to deliver. No more funny business, okay?"

"It's a promise."

So this is what the advertising business is like. Big, multi-million euro deals. High-profile accounts…the excitement, the rush, the…

"James? Busy?" a soft female voice breaks my concentration.

It's Claire, poking her head around my office door.

"No," I say, adjusting my tie, and taking a few breaths.

"Can we talk?"

"Sure. What's up?" I ask, concerned. She's been acting a bit strange this week. Distant, not focussed. Her head almost as if it's in the clouds most of the time, which is not like her.

She closes the door, and sits down opposite me, crossing her legs, and pulling the skirt down a little bit further to cover her knees.

"Can you remember the other day when you asked me about trying to help you track down a friend on the internet?"

"Yes, Monday. I was looking for 'Friends Reunited?'" I reply, immediately interested in where she's going with this.

"What? *Friends Reunited*? That's a good name…Anyway, I've been doing a lot of thinking about that idea. It's a great idea. I've done a lot of research, and the fact is that there is nothing like it on the web yet. It's a great opportunity…"

"And…?"

"And, I've been discussing it with a group of my friends, a lot…I mean, we've been doing nothing else but talk about it for the past couple of days. One's a banker…he's got venture capitalist friends, and getting V.C. money isn't a problem for him…and another one is an internet guru. Does websites, hosting and storage…"

I think I know where this is going.

"…and…." She hesitates.

I know what's coming.

"…and, we've decided to set up our own company to do it. We're calling it 'Find-a-Friend', the idea I had on Monday…so, I'm…well…"

"Well what?" I'm smiling. She's nervous. But it's best if she says it.

"…I'm resigning."

Silence.

"It's not that I'm running away from us…it's got nothing to do with us…not that there is an 'us' anymore…, it's just that ideas like this don't come along very often, and when you come across something like this, you've got to act quickly. We've done some research, and it looks like there's nothing else similar in the pipeline, so…" she waffles on, almost a little embarrassed about the decision she is taking.

"Claire, it's a great idea. And you don't have to justify yourself or your decisions to me. It's brilliant."

And it is. Maybe I should ask her for a job.

"Claire, don't ask me how I know, but I know for a fact that your idea will work. In fact, I'm so sure that it will succeed, that I want to give you another suggestion. Don't just restrict it to old-school friends. Make sure that you arrange it so that there is a version where old work-colleagues can get in contact with each other too... and while you are it, why not make sure that people can build their own little profiles and put their pictures on there, ...and express their likes and dislikes and let others post their thoughts on their friends ...", I hesitate,...maybe I shouldn't say any more...

"That's a *brilliant* idea! Excellent, thanks." A pause. "You never know James, if it gets off the ground, maybe we'll need some advertising…?"

I push back from my desk, relaxing back into my chair.

"You know, somehow I don't think you will. A thing like this will work by itself, and it'll all spread by word of mouth. Radio shows will talk about it, and journalists will write about it a lot for free, so I honestly don't think you will need to advertise it much…In fact, "I say, reaching into my jacket pocket and pulling out my chequebook, "...I think your idea is so good, that I want to be the first person to invest in it. Here is a cheque for ten thousand euros of the first shares you issue, just to get you off the ground. I want you to put the shares equally in my wife's and my children's names...And if you come back with a proper business plan, maybe I'll give you some more…Anyway, that should keep you going for the first couple of days, until some serious money comes in from your VC friends."

Before she can say anything I have written it out and handed it over to her. She just looks at me, mouth wide-open, speechless.

"I don't know what to say...."

"Then don't say anything. Just make sure that the kids get some of the first shares issued, so that they can boast about it later: 'Hey, our daddy was the first person to invest in 'Find-a-Friend!' "

She stands up, smiling, still looking at the cheque in her hands.

"So when do you want to leave?" I ask her, changing the subject.

"In two weeks' time?"

"No, let's make it a week. That'll be long enough, and you need to get to work on this as soon as possible. You've got to be paranoid that if we've---you've---had this idea, that somebody else might have it too. First one to launch wins. Get to work on it as soon as possible. I'll get the HR department to find a replacement for you."

"Are you sure?" she asks.

"I'm sure. As long as you finish that report you promised me for the Dome team?"

As she leaves the office, she turns in the doorway. "James, although I'm excited about all of this, it does feel a little weird. I mean, we've worked together for years. We've been a good team. I'm going to miss you."

"I'll miss you too," but as she turns and goes, I can't help but feel happy for her. In a few years time she's going to be rich. Very rich indeed.

About ten minutes later, Richard pops his head around the door.

"James, how's it going?" He hovers nervously in the doorway, as if not sure whether now I'm a partner he can just walk in whenever he feels like it..

"Come in, take a pew." I offer.

"Thanks", he says, sitting down. "Listen, everything going okay? Coping okay? Need any help?"

"Any reason why I shouldn't be coping?" I ask. A little suspicious. Is this a friendly chat, concerned about my health, or just that so far I've got fifteen million euros worth of business under my belt. The two biggest deals the company has, and it's my business. Business that I can take with me if I walk.

And he doesn't even know about the Olympics opportunity.

Is it possible that he knows about my meeting with PHI at lunchtime?

"No, no reason. James, I like to run a friendly, informal ship here. We help each other out. We're there for each other. We're not like other firms..."

Sure we're not. So why did I want to leave then?

"Thanks, Richard. I appreciate your concern, but I'm fine. Honestly. There's lots going on, lots to do, and I'm just really busy,..."

"Oh, sorry, didn't mean to intrude," he says, jumping to his feet.

"No, I didn't mean that. You're welcome. I meant that perhaps it may seem I've been a bit distant as of late, but we've got a lot to do in a very short time."

"Exactly. So I'd better let you get on with it then. But if you need help, you just have to ask."

"Actually, there is something you can do for me. Claire has just resigned. I need another PA."

A few minutes later, Richard leaves the office, the task of replacing my PA now delegated to someone else. Result.

Lunch time comes, and I wrap up the meeting I'm in and head out.

Helen, the woman from PHI, had called me briefly at 11am and arranged to meet downstairs in the Stock Pot, a fantastic cheap'n'cheerful café in Compton Street. Cheap, but excellent home-cooked food. And discreet. No one from Cohen's would ever set foot in there.

When I arrive she is already there, sitting downstairs at the back of the café, in one of the many two-seater tables, which are squeezed in beside each other as close as possible.

She smiles when she sees me, and pushes her chair back a little, almost as if she is going to rise to greet me. I quickly wave to her to stay seated, and squeeze into the seat beside the wall opposite from her. She is very pretty today, her dark sultry looks and expensive clothes presenting the image of a very sophisticated successful businesswoman. A far cry from the other version of her that I know, handing out magazines outside a tube station.

"So," I start. "I gather you spoke to my wife, Jane, and she explained things to you. Do you believe me now?"

"Yes, I do. And maybe I owe you an apology too. It must be very hard for you at the moment. I don't know how I would cope if I lost my memory and was in your situation."

"You live and learn. You have no choice. Life goes on. Anyway, enough said. Just let's say that, I'm very, very sorry for letting you down. Please forgive me. I'm sorry."

"Okay, enough said. Apology accepted."

"So… where do we start?" I start off. "As my father always says, I think it is better if we start right at the beginning. Perhaps you could 'introduce' yourself to me as if we'd never met before…, tell me a little bit about yourself, and then how we got to be sitting here today, talking about PHI and Cohen's…" I see the look in her eye, and pre-empt the next question. "No, honestly. It's that basic. I can't remember you, or anything we have talked about before. Best start right at the beginning."

She pauses. Thinking.

"Okay. Fine... This is a bit weird, but I'll go with it...My name," she smiles, turning a little red, as if she is embarrassed. "…is Helen Engel. I'm a Partner at Peters Hall and Irvine, who, I am sure you know is the second largest advertising firm in London. The firm that taught you a lot of what you know today, and where you worked happily for many years…"

"Five." I interrupt her."…according to my 'executive profile', that was just drawn up by our P.R. company."

"Yes, five. Then you left and when to Cohen's. A strange move, but hey, we all do these things for money. Unfortunately, it's a move you've regretted since the day you walked out of our offices, and left your incredible creative team high and dry. They were all shocked by the way…" I squirm in my seat a little. The more I learn about my former self, the less I like myself. What sort of bastard was I?

"Anyway," she carries on, reading my body language and realising she should change tack."I was your best friend at PHI. We joined at the same time, both did well. You left, I got promoted two years later. Since then we've kept in touch. Through the good times, and a lot of the bad times. Stayed friends. Very good friends. Sometimes better friends than we should have been, but we won't go there just now. Fact is, that we were, and still are, close. Very close. About six months ago you started talking about wanting to come back to PHI. About cutting loose from Richard's mad organisation, and about how you couldn't take it any longer. About how the politics and the insanity, and Richard always stealing your ideas had driven you to the point of just walking out."

"Is it really that bad?" I ask, glossing over her previous comment about being more than just friends. Best left alone.

"Bad? Come on, you must know that Richard is infamous throughout the industry for being the biggest Dick in town? How you ever managed to stick it so long, is one of the talking points of the London advertising world." She suddenly becomes very serious and leans across the table to me. "James, you're good. *Damn* good. You could work for anyone in the industry, get any client you want. Shit, you could start your own agency if you really wanted to. But you don't believe in yourself, …and you're a coward. And Richard knows that too. He's screwing you, sucking the life out of you, bleeding you dry of every creative juice in your body, and making a fortune in the process. Do you know how much of Cohen's business comes from your books? About 60%! You told me yourself. 60%. That's more than three of the Partners at PHI combined."

"So, the last time we met, you said that you had stuck your neck out for me, and that you had approached your other partners and asked them to take me back, and to give me a job. If I'm that damn good, why didn't they just jump at the chance straight away?"

"Because of what you did when you left PHI. And *how* you left. The other Partners hate you. Okay, so they respect you, but when you left PHI you took two of our best customers to Richard at Cohen's, and spread some pretty nasty dirt to some of our other clients, in the hope they would ditch PHI and come after you too. PHI aren't stupid. What's to say that if they give you another job, that you won't just do the same thing again?"

"But if, as you say, I'm so good and I have so many good customers, about 60% of the Cohen's business, surely they would see that I don't need to steal customers anymore. I can get my own." I reason.

"True. And that's what I argued. But they're scared that you might take the business from Cohen's, then join us, take our best business and then set up yourself. And besides that, there's that whole business of the slandering you did last time you left. You caused some damage. Money's one thing. But PHI can't afford to be tarred with your dirty brush again. If they take you back, they will risk a lot. It will be a big step for them."

"So if I'm so good, and I hate Cohen's, and Richard, why don't I just set up my own agency now?"

"Good question. I've been asking you that for years. But the truth is that you are probably not quite ready for it yet. In another two years maybe. You just lack self-belief. And in this business, we both know that's half the equation. You need someone to really mentor you on the confidence building side of things. And that's where PHI could come in. So I went to bat for you with the Partners, argued like crazy on your behalf that things would be different this time around, that you wouldn't screw us again and that if we gave you the opportunity and the safe harbour from where you could really develop and grow yourself even more, you would be loyal to us."

The waitress interrupts us both, urging us to order something. We both scan the menu quickly and pick something to eat. I go for an omelette and chips.

"And, so what did they say?"

"It took a lot of arguing, and I mean a lot. But eventually they came around. PHI offered you a five year contract. So long as you promise in writing that there'll be no fucking-around. With legally binding penalties if you screw us and try to take any clients from us again. But with one caveat."

"Which is what?"

"That you first show us good faith, and make reparations for some of the damage you did previously, by bringing us a couple of big clients from Cohen's when you make the move."

"Like who?"

"Like Scotia Telecom, and the Dome Deal for a start. You suggested them. They were your idea. Your sacrificial lambs. You put them on the table, PHI saw that the offer was good, and we agreed to do the deal. You give us both those accounts, we forgive you, and you come back to PHI."

"Aha...." I begin to understand.

"Exactly. Everyone's happy. Fact is, the deal was almost done. When, *after all that,* out of the blue, you get back up to your old tricks, and you sign both of them with Cohen. "Double-crossing bastard" was the term Andrew used...our Chairman, when he found out. You made me look a fool too."

"But, I didn't know anything about any of this. I had amnesia. This is the first time I've heard about it. I didn't even know I was so unhappy at Cohen's."

"I know, I know. And I believe you now. But at least you can understand why I was so pissed off with you yesterday. I thought you screwed our friendship as well as my career."

"No. Bloody hell. This is a right mess. I'm so sorry."

Our food arrives, and for a few minutes we fight with cutlery, salt and pepper and a few mouthfuls of lunch. We both sit, chewing food, digesting what has been said so far. I catch her eyes, in between a mouthful of peas and potatoes. She is looking back at me, and I can see she is waiting for me to say something.

"One more time, how much do I hate it at Cohen's?" I ask.

" '*Hate*' was one of the words you used. Another one was 'detest'. Richard Cohen, in your own words, is out to suck you dry, ...to use your creativity but not reward you for it? Did you not see the press release on the Scotia deal. He practically took all the credit for it, didn't mention you anywhere."

"Yes, " I nod. " I noticed that."

"But I don't understand why, if Richard is such a bad guy and is out to suck me dry and not give me any credit, why has he just made me partner?"

"Think about it. He's been pushing you for years. But he knows that you are not stupid, and that if you won Scotia and then also the Dome deal, then he probably couldn't get away with it anymore. You'd be so high profile in the industry that you'd bound to be a target for others to headhunt you out of Cohen...so he does a pre-emptive strike, and really muddies the water by offering you a Partnership. But I would bet that the deal you've got on Partnership is nothing like what I've got, or what you could get at PHI, say, sometime in the future?"

"What about now? Would PHI make me a Partner now?"

She puts down her knives and fork.

"Steady on. One step at a time. If PHI offer you a life-line out of there, then you first have to prove yourself loyal and show yourself to be grateful. Then maybe we can perhaps talk about Partnership in say, six months or a year. Of course, when it happens...that's a different matter. PHI are a good company to work for, and the Partners there...well, we all do well. You made a mistake, a BIG mistake, when you left PHI in the first place. If you'd stayed, you'd be a Partner now too. Definitely."

I sip some water, and wash down the rest of my hurriedly eaten lunch.

"So what happens now?" I ask.

"You think about this over the weekend, and then you call me on Monday, telling me if you want me to talk to the Board again. I'll explain the extenuating circumstances, and I think they'll understand. Then you hand in your resignation to Richard next week, which you were planning to do a few weeks ago anyway, and then you start with PHI the week after."

"Wow. Big changes."

"James, it's what you wanted. You're just lucky I was around to remind you..."

CHAPTER 31
Friday Afternoon and Tosca

As I walk back to the office, I realise that this weekend I am going to have to make some pretty big decisions. Or do I just accept the decision that I had already made before my 'C' day, and just go with the flow. Leave Cohen's, and move back to PHI, which, by the sound of it, is a much better place to work anyway.

A group of tourists pass me by, jabbering away in Spanish, and gesticulating wildly at each other.

"Ah!" I suddenly remember. "I have to call Sarah's mother in Spain." In all the excitement of this morning I had completely forgotten about it. When I get back to the office, I dial International Directory Enquiries and give them her name and the address of the house in *Sierra Sien*, a little town high in the mountains about two hours drive south-east of Madrid. I remember the address off by heart, having visited it with Sarah quite often, before her mother died five years ago. If she isn't dead now, hopefully she will still be there.

"I am sorry, 'owever, there eez no one there living there by that name." The operator tells me in broken English, when she responds to my call.

"Can you try Martha Coltrane?" I ask again, trying her mother's maiden name, which luckily I remember.

"I am sorry. The name we have for ze person who is living at theeze 'ouse, is not that name. I cannot help you."

"Can you please just give me the telephone number of the house, and I can call them directly myself. The people who live there now might know where my friend moved to?" I plead with the operator.

"I am sorry. That eez against ze rules. I cannot help you, sir."

I thank her, and ring off. Rules. There are so many bloody rules designed to stop people finding friends, it's ridiculous. Was it this bad in my world?, I ask myself, knowing full well that the answer is that it was exactly the same.

Looking at my watch I realise that I have thirty minutes free before my next meeting. I pull out my diary and look up my page of notes where I have outlined the plan to search for Sarah.

1: Find father and visit him. Get contact address from him for where Sarah is now.

2: Visit graveyard where mother is buried. Try to see if I can get contact address from curator of graveyard.

3: Contact Rosedean Secondary Modern. Maybe they have some alumni scheme?

4: Likewise for Kings College.

5: Ditto for Teacher training college.

6: Check to see if Centric Telecom still exists. If it does, maybe they have a record of Sarah working there.

7:Try finding her best friend in Telford. Maybe she's still working at the same old school?

My options are running out. Only the last two continue to offer any hope. Of these, I decide to try and deal with the second last one now, and turn to my computer, entering Centric Telecom into the Google search page.

A few entries come up, but nothing to do with my old company.

I type in the address of where Centric Telecom used to be, and a few companies come up as being listed at that location. None of them a telecoms company, or anything vaguely sounding familiar.

I'm getting used to disappointment now. Should I bother jumping in a taxi and going round to the old building to see if I can get any other clues? Would anyone there now, possibly remember if there used to be a company called Centric Telecom operating from there in the past?

Why not just call the other companies listed in that building now? I look at my watch. Fifteen minutes. I've got time and nothing to lose.

Going through the list of companies that are listed, I call the advertised numbers, and talk to the receptionists. "Have you ever heard of a company called Centric Telecom? Was there ever a company that sounded like that in your building? How long have you worked there for? Can you ask one of your colleagues? Who owns the building now?" Etc. etc. etc.

Nothing.

Zero steps forward. No steps back.

The only thing left on my list is to drive up to Ironbridge and see if Sarah's old friend still works at the school there. This was the last idea on the list and a measure of last resort, hoping that I would only end up here if I had no other options.

The idea of going there again immediately fills me with dread, even after all these years. The last time I went up to visit her was under circumstances that no man should have to face or deal with. Bad memories, painful images, a nightmare that doesn't really go away.

Not even in this new world…

I sit through Richard's 'all-hands' meeting later that afternoon, wondering what on earth I'm going to do. I take a back seat, watching his face and mannerisms, squirming at the deceitfulness of the way he goes about things. I watch his eyes, his false smiles, and think about everything that Helen has told me.

If it wasn't for her, telling me about just how unhappy I was, I wonder just how long would it have been before I came to that conclusion again. Before I would have been desperate to get out. I owe Helen a lot. A gut reaction begins to form in my belly, and I think that I already know what I am going to do. Thinking about how he has been sneaking around me, paranoid that I am going to leave, and how once he had given me the Partnership, he backdated the pay rise. He knew he should have given me a better deal earlier on, but he didn't. He was trying to screw me. Just like Helen said.

I become angry. So much so, that when Richard…the *Big Dick*…a name I now know to be wisely chosen…asks me if I want to say anything in front of the gathered company employees, I have to turn him down just in case people can hear the anger when I speak.

After a single drink down the Crown, where everyone retires to immediately after the all-hands meeting, I sneak away so that I can meet Jane for our second attempt to see "Tosca".

Having completely ruined the evening the last time, I pick up a bouquet of flowers for her from the flower stand on the corner. I am even polite to the 'penguin' at the entrance to The Ivy, where we boldly put in an appearance, so soon after the 'incident' the week before.

I hate opera, have never liked it, in this life, my past life, or any life to come. But for Jane's sake, I pretend to love it. So I sit through almost two-and-a-half hours of someone singing something in a foreign language, and prancing around the stage in tights and flamboyant garish costumes, not understanding for one moment, anything that is going on. But holding Jane's hand and smiling at all the right moments.

Still, being forced to sit still for a couple of hours, it gives me a chance to think about moving to PHI, about Sarah, and everything that has happened to me. My mind moves quickly from one thought to the next, images rapidly forming in my mind, and taking on a life of their own. Slowly my eyelids get heavier, and the warmth of the theatre lulls me into dreamland: the place I go to talk with my children and be with my wife.

It's only when Jane prods me in the ribs at the end of the show, saying "*wake up*" that I realise, that once again, I may be in her bad books.

But as we catch a cab home to Surbiton, she cuddles in close beside me on the back seat, and thanks me for a wonderful evening. "Don't worry…I'll forgive you for falling asleep. At least you didn't snore."

On the pretext of going fishing with my father, the next day I find myself in the Audi, zapping up the M6 and M54 towards Telford, resolved to find Sarah's best friend Mary in spite of the painful memories of the last time I made this drive alone, trying to save my marriage and protect our family.

Stupidly, it's not until I get to Ironbridge that I realise that it's a Saturday, and that the school where I am hoping she will still be working, will be closed.

Feeling rather stupid, but still resolved, especially since I have summoned the courage to get this far, I drive to the school and park outside. Walking up to the gates, I find them open, and hear the sound of children's voices screaming and shouting from behind the school buildings.

Aha… Saturday morning Rugby and Hockey.

I wander round to the back, and find myself amongst a group of parents and teachers, spectating from the sidelines of a couple of rugby and hockey pitches. Feigning interest I join the nearest group and cheer when they do, showing disappointment at all the right moments.

When I soon realise that I have been cheering for the wrong side, the visiting team, I move round to another group of parents and try again. After a while I start chatting to another man, a proud father whose son just scored a try, and ask him if he is familiar with the school teachers…has he ever heard of Mary Wright?

"The Head Teacher? Of course I have. Damn fine teacher too. Done wonders for the school."

Excellent. She's still teaching here. But, although that is great news, at the thought of seeing Mary again, a tingle of foreboding travels down my spine and I shiver. Clenching my teeth, I swallow and keep looking for her, scanning the rest of the crowd just in case she's here.

After searching around the rest of the pitches, I eventually return to my car, and drive to the house where I last visited her.

It's not fair to hang all this on Mary. It's not her that I am scared of. It's just fear by association. Mary is a trigger point for the worst of my past, the same feelings that I strive to keep buried, but which threaten to bubble up and spill out, bringing it all back again.

Mary has been Sarah's best friend for as long as I have known her. They went to school together, stayed friends through college, and have always been there for each other, through thick and thin.

It was Mary that Sarah ran to when she left me, six years into our marriage, leaving me to look after Nicole and Keira, and forcing me to take leave of absence from work. A whole month of playing mum with two tiny toddlers, no sleep, worry, and fear. Fear that Sarah was not going to come home. Fear that our marriage was over. Fear that our family had died. And fear, above all, for Sarah's health.

On top of the everything else, the pain and the grief,...post natal depression.

Three words that completely understate the devastation this little understood condition can wreak upon families, and the women who are struck down by it.

Sarah was always a doting mother, but after the pregnancy ..., she became a shadow of her former self, crying all the time, unable to cope, withdrawn, and blaming me for all the confusion she felt. Even though the true cause of it all was no fault of either of us and she couldn't see I was confused and upset by it all too...

Until one day, while I am giving Keira a bath, she slips out the front door and disappears. Gone into the night, the note she left behind on the table saying only three things:

"*Sorry. I'll call you. Do not try to find me.*"

After three days of pure hell, Sarah eventually did call, and I found out she was with Mary, where she said she wanted to stay until we could resolve things. Resolve things? What had either of us done wrong? It was no one's fault, although God knows, how much I have blamed myself for it all. There is not a day that goes past where I still have to fight to keep a lid on my true feelings. To control the demon fear, and the sadness.

The doctors were great. They helped me to understand as much as possible about Sarah's condition,...not mine, they did *nothing* for me.. except to explain to me that it was not my fault, and that is was equally not Sarah's. And that with luck, and with understanding, and treatment, it would pass.

During the whole time my mum and dad were great, especially my mum, helping me, supporting me, encouraging me, and looking after the girls as much as they could.

It wasn't easy, but I learned how to support and try and understand what was happening to Sarah, and eventually after a month, she did come home. A few months later, she was fine, and things were back to normal. Well almost. We never talked of it again. We buried the whole thing, both scared to talk about it, even though the doctors told us we should. Both wanting to forget the cause, and to live for the future with Keira and Nicole. To be grateful for the wonderful children God had given us.

Sarah got better. But perhaps I never did.

Looking back on it, the experience brought me closer to Nicole and Keira, giving me an opportunity to spend time with them both that I would never otherwise have got.

But driving up to Mary's house now, the memories all come flashing back, and the irony of it strikes me. Once again I am coming to Mary's to find Sarah. The sense of *déjà vu* is overpowering.

The house is a little cottage, perched high on the side of the valley on the edge of the Ironbridge Gorge. The front windows look out straight onto the valley below, and the picturesque view of the first bridge in the world to be built of iron, which still spans the fast flowing river beneath it.

I have always been very jealous of Mary, living in such a fantastic spot. Rural. Idyllic. Stress-free. None of the London rat-race here, that's for sure.

I knock, stepping back from the door, as I hear footsteps.

The door opens, and Mary smiles at me.

"Hello, can I help you?"

It's actually her. I can hardly believe it. I feel an incredible urge to grab her and hug her to bits, and it takes all my willpower to resist it. It's hard to believe that she can't recognise me. She looks exactly like the last time I saw her, the same hairstyle, the same style of glasses, almost exactly the same clothes. Surely she must know me…

The little speech I had practised over and over in my mind, just in case she was here, immediately evaporates, and I'm left floundering like an idiot on her doorstep. It's hard not to be informal with her, after all I've known her for years…but instead I force myself to pretend that I don't know her.

Which I don't. In this world, she has never met me before.

"Hi. We haven't met. My name is James Quinn." I hand her my Cohen business card to make it look a bit more official, and to help reassure her that I am not a mad axe-wielding stranger, knocking on her door without any introduction. "I am trying to track down a long-lost friend from school. Sarah Turnstone? I think she might be a good friend of yours and I was hoping that you may be able to put me in contact with her?"

She opens the door a little wider, and immediately a big golden Labrador comes up to her side, his tongue hanging out of his mouth, panting and drooling, while his nose twitches wildly as he sniffs the air around me. Mary's dog Sam. The same dog she has always had as long as I have known her. Just then Sam barks excitedly and starts towards me, pushing past Mary in the doorway. Mary immediately reaches down and calmly yanks him back by the collar.

"Don't mind Sam. He's harmless." She says in passing as she looks at my business card, as if she's said the same thing a thousand times over the years to everyone who rings her doorbell. "Sarah? Yes, I know her…"

My heart skips a beat. Literally. It's like something has just jumped inside my chest, and the feeling it leaves forces me to cough. My pulse starts to race.

"You know Sarah?" I ask in disbelief.

"Yes. She's a good friend. Does she know you?" She looks up from the card, questioningly.

"I don't know, " I answer truthfully. Is there any chance that in this world she may know who I am? "... I doubt it…" I suddenly remember my practised lines. "I was a very spotty insignificant kid at school. I don't think any of the pretty girls noticed me then." I laugh as I speak. It has the desired effect. Mary laughs too.

"Well, you certainly turned out nice enough. They probably don't ignore you now," she blurts out quickly, her face turning a little red as she realises that the compliment was perhaps just a little too forward. An embarrassed silence follows.

"Can you tell me where she is living now,...if she's married, ...a little about her?" I ask.

Mary hesitates.

"She lives in London. Divorced now. She was married to a right bastard…" she stops in mid-sentence. "...And actually, maybe I shouldn't give you any more of her details until I have spoken to her?"

"Could you give me her home number? And I could call her? If she doesn't want to meet or talk to me anymore, she doesn't have to give me her address or anything else?" I suggest.

She thinks about it for a moment. Sam barks loudly again, straining to break free of Mary's grip, his large brown eyes fixed on me, his tongue hanging out, panting heavily.

"Sam, be quiet," Mary shouts, scowling at her dog momentarily before looking back at me. "I don't know…" she says to me now, shaking her head slightly.

I reach inside my jacket pocket, and pull out a letter I wrote in the office yesterday afternoon.

"No problem. I understand. Just in case you were a little uncomfortable in handing out her contact details to a relative stranger, I thought it might be wise if I wrote a letter of introduction. Here," I say, handing the white envelope to her. "You can read it if you want. I would really appreciate it if you gave it to her, along with my card. Then when she wants, she can either call me at work, or get me on my mobile. Both numbers are on the letter too…"

She looks at the letter, taking it gently from my outstretched hand.

Now free, Sam suddenly jumps forwards and up at me, his big paws scrambling against my chest, his large, sloppy tongue starting to lick my face.

"Sam! Sam!" Mary shouts quickly, stepping forward and grabbing hold of his collar, and pulling him down.

"I'm sorry about this. Don't worry, he's only being friendly. For some reason he's really excited to see you. He's normally really shy, but he obviously likes you... it's almost as if he knows you. He must have mistaken you for someone else."

"Maybe not," I say. "But they say, dogs are good judges of character. If Sam likes me, then there's no reason for Sarah to be worried either."

"True, maybe... Listen, if you leave this with me, I'll give her a call, and send her this when she gets back from holiday. She's away for another couple of weeks."

"Somewhere nice?" I ask.

"Cuba. One of those adventure singles holidays. Not that she's looking for anybody or anything. Just that it's nice to have company."

"I understand, don't worry. Mary, if you could talk to her when she gets back that would be great."

"Okay. By the way, how did you know that I know Sarah? And how do you know my name?" she asks, pulling hard on Sam's collar - he is fighting desperately to jump up and greet me again.

"Another of Sarah's friends," I lie. Time to leave: best quit whilst I'm ahead. "Okay, thank you Mary. I'd better be going now. I've got to get back to London."

"You drove all the way up from London?" she asks, almost surprised.

"Yes."

"Wow. You must want to get in contact with her pretty badly," she pauses. "Why?"

"Because sometimes we lose contact with people and regret it, and then spend the rest of our lives, wondering what it would have been like to have known them better. I woke up one day, and realised that it was silly, always wondering...why not do something about it?"

Mary smiles back. I turn to go.

"Is that your car?" she asks.

"Yes."

"Fantastic. I haven't seen anything like it before," she says, coming down the path behind me, Sam by her side.

"Believe me when I say that until a few weeks ago, neither had I." I open the door, and turn towards her, just before I bend down and climb in.

"Thanks Mary. I appreciate it. Say 'Hi.' to her from me, and let her know that I hope she will call me."

I wave, close the door and drive off.

I've never been more nervous in my life.

Please God, please get Sarah to call me.

CHAPTER 32
Dad and Mum

On Saturday evening I am still in Jane's good books. I am even beginning to become comfortable with living in the big house, which I have now dubbed Castle Quinn. On Saturday night, I ventured up into the massive attic space above the house, and looked around at some of the rubbish stored up there.

When I came across some of my old school books, I sat down to read some of the school work and essays I did in English class in primary school, so many years before. I was eight years old. Young, annoyingly smart, and ambitious: I wanted to be the best train driver in the world, and to drive the fastest and biggest train between Scotland and England. It said so, right there in my tiny, eight-year old almost joined up hand-writing. I closed my eyes and tried to remember what my old school looked like, and laughed aloud when I recalled the day when a group of us playfully tied up the trainee teacher and locked her in the cupboard for an hour.

We got in a lot of trouble, one hundred lines of "I must respect Miss Stewart and refrain from tying her up and leaving her in the school cupboard." My parents were called down to the school, and I can't help but smile again when I remember how my father laughed when the headmaster told him what we had done.

As I sit in the quiet attic space above my house, holding work which I actually wrote with my own hand so many years before, I think back to the incident on the Jubilee Line when the sign on the wall changed from "Charing Cross" to "Westminster" and back. I think about the history of the Jubilee Line I read about at the transport museum, and about the paperweight from my grandmother that sits on my desk at work.

Strands of continuity.

I realise then, perhaps for the first time, that in this world, the life I am living now continues seamlessly right back to the day of my birth without a break. This world and my world, my real world, share a common past.

Except there must be a single point of time when the two worlds diverged. Where one world took a future that headed in one direction, and the other diverged on a completely different path. In my world, someone decided to build the Jubilee Line through Westminster to Canary Wharf, and in this world, the decision went the other way, and the line was built through Charing Cross down to East Dulwich.

When did my worlds diverge? What day? What minute? What second? And why?

Perhaps I will never know.

But for whatever reason, I somehow stepped from one world to the other. Both with the same past, but each with a very different future.

I think of Sarah, and the letter I wrote her.

Will she contact me? When she reads the letter will she be curious enough to wonder who the spotty little boy at school was that wants to meet her? Of course, I was never in her class, or her school, and she has never ever met me before, but if she reads the letter and is curious, hopefully she will call me to find out. Just one phone call, and I will take it from there.

But what happens if she doesn't take the bait?

I mull this question over in my mind, over and over again. I worry about it that Saturday evening, as I lie awake in bed with Jane by my side, and all the next day when we go over to my parents for Sunday lunch.

After the roast chicken and trifle, Dad and I disappear to the shed at the bottom of his garden. Whenever he closes that shed door behind him, he enters his own little world. A real '*Shedder*'. My mum would never dream of disturbing him here. This is where he comes to escape, to potter around, sometimes doing absolutely nothing, but at other times, making flies for fishing, or making something out of wood for his grandchildren. Or simply to sit and read, and drink a quiet beer.

The shed is more like a mini-house. Wired for sound, TV and with its own fridge, a long-spacious wooden bench, and a rack of tools and DIY gear that even B&Q would be jealous of.

"So," Dad says, as he tosses me a beer from the fridge, and we both sit down in two old armchairs with broken springs, the smell of wood and sawdust heavy in the air. "Did you find anything out yesterday?"

"Yes. I met her best friend, and gave her a letter of introduction to pass on. She's away on holiday at the moment, but she'll be back in a few weeks." I tell him, and then go on to update him on the rest of the search for Sarah.

"Dad…what do think I should do if she doesn't call me when she gets the letter?"

"Were you happy with what you said in the letter?" he asks.

"Yes," I reply. "I read it about a thousand times before I finally decided that there was nothing more I could add. It's the best I could make it."

"Then, if she reads it and decides not to call you, perhaps you should just leave it. By then you will have done your best. And there's nothing more you can do than that."

I start to protest, but my Dad cuts me short.

"Listen son, " he says, blowing on the top of the can, and pulling back the ring-pull. "My dad always used to say to me, that if something is meant for you, then it won't pass you by. I've always believed in those words. Always. You've done your best to contact her, to let her know you want to meet her…if she decides not to contact you back, then let it be."

"...But if I get to speak to her, I would be able to explain things better…"

"That's as maybe, but I wouldn't chase that through your friend. If she doesn't reply to you, and you are meant to meet, then it will happen another way. Believe me. If it's meant to be, it will."

"But, I've tried everything else I know to get to meet her. Mary knows her. She can introduce us…"

"And she might. Don't be so negative. She hasn't even got the letter yet and you're going crazy worrying about *'what if?'*. Give it some time."

"Okay…" I take a swig out of the can, and settle back in the chair.

"Listen Son, if there was anything that I could do to bring you together with the woman who could make you as happy in your life as I have been in mine, then I would. I would do anything for you son, even if it was the last thing I did. You know that don't you? You're a good lad, and you deserve to be happy." He says, leaning forward and patting me on one of my knees. "But for now, just let it be."

It's Sunday evening, and Jane listens patiently as I explain to her the whole deal about moving to PHI. She doesn't interrupt, and doesn't ask any questions. At the end, she doesn't say anything except, "You don't need my opinion. I think you have already made up your mind about what you are going to do."

"Maybe…maybe not. I just want to know what you think?"

"Does it matter?" she asks, quite openly.

"Of course it does."

"Why does it suddenly matter what I believe?" she asks.

"What do you mean?"

"I mean, you never listen to my opinions. I tell you what I think, you ignore what I say, and always do just as you want. What difference will it make this time?"

"I'm different now. *Things* are different. What you think does matter."

"Are you sure?"

"Yes."

"What things are different. Name them."

"What do you mean?"

"Like I said, I want you to name what's different?"

"My perspective on things, for a start. The importance I place on things. The way I want to lead my life. The way I want you to lead your life. Lots of things are different."

"Why?"

"Jane, what's this about?"

"Who is Sarah?"

"What?"

"You dreamt about her again last night. You called out to her again. Who is she?"

"Like I said the other day, I don't know. Some woman in my dreams. I don't know who she is."

"Are you having an affair with her?"

Suddenly this conversation is going completely the wrong direction. I can feel Jane's mood changing. It's getting ugly.

"No. How can I be having an affair with someone I've never met?"

A good question.

If only she knew I was married to her. Married to someone I have never met before.

"Jane, I can't remember anything about the dream and I don't know why I was dreaming about anyone called Sarah. Don't you ever dream about people you just make up?"

"Yes, sometimes…"

"So, there. She's just a figment of my imagination. I can promise you, that never in this life have I ever met or had an affair with a Sarah. Honestly."

Which is true.

"Okay. Fine. But next time you dream about her, you ask her what she's doing in your dreams, okay?"

"Agreed. So back to the conversation. What should I do?"

"Like I said, you've already made up your mind. You know what you're going to do. So do it."

I make the call from my mobile at 10.30 am, whilst walking from the office down to Charing Cross, on the way to Scotia Telecom. A short, but important conversation.

"Helen? Hi, it's James."

"And?"

"Draw up the papers. Get them over to me on Friday morning. I'll read them over the weekend and sign them on Monday."

"Excellent. You won't regret it."

"Neither will PHI. Thanks for your help."

"No problem. See you Friday morning, downstairs in the Stockpot at eleven? I'll hand them to you personally."

"Okay. See you there."

There are three tube trains showing on the overhead sign, no delays. All on time. A sure reminder that this world is very different from my own.

I feel nervous. This morning I decided that from now on whenever I go up to the Scotia Telecom or the Dome offices, I'm going to take the Jubilee Line up to Marble Arch, and walk from there. The connection from my old world to this one has got something to do with the Jubilee Line. I know it would be insanity to spend hours every day zipping around on the underground, just staring at the station signs and hoping that they will change again, from Charing Cross to Westminster, or East Dulwich to Canary Wharf, or something else, especially since it may never ever happen again. But there is always that 'if', that slight possibility that it 'might'.

Like Robinson Crusoe, I have to get on with my life…but just in case it might happen again, I've decided to make any excuse I can to travel on the Jubilee Line, whenever I can, to anywhere that's remotely near to anywhere I really need to go to in the normal course of everyday life. Just in case.

So, with at least three meetings a week with Scotia and two at the Dome offices, that's at least six separate trips on the underground. Maybe even ten.

The feeling I have while standing on the platform, waiting for the next tube is just like the feeling you get when you play roulette and you're waiting for the spinning ball to slow down and stop. Will it land in my number? Will this be the time?

And then when the train arrives, another thought…should I get this tube or wait for the next one? Will this train be the one that does the jump from this world to the next? Or will the next train be the one?

Realising that if I'm not careful this whole thing could spiral out of control and become a stupid obsession, a weird compulsive behavioural disorder, I step onto the first train to arrive. If it's ever going to happen again, this train has as much possibility as any other one for making the jump. The jump. That's what I'll call it from now on.

'The Jump.'

From one world to another.

I try to stick close by the entrance door as the other passengers pour on, but am pressed backward by the sheer number of people eager to get on. I end up on the other side of the carriage, squashed against the opposite set of doors, a wall of people between myself and the doors I just came through.

My heart is going crazy. Beating faster and faster with anticipation.

I find the sign on the wall outside the tube carriage. Blast, someone has moved just in front of me. I can't see it clearly anymore.

I duck down a little, my face almost level with the shoulders of the person in front. My head is at an angle, and the people around stare at me, wondering what I am doing.

The doors begin to close.

I look over at them, and blink. I turn again to stare at the sign "Charing Cross" on the wall. I blink again. I cannot find it. It is gone...

My eyes scan quickly back to the doors. They are still closing. Beyond them the station is shimmering. Fading in and out.

It's happening.

Shit…It's *really* happening.

Quick, I must jump off, I must force my way to the doors. Make the jump back to my own world.

I push against the passenger in front of me, desperate to get by.

"Excuse me, let me off!" I shout.

My shoulders meet with a rock solid object, the person now as hard as stone, a solid, immovable barrier that refuses to give way. I blink again, everything happening so slowly… so *slowly*. As if time itself is slowing down around me.

I push hard again, this time on another woman to my side.

She is smaller than me, thin, half my body weight, but she is glued to the floor. Stationary.

I look at her face. There is no emotion. No signs of life. Her blank eyes stare past me into space. Her skin like wax, the dull light in her eyes, her mouth half open, frozen in the act of breathing, her body one solid, immovable statue.

I am trapped. Hemmed in by people like metal bars in a prison.

My reactions are slow, but I can move. Unlike the human mannequins and statues around me.

I stare out onto the platform outside.

For an instant, just an instant, the shimmering stops, and the platform solidifies. I see people walking past, real people, not mannequins, people oblivious to the scene aboard my train, and the situation all around me.

On the wall, directly outside the doors, I see a sign.

"*Westminster.*"

I push again against the wall of people surrounding me. I have to get out of the train.

I have to make the jump.

But already it is too late.

The doors are beginning to close, the view of Westminster station is beginning to shimmer, to fade away, to be replaced by something else.

And then it is gone.

The doors close.

Instantly, the lifeless statues around me return to life, their rigidity being replaced by soft supple bodies. Still pushing on the person in front of me, I immediately fall forward. The woman shouts something, and in turn falls against the person standing beside her. I stumble, then topple forwards again, but a hand reaches out and grabs me, pulling me back up. I stagger a little, but recover my posture, apologising to those around me and thanking the man beside me who owned the helping hand.

The tube accelerates away.

Another chance gone.

But proof once more, that for some reason, my world and this are still connected.

And that there *is* hope.

Like Robinson Crusoe on his desert island, I have to make plans.

I spend the next thirty minutes travelling back and forwards through Charing Cross, hoping that it will happen again, but to no avail. I am twenty minutes late for my meeting, apologising that I was stuck on the tube between stations for a while, an excuse which everyone accepts easily.

I find it hard to concentrate for the rest of the afternoon.

My thoughts are dominated by what just happened on the tube. I think about it constantly, replaying it over and over again in my mind. That is the second time it has happened. Although this time it lasted for longer, seeming to stretch itself out and last for seconds. An age.

In my mind's eye I remember being able to look out onto the platform outside and notice people walking around, back and forth past the entrance to the tube doors. I remember the feeling of pushing against the people about me, struggling to get past them, wanting desperately to leave the train and step out onto Westminster beyond, but being prevented by solid, immovable, seemingly lifeless-bodies. Why was it that I could move but they couldn't?

When I catch the Jubilee Line back down to Charing Cross later that evening, nothing unusual happens. Again, like before, I ride the train back up to Green Park, and then again down to Charing Cross, but without incident. Whatever it is that happens down there on the Jubilee Line seems to be entirely random.

Except there is one thing I have noticed. On both occasions, afterwards I am left feeling tired, exhausted. Even a little sick. Whether from the excitement and the adrenaline rush, or something else, I cannot tell.

I grab a pizza on the way back to the office, and pick up a fresh cup of coffee at the local deli. By the time I lock myself in my room, and sit down in my large, welcoming, chair, it's 6.30 pm. I'm meeting Stu Roberts at 8 pm.

The pizza is a little cold, but I am hungry. The warm coffee helps to wash it down, and soon it is all gone. The box empty, and in the bin.

It's ten past eight when I finally get to Waxy's.

So what does Stu look like nowadays? It's been years since I last saw him. As I walk into the busy bar I examine all of the faces around me, hoping to spot one that is familiar. Hoping that over the years he hasn't changed, become bald, and fat. Unrecognisable.

"Hey, James!" A hand on the elbow, a voice from behind.

He's just come in the door behind me and still looks almost exactly the same as when I last saw him. Slim, energetic, good looking…all his own hair. Has no one told him that he's meant to age? To get old!?

"You look great!" I stammer. "What on earth are you taking?" I ask.

"About three hours of exercise every day, nutrients, fruit juices, and lots and lots of sex," he jokes, steering my elbow towards the bar. "And lots of beer. What are you drinking?"

We talk about old times, about our fun days in the college bar, but very soon the conversation gets round to my concussion.

"You've forgotten everything? Permanently?"

I reply, rattling off the same speech I've given a thousand times to others.

Then I ask him about the Olympics, the 400m and his Gold Medal, and then eventually we get round to the reason we're here.

"Fourteen million euros? It's a big deal. How come you're not putting it out to tender?" I ask.

"Politics. And a few other reasons. Which we won't go into. The fact is that you and I have talked a lot about this already, and from what we've gone over together, you've already convinced me that Cohen's is the agency to do the job for us. I know all about your track record. What you've done. We don't need to go into it all again. Apart from one concern, the business is yours. Take it or leave it?"

"Of course, I'll take it. But what's your concern?"

"This is a high profile deal. What with your concussion and lack of memory and everything, please forgive me for asking, but I have to,…I would be wrong not to worry about this…but, are you up to the job now? I mean, you will be leading the team, heading up the project? Are you well enough?

Have the doctors said anything about your condition that might cause a problem later on? And, honestly, has the concussion affected your ability to create the best advertising and marketing campaigns on the planet?" He reaches out, his hand on the side of my arm, concern showing in his eyes. Concern for my health, for me, but also concern for the project and the work he has the responsibility of handing out.

"Stu, I'm fine. If anything, I'm even more creative than before. I've got a whole new vitality to my work. It's a fresh approach, and its going down well. Did I tell you that I've been promoted to Partner…*since* I had the concussion? And that I've won two major deals…the contract for promoting the Millennium Dome, and one for a very large Telecommunications company, that is going to launch the first, truly safe, mobile phone network in Europe and the Middle East?"

"Yes, I know. I did some background work. Listen all you have to do is tell me you're up to it, and I'll believe you. But don't bullshit me. Me worrying about your ability to deliver is as much for you as it is for me. If you fail on this, it'll be so high profile, it'll hit you hard. But if you do well, the whole world will see your work. I mean, it's the Olympics… You can't get better than that!"

When I leave the bar, probably a few worse for wear, the deal is done. A contract, signed, and witnessed by the barman and manager of Waxy O'Connors. Unconventional, but then again, Stu was never conventional. Ever.

I decide to walk back down to Waterloo, crossing the bridge over the Thames, and stopping to admire the view. The best view in the world.

I steady myself against the rail and look out towards Big Ben and the Houses of Parliament, England's most historic buildings glowing orange in the floodlights, and casting long, jumping shadows on the turbulent water below.

A boat passes by underneath the bridge and I look down onto the deck, the sounds of a discotheque, and flashing lights pouring out of the windows. A couple are standing at the back, arms around each other, leaning against the rail.

They look up at me and wave.

And I wave back.

CHAPTER 33
Friday
Rcsigning

On Tuesday, Wednesday and Thursday I spend a lot of time working on the Dome and Scotia Telecom deals. Personal attention, ensuring that the clients know that they are my top priority. Cultivating the bond. Making sure they are well and truly cemented to me. And not to Cohen Advertising. Preparing for the move from Cohen's to PHI.

In total, this gives me the opportunity to make ten separate journeys on the Jubilee Line, but nothing unusual happens. There are no repeats of the incident on Monday.

On Wednesday morning I interview three candidates from an agency, and select one of them to replace Claire. A twenty-five year old woman called Tracy with an impressive CV. She accepts the job and agrees to start the next Monday.

On Thursday afternoon I meet with Stu and some of his colleagues at the Department of Sport in Whitehall. A low-key meeting, behind closed doors. Again, preparing the way. Before I finally signed the contract over a beer in the pub last Monday night, I had told Stu of the potential move to another agency, and he was comfortable with both the move and the reputation of PHI. So long as it meant I was still the lead man on the project, and that I could guarantee my personal attention and involvement. Which will obviously be one of the conditions I will have to make sure is in the contract with PHI before I sign it.

So far, I have not mentioned anything to Richard or Claire. As far as I know, no one else at Cohen's knows anything about the Olympics.

There have been moments during the week when I have worried about the morality behind what I am about to do. When I leave Cohen a lot of people could lose their jobs. With the sudden loss of such important business to a competitor, Cohen Advertising may be ruined. My actions could kill the company.

The thought plagues me, but then I remember Helen's words, and how unhappy I have been at Cohen's. After all, if it had not been for the concussion I would already have made the move. I have to trust the judgement I had already made. So far, I have been impressed by everything I have found out about my previous decisions. I cannot fault any of my previous business activities, so why should I question this one?

Several times during the week, I have to avoid conversations with Richard. I no longer trust the man, in fact I now find the way he sneaks passively around the office very annoying. Always smiling. Always joking with the staff. Always screwing them behind their backs.

In turn, I hear the staff joking about him behind his back, *'Big Dick did this'*, *'Big Dick did that'*, *'Did you hear what Big Dick said to what's-his-face the other day?'*. Why does no one else stand up to him? A stupid question. He would probably fire them.

The past couple of days have also given me the opportunity to properly review the rest of the work that is ongoing and on my books. I have a lot more business than I realised. Business which I have been neglecting as of late. Business which has been demanding attention, but which I have not given the proper focus.

Immediately I set about changing that, and work late, very late, three nights in a row.

This causes a row with Jane on the Friday morning, and by the time I leave home, I am already stressed. Stress which I could do without.

I meet with Richard in the morning, very briefly, to discuss some trivial detail on a prospective new client of his, and to approve some expenses on behalf of the company. Then I make my excuses and leave. Helen calls and asks me if I can meet her earlier in the Stock Pot: the contract is all ready for me to pick up.

We meet at 11 am. A quick coffee. A quick explanation of the offer, and the details of the move. And a quick reassurance that this is the best decision I will have made in years. I nod, almost in quiet acceptance, but I request that once I've read the contract, and we've agreed the terms, that I get to meet the other partners at PHI before I finally sign it. She agrees to arrange it, sensing that I am very close to signing. "Just give me a call when you're ready…"

As I walk back to the office, I am a little scared. So much has happened to me in the past month, so many changes, is there a possibility that this change is the one that will finally break the camel's back. My back. Will I be able to cope with the stress that this might cause?

In spite of this thought, I realise that that I am enjoying it. It's exciting. Far more exciting than being a Product Manager at Kitte-Kat ever was.

But, at the same time, underneath all the emotion, there is another feeling: the feeling that I am being a Judas.

I bury it quickly, and decide that the best way to do this is to get it over and done with immediately. I've spent the past week thinking about it, and I know I've already made up my mind to make the move. All I need to do is to read the contract, to make sure it's okay, and then to meet with the Partners at PHI in person, just to dot the 'i's and cross the 't's, before I hand it over to them.

So I duck into a Starbucks, grab a coffee and find a seat downstairs and in a corner.

I read the contract from start-to-finish four times. It takes two more coffees and some sandwiches before I am happy that I understand it, and that I am almost comfortable with it.

The only thing that worries me is that once I move to PHI, I am stuck with them for at least five years. There is no way out. Helen was quick to point out the small print that specified how the integration of my current clients onto PHI's books would be handled. Effectively, my clients will become theirs. And I have to sign a separate contract agreeing in advance to paying damage and impossible penalties to PHI, should I attempt to steal clients from PHI in the future. Although from what Helen has told me about what I did in the past, I understand their concerns and I am happy to sign the deal. After all, in a way, PHI are doing me a favour in getting me out of Cohen's.

When I walk back into the office, I am ready to face Richard.

"Richard, can we talk for a moment?" I ask, knocking on his door, and then walking in without waiting for a reply.

He looks up from his PC.

"Sure. What's up?"

I sit down opposite him, nervous, a little shaky, but resolved to do what needs to be done.

"Richard. There's no easy way to say this, so I'm just going to get on with it. I've been doing a lot of thinking about my future. About what I want, where I want to go, and what I think is best for me."

The smile starts to disappear from his face, and the corner of his eye begins to twitch, a nervous twitch similar to what sometimes happens when a person is very tired. The colour begins to drain from his rosy cheeks, and he becomes very serious.

"The thing is Richard. I have decided that it would be best if I were to leave Cohen's and start a new career elsewhere."

There. It is done.

He stares at me for a moment, his mouth half open. The twinkle disappears from his eye, and they glaze over.

I have never really looked at him before, properly, but now I do I see a very different person. Almost bald, a tired, wrinkled face. At one time in his life he probably smoked heavily, the tell-tale signs of a smoker rippling outwards from the corners of his mouth, the deep, narrow lines which all smokers eventually get from sucking on the nicotine sticks. There is a cut just above one eye, either from a fight or more-likely an accident when he was a child. I cannot tell. Suddenly I do not see a powerful executive in the advertising world, but an old, tired, man.

He speaks quietly at first. Almost as if in disbelief.

"Why do you want to leave? Why on earth would you want to leave Cohen's? Where will you go to?"

"I can't tell you that just now, but let's just say that I am a little unhappy here."

"Unhappy? Why? Everyone loves it here. We're the best agency in the country!"

"That may be, but…" I start to protest.

He leans forward across the desk, the palms of his hands flat on the oak surface.

"James, has this got something to do with your concussion? Do you want some time off? A vacation?…"

"No, Richard, I don't need a vacation. I…"

"It's PHI, isn't it. They're after you. I knew it! The bastards." He pushes hard down on the desk, and stands up quickly, grabbing the back of the chair with one hand and whipping it backwards away from him. He starts to stride back and forward on the other side of the desk, wringing his two hands together, staring at me as he walks. "What have they said to you? What have they promised you? Are you mad? Why would you want to go and work for them again? They're the biggest sharks in the business. That's why you left them in the first place. They steal your talent, suck you dry, and then spit out the remains, but only after they have taken every little bit of profit they can from any of the work you have done. You hated it there before… Why go back? I don't understand…"

That's funny. Coming from him.

"Listen, Richard, it's nothing personal. It's just that this is the right thing for me to do, at this moment in time."

"What? That's great. '*It's the right thing for you to do.*' You're a bloody partner here now James. You have responsibilities! You can't just walk away from them."

"I can and you know it. And you only made me a Partner because you were trying to trap me and stop me from leaving."

"That's rubbish! Rubbish and you know that too. I made you a Partner because you deserved it. And I didn't *MAKE* you a Partner. I offered it to you, and you accepted. You voluntarily agreed to take on a Partnership role in this company, and all the responsibility that went with it. You can't leave!"

"I can, and I will. Listen Richard, there is nothing you can do to stop me leaving now. I've made up my mind, and I'm going. So let's just try to make this as smooth as possible for all of us…"

He stops in mid-step, turns and faces me straight on. He stares at me. I can see the thoughts flooding through his mind, and the sudden change in emotion that seems to engulf him from nowhere.

He grabs the chair and pulls it back in front of the table. He sits down, and sighs.

"James, please don't do this. If you leave, most of the business at Cohen's will follow you. That's more than half of everything on our books."

"60%" I interrupt.

"Exactly! 60%. If you leave, ...Cohen's is finished. We won't survive this. We'll go under."

"You're overestimating this a little Richard. That won't happen." I protest.

"No. The fact is you haven't thought this through James. If you leave, within a couple of months, almost everyone here in this building will be out on the streets. For goodness sake, they have wives and children, families that depend upon them. Do you honestly want to be responsible for ruining all their lives?"

"Come on, enough of the dramatics Richard, this is life. It's the business we work in. It's advertising."

"I can't believe I'm hearing you say that. That's exactly why you wanted to work here. Because we are *not* just an advertising agency. We are one big happy family. At Cohen's we care about each other. You sometimes more than others. Don't think I don't know about you and Alice, and Claire. Anyway, that's beside the point, the point is that we are different, very different from everyone else. "

He is silent. I have nothing to say. I expected an outburst, and I got one. I'm just a little bit taken aback by the sight of him almost pleading for me to stay.

Getting up to go, I feel a hand on my arm, and I turn to face him.

"James. Please, please think about this again. "

His voice quivers as he speaks, and he coughs. His face has turned red, and as I look at him, I watch in amazement as his eyes begin to well with tears. A sudden turn of events that I find very difficult to deal with. A grown man, about to cry.

"James, my brother Marty and I started this company forty years ago. We built it from nothing. We have always tried to help people, always tried to encourage people. It's never been just about the money. It's been about the thrill of the ride, the experience, the privilege that everyone here shares to be able to work here in the advertising world and play the game. The advertising game. When you came to me you sat in front of me in this very office, and told me how much you wanted to work for us. There were a thousand CVs already on my desk from about almost every other ad man in the country. I didn't need anyone else. Marty was still alive, and we were doing fine. But I saw something in you that I liked. I took you in. I personally took an interest in you, and helped you grow. I cleaned out the garbage you had learned at PHI and made you into a real ad man. A good ad man. One of the best, if not *the* best ad man in the business. I'm not saying you owe me for anything, no, everything I did, was because I liked you. The only thing I ever asked from you in return was that you try to be the best, that you try to achieve your potential. You had great potential back then James. Great potential. A potential that you have almost realised now. Sure, in the past year you've won some of the best deals going, but there's still more out there. More that I can teach you. You could be great James. Great. But if you go to PHI, it'll all be over. And everything that Marty and I, and you, and all those people out there in this building have strived for, for almost half a century…it'll all be gone. Gone within six months."

"...James, if you leave, you'll kill us. Please don't. I'm asking you to reconsider…please. And if you still feel the same way on Monday morning, I won't stand in your way. But think, man, think! Do you really, *really*, want to do this?"

I grab his hand and shake it free from my arm. Without saying another word, I turn and leave, closing the door behind me.

I walk down to Covent Garden, and sit in the square for a while, watching the buskers and the street theatre. My mind is full of the confrontation with Richard, and I find it hard to shake off the sight of him crying. That is something that I did not expect.

When I return to the office, Alice grabs me at the door, and pulls me into the room behind her reception area.

"What on earth is going on? Richard has cancelled all his meetings for the rest of the afternoon and he has told me to make sure that your network privileges are revoked, so that you can't log onto the system anymore. What's happened?"

"Let's just say for the moment that Richard and I have fallen out."

"He told me there's going to be some sort of special announcement at the meeting this afternoon, and he asked me to get in a dozen bottles of champagne. Why?"

Interesting. Is he going to celebrate the fact that I've resigned, or toast the end of the company? It doesn't make sense.

The rest of the afternoon passes behind closed and locked doors. No one is talking to each other, and a sense of expectation, almost excitement, hangs in the air. The word gets around the office that Richard is going to say something important at the all-hands meeting in the afternoon.

Without network access there is little I can do, so I start to tidy my desk, and get some of my things in order. I'd already copied and downloaded most of the important documents that I will need when I leave, fully expecting my privileges to be terminated as soon as I resigned. I'm only surprised that Richard didn't have me marched off the premises straight away.

Five o'clock comes and the company gathers together on the floor above, in the large open area outside Richard's office. The usual buzz is more punctuated than usual, and everyone can see the bottles of champagne lined up along the wall on one of the tables, with glasses, peanuts, cakes and some nibbles.

I'm a little confused. What does he have to celebrate?

At five o'clock on the dot, the door to Richard's office opens and he steps outside. Everyone goes quiet. Richard stands on one of the chairs and speaks.

"Thanks for coming everyone. It's good to have you all here again for the All-Hands. It's been a busy week. A few more major deals are in the offing, and some pretty good work has been done by all of us..."

For the next fifteen minutes he goes through the latest and greatest, handing over where appropriate to different team members of the various projects, giving as many people as possible the opportunity to speak, to voice their achievements or their questions. It turns out one of the other young managers has just won a deal with one of the high street stores. A deal that could bring in five hundred thousand euros. It was unexpected, something that the manager had kept up his sleeve until the last moment. A good achievement.

One of the young graphic designers also just announced she was pregnant. Everyone knew she had been trying for quite a while...it was no big secret...but everyone was surprised and genuinely pleased for her when she announced she was expecting a boy next summer. A round of applause and congratulations. Almost touching.

"Which brings me to the last announcement of the day. James..." Richard looks over at me, and my heart freezes. He's going to announce it already... "James...came to me earlier in the week and gave me some very bad news. It seems that Claire is going to leave us and set up her own dot.com company. And unfortunately today is her last day. Claire, can you come up front please?"

Shit. It's Claire's last day. That's what this is all about. And I've forgotten all about it. I can't believe it. I've been so selfish, thinking about me the whole day, that I've clean forgotten to get her a card, or say anything to her. Blast.

Claire is bright red. She looks briefly over at me, and I smile back at her, inviting her to come up to the front where I am already standing close to Richard. A Partner, after all.

"Claire first joined us in 2006 when she came over from Peters Hall and Irvine with James. They've always made a good team, and when James left PHI to come to us, she jumped at the chance to come with him. She quickly settled in, and ever since she has been James's right hand man...sorry, even better than that, she's been his right hand woman. I know that James will want to say something in a moment, but before he does, I just wanted to say a few words. Everyone here knows that Cohen's is not a normal run-of-the-mill advertising company. Here we strive to be a closely knit unit, a group of friends all striving together towards a common goal, and sometimes, even though you may think it's a bit pretentious, I even like to think that we are all a big family. Although getting the deal, and doing a great job are really important,…that goes without saying…what's different about Cohen's is that I firmly believe that we must have fun in the process. Everyone here enjoys working at Cohen's, I think…in fact, honestly, let me ask you all, is there a single person here who is not happy with being here?"

There is a moment's silence, a few people look at each other, but surprisingly there is no obvious embarrassment. Then, almost en masse, everyone shouts back their approval. They all *genuinely* seem to be a happy crowd.

"Okay, okay, I know you all call me *'Big Dick'* behind my back, but I deserve it. If we can't take the piss out of ourselves, then we don't deserve to take the piss out of others. And anyway, after last year's Christmas party, I think it's common knowledge that the name Big Dick is richly deserved. It serves me right for being so drunk that I fell asleep in the toilet and got locked in the restaurant overnight!"

Everyone laughs. Some people clap.

"But seriously, though, the important thing is that here at Cohen's we enjoy our work. And because we enjoy it, we produce some of the most outstanding campaigns in the industry. If not *the* best."

Everyone cheers again.

"Claire, I'm sorry to see you leave. We all are. I know I'm speaking for all of us when I say that. So I just wanted to say 'thank you' for everything you've done for us, and for James over the years… and, as a sign of our appreciation for your hard work, I would like to offer you this." He hands over a large white envelope to Claire, who takes it from him quickly with one hand, and steps forward and gives Richard a massive hug, tears streaming down her face. While she is burying her wet face into his chest, Richard announces to everyone that the envelope contains tickets for an all-expense paid long weekend in Rome for Claire and a friend.

I look on, almost as if I'm an unwelcome observer to this whole scene. A feeling of disquiet and unrest beginning to grow in my chest.

The incredible open signs of affection from Claire to Richard, the warm response and the laughter Richard's little speech so obviously elicited. And the generosity of the gift from Richard. A personal gift, one which he paid for himself. As partner I know that it wasn't paid for by the company. It's as much a surprise to me as it is to her.

There is something very wrong here. What I have just witnessed and what my experience, at least what I *believe* my experience of working for Cohen's is, don't match up.

My mind is racing, but as I struggle to come to grips with my thoughts, I become uncomfortably aware that Richard is inviting me to say a few words too. After all, Claire is my PA. (And I haven't even got her a present…!)

Suddenly the feeling of being Judas again.

I step up on the chair, beckon for everyone to quieten down, then try to follow Richard's example. Except, I find that I have nothing or little to say. I can't quip any funny remarks about Claire, because I don't remember much about her. I feel extra stupid, because I have the feeling that everyone in the office knows that I had an affair with her, and suspect that the reason she is leaving is something to do with me. So for a few minutes I waffle on about how wonderful the opportunity is that she is going after, and how I am sure that one day soon, she may be running her own very large and successful company, and how I hope that when that happens, if I come to her and ask her for a job, she will remember me. That gets a small laugh. Best quit whilst I'm ahead.

"I'm not one for big speeches" I say, another laugh, "but I just want to say that I don't know how I'll survive without her. I'll miss her. A lot."

Everyone senses there is more behind the last words than there actually is, and I get a round of applause. And a big hug and an affectionate kiss from Claire, which draws a cheer and some raucous whooping from the rabble.

Behind us Alice is busy cracking the bottles of champagne and passing out the drinks. Richard takes over from me and invites everyone to join us in a toast to Claire's future, and the traditional three cheers for any Cohen's leaver. Everyone raises their glasses, cheers, and the evening's celebrations begin.

"And…" Richard concludes, shouting above the din of the crowd…" I forgot to mention, I've got a tab behind the bar in The Crown for Claire until 8 pm. After that, you're on your own."

Another cheer. And then the serious drinking begins.

CHAPTER 34
Help!

Shortly after seven, I finally manage to grab Claire and drag her to a corner of the pub. The rest of the company see me with her, and leave us to it. I know that they are thinking I'm having a last minute moment of intimacy with her, maybe even trying it on with her again. But I don't care. I've got other things on my mind.

"So, are you sad to be leaving then. I mean, genuinely sad? Or was all that back there just a show?" I ask her, as we sit down at a table.

"What do you mean? Of course I'm sad to be going. I almost feel guilty. Not for leaving you, ...you'll survive, you bastard...you always do. But because I love working for Cohen's. They've given me a lot, and I feel bad about just walking out."

"...but I thought people didn't like working here?"

"Who told you that?"

No one did. I just assumed it.

"Claire. I need to ask you a few things. Important things..."

"What?" she says, a little tipsy.

"I feel stupid, but did you really come here to Cohen's with me from PHI?"

Her eyes crumple up at the corners and form a big question mark.

"Of course I did. You begged me to. But I would have anyway. I wanted to leave PHI too."

"Shit. I didn't realise that you had worked at PHI too. Can I tell you a secret, Claire?"

But even as I ask her I realise that it may be a big mistake to tell her anything just now.

"No...forget that. But tell me, why did I leave PHI and why were you so happy to come with me?"

"Because it's a shit hole. We hated working there, and you couldn't wait to escape."

A twinge runs from the top of my spine to my testicles. Then a sudden sinking feeling. A feeling of impending dread.

"What do you mean?"

"Like I said. You spent most of your time there trying to escape. Most people did. It's a totally crap company to work for. You hated the place!"

Oh no.

"Have you ever heard of a woman there, I think she's probably a partner now, …called Helen?"

"Yes. Of course I have. She hated you and you hated her. She's one of the big reasons you left. You both joined PHI at the same time, and rubbed each other up the wrong way from the first day you got there."

"Are you sure?"

"Listen, you're the one with the memory loss, not me. What's this all about?" she asks, putting down her glass of wine, and raising a finger to touch me on my arm. "Actually, come to think of it, it's funny you should mention her...", Claire continues, "...because only a couple of weeks ago she called me up out of the blue. She was sniffing around for information on the Scotia Telecom deal. She'd seen the photo in one of the marketing mags, and was asking questions about it. Then last week she called me again and tried to get some information on the Dome deal. She was also sniffing around on the Olympics deal, but I didn't say anything. Someone in her company had seen you talking to Stu Roberts in a bar a couple of months ago, and she must have put two and two together."

"So you know about the Olympics deal?" I ask, in disbelief.

"Of course I do, it was me that set up the first meeting with Stu several months ago. I don't know if you've forgotten, but I am…sorry, I was…your PA. I do all your meetings for you. But don't worry, I didn't tell anyone else, just like you asked. Listen, have I done something wrong?"

"No." I stutter. "No…no, you haven't. It's just that…, listen, did you tell Helen anything about me when she called up?"

"Like what?"

"About, you know…"

"About your concussion? Of course I did. She wanted to speak to you, but you weren't in. You were off sick. Remember? We were all really worried for you. Everyone was. She was pretty insistent, and she was beginning to annoy me, so I had a go at her and I think I told her something about how if you were lucky you might have forgotten all about her too. Old bag."

"So she knew all about my concussion?"

"Yes…"

Oh fuck.

I walk for miles through the busy London streets, but like I always do when I really need to think, I end up back down at the Jubilee Bridge crossing the Thames. I stare out across the huge, dark, flowing river, watching the reflected evening lights dancing on the waves. Yellows, reds, white, blue. A bright vivid blue, bouncing off the river from the lights of the towering London Eye.

The night air is cold, and a little chilly. Just what I need to freshen me up and sharpen my senses.

It's all become clear now.

Startlingly clear.

The new world that I had begun to build around me, such a clever boy, so successful, *so fucking smart* that I am, has all just come crashing down around my ankles.

I've just been taken for one of the biggest corporate rides in history.

Twenty-nine million euros worth in fact. Twenty-nine million euros worth of business that is now PHI's!

What an idiot.

PHI don't want me. They want my clients. The Scotia deal, the Dome deal, and probably more than either of them together, they want the 2016 Olympics campaign.

And what a clever and devious woman Helen is. *Bitch.* She put this whole scam together.

I look up at Big Ben and admire it. Its famous chimes resound across the water, and I listen as it strikes ten. It's then that I realise that I have not yet signed the contract with PHI.

Richard...

Fuck, *I've just resigned...*

I rush back through the busy streets, dodging round people on the pavements, missing moving cars and ignoring their blaring horns. By the time I arrive back at The Crown, I am exhausted and soaked through with sweat, but I find him still there, sitting in the corner by himself. Alone. Almost all the others have moved on now, to a club or a party somewhere else.

He sees me as I walk in, and looks away. I can see the spirit has gone out of him now. I take a seat beside him, expecting to find him completely drunk. Instead, he looks up at me with clear eyes, and I can see that he is drinking orange juice. The man is stone sober.

"You're not drinking?" I ask.

"No... not tonight. I was just enjoying the evening. I want to remember it all...it was a good night. We had fun...Perhaps one of the last we'll have like that. Thanks to you."

Judas.

"Richard, can I buy you a drink? A real drink. I want to talk...and I think I have a lot of explaining to do..."

PART FOUR

CHAPTER 35
Monday Afternoon Physics

Sitting outside Professor Kasparek's office in Edinburgh University brings back some very interesting memories. I can remember vividly the time I came to my first tutorial, a spotty, thin, twenty-year old, full of bright ideas and a hunger to learn Physics. "*The man who understands Physics, is the man who has the key to changing the world!*" is what the old professor told us at the start of his first lecture in Quantum Mechanics, the most popular course in our second year.

He seemed old then, which must make him ancient now, twenty years later. A wonder he is still going, or can remember anything. Of course, when we were twenty, any person forty-plus was old. Sixty was ancient.

The last incident on the Jubilee Line had plagued me all weekend. I realised on Sunday afternoon that I needed to understand better what was happening to me, and I needed to be able to talk to someone who might have some insight into it all. I was playing with Elspeth in the back-garden, pushing her on the swing, when I suddenly thought about my first job referee and old tutor at Edinburgh University, and realised that he was the obvious person to discuss this with. I looked him up in Directory Enquiries, ---there are not too many Professor Kaspareks listed---, and gave him a call just after 4pm.

"Professor Kasparek? Hi. I don't know if you will remember me, my name is James Quinn. You were my Tutor and Quantum Mechanics professor for three years whilst…"

"Quinn? James Quinn…? Yes…yes, of course I do. How are you? How are you my boy?"

"Fine…"

"So, what are you doing nowadays? Did you ever go into advertising?"

"Wow…you remembered. Yes, actually, I did. I'm a Partner now in one of the London firms…"

"Excellent, my boy. Excellent. Shame about the physics though. You were rather good. One of the better ones. I really liked your fourth year project. Very, very original."

"Actually, I rather want to discuss some Physics with you. Something has come up, that I think you might be able to help me with…"

"Something to do with advertising?"

"No. No. It's, well, actually it's too difficult to talk about it on the phone. I was wondering if I were to jump on a plane and come up to Edinburgh tomorrow morning, if you might be able to give me an hour to discuss something...I think you might find it very interesting."

"Tomorrow? Okay, that is possible. About two o'clock. I have a tutorial at four, so I don't have too much time. By the way, I'm on the fourth floor of the King's Buildings now....Room 416."

"Excellent. I'll find you."

I was at Heathrow by 10 am and in Edinburgh by noon Whenever I fly up to Scotland I'm always amazed by just how quick it is. I once spoke to a stewardess who told me that the flight time as the crow flies...although no crow can fly at 500 mph... is about forty minutes. The rest is waiting for take-off and joining the holding pattern for landing.

I hired a car at the airport and drove through the city centre, past the incredible castle perched high on the plug of volcanic rock, looking out over and dominating the city below. The most impressive castle I have seen anywhere in the world. Scots people are so lucky...They have an incredible standard of living. Sun, sea, mountains and lochs (that's lakes to those south of the border.) But I lied about the sun.

As I left Princes Street, and wound my way up the Mound, across the Royal Mile, where the first skyscrapers in the world were built, and then down past the statue of Greyfriar's Bobby...the little Scottish dog who made his way into several Hollywood films...I wondered just how much Prof Kasparek will remember about me. I got to know him quite well after I had left university, through the alumni association and our common interest in hill-walking, and the reunions in 1993 and 1998. But that was in another world. The question is, did we have '*reunions*' in this world too?

I drive past the University in the centre of the city, and head out along the Mayfield Road to the science campus on the outskirts of the city. Twenty minutes later I am back in the King's Buildings for the first time in years. Memories come flooding back. Real memories. Not anything imagined or concocted by a madman.

"James. Come in, come in!" the Professor says enthusiastically, as he sticks his head around his office door and invites me in, hand outstretched.

"Thanks." I say, taking his hand and shaking it warmly. Physically he doesn't actually seem to have changed much, except his hair has gone white. Rather charming, but so typical of the classic image of any mad professor.

"I can't believe it's been ...what, twenty three years?" he says, "I looked up my notes...you were President of the Physics club in 1989, weren't you, the year you graduated?"

"Twenty three years? Wow. It's hard to believe it's been that long. Did you ever make it to any of the reunions?" I ask, testing the water.

"What reunions? I didn't hear about any?"

Ah. So that answers my first question then.

We chat for a while about nothing in particular, while he makes us both a cup of tea from the kettle at the back of his office. He asks me about my career, and I listen while he talks enthusiastically about his latest field of work. "Quantum holes, my boy, that's where it's at today. Quantum holes!"

I listen, excitedly, wondering if there is any connection between Quantum Holes and making 'the jump', although when I find out a little more about what a Quantum Hole is, I suspect there isn't.

"So what brings you all the way up from the Big Smoke? Something to do with an exciting advertising project? Is Saatchi and Saatchi going to start promoting Nuclear Physics?"

"No, nothing like that." I fiddle with the cup of tea in my hands for a moment, then put it down on his large oak desk. "Something happened to me, that I needed to talk to someone about, something very strange. And I think that you might be the person who might be able to help explain it all to me…I hope…"

"I'll do my best, my boy. I'll do my best. So what are we talking about then? Have you been abducted by aliens?"

I squirm in my seat, and distinctly feel my face beginning to glow. I must be blushing. Perhaps this wasn't such a good idea after all.

"No. I don't believe in aliens. But what I have to say is rather bizarre. Maybe even unbelievable, but I'll tell you the whole thing, and you can make your own mind up if I'm mad or not. But before I start, I would just add that I have already been checked out at the hospital, and according to the best medical science that BUPA can buy, I am perfectly sane. And I am a Physicist, so I do understand the fundamental physics behind most phenomena …it's just that I don't understand this one…"

"Which is what? What exactly are we talking about?" he asks, his interest now captured.

So, for only the second time since I made *'The Jump'*, as it were, I start to tell another person the truth about what has happened to me. My father listened, but it was beyond his scope of understanding, and at the end of it, I don't think that he really believed me.

As I speak, the old Professor switches on his desk lamp, picks up a pad, and starts to make some notes. A few times he stops me and interrupts, asking to go back over a particular point again, or asking more about something I just said. Occasionally, he looks up at me and mutters something to himself in Polish, his mother tongue, which I don't understand, and once he gets up and walks over to a shelf, picking out a book, and looking at a few pages, before putting it back and then asking me to continue.

I feel like I'm in a doctor's office, and I am telling him all the symptoms of my illness. I half expect him to turn round and tell me, that I either have terminal cancer, or that *'there is a lot of it going around'* and I should just take two aspirins, three times a day, before he then shouts 'Next Please!'

When I come to the end of the story, paying particular attention to both of the recent incidents on the Jubilee Line, he asks me to go over these two occasions again in greater depth, asking a lot more detailed questions on each of them.

"*And what time was this at?*", "*How long did it last for?*", "*Ah, so you said that afterwards you felt tired both times…that is most interesting!*", "*And you said that their bodies were solid, like statues?*", "*Can you remember any strange smells when it happened?*"… he questions everything and anything that I say around these incidents. "*And what was the weather like outside the tube station? Can you recall seeing or hearing any thunder or lightning?*" Questions about my feelings and observations before I went into the tube station, and then also when I came out.

"*Did I notice any changes to my so-called 'new world', after these incidents, that weren't there before?*"

A good question, but one to which I had to answer no.

"*Any headaches afterwards?*"

Questions about my physiology, about my feelings, my thoughts…

"I have been having a lot of dreams recently…" I answer.

"*So, tell me about them.*"

I tell him a few, without going into great detail, and he nods and makes more notes.

The two hours come to an end, and he gets up for a moment, excusing himself from the room. When he comes back, he explains that he has got someone else to take his tutorial scheduled for four o'clock, and he starts again from where he left off. Questions, questions, questions.

By the time we get to five o'clock we are almost done. Then he asks, "And what changes do you say you have noticed in this world, that weren't there in your first world?" That takes us to seven o'clock.

The time slips by and we seem not to notice it. We talk, and talk, but by seven thirty the questions have dried up, and the thick note pad is almost full.

"So, now you are just waiting to see if Sarah will call you?" he asks, finally putting down the pen on his desk, and flicking backwards through the notes he has made.

"Yes. According to her friend Mary, she's on holiday until next week, so I won't hear anything until she gets back anyway."

"And you think she may call you?" he asks.

"I don't know. " I reply. "I really hope so."

We sit for a few minutes in silence. I am really nervous now, scared almost to ask him what he thinks. ---Is the prognosis fatal? Am I going to die?---

"So," I bite the bullet, the silence just too heavy to bear." Do you think I am mad or…?"

"Or, what?"

"Or… I don't know. Maybe you believe me, and you can give me a physical explanation for what is going on, or what has happened to me?"

The Professor gets up, and walks past me to the door, flicking the light switch on the wall. It has got surprisingly dark in the room without us noticing it. We can hardly see each other's faces any more.

"The point is that you believe it. And you are, I would say, obviously still very sane. I am not a Professor of the mind….only of nature, the physics of existence. I try to stay clear of how our minds interpret and make us believe the things we experience around us. That is someone else's job. I just try to understand what IS around us, not what we THINK is around us…"

"In other words, you don't believe me. You think I may be mad…"

"I did not say that. I think you are intelligent, and as I say, from what I can perceive about you now, you seem to be sane. The problem is that what you are saying is…well, it is very, very interesting…Except…". He sits down and picks up his notes, flicking back to something he wrote before. He mutters something in Polish again, and then chucks the notepad back onto his desk, shaking his head.

"Listen," I say, getting up from my chair and wandering over to the window behind his desk. From here you can see across the fields behind the science campus on the edge of Edinburgh, on and up to the Pentland Hills, the lights of the man-made ski-slope now beginning to shine like fairy lights on the edge of the mountain range, "I asked you earlier if you had been to any of the Physics Society alumni reunions. You said no. Well, in my real world, the physics society organised hill-walking weekends, up at the university outdoor pursuits centre in Firbush, for graduates and alumni. You went to a lot of them, ...at least all the ones I went to. One was in 1998, and the first one was back in 1993. At the meeting in 1993, we got on really well, and then in 1996, you invited a small group of us to your house in Skye for a week of walking in the Cuillins…"

I am watching his face now, looking for any telltale signs of recognition.

"Go on…" he says, his elbows resting on the arms of the chair with both his hands arched together and touching his fingertips in front of his face, as he prepares to take in every word I say.

"On the trip to the Cuillins, you drove us there in your Land Rover. There were four of us, and you. We arranged to meet in your house. You were still living with your ageing mother then, up in Ravelston Dykes, who, you did explain at the time, was quite rich. Your father was something to do with importing and exporting steel from Poland to the States. He died in America, and left your mum comfortably off. …by the way, she died a year later, which would make it 1997. Bad kidney. You told us that in 1998, on my second trip to Firbush…anyway, I digress. In a room at the back of your house, you gave us something to eat before we left. You play the piano, and have a Steinway grand there. It used to be your grandmother's piano. It's very old."

His face has turned white, his mouth now half open. The hands have sunk down into his lap, and he is transfixed by my words.

"We left about six o'clock, and drove up to the house in Skye. It's a lovely house, an old Victorian house, which you bought a few years after you came to Edinburgh University. You go there a lot. You like to escape up there…you paint a lot …watercolours…and your house is covered in your pictures. Which, are, incidentally, very good."

He smiles, the colour briefly returning to his cheeks as he takes his turn to blush.

"One night, we all got quite drunk. Very drunk. Too much Glenmorangie whisky. Your favourite. I drink it all the time now, a bad habit that I picked up from you. Anyway, as I was saying, we all got really drunk, and you and I end up in this big, big discussion about life. And our lost loves…"

I see him visibly shift in his seat, suddenly getting a little uncomfortable.

"I told you all about a woman, Sarah, and you told me something that you said you have never ever told anyone else about. You told me about a woman, …I'm sorry, I can't remember her name, …but I do remember that she was an artist too…that's right, I remember now, you pointed to one of the paintings on the wall, and said that that one was painted by her…"

"What was it?" he suddenly speaks.

"It was a rose. A big, red rose!" I reply, clicking my fingers in excitement as I recall the picture on the wall.

"You're right. It is a rose." he says quietly, his voice quivering. "After her. Her name was Rosa."

I look at him, and notice that he is crying. Quietly. A few silent tears running down the edges of his cheek. For a moment I wonder if I should go on, but when he says nothing more, I do.

"It was only me you told it to, so no one else knows, but you told me then that you had loved this woman,…remember we were both very drunk…, and that she was your fiancée. After your parents came to Scotland, you went back to Poland to university, and then you both spent some time together later in another of the Eastern European countries…"

"It was Czechoslovakia. I did my Ph.D. there…in Prague…" he interrupts.

" …Then you told me that your fiancée was killed in the Soviet invasion of Czechoslovakia in 1968. She was part of some student movement in Prague, or something like that…I'm sorry, no disrespect meant, but it was a long time ago, and I can't remember all the details….I can just remember that afterwards that was the reason you left there, and came over here to live with your mother, and why you never married after that. You have always loved her..."

"How do you know all this, James?" he suddenly asks, his voice very serious. "How do you know so much about my personal life?"

"You told me."

"I did not. I have never told anyone about Rosa. It...it is my secret."

"You told me. In another world. *My* world." I insist, walking back to my seat and sitting down again. "Professor Kasparek, you told me all of this, ...and more..., over the years. To me this is all true, and it is knowledge that I have picked up about you from the other world I live in. The question is, is this knowledge based on fact, or is it garbage?"

"It is true. All true...."

"So, unless I am a psychic, which I can assure you I am not, then *ipso facto* this proves that the rest of the story that I have told you is also true!"

Silence.

A clock ticks loudly on one of the shelves, and I wonder why I have not noticed it before.

My words have obviously stirred some painful memories within the Professor's mind, and the rekindling of them has had an incredible effect on the old man. He seems sad, withdrawn, and very pensive.

"James, I need to think. There is much to ponder. What are your plans for this evening? Can you stay in Edinburgh until tomorrow, or must you catch the last flight back to London?"

"I can stay. That's not a problem. Listen, I'm sorry if what I've said..." I start to apologise.

"No. Don't. But for now, I need to think, and I would like to be alone. Can we meet again tomorrow? At my house? I still live at the same place you mentioned. Will you be able to find it again?"

"Yes. I will."

"Good. Then tomorrow morning at say, eleven?"

I take the cue to go, and to leave an old man to his thoughts. His memories of a lost love. I'm just leaving the office when the Professor asks one last question...

"Oh, by the way, James....how heavy are you?"

"80kg. Why?... " I ask, surprised.

"*Just wondered.* ...Just wondered, that's all...Tomorrow then. At eleven o'clock..." And with a smile, the Professor closes his office door and is gone.

I am just getting into my car in the car park, when my mobile rings.

It's Helen.

CHAPTER 36
Explanations

"James, where the hell are you? I've been calling your office all day. I've left you about twenty messages already!" She seems a little upset.

"I'm in Edinburgh. Something came up unexpectedly over the weekend, and I had to drop everything and catch a flight up here this morning."

"Is everything okay?" she asks, the edge of anger in her voice, not so pronounced as before.

"Yes, but I had to forget about work for a few days. Something personal that demanded some immediate attention. But I'll be back in London tomorrow night."

"Good. Have you signed the contracts?"

"Yes, I've already done it. I read the contract and I like it. It's fine. Listen, I wanted to talk to you about something really interesting that came up last week…I've been thinking about it, and I came up with a brilliant idea. I've already spoken to a few people about it, and we're setting something up for Thursday."

"What? What are you talking about? And what's happening on Thursday? I don't particularly like surprises." She sounds a little concerned.

"Okay, since you don't like surprises, I'll give you a piece of the good news now then. Have you heard anything about the bid for the Olympics campaign?" I ask innocently.

"No. The Olympics? What do you mean?"

So it's true. She's lying. From what Claire told me, she knows everything about the Olympics deal.

"Well, what would you say if I told you that I'd just won it…"

"You're kidding... I mean, you're joking, right?" she feigns a little joyous laughter, as if she was really happily surprised. "Wow, the other Partners will love this. You couldn't be bringing a better piece of business to us if you tried. They've been dying to get that deal for ages…"

"I thought you said you hadn't heard about it?"

"I haven't, I mean, of course I knew that it would be coming up, and I knew, obviously that one of the other Partners was sniffing around for it. But when I tell him it's going to be ours after all, and that you're bringing it to us when you join, he'll be over the moon. Well pleased. That's fantastic news James. Brilliant!"

What a cow!

"So do you want to hear about my plan for Thursday?" I ask.

"Yes…great. What's happening?"

"I've arranged an impromptu Press Conference. Some of the Olympic Committee are coming along, and they'll do a formal announcement that they are handing over the business into my safe hands, and to PHI. I couldn't think of a better way to announce my leaving Cohen's than this. It'll be great! Can you imagine the look on Richard's face, when he reads about it in the papers and sees the pictures in the rags next week?"

"Fantastic idea. Oh James, you are evil!" she says, laughing again.

Not half as wicked as you, my friend.

"So, I'll see you there then. The Savoy Hotel, the Osprey Rooms, at 11 am. And to get the maximum publicity, bring the other Partners with you."

"It's a date. I'm looking forward to it already.".

So am I, Helen. So am I.

Another night, another dream.

This time I am on a balloon flight. I'm in the basket with a co-pilot that I cannot see, a hood covering his face and hiding it from view. In the distance we can see another colourful balloon coming towards us. As it gets closer I begin to hear voices, and soon I recognise that they belong to Keira, Nicole and Sarah.

We are coming very close to each other, and I shout to them. They hear me, and all three reach out to me from within their balloon basket, leaning out perilously far in an effort to reach me.

I see that they are alone, being blown along at the mercy of the winds. Out of control.

We are close now. Very close. We stare at each other, and I can almost touch the fear and the longing crying out from her eyes.

Sarah is holding a bundle in her arms, and as we draw closer she reaches out to me, imploring me to take the bundle from her.

I stretch out to her, preparing to accept what she wants so desperately for me to take.

We are tantalisingly close. My fingers touch the cloth on the edge of the bundle, but I cannot yet quite reach it.

I look down, and see the ground miles below. There are small white clouds dotted around beneath us, between us and the lush green English countryside. I look back at Sarah, and now climb up onto the edge of the basket, ready to try once more to take the bundle from her as soon as the two baskets are a little closer. Just another second…one more…

We edge a little closer and leaning out as far as I can go, my fingers grasp for the bundle at the same time as Sarah pushes it towards me.

Then a sudden gust of wind, and our baskets separate abruptly, the bundle slipping from between our hands,… falling, …falling…, dropping to the earth and hard ground, far, far below.

Tipped backwards by the jerking of the balloon, I fall backwards into the bottom of the basket and sprawl at the foot of my pilot.

The two balloons drift past each other.

I am screaming at the hooded pilot, begging him to somehow stop, to turn the balloon around.

He looks down at me, and laughs. A high pitched, feminine laugh.

Reaching up a hand, and pulling back the hood, reveals a smiling, laughing face.

It is Jane.

Typically of Scotland, little has changed in Ravelston Dykes since I was last here. Tall, detached, sprawling Victorian town-houses, made of solid blocks of grey granite. Built to last, these houses will still be here in a thousand years' time. In this world or any other. Strong enough to withstand the dour Scottish climate of constant rain, rain and more freezing rain. And the occasional day when the sun shines and it snows in the afternoon and then hails at night time - summertime.

The Professor's house is on the brow of the hill, where the road levels off and sweeps round in a great curve back towards the city centre. The views from here are commanding, and hence the reason these magnificent houses command such a lofty price. The most expensive houses in Edinburgh.

I walk up the garden path, ring the doorbell, and half expect a manservant or maid to answer the door and bid me enter. Instead, Professor Kasparek greets me personally, and ushers me into the back of the house, to the reception room where the great Steinway grand piano still dominates the room.

The Professor sees me looking at it, as we sit down opposite each other in the large comfortable chairs around the open fireplace.

"Aha…so, you see I have the piano in this world, just as in the other. Although, in your world, I probably play it somewhat better."

I laugh.

"So you believe me then. You accept that I have somehow made a jump from one world to another?" I ask him, seizing upon his words.

"My dear boy, I have been up half the night, pondering what you told me yesterday. For the life of me, I cannot understand how you came to know the things you somehow did. I invite so few people back to my house, and nowadays I live the lifestyle of a virtual recluse. I have few friends, real friends, and seldom get drunk. To the best of my knowledge, ---and believe me, such things you do not discuss lightly,---I have never told anyone about my loss. I have loved only once in my life, and never again. I just want to ask you a few questions though, and I want to see your eyes when you reply to me. So come close to me, so that I can see you properly."

I respond obediently, moving onto the edge of my chair, and wiping the hair away from my face and forehead so that he can clearly see my eyes.

"James, I will ask you just a few questions, and by watching your response as you answer, I will know whether you are lying to me, or telling me the truth. So don't lie. It will serve no purpose."

"Ask away…"

"James Quinn, Tell me,…is everything that you told me the truth?"

"It is." I answer effortlessly.

"Is this a strange game that you are playing with me or are you sincere?"

"I am sincere."

"To the best of your knowledge, do you come from another world, one very similar to ours, but with a common past and different future?"

"I do." I add. "But I do not understand the how, or the why. I was hoping that you may be able to explain it to me…"

The old Professor sits back, an excitement burning fresh in his eyes.

"Amazing. You did not lie. You have told the truth. I have studied the art of NLP…that's Neuro Linguistic Programming…a little hobby of mine, and when someone lies, they signal the lie with tell-tale unconscious facial muscular movements and with a movement of the eyeballs. You did not. You told the truth." He stands up and goes to a drinks cabinet near the window. "Would you like a drink? I think I need one myself."

"Please…"

"….a Glenmorangie?"

"Exactly."

As he hands me the glass he says, "Everything you told me about my past, that is the common past we shared before the time at which our two worlds must have diverged, is true. But after the divergence, things were a little different between our experiences. For example, you said yesterday that in your world, my mother died in 1997. In this life, she died in 2001. After Rosa died, I spent most of my life dedicated to looking after her. Since she has gone, I have been very alone, but I do not know how to change. I am as I am.

A recluse. I have my physics and that is my passion. That is why I have not retired yet. That and the sad fact that I really have nothing to retire to."

I am looking around the room now, admiring the paintings on the walls.

"Which brings me to another small difference between your world and mine. In this world, the picture of the Rose now hangs in my bedroom upstairs. True, it used to be my favourite in Skye, but when my mother died, I moved it down here. It helps me remember…"

The whisky is so smooth that as I sip it, I hardly notice the liquid pass down the back of my throat and into my stomach.

"Special Reserve. Over thirty years old," the Professor announces, as if he is reading my mind. "...But now to business, my boy, now to business." He picks up a notepad from the coffee table which separates us, and starts to looks at his notes. I recognise the notepad as the same one he scribbled on so actively yesterday afternoon.

I know that now is the time for me to be silent and follow the Professor's lead. Speak only in reply to his questions. He is silent for awhile, and then he starts.

"I have thought a lot about what you have told me. I do not pretend to understand what has happened to you. But, assuming that it actually has, then there must be some sort of explanation…there always is."

"I have studied Quantum Mechanics for a long, long time. I was a good friend of Professor Higgs at Edinburgh, and marvelled at his ideas and his postulation of the Higgs Boson. A genius. More of a genius than I will ever be. I digress, I am sorry. Anyway, I know a few other physicists who have been working on an interesting theory which could explain the experiences that you claim to have had…In a new branch of quantum mechanics, which I must admit, even I found a little hard to understand when I first looked at it...What's interesting is that they have described the theoretical existence of an event such as that which would apparently seem to have happened to you. I will try to explain what they mean…James, you will remember, will you not, the equation of Heisenberg?"

"His *'uncertainty principle'*?" I ask.

"*Exactement…*" he says in French, which sounds rather odd, spoken with his Polish accent. "His fabulous theorem which in one way states that matter can either be described as a wave of energy or a physical particle with mass and velocity, but where we can never be sure of the exact state of both…"

"...Where we can only have true knowledge of one state of existence, and whereby if we conduct research to gain an insight into the condition or possible condition of the other state, that we thereby lose all knowledge of the original state that we knew of?" I add.

"Yes. And you will also recall, what a gluon is?" he asks.

"Yes…"

"Or that all matter exists, but is constantly transforming itself into energy, and changing its state from a physical reality, to a wave of pure energy, before it retransforms itself back into matter again. Essentially that we are constantly recreating ourselves?"

"Yes…"

"And that at the point when matter has become energy, and is in the process of transforming itself back into matter, it has a myriad of options as to how it can recreate itself. The biggest mystery being, the how and the why of why it actually transforms itself into essentially the same identical particle it used to be…when in fact, it could become so many other things…are you with me still?"

I nod.

"Another way to look at this, is that at any point in time, when we recreate ourselves from what we were before, we have a million, a trillion, no, an infinite number of different possible futures. At the quantum level, each of these particle futures will occupy a different point in the space-time continuum, and will lie on a different time-line. In other words, each particle has an infinite number of different futures that it can follow. Now, each time a particle destroys itself, transforms itself into energy, and then recreates itself, it takes a little step forward in time, on its individual time-line, into its chosen future. When we connect up all the little events it undergoes, the line we draw connecting its past events to its future events prescribes the *'time-line'*, or the *'life-line'* or *'life'* of the particle. Whatever you want to call it."

I take another sip of the whisky, mesmerized by the Professor's words.

"Now that is all on a quantum level. If we step backwards to the classical level, and onto a much larger scale, where we no longer see particles or quarks but rather humans and mountains and planets, the world around us, we can now see that at any point in time, before we take a step forward into the future, there are an infinite number of different possibilities for that future. In other words, there are an infinite number of timelines that we can take. Each one different from each other. But all sharing a common past."

"Now, according to many leading theorists, many of whose work you studied with me at Edinburgh, such theorems have always conjectured but never proven, that each of these myriad of different possible timelines actually co-exist together. Multiple, parallel existences. The stuff of 'parallel dimensions' much heralded about on TV in the Z-Files and such like. "

"You mean the 'X'-files…?"

"No, I mean the 'Z'-files. I should know. It's one of my favourite programmes. You can pick whatever letter you want in your world, but in this world, on this timeline…the letter is 'Z'! We call it the 'Z-files'."

"A case in point. A good example. Thanks…" I add, humbly, resisting the urge to re-emphasise that in my world, we call it the X-Files.

"Now, getting back to where I was..." the Professor continues. "I was saying that even as we speak, in this room, all around us, there are a million different parallel timelines running, each line threading its own path through time. Now what would happen if at some point, for no apparent reason whatsoever, two of these different timelines were to cross paths, or to intersect? And at the instant they intersect, is it possible for particles from one timeline to innocently cross over to the other timeline and continue onwards into a new future on the other timeline? A future with a different past than all the other particles on that new timeline?"

"To 'jump' from one timeline to another? From one world to another parallel world?"

"*Exactly*...spot on."

"Now, let me ask you another question. Have you heard of String Theory?"

"Yes… but I don't know much about it." I reply.

"Well, James, basically, for a while it was all the rage. People used to think that particles, dimensions, time itself was explainable in terms of strings. Now, using that analogy, imagine for a second that the timelines themselves were strings. Imagine that they bump into each other, and cross each other's paths. Once they touch, perhaps it is possible that two timelines get tangled up, or intertwined…maybe not permanently, perhaps just temporarily,…who knows…"

"Perhaps it is possible that for a while the two timelines are attracted to each other, each continuing to exist independently but spiralling and circling around the other as they move forwards in time. Spinning around each other in some form of quantum dance. Now, the question you may ask is, why would they continue to spin around each other…and perhaps an answer to that question would be that when the particle from one 'timeline'…let's call it 'Timeline A',…when the particle from 'Timeline A' jumps to 'Timeline B', it still manages to exert some kind of force on its friends that remain on the other timeline -'Timeline A'. In other words, the two timelines attract each other, and begin to tangle up again."

"But as time goes on, the effect that the particle which has jumped onto the new timeline continues to have on its friends left behind on the other timeline, begins to diminish, and the attraction between the timelines begins to fade."

I hold up my hand, interrupting him.

"I know where you are going. In other words, you are saying that for a while, the two timelines will spin around each other, and occasionally bump into each other and perhaps intersect, but the longer the particle remains on the new timeline, the less it will happen. The attraction decreases with time. So eventually the two timelines will separate completely and become independent again."

"Almost," the Professor takes over again, "...except for one thing. At first the intensity by which the timelines will tangle with each other will increase, but then after a number of collisions, the intensity will decrease."

"I don't understand."

"And why should you? What I am saying is only an idea, one of many possible explanations that may be true," he says, waving his hand gently in the air.

"But, it makes so much sense," I argue.

"That it does my boy. Or it may be complete and utter crap. Shit. Merde. The same thing, in whatever language you may choose to describe it.... But let us assume for one moment that it may be a good description of the events we are questioning and not a bad one... Now, in that case, what would our new idea tell us?"

He looks at me with raised eyebrows. I shrug my shoulders.

"I don't know…what? You tell me."

"The model, if we can call it that, would tell us that a particle that makes the 'jump', as you say in your parlance, would have, ...'*may*' have, several opportunities to make the 'jump' back to where it came from. To rejoin its original timeline. The model also tells us, that at first, the intensity of the collisions between the timelines would seem to increase…this is borne out by your experiences so far…but after awhile, the intensity will decrease, and the lines will separate. Perhaps for good. In other words, you could almost say, that once the particle has accidentally strayed from one timeline to another, that mother nature will give it a few chances to 'jump' back to where it belongs. But if the particle does not make the 'jump', the opportunities will stop. There will also be an optimal time, at which the 'jump' should occur. On either side of this optimal time the 'jump' may be possible, but at some point afterwards a safe 'jump' will no longer be feasible and should not be attempted."

The Professor stands up and walks back to the drinks cabinet, waving his glass at me to ask if I too want a refill. I shake my head.

His last few words hang in the air, their significance not lost on my ears.

"So how many opportunities will I get to make the jump? Before it is too late? And when will the optimal time be to do it?" I ask.

The Professor fills his glass and returns to his seat, picking out a small red notebook from the breast pocket of his shirt, and flicking it open.

"Good questions. For you I imagine, they are the most important questions. I too, wondered how many times the timelines would cross, and I have done some calculations to model their possible behaviour. Of course, we are not talking about particles here, we are talking about you, a grown man. A man who is made up of untold billions of tiny atomic particles, each of distinct energy and mass… But, based upon your weight/mass, I have calculated your equivalent energy, and estimated the attraction between the timelines..."

"And?"

"And my calculations would suggest that there is enough attraction between your timeline and mine for them to intersect eight or nine times. No more. The optimal time to cross over being the fourth time it happens. After that, there is a danger the lines will diverge before any jump could successfully be completed."

"What do you mean?"

"I mean, that after the fourth time, the attraction may not be great enough to enable the jumping body to recreate itself properly on the original timeline. In other words, the body may try to cross, but be lost in the translation between the events…or it may cross but reassemble itself into some other form. Perhaps not a form that could sustain life. In other words, if you to try to make the jump too late, you will die."

He leans forward and pats me on the thigh. "Now, don't dwell on that. Think rather about what is important. The thing is that from what you have told me, you already have had two possibilities to jump back. That's two out of four."

"But the first time was far too short. And the second time I couldn't get to the door…"

"I know. You said. But, to a certain extent what has happened to you, backs up the model. You see, the first time it happened, it lasted only a fraction of a second. The next time it lasted longer, although still only momentarily. I would predict that the third time it happens you will experience it for even longer. And the next time, it will last long enough…although perhaps still maybe only a minute, perhaps two, for you to complete the jump. After that, though, the next time it will last only a fraction of that, and then by the sixth time, you may not even notice it…"

"But when it happened last time, I could not make it to the doors, because the other people prevented me."

"So, from now on, you just make sure you are always the closest to the doors!"

An obvious solution.

"But why do the others not see what I do, and why am I not affected like them? They are frozen solid, almost as if time is standing still for them."

"And so it is. You see, for them, they are on the correct timeline. For them, there is no attraction to the other timeline. They do not experience it as you do. This is, after all, their world. It is you who are the stranger. Nature is not inviting them to leave. Only you."

"Why do I get the sudden feeling that I am like an asylum seeker, seeking sanctuary in this world. I've lost mine, and have wandered into this one. Only you don't want me here, and someone is trying to gently prod me to leave."

"Aha. A good analogy. And if I may, being the good customs official that I am, I should just warn you, that if you do not go home on either of the next two timeline collisions, you will lose your physical passport and be stuck here for good."

"But how will I know when these timeline collisions will take place again, or that they haven't happened already?" I ask, suddenly worried that they may have already happened but I wasn't travelling on the Jubilee Line at the time when they occurred.

"Ah… I know what you are thinking. Don't worry. These events are *centred* around *you.* They will not happen when you are not there. The fact is that you *will* be aware when it happens. You will be at the *centre* of the timeline collision. You will be the cause of it occurring. We know it seems to happen on the Jubilee Line, but as to the question of when? That I cannot tell you. It will be random. The stupid thing is that it could be tomorrow, next year, or even in ten years' time. Time is, after all, relative. In the great scheme of things, there is little difference between tomorrow or next century. All I can say is, watch, wait, and be ready. You have two more chances, James. That's all. Miss them and you are stuck here for good."

CHAPTER 37
Tuesday night

The flight back down to London passes quickly, my mind lost in a forest of thoughts. The Professor has given me hope, hope which he has dangled in front of me like a carrot, but at the same time, depressing me with the threat that such hope comes with a warning: two more chances. Miss them and I can forget my old life forever.

Thoughts of Sarah soon lead me to pondering once again, why on earth it was that I started looking elsewhere, and why I started to feel the necessity for chasing after another woman. I *love* Sarah. Why did I do what I did??? Why?

I'm old enough and ugly enough to know that somewhere there is a good reason. And although stupidity was my middle name, I know now that I must figure out the 'what' and the 'why' of Sarah and my relationship. There is no point in finding Sarah again, without first understanding why it went wrong the first time around. If I find her… I have to make sure the same thing doesn't happen again. That I do not make the same mistake twice.

As soon as I start on that track of thought, I find myself conjuring up the smiling face of Sarah in my mind, and once again I see her running down the garden path at home, laughing, hurrying to answer Keira's calls, who is screaming for mummy to push her on the swing. I smile at the memory again, the same memory I had not so long ago, and I long for Sarah. I need her.

Then she turns towards me as I call out for her to let me take a photograph, and as she turns towards me her swollen womb swings into view.

The smile dies on my lips, and sadness fills me again, a feeling of dread surging through my mind and body. The attraction I felt to the vision of Sarah, so strong and so physical, vanishes in a flash, and I quickly switch off the picture, fighting to bring my breathing back into line, adrenaline pumping through my body.

Worse than before, far worse. Is this what a panic attack is?

As the plane turns in a sweeping arc high above Heathrow, the passenger beside me notices me gripping the hand-rest tightly and breathing heavily. He turns towards me, touching me lightly on the arm.

"Excuse me, are you okay? Are you scared of flying…" he asks, genuinely concerned for my well-being.

I stare at him, without replying, the face of Sarah being replaced by that of the man beside me.

"Don't worry mate. I promise you, there's nothing to be afraid of… and we'll be on the ground in a few minutes…"

Rather rudely, I turn away from him, muttering a word or two of thanks, and start to stare blankly out of the little porthole beside me.

Far below, the little cars dart up and down the M25, thousands of people heading home from work. Driving home to loved ones, and to their families.

So just what is it in the mental picture of Sarah being pregnant that causes me to react to so physically?

What?

On Tuesday night we were all invited around to Jane's parents to celebrate their fortieth wedding anniversary. My parents were invited too.

I made it back to the house just in time to shower and change, and then drive the family over to Chiswick for 7 pm. Jane was in a good mood, excited about the evening, and pleased with the presents she had bought them. Presents which she had bought several months ago, apparently with my help, although I have never seen them before.

This would be only the second time I had met Jane's parents, the first being last week, when they popped around to our house briefly one night. Her mother was all over me, showing genuine concern for the state of my health, but probably more worried about her daughter, and worrying about the future of our marriage. I wonder just how much Jane has told her about our relationship and my affairs?

About forty people had been invited to the party, and an excellent buffet had been laid on, along with copious amounts of drink. About half way through the evening, Jane's dad made an emotional speech about how lucky he had been in love, and how important and wonderful it was to find the right person. Something he wished everyone else could do too. Perhaps not the best advice he could be giving me, his son-in-law, given the circumstances.

As the evening drew to a close, I offered to take my parents home, after dropping Jane and the kids off first. I wanted the chance to talk to my dad alone, and to tell him about my visit to Edinburgh once mum had gone to bed.

Over a cup of hot chocolate I went over everything I had learned.

"…so you see…there could be some sort of weird physical explanation for all of this after all," I said, finishing up.

My father got up from our seats in front of the fire, and went to get some fresh tobacco for his pipe. He came back, filled it, and then sat silently a little longer. Eventually, the silence began to annoy me.

"So, dad. What do you think?" I ask.

"What do you want me to think? I'm both scared and happy for you."

"What do you mean?" I question, puzzled.

"Listen, James. I'm a simple old man now. I don't understand all this science stuff. I was born before they invented the helicopter or the hovercraft or colour television or spacecraft. My generation just had bicycles, spam and black and white movies. And to be quite honest, I still don't know if I believe all this stuff you are telling me. I mean, how can I? I know it is real to you, but to me? It's just way beyond anything I can ever grasp. No, stop, listen and let me finish," he says, raising his hand to stop me speaking when I try to interrupt him. "…but I will do everything I can to support you. You are my son, and I love you. I want you to be happy. Okay, now just imagine for a second that this is all true. Imagine everything you have said to me is correct. Then the way I see it, we have two problems. Two big problems. Not the least of these is that, if your happiness now depends upon making 'the jump', as you so quaintly describe it, and this professor chappie of yours is correct, then you now only have two more chances to 'jump' from this world to your own. Two. Miss them, and you are stuck here for good. And then you lose what you perceive as the only chance you have left for happiness. And that is the last thing I want to happen to you. I want you to be happy, son. And I'm scared that if you miss either of these opportunities, then you will never find happiness again in this life. And that is something that would make me very, very unhappy. Which means that I must then advise you, to make as many preparations as you can, to make sure you are ready whenever the next occasion arises…"

I try to speak again. But he cuts me short once more.

"No. I've not finished yet. This all leaves me with a big dilemma. I'm encouraging you to go after something which you believe to be real. But from my side, I can't see how it is. So, in a way I'm encouraging you to go after something which I don't think can happen, knowing full well that when it doesn't, you will be heartbroken! I'm in no-man's land here, son. So, what do I do? Support you on your holy quest, or encourage you now to give it up? Of course, there is the possibility that you're right, that I'm wrong, and that this 'jump' thing is completely possible. Which takes us into a whole new area. James, what happens if you make this 'jump?' What happens if you do successfully cross over to your other world? What happens to us? To your mother and I? Did your professor friend tell you what happens to the people you leave behind? It would kill your mother if you suddenly disappeared from her life. One minute you're there, the next you're gone! And who would look after Jane and the kids?"

Ouch. I hadn't thought of that.

"James, if your marriage is over with Jane, that's one thing. But are you sure that you and your subconscious are not just making this whole thing up to help you run away from your problems, and from your marriage? Think about it, the mind is a very powerful thing. Have you thought..."

"Dad, I have thought about all these things. And I'm not mad. Honestly. Please, please believe me. But what can I do? This is *not* my world...I don't belong here!"

Emotions are beginning to rise. Both of us are on our feet, pacing the room, my father puffing furiously on his pipe, blue smoke filling the room. My father's face is red, and for the first time I wonder if I should be bothering an old man with all of this. Am I asking too much of my dad?

I'm a man of science, and if *I'm* struggling to get my head around this, what hope has my dad got?

"James, please, come sit down." He waves at my seat. "Let me ask you one question. Do you think you can save your marriage to Jane? Honestly..."

"No dad. I don't think I can. All I can do now is to prepare her for the future. I just don't think that I could continue in a marriage that is not one of my own choosing. For a start, I never proposed to her..."

"Okay. Okay. If that is what you seriously believe, then my advice to you now is still the same as I gave you before. And I think it's the only way to go that keeps everyone as happy as possible. You must find this woman Sarah, your real wife. And you must make a life with her here. In this world."

"But what if she doesn't call me when she gets back from her trip to Cuba?"

"What did I say before?"

"One bridge at a time?"

"Exactly."

I decide two things on the way home in my car.

Firstly, I can't talk to my dad about this anymore...

And secondly, despite the concern my dad might have about me going back to my world, I have to do everything I can to tie up my affairs here, and to make all the preparations I need so that I can make the jump back at the next opportunity that presents itself.

Whatever the cost, whenever it happens, whether it's this year, next year, or in ten years' time, I'm going home.

CHAPTER 38

Thursday -The Osprey Rooms

With the arrangements and all the final preparations for the Olympics PR conference completed by the end of play on Wednesday, I wake up on the Thursday morning, and am looking forward to the day ahead.

Really looking forward to it…

Stu Roberts and some of the other important officials from the British Olympic Committee all arrive promptly at 9.00 am, and I immediately recognise the faces of a couple of them, one a famous Olympic medal winner from my university days, and another a famous politician. Both as famous in this world, as they are in mine.

The Osprey Room is well organised, rows and rows of seats lined up in front of the raised stage, above which an impressive overhead presentation system proudly projects the famous five rings of the Olympics and the words LONDON 2016 underneath.

The press begin to arrive at 9.30 am, and my new PA, Tracy, runs around like mad, making sure that everyone is happy, has some refreshments, and has received a copy of the Press Pack she has put together. It's her first big job for me, and I must say that I'm really impressed. She worked with Stu to pull this all together at a moment's notice, and giving credit where credit is due, she has done a marvellous job.

By 10 am people are seated, and Richard gets up and welcomes everybody to the meeting. A short speech then it's over to me. Without enough time to become as knowledgeable on all the details as I would like to be, I have arranged to quickly hand over to Stu, so that he can field most of the questions. His presentation is flawless, and the press lap it up, every drop of it. By the time the Chairman of the Olympic Committee -Sir Alexander Breston O.B.E-, gets up, all of us are really excited about the coming Olympics, Britain's chances, the benefits it will bring to Britain, and the opportunity that Cohen's have to run the whole promotion and advertising campaign, ...both here and abroad. A truly international affair. As I sit listening to the presenters I begin to tot up the figures in my mind, and with a shock, I realise that our previous estimate of how much it might be worth to us is a gross miscalculation. More like double, the international rights being something that I had not properly thought through. What's more, Cohen's will become internationally famous into the bargain: the Saatchi and Saatchi of the new millennium! Impressively, the press pack that we give out to the assembled media, PR and journalists, contains a comprehensive breakdown on the success of Cohen's over the years, including substantial emphasis on two other recent wins: the Scotia Telecom deal, and the Dome deal.

The session breaks up at 10.38 am and everyone starts to mingle and circulate, helping themselves to the plentiful supply of champagne and orange juice which has just been brought in.

At 10.48 am precisely my mobile goes off. It's Helen. She's in reception with the rest of the Partners from PHI.

"Come on up." I invite her. The Osprey Rooms. We're all up here!"

Three minutes later, the doors at the back of the conference room open up and Helen walks in, followed by four of the firm's Senior Partners. She is smiling broadly, looking as happy as ever I have seen her. She steps aside just inside the door and lets the other Partners file past her into the room. I walk over to her to greet them.

There is, by this time, quite a lot of commotion going on in the room, everyone present taking as much advantage of the free alcohol as possible. It's turning into quite a party. And I suspect, it's just about to get somewhat hotter.

"Welcome. Welcome. I'm glad you could all come," I announce as they form a small semi-circle around me. Helen starts introducing them all to me, and I shake their hands and smile, enjoying the moment immensely.

"So, when do we begin?" Helen asks loudly, and then stepping forward and speaking a little more quietly into my left ear, "...And wouldn't it have been better if you had kept the drinks until the end?"

Suddenly, there is some loud laughter coming from the side of the stage, and we all look to its source. A little gap opens up amidst the people in front of us, who were previously shielding the other end of the room from sight.

Another laugh, and we all see its owner. Richard. He's patting Sir Alexander Breston on the back, and they are both shaking hands, and smiling, whilst a round of camera flashes light up the room.

Helen's jaw drops, and she turns to me, ashen faced.

"What's Richard doing here? What's going on James?"

She sees a Press Pack lying on one of the chairs in front of her, leans forward and picks it up. She opens it to the front page, reads the first couple of paragraphs, and drops it on the floor.

"You BASTARD!" she screams, stepping forward, her right arm swinging upwards to my face, as if to slap me.

I grab her arm in mid air, catching it just centimetres from my cheek, my grip on her wrist tight and strong.

"So, I'm a bastard am I? That's interesting. Now, if you'll excuse me, I think I must go and join Richard and the Olympic Committee, ...and the international press. I think they want to take some pictures for tomorrow's newspapers. And I get the feeling you might have a little bit of explaining to do to your Partners? So I'll leave you to it. Anyway, thanks for coming. So refreshing to see our competition willing to come along and celebrate our good fortune with us. Help yourself to drinks. Stay awhile..."

I nod briefly to Helen's speechless colleagues and turn and walk towards the others. As I join Stu and Richard I smile for the cameras and turn to see the last of the PHI Partners walking out the door, Helen following quickly behind them.

CHAPTER 39
Time Rolls By

The next two weeks roll by, the days blending quickly from one into the other. Work intensifies, Jane and I improve our relationship in many ways, but become more distant in others. And I become friends with the children. Yet, try as I might, I make no progress in developing any paternal feelings towards them. True, I laugh and smile when I play with them, and Elspeth is a real cutie, but at the end of the day, I am happy when Jane takes them away, puts them in bed, and they are gone. Not once have I found the desire to stand at the doors to their bedrooms and gaze silently at their pretty little faces as they sleep, full of any sort of pride. A stark contrast to how I feel about Keira and Nicole.

More nightmares. Each one more desperate than the other. I wake up sweating, my heart racing with fear and longing, my hand reaching out into the night, trying to touch the vision of a family, my family, waiting for me and crying my name, in a world beyond my reach.

Each time it becomes more difficult to explain to Jane who Sarah is. And now she is asking who Keira and Nicole are too, and I feel that the time is soon coming when I must tell her the whole story. Yet, I know that to do so, would be to give up all possible hope of any normality in our relationship, and would lead to more problems than it would solve.

What if I never ever have the opportunity to make the journey back to my real life and my own world again? Should I divorce Jane and seek to start a new, separate life, or should I stay with Jane in the hope that I will learn to love her? I know the answer to that is no, but I cannot bring myself to face it. The truth of the matter is, that for now, she offers me support and comfort, and to walk away when she is trying so hard…I am a coward, and perhaps, if I admit it to myself, I am beginning to lose respect for myself. I should do what I know is right. I should. But I don't.

The waiting increases the worrying, and my mind begins to ask questions, not all of which are helpful. Some of which I cannot answer, but which scare me just by thinking them.

The worst of the these questions is one that comes to me in the middle of one night, and does not leave. It haunts me and does not go away.

The question is simple.

'When I made the jump into this world, what happened to the James Quinn who was here before I arrived? Where is he now?'

After a day I cannot stand it any longer, and I call the Professor.

"Ah," he says as the listens to me unfold the question, " I wondered how long it would take for you to come up with that one. I'd rather hoped you wouldn't think about it."

"You mean, you've already thought about it yourself?" I ask.

"Yes. Of course. It's a natural question to ask…" He replies.

"And? What is the answer?" I interrupt him, eager for him to put me out of my misery.

"Well, actually, there are only two really feasible answers that I can come up with. Firstly, and this is the most likely, there is no other James Quinn. You are him. After all, you look like him, you have all the same physical attributes as the James Quinn who occupied the world before you got here, so, *ipso facto*, you are him. It's just that, for some reason, you have adopted the memory patterns of a James Quinn from the other timeline. A timeline, which to us, does not exist. Only to you does it have meaning, and only to the grey matter in your mind. There is no physical manifestation of the James Quinn from another timeline, only a rearrangement of biological matter in your mind, a spontaneous shuffling and realignment of the neurons in the brain which, once complete, has formed another consciousness and a new personality with a whole new set of memories."

"Which means what? That the other timeline no longer exists, or that the James Quinn in the other world, where I used to be, has just ceased to exist, and has gone missing?" I ask.

"The latter, my boy. The latter. Which is the most likely answer. I mean, who's to say, that this sort of thing doesn't happen all the time. After all, hardly a day goes by without the news reporting some person who is missing or has simply disappeared and is never seen again. Perhaps…"

"And what is the second likely answer that you found?" I push.

"The second? Oh dear, that one is a little more complicated. The mathematics show that perhaps you are physically the James Quinn from the other world, that you did physically cross over. And that the James Quinn that was here before you, could have been bumped into another world, or another timeline. Or simply ceased to exist."

"What do you mean 'bumped' into another world? You mean, he might have swapped with me? He might be back in my world, and he might be living with Sarah right now?"

"An interesting thought. But one which is not possible. And I mean not possible. You see, the James that was here before you, may now be somewhere else, but he is most certainly not in your old world, with your old Sarah. That is proven by the fact that your world and mine, your new world, are still attracted to each other and intertwined. As I explained before, the attraction between your old world and this one is that your old world is missing your physical makeup. It wants the physical matter back. There is a hole in the energy/ matter balance of the world you used to exist in, and the timelines are still interacting with each other in an effort to fill the void where you used to be. If the James who used to be here, is now there, there would be no such hole, no such void. There would be balance. With no more timeline intersections occurring down on the Jubilee Line. No, that much is clear, perhaps the James who was here, is now in another timeline, or another world, somewhere else, but for sure, he isn't in the world where you used to be. And you should be very grateful for that. Because otherwise there would be no opportunity for you to jump back. You would be here for good."

I am silent for a moment. I am not too sure that I have completely understood what the Professor has just said, but I catch the sense of it. Especially the part about the hole that obviously still needs to be filled.

"James," he eventually says. "Do not worry about this thing. There is much that is strange about this phenomenon. But, I promise you, worrying about whether there is another James in your world, just now, is pointless and wrong. He is not there. There are only two things that you should think about: either you are here only temporarily, and that the family you love is alone and waiting for you in your other world, and that you will return to them soon, or…, that if you are stuck in this world for good, how you should adapt to your new life here, and for that, you should focus only on your search to find Sarah here, in this world."

I feel reassured by the Professor's words, and his logic. So, I decide that I must not worry so much about Sarah being alone in my old world…at least I shall try to think less about that, since there is little I can do but wait for the opportunity to jump back..., and when that will happen does not seem to be anything that I can influence. Instead, for now, I will worry whether or not she is going to respond to my letter in this world.

As the days roll by I become more nervous and more impatient. I carry my new Scotia mobile around with me at all times, permanently switched on, and I check it constantly, just in case I have missed a call, or I have accidentally switched it off.

Sarah will be back from holiday by now. She should have talked to Mary. She should have my letter. If she is going to, she should be calling me now, sometime soon. And yet, she doesn't. I don't hear from her. My mobile is terrifyingly quiet.

The only people who really call me are other people in advertising, Jane, or Scotia Telecom. So few people have yet bought mobiles in this world. Which all means that the market opportunity for growth in mobile sales is vast. I'm not a gambling man, but knowing what I do, it would be foolish not to do something with the knowledge, so I start to invest heavily in Scotia Telecom stock. For a while I wonder if it is wrong, and feel a little guilty, as if I could be accused of insider-trading. Not because I work with Scotia, but because I know just how successful the whole industry is going to become. If there is anything I can learn from my world, I know that now the mobiles satisfy the Health and Safety requirements of the European Union, that sales will soar. Soon everyone will be carrying one. Soon the industry will become one of the largest in the world. Mobile phones will become the new tobacco. Within two to three years, the stock will rocket, and I will be rich. Very rich. Enough money to support Jane and the girls… and any new family I may have with Sarah, should I ever find her…With my thoughts moving to Sarah, I decide to put half the shares in the names of Jane and the girls, and I feel a little better, knowing that I am helping secure their future, whether or not I am part of that future.

In the meantime, as the weeks pass, I ride the Jubilee Line as often as possible. Watching. Hoping. Ready and waiting...

Nothing.

The third week comes.

I am walking down the road from our offices towards Covent Garden, on my way to meet Stu Roberts in a pub after work.

My mobile rings.

I pull it out of my pocket, and look at the LCD display. "Unknown Number calling".

Interesting...

I hit the little telephone on the keypad, and speak.

"Hi, it's James."

There is silence at the other end of the phone, the sound of air.

"Hello?" I ask again.

More silence. I stop in the street and focus on the sounds at the other end of the phone. I hear breathing. Someone is there…

Click.

They hang up.

I go to *Call Register*, but there are no clues as to the number that called me. A wrong number? Perhaps.

The next day I am in my office. It is 1 pm I have just returned from lunch, and am about to review some files that Tracy has left on my desk.

The mobile rings, and I pick it up. *Unknown Number Calling.*

"Hello?"

Dead air.

A slight sound of breathing.

"Hello? Is there anyone there? This is James Quinn."

Click.

I am crossing the bridge above the Thames, midway between Embankment and Waterloo. It is 7 pm later that same day, and I am on my way home.

Phone rings.

Unknown Number Calling.

Pick it up. "Hello?"

No one.

This is becoming annoying. Who is it?

Then a thought hits me. A long shot. But maybe?

"....Sarah? Is that you?"

I can hear the sound of heavier breathing. Almost as if the name has got a response...

"Sarah, is that you?"

Silence.

Then "Click".

And then it hits me, that perhaps it was Jane.

Testing me.

I worry about this all the way home, but when she picks me up at the station she is in a good mood. I ask her if she tried to call me today, this evening, an hour ago. She says no.

"Why?"

"No reason. Someone tried to call, but couldn't get through. I thought it must be you."

Is Jane telling the truth? And if she is and it wasn't her...who was it?

By the end of the fourth week, I am very nervous. Sarah has not yet contacted me. Which means, that if she has chosen not to call, and if she has received the letter from her friend Mary, then my last chance of establishing contact with her is gone.

I'm 'at the bridge now'. And it's time to cross it.

Maybe Mary hasn't talked to her yet? How do I know if she has given her the letter? There's only one thing for it. I have to talk to Mary again…just to check…and to see if Sarah gave any reaction to Mary when she read the letter…

So Saturday morning finds me in the car, my dad being my alibi once again, and the pretext being a fishing trip somewhere north of the M25. Except this time, he actually comes with me. When we get to Ironbridge, it'll only take about twenty minutes to talk to Mary. The rest of the time, I could do with his company. In fact, why not get in a bit of fishing on the river while we're there?

The weather is surprisingly good for this time of the year. Next week will be the first week in November, and yet it's still warm, and the sun is shining.

It's two-and-a-half hours drive up to Ironbridge, and once again, the journey to see Mary brings with it a sense of foreboding. In my subconscious I can feel the stirrings of dark memories, even fear, an association to do with the time Sarah left me to stay with her, and the reasons she did.

I try to steer my thoughts away from this by talking to my dad, and for what I think must be the first time in my life, I ask my dad about how he courted my mother. How long did they go out for, what was dating like in his day, how did they get engaged? My dad, relaxed and enjoying the trip, the first time he's been out of London for months, opens up and tells me a lot that I never knew. I learn about their romance, the first time they kissed, and the night he got down on one knee during dinner in a restaurant in Paris, the first time they had been abroad together. We laugh together, we joke, and it's like talking to a good friend.

As we approach Birmingham, I fight with the temptation to ask him about the affair, who the other woman was, and how he met her. Then I remember the promise he made me make, and I manage to suppress it, and the conversation moves on.

The only time the conversation sours a little is when we briefly discuss the plan of action for the afternoon. My father is still uncomfortable with me pursuing another conversation with Mary. "Let it be", he says. "That avenue hasn't worked. You have to find another. If she got the message from Mary, she would have called you if she had wanted to."

We stop for lunch in small village somewhere outside Telford. Steak and kidney pie and mash. Good home cooking, washed down by a pint of Guinness.

We park down the road from Mary's house, and I walk along the street, leaving my dad in the car with a newspaper, but pretty sure that he'll soon close his eyes and take an afternoon nap. He won't miss me.

I knock on the door, and wait for the sound of the dog barking.

Silence.

I knock again, and then once more, but it soon becomes evident that no one is at home. Blast!

I am just about to turn and leave when a big wet tongue licks my cheek, and the weight of Sam jumping up on me from behind catches me off balance and pushes me against the door.

"Sam! *Sam!..Down boy!*" Mary is shouting, as she hurries up the garden path behind him. "Sorry," she says, grabbing his collar and pulling him off. "It's strange, but he really seems to like you…Sit, Sam, *Sit!* Good boy…" And now, turning to face me, "Sorry, we were just out for a walk, it's a fantastic day." She says, while her eyes ask *'What do you want?'*

"It's a lovely day. It's more like July than November." I reply. Small talk.

Then silence.

"I gave her the letter, James. She read it."

"Thank you. I just had to be sure…"

"So she didn't call you then? I didn't think she would," she replies.

"Why not?" I ask.

"Because we don't know you. Try as she could, she couldn't remember your name and when she looked through her old school photographs she couldn't find you."

"That's because I was sick the day the photos were taken. I couldn't stand being photographed when I was younger because I had so many spots…" I lie.

"James, I like you, I don't get any bad vibes from you, and Sam likes you too, and he's the best judge of character I know. But the thing is, it's up to Sarah, and what with all the shit she's been through with her ex-husband, she doesn't want anything to do with men just now."

"I was really hoping that maybe, you could have another word with her?"

Her look changes again, a few lines appearing on her brow as she becomes quite serious.

"Why are you so desperate to meet her? Is there more to this than you are telling me? Something else that I should know?"

I feel myself turning a little red.

"No." I reply quickly. "No, nothing…"

"Then just leave it James. I'll tell her you came up again, but I'm not going to push it. It's up to her. To tell you the truth, if it was the other way around, I don't think that I would call you if I hadn't met you before. Not because you're not nice or anything, but just because,…well, you know…you can never tell, can you?"

"I'm not an axe-murderer, I can promise you…*"I'm her husband!*

I'm wasting my time. The more I press it, the more desperate I'm going to sound, and the less likely it'll be that she'll say anything positive to Sarah. The best thing to do now is to bow out gracefully and try and leave her with the best impression possible.

"One last favour then, please" I ask. "Can you tell me where you think the best place is around here that I could maybe take my dad fishing. He's in the car, over there, and I brought him along for a bit of moral support and the promise of an hour spent on the river."

She turns and looks towards my car, seeing my dad asleep in the front seat.

"You brought your dad?"

"Yes, it's a nice day. Why not?"

"Well, I suppose you could try down underneath the bridge…there's a few big pools there, and you often see people down there…"

"Thanks." I pat Sam on the head a few times, smile at Mary, and start to back away, down the path. "…and I'm sorry to put you in an embarrassing position Mary. I didn't want to make you feel awkward. It's just that you were my last hope…"

As I close the gate, she is opening the door to her house. I'm a few steps away down the road, when she calls after me, "Okay, I'll call Sarah tonight. But if you don't hear from her next week, I would just drop it. Okay?"

I turn and shout back. "Fantastic!...And thank you, Mary."

But Sarah doesn't call.

That week.

The next.

Or the week after that.

CHAPTER 40
Farewell

November turns into December, and I slowly begin to resign myself to the inevitable. There will be no Sarah. She has chosen not to contact me, and except for one last avenue of hope, I can think of no other way to find her.

So, out of desperation, rather than anything else, I spend the last weekend in November driving round several more graveyards trying to see if I can find the grave of Sarah's mother-in-law, wherever it may be, and obviously assuming that she is already dead.

The graveyards bring with them that darkness that always descends upon me whenever I go near them, but I know I have no choice and I strive to overcome the urge to run as far away as possible from them. Systematically I tick them off the list.

But I come up with nothing, and eventually realise that it is a hopeless task. Who is to say that she isn't buried in Spain, or Norwich, or somewhere else? There are hundreds of graveyards in London. Hundreds. Without really knowing where she could be buried, I have no hope of finding her. I can't even find someone that is alive, so what chance do I have of finding someone when they're dead and not going anywhere fast.

It snows in December. Heavily, and incessant, and soon we are in the midst of the coldest winter I can ever remember. Winter bites hard and Britain grinds to a halt. The snow, several feet deep in places, blankets the cities with a mantle of white, the like of which I have never seen before.

It lasts two weeks, during which the only transport that functions reliably in London is the underground. Trains work only as far out as Wimbledon, and beyond that the tracks are covered beyond all help. Most people cannot make it into work, and few try. The schools close, and families find themselves with a long unplanned holiday.

In the second week, when the snow stops and the sun comes out, something magical happens.

Grown-ups rediscover the children hidden within us all. The streets turn into sledging tracks and skiing paths, and parents play with their children in the white manna, building snowmen and losing snowball fights to their sons and daughters who run around screaming and shouting, laughing and enjoying themselves like they haven't for many a year, the television and the Xbox a poor second to the magic white powder from the sky.

During this time I get to know Allison and Elspeth better, and I endeavour to be the father they wish I was. I try hard, but when I hear them screaming with excitement as I chase them around the garden with two big white snowballs, I cannot stop thinking of Keira and Nicole. Memories which build a wall around my heart, and leave it cold and unloving.

On the 28th of December I finally move into a separate bedroom from Jane. The result of a family Christmas which I find hard to endure. I find it difficult to continue to sleep in the same bed as her, the memories of Sarah, and Nicole and Keira unbearably strong, the smell of the pine needles on the Christmas tree bringing back far too many memories for me to run away or hide from. The dreams are becoming more frequent, and I can no longer endure the guilt I feel when I sometimes lie in bed with Jane in my arms, and think of Sarah.

"Just for now," I say to her, promising that it is only a temporary measure. "I just think it's best for now."

Jane takes it hard. She doesn't understand. And how can I expect her to?

"Just for now..." I promise. But we both know it is a lie.

Jan rolls into Feb, March comes and April showers rain down.

My life has become my life. A funny thing to say, but such is as it is. The life that I walked into one day has become my existence. I am resigned to live it as best I can. I have no other choice.

Jane and I live together, the two children keeping us together, along with convention and a fear that to leave them would be wrong. In some ways I find myself making atonement towards them for the cruelty and mistreatment I discover that I had wrought upon them in my past. Not me, but, well, me. For it was I that had the affairs with other women, it was I that belittled Jane and slowly took away her confidence, and it was I that neglected the children when they needed me most.

I have lost count of the number of people who have commented upon the new me. The *improved* new me. The new *caring*, sensitive me.

So the new caring sensitive me makes it my mission to build up Jane's confidence, to return to her the woman that I took away, and make her strong, reliant, and independent. In doing so I know that it is just a matter of time before one day she takes the decision to ask me to leave. A decision that will come probably sooner rather than later.

By April she is a different person than the one I came to know last August. We become friends, and truth be told, once again I start to become attracted to her. But only physically. I feel the lust of old returning. The desire. The strange feelings in my loins when I see her bath, or shower, or when I notice how attractive she looks in a new dress, or when the light catches her eyes just right, and I see a sparkle there that was missing only six months before.

Yet, this attraction I know now is only lust, and if there is any lesson I have learned over the past months, it is that lust and friendship are not enough. There must be something more for a relationship to work, something deeper, a connection, an understanding, a joining of the souls. Something that I only ever had with Sarah, but which I did not realise I had until too late. A magic which was once there, but which I lost, no, we both lost, when… but with this thought my thinking edges too close to the edge of the bottomless pit of despair, which once engulfed and almost drowned me. Almost.

I managed to climb out of the misery eventually, we both did, but now, for the first time since Sarah's post-natal depression, I remember how lost I was, and I realise how much both of us suffered. And I see for the first time, that perhaps as a couple we never did recover after all.

I must,...I have to..., understand why I started to lose interest in Sarah. Although every time I start to ever wonder about this, I start to remember feelings that are too painful to relive, to endure again…

A tear forms in my eye, and I swallow hard, then cough. Time to look away again, to think on something new. I think instead about the time I used to travel in to work, wondering about the lives that other people lived. Wondering, day after day, how green the grass would be on the other side, but naively not realising that there are many thousands of different types of grass. True, the grass I have now is green. But it is only a different shade of green. I realise now that a person should be careful what they wish for, and I long for the strong, vivid green grass that I used to feel beneath my feet and picnic on with Sarah and my girls...

Occasionally, *in spite of myself*, and truth be told, the blame does not lie entirely with me,---should there be guilt at all---, occasionally Jane and I have reached out to each other when passing in a room, or after a nice meal, or when the rain lashes against the window sill and inside the house there has been an abundance of warmth. Occasionally we have sought solace in each other's caress, and I have lost myself with Jane in the act of sex. Though not the act of love.

The word love is one that I have learned to respect and guard, and when we have woken in the morning in each other's arms, I have often tasted the tear that has trickled from my eye, and suffered from the guilt I have felt from sleeping with Jane, who is not my wife, yet is.

And so it is that the days and weeks turn to months, and the seasons swing around. When April appears, when the flowers begin to bud on the trees and the winter clouds begin to blow away, a new spring calls to us all.

Then one day the sun shines, and my dad calls on the phone.

"Let's go fishing," he says. "Let's go see Old Ralph!"

It's Sunday morning, and we decide to make it a family affair. We load up Jane's car, and drive down to the Riverside, parking the car at the front of the pub, and carrying a large picnic down to the river bank. Dad and mum are already there. My dad already has three small fish in the net, and he pulls them out of the river to show the children, who squeal and run away. We all laugh.

Jane and mum spread out the tartan rugs, and start to lay out the picnic. Dad and I chat, and I listen to my father recounting the tale of this morning's catches.

It's soon lunchtime and we all stretch out and start the feast, washed down by a couple of beers from the cooler. Occasionally my dad looks across at the rod, checking to see it's still okay, and watching for a bite, the line cast out into the deep pool on the other side of the river. After lunch I stretch out on the grass and bask lazily in the sun. I close my eyes, and begin to sleep.

I am woken roughly by the sound of my dad shouting with excitement.

"James, *James!* Get yourself over here now. It's Ralph!"

I jump to my feet, and rush to his side.

"How do you know?" I ask.

"It's him all right, son. Only he's that strong, and I can tell by the way he plays the line. He knows exactly what he's doing…You know, sometimes I can't make up my mind, if he's trying to catch me, or I'm trying to catch him."

He's smiling, and as he works the line, pleasure is written all over his face. This is what he loves doing best.

As I watch him in his eternal game of chess, a game of patience and cunning played between him and his old friend Ralph, I envy him. I have no such hobby that consumes me, that I enjoy as much as he obviously does this. Nothing that gets me out of the bed at the weekend, and away from the house.

For a whole hour I watch my father fight with his arch-rival. One moment he is reeling the line in fast, the next he lets it out and plays it in slowly. In the depths of the water, Old Ralph moves up and down the river, making full use of his space and his territory.

Twice, we refuel my dad with a bottle of cold beer. As the afternoon heats up, dad strips down to his vest, and soon the sweat is rolling off his head.

At first we all watch, excited and full of anticipation. Is this going to be the day, after twenty years of waiting, that dad will catch Old Ralph? Not unexpectedly, the girls quickly get bored, and mum and Jane take them along the river bank, in search of some ice-cream.

"There…there, look!" My father suddenly cries aloud, pointing to the water on the other side of the river. "Look, you can see him on the surface."

There is a splash, and I see a large fish thrash in the water. Then suddenly he jumps completely clear of the surface, clearly visible in all his majesty for a full second before he disappears back into the pool.

"Wow. He's massive!" I shout aloud and laughing.

"Bigger than before…he's grown…" my father shouts. "Blast! Bugger it! Bugger! He's jumped the line. He's free. The crafty beggar. He did that deliberately. Blast. He's gone."

The look of disappointment on my father's face is acute. He sits down on the grass, and lies back, breathing heavily. Now the effort is over, I can see how tired he is, and how exhausted the battle has made him.

"I almost had him. *I almost had him.* About twenty minutes ago, he was just about close enough to use the net. I can't believe it. I really thought that today was going to be the day!" he exclaims, whilst gasping for breath, lying flat on his back.

I sit down beside him, and offer him another cold beer. "So did I. I thought that this was going to be the day. I'm really sorry Dad. I really thought you'd caught him."

Then he is all smiles, and he begins to laugh.

"The crafty old beggar. He got away. I swear, that fish is cleverer than half the people I know." He says in-between laughs. "Never mind, I think that was officially another draw. You know, in a way I'm glad he got away. It means the battle goes on…Anyway, what would I do if I did catch him? No, perhaps it's better this way. We both live to fight another day. Here's to you, Ralph. You crafty old bastard!" he shouts at the river, lifting the bottle to his mouth and gulping down the beer.

The call came at 4.23 in the morning. The shrill tone of the phone ripping into my dream and tearing me away from the beach where I was playing in the surf with Nicole and Keira, throwing a ball back and forth between us and splashing in the waves.

As I scramble for the phone, reaching out to the side table beside my bed, I become quickly alert.

A phone call at this time in the morning can only be the bearer of bad news.

It's my mum.

"James…" She is in tears. I can hear her struggling for words, fighting an overpowering emotion. I jump up in bed, and flick the side light on. I know what is coming next. I have been here before. The same conversation, many years before.

"James. Please come quickly…it's your father. He's not moving…I don't know what to do."

"Is he still breathing?" I ask, already getting out of bed and grabbing my clothes, pulling on a pair of trousers.

"I don't know, I don't think so…he's lying face down."

"Where?"

"In the bathroom…he got up in the middle of the night and went to the toilet…he was taking ages, and he didn't answer when I called him…so I went to find him." The tears overcome her.

"Have you called the ambulance?"

"No…Just you. Oh, James, I'm scared…I think…I think he's dead!"

I stop for a second. The inevitability of the words and their finality bring me to a halt. They were not unexpected. I knew they would come. But to hear them again…

Now the nightmare starts. Except this time it is real.

"Listen, mum. *Listen* to me. He may still be alive. I want you to pay careful attention to what I say. Please take a cushion and some blankets into the bathroom. Cover him up and keep him warm. Make sure you're warm too. Lift his head slightly and make sure his face is clear of the floor…

"There's blood on his head…I think he hit it against the bath when he fell…"

"Mum, I'll be there in five minutes. No more. Hold on. I'm going to call an ambulance now. I'm hanging up now…I'll be there soon."

I call an ambulance, and tell them it's a heart attack. I run to Jane's bedroom. She is stirring, wakened by the sound of my loud voice on the phone, and my crashing around the bedroom trying to put on my clothes at the same time.

"Jane. It's my dad. He's had a heart attack. I have to go. I'll call you as soon as I know anything…look after the kids…Stay here. There's nothing you can do for now..."

I'm down the stairs and out the door within seconds. I take the Audi, and race through the suburban streets at seventy miles an hour. As I drive, my heart is beating out of control, thoughts rushing through my head.

When my dad died last time, I never made it to the hospital until he was gone. I never had a chance to say goodbye. To tell him I love him. *"Please God, Please let me get to him in time!"*

I glance at the clock. 4.36 am. The dying time. Statistically speaking, more people die between the hours of four and five in the morning, than at any other time. The time when the human body is at its lowest ebb.

I'm driving crazily and I know it, but I don't care. I have to get there.

Minutes later I swing round into my mother's street, and screech to a halt, slamming the car door shut without locking it and running up the garden path. I fumble with a key in the door, and take the stairs two at a time.

"Mum? *Mum?*"

I'm in the bathroom and by his side within seconds. My mother is a mess, crying uncontrollably, kneeling beside him, holding my dad's hand and stroking his hair. I put my arm around her gently and move her to the side, so that I can get access to my dad.

I touch his face. It is still warm.

Turning him gently on to his back, I put my head against his chest, desperately searching for a heartbeat.

Nothing.

I pull up his vest and put my ear against his white hairy chest.

A pulse, very faint, but still there.

I put my cheek against his nose and wait. A few seconds later, I feel the slightest current of warm air against my cold skin.

"He's still breathing mum!"

She looks at me and cries aloud, then leans over and whispers something in his ear that I can't quite make out.

I look at his head, a deep gash showing on the side of his temple, dried and caked blood covering the side of his face.

Suddenly the bathroom at the top of the stairs is filled with a pulsating yellow light coming from the street outside, and a few seconds later the doorbell rings.

"The ambulance is here mum. I'll let them in."

I rush down the stairs, and open the door. When I point to the top of the stairs, two paramedics rush past me, and by the time I follow them up, they are already kneeling by his side and at work.

"Is he okay?" I ask one of the paramedics.

"He's still breathing, but his pulse is faint and irregular. We need to get him to hospital immediately."

A few minutes later my mother and myself are in the back of the ambulance, sitting on a green bench holding hands while the paramedics attend furiously to my father. A drip. Oxygen. The works.

We're only a few minutes from the hospital when my dad opens his eyes.

My mother and I both stand up and reach out to him.

He tries to say something, but we can't hear what he says because of the oxygen mask. I grab his hand and lean closer. He tries to say something again, but I still can't hear. The sound of the engine, and all the machinery in the back of the ambulance creating such a din that it drowns out his words.

I squeeze his hand.

"Dad, I'm here with mum. We're right here with you…"

He turns his head a little towards us, and I see the corners of his lips turn up into a smile.

"I love you dad. I love you!"

He smiles back, and squeezes my hand, acknowledging that he heard what I said.

Then his eyelids close, and his body relaxes.

"I love you dad…" I whisper in his ear one last time, but this time he doesn't hear.

He is gone.

CHAPTER 41
The Funeral

There are not many people in this world who can claim to have been through the death of the same father twice. And it is no privilege.

The pain the second time around is every bit as great as the first, perhaps more. To have lost someone, then to be given them back, so that you have the opportunity to get to know them even better, to get closer, to bond with them on a new level…and then to have them taken away once again…Words cannot describe the feeling.

Instead there is just a dull, empty pit.

I would like to say that I am a grown man, that I know what life is about, and that I possess the secret of why we exist and what we are here for. That I can accept the passing of a friend and father, and accept it as being part of the great cycle of life. An inevitability. A natural, unstoppable moment in the sequence of existence.

But I can't.

The fact is, my dad just died. So I handle it the best way I can and I cry like a baby.

Tears shed more freely than before, for a father that helped me through not only one life, but two.

The suggestion to hold the wake at the Riverside was my mum's. A good choice, one that we all knew would make my dad smile.

So I drive down to the pub to discuss the arrangements on the Thursday evening, four days later and Gavin, the owner, meets me in the car park and shakes me warmly by the hand.

"I'm sorry. He'll be missed by us all," he says, his sentiments obviously very genuine.

He walks me into a private room at the back of the pub, and sits me down. Coffee appears, and we begin to look at menus, costs, and table decorations, the latter of which I decide against, because I know my dad would hate anything pretentious.

When it was all done, Gavin says he has something to show me, and I follow him to the back of the pub, to the edge of the river, each of us carrying a glass of whisky.

"James," he says, as we stand overlooking the water, the river black and still, and almost invisible in the dark of the night. "I've known your dad for about five years now, ever since I took over the lease of the pub from the last landlord. The number of times we've sat down here together talking about Old Ralph…" He takes a sip of his whisky, and I join him. "How long is it that they've been chasing each other for?" he asks.

"About twenty years, give or take a year." I answer.

"Wow. That must be some kind of record."

"Probably. I've always wondered how long catfish are meant to live for."

"If it is a catfish…?"

"My dad was quite sure it was."

"Who really knows? But once thing's for sure, they've known each other for longer than most people do, or most husbands and wives ever stay married for," he pauses. "Look, there's something that I was wondering about, James. When did your father die?" he asks, quite matter-of-factly.

"Early Monday morning. The death certificate says 4.52 am. Why?"

"James, something strange happened on Monday morning,…down here. Perhaps it's coincidence, perhaps not, but I know how I would like to think of it."

"What?"

"I came out here on Monday morning, to throw some scraps into the river…We always feed the fish with our scraps, it encourages the fish to stay round here…and I found Old Ralph. Dead. Floating on the water."

"How do you know it's him."

"I don't. But I'm pretty sure it is. He's the biggest and the oldest looking fish I've ever seen. He's massive. A real beaut."

"What killed him?" I ask, a bit taken aback.

"Old age?" he looks at me, and shrugs his shoulder. "I don't know. Maybe best not ask. If you think about it too much, it's a bit strange isn't it?"

"Not really. Actually, it doesn't surprise me. In some ways it makes perfect sense…" I realise. Equals until death, and all that. Neither the victor. "So what have you done with him?" I ask.

"Well, if you don't mind, I was thinking of having him stuffed, and I wanted your permission to hang him in the pub. Sally and I, that's my wife, and a couple of the regulars who knew your dad quite well, we were talking about it the other night, and we came up with the idea of naming the corner of the pub where your dad used to sit '*Charlie's Corner*'. It's got a good ring to it, don't you think? We want to hang Old Ralph in the corner above the window, and put a photograph of your dad in a frame underneath it. With some words."

My eyes start to mist over. I'm touched.

"I think we would all be very proud. And I know my dad would be too. If you don't mind though, can we read the wording before you frame it? I just want to make sure that you don't imply that my dad caught the fish. He would hate that. Ralph was his friend. A good, life-long companion. It's no coincidence that they both died on the same day. The question is, who died first? My dad, or Old Ralph?"

"I'm glad you like the idea. I've already sent the fish off to the taxidermists, and I'm hoping that we'll be able to unveil him along with Charlie's photograph at his wake? Would that be okay with you?"

"I can think of nothing better. Thank you."

I give him my hand, and I shake his in gratitude.

"So," I say, raising my glass to the river. "Let's drink a toast to friendship. To the fish and the fisherman. To my dad, Charlie Quinn, and to his best friend, Old Ralph!"

"Cheers!"

We both swallow the whisky, and after glancing briefly at each other and agreeing without speaking, we toss our empty glasses out into the middle of the river.

In the still of the night there are two quiet splashes.

One for Ralph, and one for my dad.

The funeral is set for 11.30 am on the Friday morning. It's a grey day, depressing, no sunshine. Low dark clouds drift across the sky above, threatening us all with rain. The dullness persists throughout the morning, and eventually it begins to drizzle. Horrible.

We all gather at my mother's house, and when the hearse arrives with my dad, my mother, myself and my dad's only surviving brother, Peter, climb into the second car. The rest, distant cousins, family and friends, fill the cars behind: one more black limousine, and five family cars.

The cortège makes its way slowly through the streets where my dad used to walk, past the local shops, the corner pub, and the British Legion, where he sometimes played darts with his friends.

Then we hit the main road and we pick up speed.

The service at the local church, where I used to go to Sunday school as a child, tries to be a celebration of my father's life, but I can find little to celebrate. My dad is dead. The service passes me by in a haze of emotion and I find it hard to concentrate. After an hour, following some words of comfort and a small sermon from the minister, some hymns which were my dad's favourites, and a Eulogy delivered by my uncle, we file out to the cars, and head off to the cemetery.

Tears fill our car, and I sit with my arm around my mother. Thoughts of my dad fill my head. There is only sadness. I can think of nothing to smile about this morning.

Déjà vu does not apply here. There is no 'feeling' that I may have done this before. I have. Five years ago.

More than anything since I arrived in this world, I find this the hardest to deal with. Images of my dad's last funeral flash constantly through my mind, and I know what is to come. The focus of all our attention, a single wooden box, covered in flowers and riding alone in the car in front.

There is one large difference this time around. He is to be buried not in Kingston, but in a small cemetery in Twickenham. Apparently, business has been too brisk since the time when my father first died. This time around, Kingston is full up.

As we pass through the gates to the cemetery and drive around the gravel path to the back of the graveyard, I try to be a man. I try to swallow my emotion and to hide my tears. Why?

Because that is what we are told to do. That is the image that we expect of a man. A real man does not cry.

The cars come to a stop, and we filter out of the black limousines, and form a line behind the coffin. My uncle and I help form one side of the pall-bearers and we carry my father's body to the grave. The hole in the ground where he will spend the rest of his days. The place he will rot, and turn to dust.

Dust-to-dust.

None of us believe that we will ever die. We are all immortal. When we visit graveyards, we see the headstones, the markers of past lives, lived and gone, shadows on the edge of time, and still we fail to believe that we will ever end up in the ground ourselves.

Only when we stand on the edge of the hole, and look down onto the coffin of someone that we have truly loved and laughed with, do we ever start to realise that one day, we too will end up down there. All of us. No exception.

The cause of death?

Birth.

I have done this twice. I am angry now, my thoughts becoming strange and a little bitter. Why, why does this have to happen…

This is the third person I have had to bury in five years, and two of them have been the same person. And the third, …no, even to this day the memory remains so painful that I cannot allow myself to think of it…*not at all!* So, as I have done for so long now, I completely blank the other funeral from my mind, and focus instead on my father, and today. I will bury him today for the second time around…

…And now it's my turn to say something at the graveside.

I calm down, step up to the edge of the deep hole and think of my father.

I speak without hearing what I say, but conscious that I want to say something that would make my dad proud. I am his son. He is my father, and here I am to say, in a few words, what he meant to us all.

Impossible.

I say some words that I had prepared in my mind, and hope that I have done him proud. I finish up by telling them all the story of Old Ralph. Two friends that died the same day.

By now it is raining harder, and we are all standing around under black umbrellas, hiding ourselves from the sky.

The world is grey. My emotion is grey. My heart is grey.

At the end of the short service, we mingle with the other mourners who have come to the graveside, shaking hands and hugging each other. I find I cannot cope any longer, and I sneak off to catch myself. I need some space.

I walk in a daze, getting slowly drenched in the rain, but finding the cold water refreshing and exactly what I need. For a few moments I cry like a baby, the release welcome and needed, and as my shoulders shake with the flow of emotion, I steady myself on a gravestone. No one hears me. My tears are lost amongst the pillars of past lives, each one marking a human story, most long forgotten, past and gone.

When the sobs subside, my mind begins to clear, and sight begins to return to my tired eyes. The rain is getting lighter now, and I turn to walk back to the car.

I stop.

I hesitate.

A feeling, a tingling sensation on my neck. A sense of something that I should do…

Something urging me to pay attention…

I turn around and look back at the headstone where I have just stood and rested in my moment of grief, looking down at the black granite stone, and reading the light blue, chiselled lettering:

"Martha Turnstone.
Born 3rd April 1939
Died 4th June 2008

Mother and friend, and
Sorely missed by
Daughter Sarah."

Sarah's mother!

A sudden overpowering sensation of my father by my side, a warm feeling of love, of his presence. A moment, where, stupid though it may sound, I feel almost as if his hand is upon my shoulder.

And then I hear his voice, coming to me from deep within, a memory taken from only a few months back, when we last spoke of Sarah.

"Listen Son, if there was anything that I could do to bring you together with the woman who could make you as happy in your life as I have been in mine, then I would. I would do anything for you son, even if it was the last thing I did..."

I walk back to my father's grave, and look down onto the casket below.

"Thanks dad." I say.

And for the first time today, I smile.

CHAPTER 42
Hope

In the weeks following my dad's 'first' death, my mother turned in on herself, and began to lose interest in everything, except mourning my father. She locked herself in her home, didn't eat, and shut herself away from her friends.

I have been here before, the last time my father died. For three years she was a shadow of her former self and if it hadn't been for the understanding and constant attention from her friends and neighbours, the local nurses and home helps, and whatever I could do for her too, she would have died soon after my dad. I'm sure of it.

I am also mourning my father. But the strange experience in the graveyard when I felt his presence and his hand upon my shoulder…it has given me something to hold on to, something to focus on.

Hope.

The hope that I will find Sarah, and the knowledge that my dad has led me to her, is a great comfort. I feel as if he is with me now, by my side, watching over me, and waiting for me to find Sarah and start the rest of my life.

The unfortunate thing is that I cannot tell my mum about this. Even though it would give her great comfort if she knew what he had done, it would generate more confusion than it was worth. Instead, the best I can do, is to be there for her as much as I can. When my father died for the first time almost six years ago, she behaved the same way. After three years of isolation, and being withdrawn, constantly tearful and weak, she only began to take an interest again, when one night we persuaded her to go to an event organised at the British Legion. A bingo night.

It sounds really sad, very unimaginative, but there was something there that night that she latched onto. She lost herself in the excitement, in the thrill of the balls coming up with her chosen numbers, and the company of a hundred other silver or purple-haired ladies, most of them in the same situation as her. The thing is, it worked. So I didn't mock it. But this time around we won't wait for three years. I'll give her several months to mourn, then I'll take her to an evangelical Bingo night. Out of her front door, back into the world, and with other people again. Even if I have to kidnap her to do it.

As time slowly begins to fill in the widening space between the night dad died and now, thoughts of making 'the jump' are still ever-present. I still dream, almost every night, of my children and Sarah, and my little house where I used to live, but there is little I can do about it. I continue to travel on the Jubilee Line at every possibility, and I feel frustration when nothing happens. The opportunity to 'jump' seems highly elusive. Perhaps it will never happen again. So instead, I focus on the future in this world. And Sarah.

A week after the burial, I go back to the graveyard, carrying two bunches of flowers. First of all, I go to see my dad's grave. We have already decided on the headstone, and the epitaph that will go on it: black, polished granite, with little flecks of mica that will catch the sunlight and sparkle, the words in the stone glistening gold and etched deep into the granite so that they will not fade with time.

"Here lies Charles Edward Quinn.
Father, Friend, and Fisherman.

Born 5th September 1947
Died 8th April 2013

Much missed by his wife and family."

Except for the dates, it will be the same epitaph as he had on his other stone, which was also black polished granite.

I imagine how the stone will look, and laugh when I remember how I once overheard my mother arguing with my father one night, a long time ago. My father had read a joke in the paper, an epitaph on some cartoon, which said,

"*Here lies Joe Smith, Hypochondriac and worrier.
I told you I was ill!*"

And, in between laughs, he was suggesting that he should have the same thing written on his gravestone. "Over my dead body," my mum had argued. "No, over mine." he had replied.

Well, my mum won, as she always does. Instead, he got the respectable epitaph he deserved. Both in this world and the other.

After placing the flowers gently on the ground where the headstone will go, after a few minutes of silent thought, I wander over to the grave of Sarah's mother.

Last week, after the funeral, there was so much emotion going through my head, that I hadn't noticed if there was a vase at the base of the stone. But thinking about it over the past couple of days, I was sure that there would be one. And I knew that if there was one, there would be some dead irises in it. Sarah's mother's favourite flowers. Which Sarah always made an annual pilgrimage to replace on the anniversary of her mother's death. One visit each year. Which in this world will be on the 4th of June.

Less than seven weeks away.

As I approach the headstone, my heart leaps as I see the vase, lying on its side, blown over by the wind. I kneel down, lifting it up and setting it down firmly again, steadying it with a small rock. Taking out the dead irises, I lie them neatly at the base of the headstone, and replace them with my large bouquet of carnations. Her next favourite flowers.

They look good.

I stand by the grave for a while, full of hope. I close my eyes and try to think of Sarah. I see her face fill my mind.

She is smiling.

Then slowly, she starts to move away from me, running towards the swing at the bottom of the garden…

I open my eyes quickly, my heart beginning to race… It's the vision again, that same sequence of memory that starts to run whenever I conjure up Sarah's face in my mind. I know what will happen next. I *know* that any moment now a rush of emotion will hit me, and I will start to feel bad. *Very* bad.

Feeling a little unsteady, I move towards Sarah's mother's headstone, and steady myself on the cold granite, catching my breath.

"Why?" I almost shout aloud. "What is it that makes me so scared? And why do my feelings for Sarah change so dramatically as the sequence rolls forward? Is my subconscious trying to tell me something?"

Clenching my fists into tight balls, I wrap my arms around my chest, and throw my head back to the sky. I know what I have to do. The only way to find out what scares me so much is to let the sequence finish, to go where it is going, and to ride the wave of fear until I see what lies on the other side.

So I close my eyes, picture Sarah again, and a moment later she is running down the garden path towards Keira, who is, like before, crying for her mummy to push her on the swing.

I call to her. "Turn around, smile at the camera!"

Sarah turns.

The fear, the dread, the sadness hits me like a wave.

Sarah is pregnant.

My fists tighten more, the muscles in my arm straining with the pressure, my eyelids flickering as I fight the urge to open them and let it all end.

I fall to my knees, still riding the wave.

…Sarah is facing me now. Large, beaming with happiness, so motherly, her pregnancy almost full term…Keira behind her…

And then it happens. I hear another voice. Behind me.
"Daddy. Daddy…wait…photograph me too…"
It’s the voice of little Nicole.

CHAPTER 43
The Dome Bash

Two weeks later Jane and I are on the train on the way into London. Tonight is going to be the first of several large events that we have put together to be staged at the Dome, the first of a programme in which we will re-launch the Dome as *the* Entertainment venue for London, for concerts, stage-shows, and large conferences.

And what better way to start than with a Concert to launch the campaign for the British Olympics in London, with all the money raised going to a new charity providing sponsorship to encourage and support future British Olympians. The concert has taken months to organise, and will be attended by King Harry, Sting, Elton John, the Mayor of London, a string of famous world athletes, and a host of entertainers and singers taken from the current West End musicals.

It promises to be a fantastic evening and we are both really looking forward to it. I'm proud of what has been organised by my team, along with help from the Dome, and the British Olympic organisation.

We arrive at Waterloo, and decide to walk across the bridge, instead of catching the Jubilee Line straight up to Hyde Park. It's a fantastic evening, and the evenings are already beginning to get very warm.

Recently Jane and I have been getting along well, and our relationship has been very cordial. No more arguments---not that there were many in the first place---, and we have been laughing and speaking about important subjects, not just about the children. I can see her confidence building, and I like it. She is blossoming, becoming a better Jane, and I sense that she can feel it too. She likes the new her.

Jane walks beside me, arm-in-arm. We walk through the station, down to the river's edge, and then up on to the bridge. The view is wonderful. A good evening to be up in the London Eye. The sun is on the way down, the sunset flooding the river with incandescent oranges and yellows, which bounce off the undulating surface and wash over the buildings all around, the vista becoming one single, vast Monet landscape. Boats are passing by underneath, people waving from the upper decks, people in evening dress walking along the embankment, making their way to concerts or theatres on the South Bank.

As we cross the bridge, passing the spot at the top of the stairs where I habitually hurry past to avoid the "Good Evening, have you got any spare change?", followed by the standard "THANK you, And HAVE a GOOD EVENING", delivered in that ultimate line of pure sarcasm that they all seem to master, it dawns on me that I have never once been accosted by a single beggar since I arrived in this new world.

Not once since last August have I passed someone crouched beneath a blanket at the top of the stairs, stroking a dog, and nursing an almost empty can of cider. Not once I have been offered a "Big Issue" and not once has someone paraded up and down the night train from Waterloo to Surbiton, saying "Excuse me Ladies and Gentleman, I'm not going to ask you for any spare change, but can you lend me a tenner till next Tuesday? I need just a few pounds to get into the shelter for tonight?"

What, you mean the shelter that officially closed an hour ago?

I'm dying to ask Jane what's happened to all the beggars? Has she ever heard of the *Big Issue*? Surely, the problem hasn't just gone away?

I can't believe I haven't noticed it before.

But I can't ask her about it and I can't mention it. So I just have to pretend as if it is normal, and just add it to the growing list of differences between my world and this.

When we get to the other side of the river, we cross 'underneath the arches' and walk up the pedestrian precinct to Charing Cross Tube station, then down into the Jubilee Line.

The trains are almost empty. The rush hour is gone, and most people tonight are taking advantage of the beautiful evening and are walking to wherever they are going.

A tube arrives, we let an old lady off, and we get into a carriage in the middle of the train.

For what seems like the thousandth time since my big "C" day, I nervously watch as the doors on the Tube begin to close. A moment of anticipation, while a swarm of butterflies fly around my stomach.

Then the doors close, a lurch forward, and the tube disappears into blackness.

Nothing.

By now, I am used to it, and the moment of hope disappears instantly and is replaced with conversation with Jane. I have almost given up hope of anything happening again. It may never do. And the momentary pulse of expectation followed by the continuation of my life in this world, is as automatic to me now, as the sound of air hissing from the doors when they close, and nothing happens.

It's just another normal evening. Except not quite.

It's not every evening you get to meet Elton John or Sting or Andrew Lloyd-Webber. In fact, I must admit that this is probably the only time in my entire life, ---and I can take my pick from two---, that I have partied with the stars. But at the after-show party, I mingle with them as if it's an everyday occurrence, laughing and joking, and resisting the incredible temptation to whip out a ballpoint pen and ask someone to sign a napkin. Not for me, please, but for a friend, you understand...

Jane of course, is ecstatic.

"I can't believe I just shook hands with the King!" she says, still almost speechless, a whole hour after we are introduced to King Harry.

"He's just a normal human being," I say," ...except for the fact he's richer than almost any other human being on the planet." I still find it amusing that the freckled 'ginger' from Eton is now the head of the European Monarchy. How on earth did that happen?

Call me a Republican. And call him a Publican. After all, that's where he has spent most of his life so far. Drinking beer, and chasing women.

'Nuffsaid.

Except Jane won't let it lie, and we end up in a group of semi-plastered guests, all wearing Black Tie and Evening Gowns, discussing the ultimate question: "*The King? Parasite and tax-dodger, or the Ultimate Ambassador for British tourism and trade?*"

Knowing that Jane and I will never agree on this one, I side-step the group and wander round the inside of the Dome, swiping another couple of sparkling champagne flutes from a nearby passing waiter.

"Stu?", I call, spying him in the middle of the arena, surrounded by a gaggle of beauties. I hand him a fresh glass, and drag him off to the side, and soon we are discussing the old days again, chatting about our old girlfriends, and reliving our uni conquests.

About two o'clock, the party starts to wind down, and Jane and I decide to leave. My mother is sleeping over at our house tonight, babysitting the kids, so we're in no rush to get home, but I'm tired, and I want to catch the tube back to Waterloo.

Which is another of the positive differences that has pleasantly surprised me about my new London. Twenty-four hour drinking licences, so you can always find a decent pub whenever you go out, no matter what time of day, and transport links that run throughout the night, and which don't shut down and leave people stranded in the middle of the city, pissed and with no way to get home.

In other words, this London is a truly cosmopolitan city, right up there beside Paris, and Rome. You can enjoy it at any time of the day or night, and you're never under pressure to drink two pints of beer quickly before closing time, before you run for the last train, and find yourself bursting for the toilet and nowhere to go when the old train breaks down half-way between Waterloo and Clapham Junction.

This London has come of age.

So why do I still miss the old one?

By now the alcohol has begun to wear off, and I am almost sober. Jane, on the other hand, is quite merry. Which is putting it diplomatically. Pissed as a fart, would be a more accurate description. So we walk down into the tube station, her giggling away and me supporting her with one arm around her waist and the other holding onto her hand.

When a tube finally arrives, we climb onto an almost empty train, and sit down in a seat close to the door, on the opposite side of the carriage, not because I choose to, but because that is where Jane quickly falls. I sit down beside her, prop her up, and she nuzzles in against me. She is wrapped around my arm, cuddling it, her eyes closed, and contentment written all over her face. She has had a good evening.

The tube pulls into Green Park, and the only other people in the carriage get off. We pull away, and hurtle off towards Charing Cross, where the platform is a little more busy, and a motley ensemble of drunk Londoners and red-eyed tourists clamber aboard. Only two people get into our carriage, a man and woman, who sit as far away from us as possible, and proceed to start snogging as soon as they sit down.

A tingle goes down the back of my neck, and I feel slightly strange. I look up, immediately alert. I know this feeling.

The doors are beginning to close.

Quick. Find the name of the tube station. Where…where…Yes! There it is…Charing Cross. Charing Cross. Yes, there! The words are beginning to shimmer, to change…

Already it is happening. Time slowing down. Beginning to freeze.

The doors are half of the way closed, but now moving almost imperceptibly slowly.

I glance across at the couple, still kissing each other at the other end of the carriage, but already they have become mannequins, joined at the mouth, their tongues stuck deep into each other's throats, frozen saliva glistening on the edges of their tongues, the man's hand motionless and solid, the fingers of his hand caressing the woman's right breast underneath her jumper.

I react instantly. This is the moment I have been waiting for and anticipating every day that I have travelled on the Jubilee Line for the past five months. This is it…

Already I can see onto the platform outside, the friendly, much missed colours and design of Westminster station platform, two people walking past the open doors. In the other world. My world.

Without further thought I lunge forward, surging upwards from my seat, the path between me and the open doors clear, and unimpeded.

I leap up, but am immediately jerked back down into my seat. I turn in panic, pulling at my arm, realising with horror that Jane, frozen solid and immovable, is firmly latched onto my arm, in a death-like grip that I cannot shake off, violently as I try.

I look back to the door, the sign on the wall outside "Westminster", clear and steady. The doors half-open, but frozen still. An open gateway back into my world.

I pull again, as hard as I can, but nothing gives. I'm left panting loudly, my own loud breathing the only sound I can hear. Around me everything else is eerily quiet.

I am trapped in a soundless void. Lost in a world of deathly, cold, silence.

"*Shit!*" I shout, turning to Jane, contorting myself and pulling, pushing, jerking, trying everything and anything to free myself from her.

Her eyes are closed and she seems totally oblivious to my attempts to break free and escape. Her face and body, wax-like in appearance, neither alive, nor dead.

"Jane, please let me go. *Please...*" I beg of her.

But she cannot hear me.

And then the sound of the doors beginning to move again.

Closing.

Accelerating together.

I turn quickly and watch in a mixture of pure panic, horror and indescribable frustration as the two metal doors meet in the middle.

Suddenly a wall of sound hits me, and I fall forward onto the floor, my arm whipping itself free from Jane's grip. Jane falls sideways onto the padded seat where I was just sitting and wakes with a jolt.

The couple further down the carriage momentarily break off from their passionate fumbling, and glance over at me sprawling on the dirty carriage floor.

"James...?" Jane says, "What's going on?", pulling herself upwards, and pushing out her chest and breathing deeply as if she was just waking from a hundred year sleep.

"Nothing, I tripped."

I sit up beside her, and she snuggles up again, eyes immediately closed, and asleep by the time we pull into Embankment tube station.

Close to tears, I bite my lip, and count.

That was the third time it has happened.

Which means that I have only one more chance.

One more chance to cross back to my world.

Or be trapped here for good.

CHAPTER 44
Paying it Forward

The irony of it all is not lost on me as I spend the next few days repeatedly going over the whole event in my mind. Over and over again. And then some more.

I was free to leave…the door to my world was there, right before me. But Jane held me back. My wife in this world prevented me from going back to my wife in the other.

I can't help but feel some inner anger at this, even though I know it was not really Jane's fault. She didn't know. It was just an unfortunate turn of events.

Still, the anger boils over a few days later, and Jane and I end up having a massive row. The children hear us and dissolve into tears upstairs in their bedrooms, and Jane doesn't speak to me for a week.

I feel bad.

It wasn't her fault. So why do I take it out on her?

The silence in the house becomes unbearable. *Jane's* children,…Jane's children…want to speak to Daddy, but their loyalty to their mummy zips their mouths closed, and they trail around the house after Jane, following her from room to room, avoiding big bad daddy, but really not understanding why they must.

Walking the empty streets of Thames Ditton, Hinchley Wood and Surbiton at night seems an easier option than hiding in one of the rooms at home, and it gives me the chance to think. I seem to have lost control over everything in my life, and my mind is in turmoil, perpetually dredging my subconscious for the links that will pull it all together and help it make sense.

There is so much to think about…so much…The recent events on the tube, the search for Sarah, and the aftermath of the memory I forced myself to relive at Martha's grave…

It scares me. I am an emotional mess.

The next night I am returning from work, and a woman and young boy get on the train at Clapham Junction. Sitting down opposite me, the blonde boy, probably not more than four years of age, plays with a little plastic soldier for a while before closing his eyes and resting his head against his mother's arm. A moment later he is fast asleep, his mother gently stroking his face as she stares vacantly out of the window.

His hair is soft, and there is a little scar above his left eye, freckles on his nose, and a scratch on his knee. Without realising it a tear forms and slowly rolls down my cheek.

The woman opposite me turns from the window and starts to watch me.

"Are you okay?" she asks, gently.

At first I do not notice that she has spoken to me, but when she asks again, I blink and turn my head slightly to return her gaze.

"Yes…Thank you…I'm fine…" I reply quietly, but then continue, feeling compelled to explain further to this mother…"I'm sorry. It's just that your son,…he…," I mumble. "...I've always wanted a son…and your boy looks just like what I thought my son would look like…if…*if...*"

The little boy stirs, his hand rising involuntarily to rub the tiredness in his eyes.

I feel uncomfortable, embarrassed, and dangerously close to the edge. Time to leave.

I rise quickly to my feet, muttering something more to the woman before walking along the train to the next carriage.

I find a seat and sit in silence for the rest of the journey home.

Two days later I arrive at work to find that Claire, my ex-PA is waiting for me in reception.

"I have a job for you, James. I want you to handle the advertising and marketing for 'Find-A-Friend!' We are launching in two month's time, and we want you to manage it."

I'm pleased for her. I honestly am. It's exciting. I agree to the job, and we even quote her a 'special' price. After all, Cohen's looks after its employees, past and present.

Later that afternoon I call Professor Kasparek up in Edinburgh and tell him about the incident on the tube a few days before. One of my parting promises to him when I visited him up in Edinburgh, was that I would keep him up to date on anything else that might happen to me. We had both joked, that if he never heard from me again, then I must have done the jump.

He is excited, and listens in great detail as I explain to him what has happened. I can hear him furiously scribbling down notes, and I can tell he is genuinely concerned when I explain how the opportunity was there, but how I was prevented from taking it by Jane hanging on to me, anchoring me to this world.

He also finds it particularly interesting when I tell him how there was a complete absence of any sound, except for my own breathing. He hadn't expected that, but as soon as I mention it, he agrees that it makes some sense.

Equally exciting to him is my observation that although time had seemed to stand still on my side, I could see movement beyond the doors on the Westminster platform: people walking past the doors normally, time passing for them at the same rate that I alone was experiencing it in the other world.

We talk for an hour, and I tell him about my father, the graveyard, and finding Sarah's mother's grave. When we finish, I promise to call him again in a few weeks' time, after I have been to the graveyard to meet Sarah. Before we hang up, I ask him if he can check his calculations again. Is there really only one more chance for me to cross back to my world? Please can he verify it?

When I leave work that night, my mind is alive. Full of thoughts, and worries.

On the negative side, I am worried shitless that the next time it happens, I won't make it in time to cross over. What if something else prevents me like Jane did this time. I kick myself for ever having relaxed my vigilance, for sitting with Jane and letting her hold onto my arm. It was the alcohol that relaxed me, and the fact that I had ridden the tube a million times without incident. I had got complacent. I think about how in future, I must take every precaution when riding the Jubilee Line. I even consider giving up drinking alcohol, and joining a gym, just to ensure I am as strong as possible, and fit and sober, whenever the next time occurs.

I am convinced now that it will happen again. I can feel it in my bones. I promise myself, no I swear to myself, that I will not make any more mistakes.

The next time it happens I *will* cross over. I will react instantly whenever the opportunity presents itself, and I will not delay by thinking about anything else when it does. The moment I see the doors slowing down, the moment time starts to grind to a temporary halt, I am jumping through those doors. I'm out of here.

Buoyed up by my new found self-determination and courage, I turn my thoughts to Sarah, and I start to plan for my meeting with her on the 4th June.

Only a couple of weeks away.

The days tick slowly by, and my nights becoming increasingly more restless. I toss and turn, and cannot relax. My dreams become confused, and I dream over and over again, about what will happen on the 4th June.

There are basically two different dreams. In one of them I am driving to the graveyard, when my car breaks down. I try to fix it, but cannot. So I abandon the car, and start to walk. Although in real life I know exactly how to get to the graveyard, in my dream I become hopelessly lost. I am walking through streets I don't recognise, going round and around in circles. I ask people where the graveyard is but no one has ever heard of it. The hours begin to pass, and I begin to panic that I won't make it. By the time I get there she will have come and gone…I will miss her! I become more and more desperate. I start to run, faster and faster, but I get nowhere. A feeling of dread permeates the dream, and eventually I break down in tears in a street I do not recognise.

As I am standing in the middle of the street, I look up and I suddenly find myself in front of the gates to the graveyard. A car is coming out of the entrance, and as it passes me I see the faces of Nicole and Keira peering out of the windows from the back seat. Sarah is driving the car. And another man is sitting in the passenger seat. I hear Nicole shout at the man, and the words "Daddy, please can I have an ice-cream?" come through the window.

Daddy?

But the man in the front seat is *not* your daddy… *I am*!

I try to wave the car down, but I cannot move. My body is frozen solid, like the statues on the tube when time slows down. As the car sweeps past me, Nicole and Keira press their faces against the windows and make a face at me. They do not recognise me.

And then the car is gone.

I always wake up sweating, the bed drenched through, and twice I have had actual tears rolling down my cheeks.

Once, Jane is sitting on my bed, watching me.

"Who is Sarah?" she asks when I open my eyes. "*Please* tell me…"

The other dream is altogether much more pleasant. I drive right into the graveyard in my car…which curiously enough is my old car, the trusty Ford Mondeo, …and park near Sarah's mother's grave. Sarah is already there. Her back is turned to me, but as I get out of the car and walk towards her, she turns, sees me and smiles.

We rush towards each other, hug, kiss, and make love.

I prefer the second dream.

Give credit where credit is due, and praise those that deserve it. That's my maxim.

So, in all this time, why haven't I personally contacted John, the taxi-driver that showed me such a friendly helping hand on my big 'C' day?

No excuses.

But today, I'm going to rectify the situation. Something has come up, that could just be the way to say thanks.

Breezing into reception, surprisingly happy and chirpy, June 4th only one week away, I walk up to Alice behind the reception desk, and greet her with my best smile.

"Morning wonderful. How are you today?"

"Good. And you? And what do you want?" she says, cocking her head to one side, a playful smile on her lips.

"Oh, nothing. Just wanted to see how you were." I protest.

"Rubbish. I know you. I'm Alice, remember. So, what do you want?"

"Okay, okay. Can you remember last year I gave you the card of a taxi-driver, and asked you to use him as much as possible? Have you used him at all?"

"John? Yes. Lots. He's very reliable, and very popular. Richard likes him especially. Why?"

"Good to hear, but it doesn't surprise me. Can you do your best to get him for me this morning. I need to go up to Hyde Park. Anytime between 10 and 11am. Just let me know when, but try to make sure it is him."

At 10.32 am I walk out of the office and get into the back of John's cab. John turns around when I climb in, and starts to say "Hyde Park, Marble Arch end or Buckingham Palace end?", but when he sees my face, he bursts into a broad smile.

"Morning, guv'nor…Excuse me for saying so, but don't I know you?"

"Yes, you do. Morning John. About eight months ago you came to my aid when I was throwing up outside Waterloo, and you took me to Canary Wharf, and then up to Portman Square?"

"Yes…Yes.. Now I remember. Hey, you look a lot better today than the last time I saw you," he replies, already driving down to the Seven Dials monument and turning towards Tottenham Court Road. "How are you?"

"Fine. Very good in fact."

"Sorry, I can't remember your name, but you've remembered mine. What is it, mate?"

"James."

"James. Say, James, do you work at Cohen's then?"

"Yes, I do."

"Right…Now the penny's beginning to drop. You wouldn't have anything to do with all the business I've been getting from them, would you?"

"Maybe, maybe not. I just gave your card to our receptionist and asked her to use you whenever we could. You seemed very reliable to me, and from what I hear, you are."

"Thanks mate. It's amazing. Cohen's have practically adopted me, and I get lots of calls. A lot of business. You guy's sure do spend a lot on taxis. But how come I haven't seen you at all then?"

"Oh, these days I mostly go by tube. It's much quicker." I reply, but move quickly on. "John, do you mind me asking, do you work for yourself, or for a company, or taxi-firm?"

"I used to. But when they changed the taxi licence laws, way back then, I bought my own black cab, and nowadays drive for myself. Hence the card…"

"Good. I thought so. That's what I wanted to talk to you about. Listen John, I can't explain why, but that day when you came to see if I was okay at Waterloo, and the way you showed genuine concern for me afterwards, it really meant something to me. I, …let's just say, I was going through a pretty bad patch then. Things weren't exactly going well for me that day. You could say, in fact, that it seemed as if my world had just come to an end…Anyway, the thing is, you did me a big favour and showed me some real human kindness at a time I really needed it…so I want to thank you. The point is, Cohen's is an advertising, PR and marketing agency, and next month we are running a full page ad in the Sunday Times. It's already paid for, along with the cost of the artwork, although that has not been created yet. The only thing is the customer who paid for it has just gone bust. It looks like the space is just going to be wasted."

John is listening. I have his attention.

"So… since I owe you a big favour, I was thinking maybe that I could run an ad for you?"

"What do you mean?" he asks, sounding a little nervous.

"I mean a full page ad in the Sunday Times, saying anything you want it to say. How about something like: *'Need a friendly taxi? Reliable. Discreet. Respectable rates. Call the Personal Cab Company on blah blah blah.'*, or something like that. Or anything else you want it to say. It's your ad.. So you tell us what to print and we'll do it. The way I see it, this is your chance to get a lot of business, maybe even start your own company, or just do it for a laugh, if nothing else. The thing is, the space is going to go to waste, so I thought you might want it?"

"Are you serious? It's not April the First is it?" he laughs.

"Totally serious. All you have to do is say yes, and then come into our office next week, and tell us what wording you want in the ad and we'll do the graphics and the layout for you for free."

"You're not kidding?"

"Nope."

"Blimey…"

It's the first time I've heard him speechless. That's a first. A taxi driver with nothing to say.

CHAPTER 45
Sarah

I wake up on the morning on the 4th June, both excited and scared.

Today is the day.

If Sarah turns up at her mother's grave, and we meet, the path of my future in this world will change. Either for good, or for bad. And the latter is not something that I can contemplate.

But, if she doesn't come today, then I am destined to wait for another whole year, another 365 days of thinking, wondering, hoping. My life on hold for another twelve months.

For now though, there is only one possibility that I focus on. Sarah will be there.

It is a Tuesday, and officially the office believes I am on a speculative visit to a new client. My mobile will be switched off. I will not be contactable.

I arrive at the graveyard at 8.55 am. The gates open at 9.00 am. On the way over, I stop at the flower seller in the middle of Surbiton High Street, and buy several bunches of flowers, including one of irises.

Last night, I put several garden tools into the back of my car, and when the cemetery gates open, I drive close to my father's grave, unload my tools, and slowly start to clean up the plot, cut the grass, and do anything I can around the grave to drag out the time: I don't want to be arrested for loitering with intent, so I need some reason to be here for as long as it takes.

All the while, I am keeping a keen eye out for anyone approaching Sarah's mother's grave, which is only about twenty yards away.

By eleven o'clock, it's starting to get really warm, and I strip off down to a t-shirt. I take another break, probably my third so far, and pour myself a cup of tea from my flask.

By three o'clock, I've had eight breaks, have eaten all my Mark's and Spencer's sandwiches, drunk all my tea, and I'm in imminent danger of completing everything I can think of doing around my dad's grave. One thing's for certain, it's got to be the cleanest grave in London.

Three times I have false alarms, and three times I almost die from excitement, stress and disappointment, all rolled into one. Her mother's plot is between myself and the entrance to the cemetery and three times I see women walking along the path, towards her mother's grave.

I strain to see their faces, but as they come closer, then continue walking past, I see that they are not her, and that one of them is even in her sixties.

By quarter to four, I am beginning to give up hope.

Surely, if she was going to visit the grave she would have come by now. Is there any way I could have missed her? The only time I have been away from the graveside the whole day, was when I spent two minutes in the toilets, near the entrance to the gates, but realistically, there was no way during that time that someone could have come in the gates, got to the graveside then left without me seeing them.

At four o'clock, I start to work on clearing yet another grave beside my father's. As I kneel beside the worn and darkened tombstone, a feeling of dread overcomes me.

It is not going to happen. She is not coming.

Then at five minutes past four, a car drives through the gates and comes up the gravel road towards me.

I look up. Expectantly.

It's a Saab 95.

Sarah loves Saabs. She used to have one a few years ago.

I stand up, brushing down the dirt from my trousers.

My heart is beating faster. My stomach is jumping. I wipe the sweat off my forehead with the back of my hand, and follow the car as it drives closer.

Blast. Sunlight reflects off the car window as it passes, and I cannot see the face of the driver, although I think it was a woman.

The car drives on another ten yards, then slows down and parks on the side of the gravel path. For a few moments I hold my breath as I wait nervously for the driver to step out of the car, my heart beating so fast that I think it will explode.

The door of the car opens, and a woman slips out of the driver's seat, her back to me. She is wearing a brown, woollen jacket that goes down to her knees, and her hair, blonde like Sarah's, is drawn up into a stylish, sophisticated bun on the top of her head. Before I can see her face, she bends forward back into the car, reaching across the driver's seat and picking up something from the other side.

I step a few feet closer.

The woman pulls a large bouquet of flowers out of the car, and turns.

Irises.

She looks wonderful.

Her skin, soft, and gentle. A white lambswool jumper, an elegant green skirt, and dark-brown sunglasses.

An immense feeling of yearning blossoms within me. I feel a rush of blood to my head, and I swallow hard, tears brimming in my eyes. I struggle hard with the temptation to run over to her, to sweep her off her feet, to smother her with kisses, to hold her tight, to capture her in my arms, and never, ever, let her go again. Never in a thousand years, or a million different lives.

The woman walking away from the car towards the gravestones is the woman I have dreamt about and cried for every night for the past eight months.

She is the woman of my dreams.

She is my wife.

It is Sarah.

I watch as she walks up to the grave and kneels by the headstone. She picks up the vase with my flowers in, and takes them out, replacing them with her new irises.

I go back to my car, and open the boot, taking out my own bunch of irises, and another vase which I have brought with me from my garage. I pull on my shirt and sweater, tidy my hair, and walk slowly over to the grave.

The gravel crunches under my feet as I walk down the path and approach her mother's resting place. I step up onto the grass and I am only a few feet away from Sarah, when she turns and sees me. Her eyes immediately go to the large bunch of irises I have in my hand, and she smiles.

"Hello." I start on my little speech. "You must be Sarah, Martha's daughter?"

"Yes, I am." She smiles back, I think a little surprised. "I'm sorry, I don't think that we've met before…"

"No. We haven't. I'm a friend of your mother's. I knew her quite well."

"Oh…I didn't know she had anyone else that visited her…May I ask how you knew her, or where you knew her from?"

"From Spain. I visited her house in Sierra Sien many times. She loved it there…"

"Yes, she did…I see you've bought her some irises too." She laughs, waving at her own bunch.

"Yes, I hope you don't mind. They were her favourite flowers. I came a few weeks ago, and I wanted to drop some off then, but I couldn't manage to buy any, so I left some carnations instead. I know she liked them too, but this morning I saw these in Sainsbury's, and, well…I thought I'd drop them off quickly. Since it's the anniversary of her death today."

"That's very nice of you and very thoughtful, Mr…?"

"It's no problem. Look, I brought another vase, just in case the other ones were still fresh. Here, I'll put mine in this, and you leave yours in that one."

I kneel down beside her, and pull the irises out of the wrapper and put them in my vase. I am very close to her now, and I can smell her perfume.

'*Pleasures*'. Her favourite. I breathe it in deeply and savour it, tasting it like a fine wine.

The moment reminds me of many other visits that we have made to her mother's graveside. Sometimes with Keira and Nicole.

"So Sarah, is this just a very nice coincidence or do you come every year to visit your mother's grave on the anniversary of her death?"

Still kneeling, she turns her head and looks at me quizzically. She seems a little surprised.

"It's almost a small pilgrimage for me." She replies." I do it every year, and I always bring a bunch of irises with me. When I saw the carnations, I wondered who else had been here. It's funny, I thought I knew most of my mum's friends. I don't think she ever mentioned you, Mr ….?"

"She probably didn't. I used to play poker with her every now and again. It was her favourite game, but she probably didn't want to broadcast that she was addicted to it." I laughed back.

"You're right. She did love poker. You certainly seem to know a lot about my mother. And I still don't know your name. You know, you're very mysterious. You are expertly avoiding my question as to what you are called. Now come on, cough up. Your name please, sir!" she laughs aloud.

"You're right." I reply. "I do know a lot about your mother. And I also know a lot about you, too. You'd be surprised how much. For example, I know that you love skiing, and that when you were eleven you broke your leg in St. Moritz. And…and I know that when you used to sleep in a caravan on holiday and when you were all tucked up safe and snug inside, that you used to love it when it rained really hard, and you could listen to the sound of the raindrops falling heavily on the metal roof. And…and I know that your favourite colour is red, and that even today you are probably scared of going to the dentist…"

She has stopped smiling, and is staring at me, open-mouthed.

Ouch. I think I just overdid it.

"Your mother was very proud of you, Sarah. She used to talk about you all the time whenever we played cards. I've listened to her describe your whole life. I feel that I practically know you."

She is sitting back on the grass now, watching me, her head cocked at an angle.

"It's strange. Very strange. Do you believe in déjà vu?" she asks me.

"Sorry, "I pause. "Didn't you just ask me that question?" I ask seriously. Then smile.

She looks at me blankly for a second, then gets it.

"Aha, very funny. No, but seriously. I can't explain it, but sitting here talking to you, Mr…whatever-your-name-is-but-won't-tell-me, I have the strangest feeling that we've done this before. That we've been here together, and talked like this at some other time. I know it's weird, but it's true. " She pauses. " Are you sure we haven't met before?"

"Believe me, if I'd met anyone in this life as attractive as you are, I would have remembered it!" I reply quickly. Then immediately regret it. Idiot.

She blushes, but doesn't break eye contact. I feel a twinge inside me. I feel myself blushing too, but I don't look away. Neither does she.

For a second or two, we both look directly into each other's eyes. Deep inside each other.

And in that moment, something happens. There is a connection. A meeting of the souls. Something happens that I can't put my finger on, but which I know both Sarah and I felt.

The seconds seem to stand still, until Sarah blinks, and shakes her head slightly, looking away and deliberately breaking off our eye-contact.

"I'm sorry." She says, laughing,

"No, don't be." I reply. "Your mother always used to go on about you, and she was always saying that you and I should meet. So now we have."

A few raindrops start to fall, and we both look up at the sky at the same moment.

It's about to pour.

I pause. This is the moment of truth.

"Sarah, it's very nice to meet you at long last. I was wondering, could you do me a favour?"

"Maybe, if I can." She replies, beginning to stand up, and brush down her skirt.

"Since it was your mother's wish that we should meet, I was wondering if you would help me fulfil that wish properly by allowing me to take you to dinner this evening?"

She picks up the crumpled flower wrapping paper, and the old flower heads, and turns to face me.

"Yes. Yes, I would like that. We can talk about her, and you can tell me about when you beat her at cards. "

"Good!" I reply, perhaps a little too exuberantly.

"But on one condition," she quickly adds.

"Which is?", I ask, turning to escort her back to her car.

"That you tell me what on earth your name is."

"Okay, I will. I promise. But only after the coffee and mints. Until then, at least I'll have some sort of bargaining chip and a hook with which I can keep you from leaving."

"In which case, My Mystery Man, you have a deal. I would be happy to let you take me somewhere very exciting and extremely expensive for dinner." she laughs, her eyes twinkling.

"Great."

I offer her my hand to seal the contract and she takes it. We shake, our hands lingering in each other's for just a moment longer than normal.

"So where do you want to meet?" I ask.

"You're inviting me. You decide."

"What about *Il Taglione* in Wimbledon High Street?"

"You know *Il Taglione*? That's my favourite restaurant!" She replies, surprised.

"I know." I reply. Grinning. "I'll meet you there at 7.30pm. Do you have a number that I can reach you on, just in case there is a problem?"

"I'm sorry. Not really. But don't worry, there won't be a problem. I'll see you there at 7.30 pm."

I open the car door for her, and she gets in.

As she drives off, the heavens open, but I almost don't notice. All I see is her turning around and looking at me over her shoulder as she drives away. Then she waves and I wave back.

CHAPTER 46
The Date

Jane does not deserve this.

I hate lying. I detest it in others, and yet here I am doing it. Already the deceit has started, already the guilt. The sickening guilt.

"It's corporate entertainment. Can't avoid it. You know the score…" I argue with her as she stands in the doorway to my new bedroom, and I fiddle with a tie and smooth down the jacket to my suit.

"I just hate it when you do this at such short notice. You know I don't like to be left alone at home so much, especially now Margareta has gone. I want us both to be together. You know how much I hate you having to work so hard all the time…"

"And what do you think pays the bills? Keeps you accustomed to the lifestyle you live!"

"Screw the lifestyle. I want you. We were happier when we lived in the two-bedroomed cottage in Teddington."

"That's before we had the kids. Before you started going on expensive holidays every year. Before we had…"

But already she is gone and the doorway is empty. The same argument, played out a thousand times, but with one problem.

Jane is right. I am wrong. And I am hurting her.

Il Taglione is a quiet restaurant, small, pretty and unassuming, with twinkling candles, the smell of cheese and garlic, and a real, authentic Italian atmosphere. It's tucked in at the end of the high street, seemingly transported directly from the streets of Napoli, but most people pass it by without ever noticing it is there. It's been one of Sarah's favourite restaurants for years.

As I approach the restaurant I am a mess of nerves and conflicting emotions: anticipation, excitement, fear, and arousal. A deadly concoction. My 'first date' with Sarah. Will it be the start of a new life? What happens if when we finally sit down, face to face, Sarah is not attracted to me? What happens if she is in a serious relationship with a new boyfriend, and doesn't want to be anything more than friends?…What happens if there is no chemistry? What happens if, for some highly unlikely reason, I discover that I am not attracted to her? No…that's stupid…But what happens if…? I shake my head. Calm down, James. Calm down.

I swallow hard, and open the door, quickly scanning the restaurant inside. My heart skips a beat when I see that she is already sitting at a table in the middle of the restaurant, a glass of red wine in her hand, and a sparkle in her eye.

As I walk up to the table, she rises to greet me, leaning forward slightly to allow me to kiss her gently on her cheek.

The touch of her skin against my lips sends a small shiver down my spine, and as I taste her perfume on the back of my tongue, subtle and not too strong, I close my eyes and swallow hard. A memory flashes in front of my eyes, and I remember the feel of her body against mine, her head against my chest, sleeping together in our bed at home.

"Hi," I say, as I step back and make a point of looking at her. "You look great!"

And she does. Her hair is down now, small diamond earrings catching the candlelight and sparkling in sympathy with an elegant diamond necklace. A matching set, given to her by her father on her 21st. Her dress, white and almost virginal, graces her slim, voluptuous figure, and I feel a sudden sexual longing as I realise just how attractive she truly is.

I realise then for the first time that she is, in reality, much more attractive than Jane, and I am surprised that I could have become so used to her body and her looks that I must have become blind to her beauty. How sad it is that in the day-to-day living of our lives we lose the ability to see each other properly, how security and familiarity blind us, and prevent us from seeing what we really want to see.

She smiles, and sits down. I look at her for a moment, and she looks back. My eyes meet hers, and she does not look away.

Inside my chest, I feel a warmth that spreads throughout my body, and for a moment I feel good.

But then, looking deeply into her eyes, I feel a flash of pain, and a picture fills my mind that I instantly dismiss and erase. The picture of Sarah standing half way down the garden path, pregnant, Nicole running towards her, Keira on the swing. I look away quickly, pretending to wave for the waiter, but desperately trying not to show the grief that must have been so obvious on my face. This is not the time or the place. Not now.

"Shall I order for you?" I ask, recovering my composure. "Why not let me guess what you would like?" I offer, knowing full well what she would choose. The same thing she chooses every time we come here.

"Okay." She replies, leaning forward with her elbows on the table, intertwining her fingers and cupping her hands together in front of her face, resting her chin on the back of her wrist. "This will be interesting…"

"Aha. The pressure is on. Now, let me see…" I say, looking at her pretty face again, and pretending to study her thoughts. "…I would say, that being the kind, gentle, warm-hearted lady that you are, you would probably start with the Antipasti, then, because you are probably a very passionate, affectionate woman, you would probably go on to have the Fish Lasagne."

"And why would you say that?"

"Because, underneath each layer, there is something delicious and warm. Hidden, but waiting there to be discovered and enjoyed. One layer at a time."

She laughs.

"I am impressed. And also a little scared. You have chosen exactly what I would like to order. You are either a very perceptive man, … whoever you are, my Mystery Man…, or you are a wizard."

Or maybe I am just your husband, and we have done this a thousand times before?

It's almost criminal, but when the waiter comes over and I pick up the wine list, and choose a Cabernet Shiraz, which I know is her favourite, she laughs again.

We both know that we are now flirting, that we have quickly moved from two strangers who have just met, to two people who have started to dance around the flame of passion, a sexual chemistry growing between us, drawing us together, teasing us with promises and anticipation of what is to come.

"So, Mr International Man of Mystery. What do you do?"

"I work in advertising. But that's enough of me, let's talk about you…." I lift up my glass, "Here's to your mother, and to her favourite daughter, Sarah."

Our glasses clink.

"That's not fair. You must tell me a bit more about you. I must be crazy sitting here having dinner with you. You're a complete stranger. You could be anybody."

"True. But I'm not. Okay, so what do you want to know?"

"Your name?"

"Aha, now that's unfair. You know the rules. Only after the dessert."

"Alright, alright. So,…Are you married? Do you have any children?"

Yes. To you. Two. Keira and Nicole.

"Yes, I am married. I won't lie. And I have two children. Two girls. Although, things, well,…" I stop myself. What am I going to tell her? That my wife doesn't understand me? How pathetic.

"Well, what?"

"Well, nothing. I'm married. Perhaps I shouldn't be here. But I am."

There is a heavy pregnant pause. I look across at Sarah, not smiling, not speaking, just praying that she won't get up and leave. She looks at her glass, and I can see her eyes thinking. Considering how to respond. In the end, she doesn't. The moment passes.

Then a waiter comes to our table, delivering our starters.

Sarah hasn't left.

"And you? I think you were married, weren't you?"

"Yes. Yes, I was. But we divorced about three years ago. A long time ago."

"And where do you live now?"

"In my mother's house. In Sierra Sien."

"But…ah..., have you kept your married name?"

"Yes. Why?"

"I tried to find you a while ago, but the international operator told me the person who lived there now wasn't called Turnstone."

"No. My last name is Sanchez. I kept my married name, because I couldn't be bothered changing all the documents. The legal system in Spain is a nightmare."

We eat a little.

"So, why were you trying to contact me?" she asks.

A good question.

"Because I wanted to send you some copies of some photographs of your mother. I thought you might like them."

A lie.

"Thank you. I would…"

We finish our starters, and the main course arrives.

As she lifts the first mouthful of lasagne to her mouth, I watch as she opens her lips and I see the tip of her tongue. I remember how it feels to kiss her, her taste, the touch of her fingers against my cheek, and I feel an immediate twinge of arousal. I look away and concentrate on my own plate of food.

We sit in silence for a while, appraising each other as we eat. The silence is comfortable, and there is no rush to converse.

Her makeup is done perfectly, and when I realise this it immediately pleases me that she has obviously gone to a lot of trouble to look good for me. Which is a good sign. I think…does it mean she wants me to find her attractive?

As I look at her more closely, I notice that she has a few more lines around the eyes than the last time I saw her. Worry lines? Has she led a harder life in this world? The results of a bad marriage? Or simply, that she is a year older now than the last time I saw her.

As she raises her glass to wash down a mouthful I suddenly see Nicole in her face.

It's incredible. Nicole and Sarah have the same nose, eyes and ears. And as she bends her head slightly to dab her lips with her napkin, I see her Keira in her chin, and her eyebrows, and the mannerism of the way she moves her hand. It's funny, I never noticed before just how much our girls have taken after Sarah, and as I see my children in her, I feel a sudden longing. Almost a pain, so sharp it constricts my chest, and I almost struggle for my next breath.

"Are you alright ?" Sarah asks.

"Yes." I reply. "Sorry, it's just some pepper." And I reach for my glass of wine.

"Have you ever thought of having children?" I ask her rather abruptly.

"Children? Wow. That's fast." she laughs. "We've not even got to the dessert…"

"Sorry…it's just that when I looked at you just now, it occurred to me how beautiful your daughters would be, if that is, you were ever to have any."

In spite of the subdued lighting, I can see that Sarah immediately starts to blush.

"I'm sorry, I didn't mean to embarrass you." I immediately start to apologise, feeling rather clumsy.

"No, don't apologise. I'm flattered. Thank you." She looks at me and her eyes twinkle. My heart skips a beat again. At this rate I'll be in Intensive Care by the time dessert comes…

"Actually, I've always wanted to have children. But, it's just never happened. At first I was disappointed, but after a few years of marriage I realised it would have been wrong. And in a way, I was lucky we didn't, considering." A pause. "Tell me about yours…?"

Mine? I pause, thinking about Elspeth and Allison, but realise that I cannot speak that warmly about them. And Sarah will surely notice my lack of warmth when talking about them, which will not be good. Instead I start to describe Keira and Nicole and telling Sarah about some of the antics they have got up to.

"Were you present at their births?" she asks.

"Yes…" and when I begin to describe the day Nicole was born, a tear leaks from my eye. I blink and look away.

"You obviously love them very much. They must be very lucky children to have a father who cares about them as much as you…"

It's too much. I have to change the conversation quickly.

"So, enough about me…more about you. What do you do in your spare time? Any hobbies?" I ask.

"Well, when I was at university I used to love…"

"Curling?" I cannot help but interrupt her.

She stops dead in mid-sentence. Staring at me.

"How on earth did you know that? I mean, curling isn't exactly a popular sport…" she asks quickly, sitting up a little in her chair, a slight edge in her voice.

"Your mother…" I lie. Blaming it all on her again, which probably isn't fair, given that she can't defend herself.

"What didn't she tell you?" she asks.

"Not much…she was very proud of you, and rightly so. You take after her. She was a fine woman too. I can see where you got your looks…"

Another blush, but this time not as pronounced as the first time.

"Tell me about my mother?" she asks "You seem to have known her quite well."

So I tell her everything I know about her mother, making up a little where I know it is safe to do so. Playing with the truth, expanding it a little. Adding to the web of lies I have to spread, dancing around the flame.

The game I play is dangerous. To talk to someone I have known intimately for many years, without revealing too much, without alarming her that I know things that I shouldn't, but at the same time, using exactly that same knowledge to entice her, and interest her. To lure her.

But I don't need to try too hard. When Sarah and I first met in the sandwich queue that lunchtime, so many years ago, the attraction between us was instant. And mutual.

As it is now. All these years later.

While I talk about her mother, Sarah is quiet, a pleasant smile gracing her face, relaxed, peaceful, her soft eyes studying me as I speak, following my lips as they move, running around the contours of my face, studying me, before eventually returning to meet my gaze.

As I look into her eyes, I feel a warmth, a comfort. A promise.

And without realising it, I stop speaking, and for a while we sit in silence, neither looking away, both of us lost within each other.

Someone laughs loudly on the other side of the restaurant and for the first time since I sat down at our table, I look around me. The restaurant is full now, lit only by the warm, flickering glow of table candles. Couples and families are enjoying the wonderful ambiance, the wine, and each other's company.

I look back at Sarah, and find that she is still looking at me.

And without thinking, I reach out across the table and gently touch her hand, my fingers resting lightly on hers.

She smiles.

With impeccably bad timing, a moment later the waiter arrives to ask us what we would like for dessert, and the spell is interrupted…but not broken. For a few minutes we both retreat to looking at the dessert menu and each make our choice.

Before Sarah says anything I choose the Black Forest gateau, which I know is Sarah's favourite. She laughs as I speak, and then orders the same.

"Okay, so now it's my turn," she volunteers, as the waiter walks away. "It's time for me to guess something about you. Since you're not exactly telling me much yourself."

"This will be interesting…," I smile back.

"Well, for a start, when you were a kid, I bet you were the one that sat at the back of the classroom and daydreamed of one day growing up and driving a train!"

"What? That's not exactly hard to guess is it. All little boys wanted to do that."

"True..." She looks at me, studying me harder. "Okay, so you played rugby. For quite a few years…"

"That's better…how did you know…is it a guess?" I ask.

"Not really. When you smile, …and it's a nice smile, if I may add..." she says, blushing a little, "...I can see that the tops of your front teeth are chipped. Just like one of my first boyfriends. He played rugby a lot…"

"Good guess, Sherlock." I say, running my finger along the top of my front teeth, suddenly a little self-conscious. "So, does that mean you played hockey?" I ask, knowing full well she was captain of the school team for the last two years she was there.

"Come on, there you go again, trying to turn the conversation around…"

Just then the desserts come, and we eat slowly. In-between mouthfuls, Sarah continues trying to guess what I was like as a teenager, and which pop groups I liked, before we move on to talking about lots of different things and nothing in particular. Just enjoying each other's company and each other.

The coffee arrives.

"And now, the time for truth," Sarah announces. "Please tell me your name."

"Ouch. The witching hour has come…and being a man of my word, I suppose I can't avoid the question any longer…"

"So…?"

"So, my name is James Quinn," I say, handing her over my business card.

Immediate recognition in her eyes. Wide now, and alert.

"James Quinn?" She cries, reading my name aloud from the card, then looking up. "It was you that sent me the letter last year!"

"I'm afraid so. I really wanted to contact you, and I'm afraid I made up the little story about going to the same school as you. The thing is, after hearing so much about you from your mother, I started to think a lot about you, and over the years, something just built up inside me until one day I felt I had to meet you. But I didn't know how…"

"So how did you know about Mary?"

Good question. Again.

"Does it matter? Sarah, I wanted to meet you. I mean, I really wanted to meet you. Your mother wanted me to meet you too. She often said so."

"So, why didn't you just say you were a friend of my mother's? The truth?"

Because you wouldn't believe the truth!

"I don't know. It seems the obvious thing to have done now. I'm sorry."

She is silent. Her eyes quiz me, probing me, exploring me.

"I'm confused, " she says. "And I'm feeling a little foolish…"

"Don't."

"So, was the meeting this afternoon an accident, or did you plan it?"

"Does it matter?"

"Yes. It does. I just want to know."

"The truth?"

"Yes." Then, softly. "*Please…*"

I reach across the table and rest my hand on her slender fingertips.

"The truth is a bit of both... I was waiting in the graveyard all day. Since the moment the gates opened, hoping that you would come."

"All day?"

"Yes. I've been trying to contact you for a long time, Sarah. A long time. I even told my dad all about you, and he encouraged me to search for you…which I did, *everywhere*, but I didn't know your last name, which made it that little bit harder. How was I to know it was Sanchez? I just looked for Sarah Turnstone, hoping that you were using your own name again..."

"... The letter I sent to you through Mary was my last hope. I almost gave up when you didn't call. ...Then my dad died a few months ago, and he was buried in the same graveyard as your mum. It was unbelievable...Finding your mum's grave was one of the strangest coincidences of my life. Or was it coincidence? I'm convinced it wasn't...I had almost given up hope of finding you. I never knew where your mother was buried. Then my dad dies, and bingo, he is buried only a few metres away from your mother! It was like my dad was giving me a message. He was showing me where to find your mother, and where to find you...And I just knew, don't ask me how, I just knew that you would come to visit your mum's grave on the anniversary of her death…So, I waited till today, then camped out and hoped…"

"Why? Why did you want to meet me so much? Should I be scared or flattered by all this attention?"

"Sarah, don't be scared. Please don't be scared. I can't explain why I had to meet you so much, just that I had to. It's just one of those things that is weird in life. There is no explanation, apart from the fact that when I saw the photographs of you that your mother showed me, I fell for you. Then and there."

"So, why didn't you contact me when my mother was alive?"

Help. I can't keep up this lying.

"Because, I'm married," I reply. "But my marriage hasn't being working out. We live almost two separate lives, sleep in separate rooms. We haven't made love for months. We're not man and wife anymore…And the more my relationship with my wife got worse, the more I thought of you."

Sarah is silent.

"I tried to call you," she says quietly.

"When?"

"When I first read your letter, I was a bit taken aback. I was really nervous. I wasn't going to call you at first, but there was just something about it.

Something that kept speaking to me from between the lines. And then I just had to…"

"So what happened? I never got the call."

"You did. You answered it several times. Once, the last time, you asked for me by name. I hung up."

"That was you?" A sudden flashback to the phone ringing as I crossed the Jubilee Bridge, and hearing someone breathing at the other end. Then the 'click' as Sarah hung up.

"Why did you hang up?" I asked, reaching out to touch her hand across the table.

"Because I didn't know what to say. I'm shy. Before I called you, I tried to find out a little more about you from the school, but no one had ever heard of you. No pictures, nothing. It was weird. So who were you? A stalker? A mad axe-man? *Who?*" the last word emphasised, revealing some touching emotion behind her words.

"So why did you call?"

"Because, there was something…I can't explain it, James. Something made me." She looks up at me, then takes hold of my outstretched hand across the table. "I'm scared, James. I don't understand what's going on here. You're married, and if you knew me better, you'd know there's no way I'd ever get involved with a married man. Never. But I have this incredible feeling about you. This whole thing..., meeting you at my mother's graveside,...how you know so many things about me that you shouldn't know, unless my mother really trusted you. ...And I like you. A lot. I won't deny it."

"I'm glad. I like you too. A lot."

I wrap my fingers around hers, giving them a gentle squeeze.

"James, this may sound daft, but…I have this strange feeling about us…it's really bizarre…"

"What? Tell me."

"I can't really explain it, but, I have this really weird feeling that we've met before. As if, well, as if we know each other already?" She reaches across to me with her other hand, and I take it quickly. "How can that be, James?"

"Maybe we have, Sarah. Perhaps in another world, who knows? Perhaps somewhere else, you and I are good friends, soul-mates, or lovers...What you feel, I feel too. Maybe it's best not to ask too many questions… There's something special here, and maybe we don't have to understand it. Perhaps we shouldn't even try...I think we should just accept it."

After dinner, I drive her back to her hotel in Richmond. We park the car, but neither of us seems in a hurry to get out. For a while we sit there, both reluctant to let the evening end, both happy to spend more time together, talking, learning as much as we can about each other. I ask her more about her life, finding out what she has done since she left university, and even though I already know the answers, I ask about her childhood and what she was like as a little girl. Sarah also asks about me. A lot of which I cannot tell her, since I have no memories of this life and this world. Instead, where possible, I answer by drawing upon and describing experiences from my real life, in my other world, and where I cannot give an answer without lying or making it up completely, I turn the question round to deflect from me and learn more about her.

Only when another car pulls into the car park, its bright headlights making us both blink do I realise how late it has become. We both sense the moment has come, so I step out of the car, and walk round to open her door. We walk slowly to the entrance of her hotel.

"So..." she says, as I stand with her in front of the doorway.

"So..."I reply.

"I'm leaving London later this week. Can I see you tomorrow?"

"I would like that."

"So would I. Eight o'clock?"

"Eight."

I squeeze her hand, then kiss her gently on her cheek.

"Goodnight, James Quinn. Man of mystery..." she says, then turns and walks through the door of the hotel.

She is gone.

The light in the hall is off as I unlock the front door and slip in. It's one o'clock, and Jane will be asleep.

Or maybe not.

"Where the hell have you been?" she screams at me from her seat at the bottom of the stairs.

"Out with a client! I told you." I reply, reeling from the sudden attack.

"Like hell you were. Richard called. He wanted to talk to you about tomorrow. I told him you were out with a client, and he didn't know anything about it."

"So? He's not my keeper. He doesn't keep my appointment book, and I don't keep his. Jane, what's this about?"

"So, what was this client's name? Sarah, was it? By any chance?"

Bullseye.

"Don't be silly. Jane, this obsession has got to stop. Please. You can't get so upset every time I have to go out. It's work. And I have to do it again tomorrow and probably the next day too. It's a big client. You know how it works!" I argue, as I walk past her into the kitchen to fix myself a drink.

"No I don't know how it bloody works."

She steps up beside me, and puts her hand around my neck, pulling me to her, so that she can sniff my cheek and collar.

"*Pleasures*? How the hell did that get on your collar and face then? Explain that, you bastard!"

I splash the whisky into my glass, then turn and stare at her, anger beginning to rise within me.

"I don't know. Maybe when I kissed the lady goodnight. ...And if you smell hard enough, maybe you can smell the aftershave of the men I kissed goodnight too. What do you want Jane? To drive me away? I'm just doing my job. And no, before you ask, I didn't shag the clients either." I whip the whisky into the back of my mouth, and pour another one quickly, picking the glass up and pushing past Jane into the front room.

She comes in and closes the door behind me.

"This can't go on, James. It's got to stop. You've got to stop lying to me."

"I'm not lying."

I am.

"We need help. I want us to go to see a counsellor together. I've made an appointment for Tuesday night at 8pm, not next week, but the week after. The earliest they could see us."

"I'm not going."

"You are. James, I love you. I fucking love you. Doesn't that mean anything to you? You gave me back my self-respect. You taught me to stand up for myself again, to fight for what I believe in. Well, I believe in us. I love you, and Allison and Elspeth do too. But ever since you banged your head, you've been different. One minute you're nice to me,- nicer than before-, but then the next, you're ignoring me. We're drowning James, and I don't want us to. Please, help us to stay afloat. Please come on Tuesday night."

"Is there really any point, Jane? Really?"

We stare at each other for what seems like an age, then she simply turns and walks upstairs. A moment later I hear her bedroom door close.

I collapse into the leather sofa, close my eyes, and curse myself.

Jane doesn't deserve this.

CHAPTER 47
A Date with Destiny

Richard pops his head around my door the next day, as soon I sit down and switch on the computer.

"Sorry, did I drop you in the shit yesterday?" he apologises.

"No, don't worry about it. You weren't to know that I was out with a new potential client, but Jane is getting fed up with me working so hard."

"So take a holiday. Go to the Caribbean for a week. Spend some time together. We can hold the fort while you're gone."

"Maybe. Perhaps in a month or two."

"Is everything all right between you and Jane?" he asks, innocently enough.

"Listen, maybe we can chat over a beer later in the week, but right now I need to get ready for my ten o'clock. Do you mind?" I snap at him.

Blast.

That was uncalled for.

The thing about guilt, is that you always take it out on everyone else. Although you feel guilty because it was you that did something wrong, suddenly everyone else around you becomes the guilty party, and everything turns into a fight. The less people I speak to today, the better.

I click on the email icon, and start to read my messages. Fifty new emails since Monday, most of which I quickly deal with or delete. Half an hour later, I'm down to the last two, which sit beside each other on the screen, side by side, calling out for my attention. If anything ever was, this surely must be a definite case of 'déjà vu'.

The email on the left is from Jane. The one on the right is from Sarah.

I open up the first one.

"*James,*

I'm sorry about last night. I was out of order.

But, please can you try to make it for counselling with me on the Tuesday night, not next week but the week after. It would mean a lot to me. And I think it will mean a lot to us. 8pm. Okay? The address, directions on how to get there, and the counsellor's name is below. All you have to do is turn up…Jane."

I don't reply, and ignore her meticulous instructions on how to make the appointment. I can't wait to read the next email.

I've saved the best one for last.

"*James,*

Thank you for last night. I enjoyed meeting you, very much. Perhaps a little too much. Help! What is going on?

I'm looking forward to seeing you tonight...8pm.

Sarah."

I hit the reply button.

"*Me too. See you at 8.*"

I stare at the words for a few moments, thinking that I should perhaps add something else, should say something more, but after a few minutes I still can't think of anything else to say, so I send it as is.

When I get back to my office after lunch from my 10 am meeting with the Scotia creative team, there is a large yellow stickie on my desk.

"*James, Professor Kasparek from Edinburgh called. Please call back. He says it's urgent.*"

When I call him back, he is not there. I leave him a message, and then call back twice more, leaving a message on his number at the university, and one on his home number.

Come six thirty I try his number one more time, but he is still not there. What can be so urgent that he is not around for me to call him back? At seven o'clock I leave the office and head off to Richmond, switching my mobile off so that Jane will not be able to call and interrupt me with Sarah. She knows that I won't be home till very late, having left her a note in the kitchen this morning.

She is already waiting for me outside the hotel when I arrive, sitting on a seat in the garden. I arrive at 8pm on the dot. I know that Sarah is a stickler for punctuality, and I know that if there is one way to win brownie points, respecting her time is one of them. Of course, the flipside of that is, if I were late, it would be a big, big negative.

We greet each other with a quick kiss on the cheek, and walk along the edge of the river, stopping at the Slug and Lettuce for a drink before dinner. I have booked our table at Chateau Pierre for 9 pm, and as requested, our table is at the back in one of the quiet, more private rooms.

Sarah is relaxed, and soon we are laughing and joking, getting on with each other as if we had known each other for years, and not just days. In response to the questions she asks I tell her a little about Jane and the children, but in the main, I manage to avoid much conversation about them. Instead, we talk a lot about her, her life, and her marriage. Occasionally, I drop in a piece of special '*acquired*' knowledge, for example, that I would guess that her favourite singer was Lionel Ritchie, and that her favourite place in the whole wide world was Yosemite Valley in California, and that her biggest turn-off in a man was socks and underwear with holes in them. Right on all accounts, stunning guesses which amaze her, but come easily from the years of marriage that we have spent together.

By the end of the meal we are much closer, and by the time it comes for me to walk her back to her room, we are holding hands.

We kiss at the doorway, her lips soft and warm, and instantly I am reminded of our first kiss, so many years before. But then the vision passes, and I find myself still kissing her, enjoying the experience now, with no comparisons to any other time. As I slowly start to back away, I feel her hand upon my shoulders, pulling me back, and I do not resist.

The kiss becomes more passionate, and I can feel her heart beating fast against my chest. And then I cheat.

I kiss her on the neck, just underneath her chin. Slow, soft, small kisses, that trace a path from her chin to underneath her ear.

She moans, and I feel the pressure build on my back, as she pulls me tighter into her. Almost involuntarily her hips thrust slightly forward, and her other hand wraps itself deeply into my hair, pulling gently downwards as she angles her head away from me, exposing her neck further to my advances.

Perhaps, to use the knowledge that I know this kiss will drive her crazy is a little unfair. Perhaps, having spent over ten years perfecting it, the fact I know just what it does to her body, might give me an unfair advantage that might make this wrong.

But I feel no guilt.

And as she whispers in my ear, "James, come upstairs with me to my room..." I only smile, and obey.

Perhaps it is a common thing for a man to do, perhaps it is not. But three times in my life when I have just made love to a woman, I have started to cry. For no apparent reason tears will stream down my face, and I will sob.

Not from sorrow, sadness or regret. And not from happiness either.

Maybe 'sexologists' are able to give it some sort of Latin, technical name, and maybe even some people are able to explain it, to point to it, and say, "Ah yes, that's a typical auto-sensory response to male ejaculation, quite common whenever *blah blah blah* occurs and a clear sign of *etc. etc. etc...*"

For me, I have never understood it. One moment I am in the throes of passion. Blinding light sweeping away all my thoughts and feelings, before being replaced by a euphoric sense of fulfilment. The next I am in tears, weeping onto Sarah's chest, shaking as the tears bubble up from deep within.

The first time it happened to me was with my third girlfriend. A French woman, whom I met on a university field trip to France, and then spent the whole of my second summer at university with, besotted and in love.

The second occasion immediately followed the moment I collapsed, exhausted and satisfied, into Sarah's arms, the first time we made love, thirteen years ago.

And the third time was in a hotel room in Richmond. Just now.

One common thread links the three events. Each time it happened, my companion accepted the tears without questions, stroking my hair, and soothing me, holding me tight. No questions ever asked, no explanations ever given. No words required.

It is three o'clock when I get home from Richmond. Parking the car and letting myself in, I dread the imminent onslaught of questioning from Jane, but none comes.

I shower downstairs, cleaning myself, and washing away the smell of Sarah. Her perfume, her taste, her touch.

When I hit the pillow shortly afterwards, I feel no guilt. I sleep well, and for the first time in months, there are no dreams. Just sleep. Deep, deep sleep.

When I wake in the morning, I feel good. I still feel no guilt, but I decide not to face Jane, and I dress quickly, and leave before 7am, propping up a short note on the island in the kitchen, reminding her that once again I will be out late, and saying hello to the children.

The first email arrives at 10am. It's from Jane.

"James, I'm taking the girls away for a while. We need a little space and I want you to have time to think over the next couple of weekends. By yourself. I'll be back on Tuesday evening, not next week, but the week after, in time for the appointment with the counsellor. Please take the time to think about what it is you want for us in the future, and why we

aren't working anymore. And remember to be there on the Tuesday night? It's important to me..."

"*Where? Where are you taking the children? Where are you going?*" are my immediate thoughts, and then, perhaps not exactly the reaction Jane would want, "*Good. It'll give me some breathing space, and some more time to think about Sarah.*"

The second email is from Sarah.

"*Hi.... Wow! Thank you for last night. And I mean, 'thank you!'. Can we do the same again tonight? I've changed my mind about going out for a meal. Let's just order room service, and stay in bed. I'll see you at six? I'll be in bed, waiting for you...Don't be late...*"

I reply.

"*Looking forward to it. See you at 6. Don't worry, I won't be late.*"

Tracy brings me coffee and breakfast at 10.15 and we spend the rest of the morning, planning the next few weeks. There is a lot to be done, and the workload of the firm is increasing. The publicity from the PR event for the Olympics and the concert at the Dome has brought in a lot more work, and Richard and myself have agreed that we have to expand to cope with the increased demands. That means recruiting another ten people across the company in the next three weeks, followed up with another four or five a few months later. Maybe more, especially if things continue to grow as they are. Business is booming. And, all modesty aside, the truth of the matter is that a lot of it is down to me.

My mood today is excellent. Things are going great, both at work and in my private life. And I mean great.

I move around the office feeling as if I am walking on air, and every time I think of Sarah, which on average, is about every two seconds, my heart skips a beat and I smile. Word quickly makes its way around that *'James is in a great mood'* and by lunchtime I have already had three people come into my office and ask for a pay rise. I even agree to one of them.

Then the red phone rings just after lunch, and my heart skips a beat. The red phone, I now know, is the private, direct number, that I only ever give out to a few, trusted, important people. Like the Chairman of the Olympic Committee, the CEO of Scotia Telecom, or Jane. And now Sarah.

A moment of dread. Will it be Sarah, calling to cancel this evening?

"James!" the man's voice booms down the phone. "It's Professor Kasparek."

I relax.

"Professor, I tried to call you yesterday, and I left a few messages, but…"

"I know, I know. I'm so glad I've managed to get hold of you, my boy. I have some news for you. Very important, urgent news. But don't worry,…it's good news!"

"Can you wait a minute please?" I say, putting the phone down, getting up and closing the door to my office. "I'm back. Just putting the *'Do Not Disturb'* sign on the door." I joke. "I'm all ears. What's up?"

"James, I've been spending a lot of time thinking about your problem and about what we talked about, and I've been working with a few other colleagues on updating their ideas to capture and encompass some of the empirical feedback you have given us. We're all very excited about it. We've revised the theories and the maths quite a bit. Actually, thanks to one of the observations you made, which you described to me very clearly, we managed to find a mistake in the theory that no one else spotted. We corrected the mistake, and have refined our thinking. The bottom line, is that when we worked through the maths, we were then able to actually predict all the events that you reported happening. We started with the original date and time of when the first event occurred, and from that we were able to successfully determine the predicted times of the next ones in the sequence, give or take a few hours. It's brilliant. I've never seen anything like it. The theorem is so accurate…"

"That's fantastic news!" I almost shout down the phone, sitting up straight and reaching for a pen and paper to make some notes. "So are you able to predict when it will happen next?", pen poised, expectantly.

"Yes." He replies, his voice quivering with excitement. "And that's why I had to contact you urgently. *Urgently!*"

"Why? When will it happen?"

"James, the next, and incidentally the calculations also show that it will be the last viable opportunity for you to cross over,… the next time it will happen James, ….is tonight. At 8.12pm. Give or take a few hours. James, *tonight is the night. You're going home!*"

CHAPTER 48
The Jubilee Line

"Tonight? Are you sure?" I ask, immediately excited. "Are you certain about this?"

"As much as I can be. The model has predicted all the other occasions to within hours of them happening."

"But that's only hours from now!"

"Exactly, my boy. Exactly. That's why I needed to contact you urgently. To warn you."

Shit. I'm meeting Sarah tonight. I don't want to miss that.

What am I talking about? I'll be going home to LIVE with Sarah. And Keira, and Nicole. My family. Back together. Happy!!!

On the other hand, last night was incredible. Better than any night I can remember spending with Sarah over the past five years. If only I could have one more night with her like that before going home. Just one…

"Tonight's not a good night," I hear myself say. Stupidly.

"What? What do you mean *'tonight's not a good night.'* You don't exactly have much choice in the matter, my boy. It's going to happen whether you like it or not."

"Professor, I've found Sarah! I met her last night, and I'm meeting her again this evening. Is there any way we can delay the event from happening?"

"No. Don't be silly. You're a physicist. Think boy, think. We can't influence the laws of nature. They are as they are."

"But what happens if I'm not on the Jubilee Line tonight? You said before that these events are centred around me, that I can't miss them, because I'm the star. Without me they can't happen..."

"Exactly. That's true. But you *will* be there when it happens. You can't avoid it."

"So why are you warning me?"

"To give you time to *prepare*, to get your things in order in this world. To make sure that when it happens you are beside the doorway, with no one holding on to you, and no one in your way between you and the exit from this world to the other!"

"I still don't understand. Don't I have any free choice in the matter? What happens if I just don't go down on the Jubilee Line tonight?"

"Ah, but you will. Think boy. Think about everything you learned about Quantum Mechanics and about Causality. About Time. Remember everything we discussed, and what I told you in my house. Like it or not, if it's meant to be, events *will* lead to you being there at the time it happens, so you don't need to worry about missing it. The only thing you need to worry about is that when it happens you need to be prepared. This is your last chance! Think about lightning in a storm. The lightning and the thunder can't take place without the storm, the storm is always the first thing to happen, but the lightning and the thunder are the main event."

"But if it's predetermined, how can I be sure that I will be able to cross over? How do I know that I won't be stopped from crossing again?"

"You don't. That's the whole point. You have to make sure you can. You have to maximise the conditions for the right outcome. Think about a bolt of lightning in the storm again. The lightning is unstoppable. It will happen. As soon as the conditions are right, there is nothing that can stop it. But where the lightning bolt will strike is never pre-determined. It goes for the best conductor at the highest point on the ground. Imagine a man playing golf on the green. He swings his metal golf club into the air, and if at the point the lighting jumps the golf club is the highest point of metal in the sky, the lightning will strike the golfer. A second later, and the golf club may be on the ground, and the lightning may strike a tree or a bush instead."

"So, what are you saying?"

"James, my boy. Tonight is the night. You can't stop it. It will happen. But you have to make sure that when it does, you are beside the door with no one standing in your way. And then, when it happens,…jump. Don't think. *Just go.* It's your last chance."

I'm silent now.

"James, are you there?"

"Yes. I'm just thinking."

"There's nothing to think about, my boy. Nothing. This is what you have waited and prayed for, and now it will happen. Tonight, my boy. Tonight!"

I have never heard the old Professor so excited. Never heard him so enthralled. I can picture him in my mind, pacing his office, waving his hands in the air, gesticulating wildly as he speaks.

"Professor. Thank you. I appreciate it. So, I suppose that if you're right, we won't be talking again…at least, not in this world."

"I hope not, my boy. I hope not… James, I wish you luck. I hope you find the happiness you want in your own world."

"So do I." I hear myself say. "So do I".

When I hang up the phone I am a bag of conflicting emotions. On the one hand, I am incredibly excited. The thought of seeing my children, Sarah, my friends…my own home! The prospect of starting to live my own life again…

Then I think of Sarah waiting for me in the hotel room, lying there on the bed, expecting me, ready for me to walk through the door and ravish her, to hold her, to kiss her…

The office is suddenly too claustrophobic, the walls too close. I need air. I need space. I need to think…

I grab my jacket and walk out, past Alice in reception who waves a piece of paper at me, and shouts after me saying that Richard would like to meet with me this evening after work. I ignore her, and rush out onto the street.

Looking at my watch I see that it is already 3.05 pm. I haven't much time.

After waiting almost a year, it's now only a matter of hours before I will be able to go home.

Home…

Energy courses through my body, and I walk quickly, down Monmouth Street, towards Covent Garden. My mind is awash with thoughts. Thoughts of home, of what I will do when I see my children again. Thoughts about what I will say to Sarah when I see her.

And then a strange thought hits me.

It's been almost a year. What happens if they have accepted the fact that I am dead? What happens if they have got used to me not being there anymore? What happens if they haven't missed me, and don’t want me to come home after all?

What happens if Sarah has met someone else?

I walk faster, confused. Worried. Scared.

Then I think of my work, at Kitte-Kat. For the first time it dawns on me how unhappy I really was whilst working as a Product Manager in telecomms. Conversely, I realise how happy I am now, running an advertising agency. I have a natural flair for it. I love it. I feel at home doing this. And it's what I have always wanted to do.

I decide that when I get home, I am going to make some very big changes to my life. There's no question that Kitte-Kat will have fired me by now. After all, I haven't turned up for work for ten months! I'll be free to spend some time with Sarah and the children, a few months off, then I'll start to look for work in advertising. A big career change, but it'll be worth it so that I can start to live the life I've always wanted to.

Covent Garden is full of tourists, and the atmosphere is fantastic. Everywhere people are milling around, filing past the little stalls of crafts and London tourist memorabilia. London is alive, and so am I.

But what about my mother?

She is only now just beginning to get over the death of my father. If I were to disappear now, she wouldn't be able to cope. Can I do that to her?

But then, who needs me most? My mother in my real life, or my mother here, in this life?

And then a very bizarre thought surfaces from nowhere, catching me unawares, knocking me sideways.

Where is my real life now?

What?

I stop dead in my tracks. The person behind almost bumps into me, and a few people cast me an odd glance as they walk past. But I do not see them. Instead, I find myself going over the question, again and again.

Where is my real life now?

It's been ten months since I saw my family. Ten long months. For ten months I have been existing, everyday, day in, day out in this world. Going to work, breathing, eating, going to the toilet. Living. I have a new job here, a job that I love. A career that I have always wanted to be involved in.

I think back to my old life, where every day I used to ride the train into work and stare at other people, trying to guess what it was that they did for a living. Wondering if their lives were better than mine, wondering if the life I was living was the right one. Wondering if the grass, green as it was where I lived, could actually be greener elsewhere?

And then I realise that I don't do that anymore. In ten months, I haven't once thought about whether or not I have the right job or not. I love what I do. *I love it!*

But I *do* miss Sarah. I miss the children. I miss my friends.

Then I think of Sarah and how she will be waiting for me in Richmond tonight.

I start to walk again. Faster and faster. I lose myself in the streets. Walking. Thinking. Around and around. I walk for hours, along the river, past St Paul's, almost as far as the Tower of London. Then all the way back to Covent Garden, and then down to the Strand, across the river, along the South Bank, and into Waterloo Station.

What should do I do? *What?*

As I stand on the main concourse of Waterloo, watching the people scurrying past me like little ants, everyone intent on making sure they get to where they are going on time, I realise for the first time since my big 'C' day, that the letter '*C*' not only stands for Concussion, but that it also stands for 'Choice'. I have a choice.

Do I want to go home?

Now that I have found Sarah again, are things so terribly wrong here?

Before, perhaps, if my father had still been alive, maybe there would have been another big reason to stay here once I had found Sarah. But that was before. Now my father is dead. Gone. Just like in my other life.

My other life? Do I not mean my real life?

So which one is my other life now, and which one is my real life?

Which one?

A voice from behind me. A little girl, laughing. I turn and look at her. I see that she is about the same age as Keira, and almost as beautiful.

She is pulling on her mother's hand, and jumping up and down, excited to be in London. In her free hand she is holding a red helium balloon, which bobs around in the air above her, dancing at the end of the string every time she pulls it.

I think of Keira, and all my doubts disappear.

I know that I have to go home.

My home. My *real* home. The home where my family is.

My children need a father.

And I need my children.

I look at my watch.

Shit. Where has the time gone?

It's already 6.05 pm.

I remember the Professor's words, ringing in my ears.

"...James, *tonight is the night. You're going home*! At 8.12 pm. Give or take a few hours."

Quick. I have to get to the Jubilee Line.

I hurry through the growing masses of people surging onto the platform now rush hour is on. A flood of humanity, all going home.

"Out of the way, mate. I'm going home too!" I hear myself shout at someone who stops in front of me to look up at the overhead screens.

I dodge around him, through the crowds and onto the escalators, and following the signs for the Jubilee Line, take the steps two at a time down into the underground. As I reach the bottom, I hear a train arriving at the platform, and as I hurry towards it, another surge of humanity streams towards me through the connecting tunnel. Like a salmon trying to swim upriver, I edge past them onto the platform beyond, and emerge just as the doors close on the train and it accelerates away, leaving me behind.

Shit.

The next one is in two minutes.

I wait, nervously, then step aboard as soon as it arrives. Stepping inside the last carriage, where the least people should be, I grab hold of the rail at the edge of the door, positioning myself so that I am almost pressing against the doors themselves, ensuring that I will be the first person off when the doors next open.

My pulse is racing now. I feel light headed. Almost euphoric.

Now that I have made up my mind, I am entirely focussed on what I am going to do: on making the 'jump' as soon as I can, and going home.

The train shoots into darkness, and I stare out at the blackness behind the doors.

Light suddenly floods through the glass, and we pull into Charing Cross. The doors start to open, and I pull myself up straight, tensing the muscles in my body, readying myself, preparing myself to shoot forward through the doors, the moment time starts to slow, the moment the sign on the wall begins to shimmer. The moment the door opens from this world to my own.

A man, a large American, steps onto the train, and stands in front of me.

I push him gently, urging him to move to the side. He stares at me.

"Hey kid! Where's your manners?"

He doesn't budge.

The doors start to shut.

I panic, stepping around to the side of him, ignoring his demand for an apology and focussing on the sign saying "Charing Cross" on the wall.

Woosh...

The doors close completely, and the train jostles forward, catching me off-balance. I fall to the side, banging into the woman beside me.

I hear myself mutter an apology, but inside I am fighting with the wave of disappointment that surges through me.

Nothing happened!

I look at my watch.

6.23 pm.

Too early. No wonder.

It probably won't happen for another hour or two.

"*8.12 pm. Give or take a few hours...*"

What does that mean? Anytime up till 10 pm? Does that mean I have to stay on the tube, riding back and forward between Green Park and Waterloo until 10 pm? Four hours?

No, it will happen sooner than that.

I get off the train at Green Park, and catch the next one south to Waterloo.

Again, adrenaline floods my system, and I take pole position by the doors. Anticipating. Expecting. Praying.

The doors open at Charing Cross.

The doors close at Waterloo.

The train leaves, we are in a dark tunnel, then a bright station. Waterloo.

I get off. Get the next one north.

Tunnel, Charing Cross. Green Park. Bond Street.

Get off.

Next one south.

Doors open. Doors close. Doors open. Doors close.

Next one north.

Doors open doors close doors open doors close doors open.

Get off, get on, get off, get on…Nothing.

Over and over again.

For hours.

And still nothing.

Nothing!

At 11 pm I feel faint and sick. I cannot take it anymore. I get off the tube, and practically stagger upstairs at Waterloo. I am physically and emotionally exhausted.

I wander out onto the station concourse.

I almost collapse through the main doors out into the night air, breathing deeply and trying to fill my lungs with oxygen.

I missed it! I missed the jump. It must have happened at 6 pm. The bloody professor was wrong. It happened without me. I've just missed my last, and only remaining opportunity to go home.

I am stuck here. I will never see Keira and Nicole or Sarah again…Never!

Sarah…?

I look at my watch…it's 11.15 pm. Blast!

Two minutes later, I am in the back of a cab, heading towards Richmond.

CHAPTER 49
No Mercy

The taxi pulls up in front of the hotel and I get out, leaving the driver with a fifty euro note. His lucky day. Collecting the change is the last thing on my mind.

12.05 am.

The door to the outside of the hotel is closed, so I ring the doorbell. The receptionist behind the desk looks up, presses a button behind the desk, and the door slides open in front of me.

I walk over to the lift confidently as if I am a guest and press the call button. The little red indicator above the door takes an age to change from '2' to '1' to '0', and when I walk in I press '3', urging the doors to close and the lift to hurry up.

Rushing along the corridor to room 320, I start to wonder what I am going to say to her. I know Sarah. She hates people being late and she can't stand being kept waiting. And the fact that I didn't call her to apologise in advance for not managing to make it, is totally inexcusable. I can just picture her, lying on the bed, checking her watch every few minutes and calling reception to ask if I have left any messages. No, no, no. Nothing yet Mrs Sanchez. We'll let you know if we get anything.

As I knock on the door, I fear for the worst.

No reply.

I've blown it.

Sarah will never talk to me again.

I knock again.

Silence.

I knock again, and this time I speak.

"Please Sarah, it's James. If you can hear me, please let me in. I need to apologise to you. Please. I'm so sorry."

I put my ear against the door. I can't hear anything.

"Sarah? If you can hear me please open up. I can explain…"

Nothing.

One of the doors further down the corridor opens up and a large American steps out into the corridor.

"Hey Sonny, can you keep it down? Some of us are trying to sleep!" He stops and stares at me. "Hey, don't I know you? You're the one that still owes me an apology!"

It's the American from the Jubilee Line. The one that had blocked my exit and I pushed aside.

"I'm sorry, sir," I lie. "I'm having one of the worst days of my life. It's nothing personal."

"Well, keep it down out there, or I'll call the manager."

Go home, yank...

I put my mouth against the doorframe and call Sarah's name a few more times. Nothing.

After ten minutes, the American opens his door again and walks towards me.

"Sorry," I pre-empt him, lifting my hand up, and showing him the palm of my hand. "Listen, I'll go. But could you do me a big favour? Any chance you could give me a pen and some paper? I have to write a note to the lady inside this room..."

He looks at me as if I am a Martian just about to abduct him, then he steps back into his room and re-emerges with some hotel stationery.

"Here. But please, keep it quiet. The wife can't sleep. "

I thank him, and start to scribble on the pad.

"*Sarah,*

I am so, so sorry I didn't make it on time. I didn't get here till just after midnight. I tried to wake you, but you were fast asleep. I can explain. I got stuck in a lift at work as I was leaving the office, and no one noticed I was there until the night watchman did his rounds. I haven't eaten or drunk anything since lunch, but I came straight here. You are important to me, and I do respect your time! Please, please forgive me. I know how important punctuality is to you, and I know that you split up with your third boyfriend at university because he stood you up one night. Please don't do that to me! Please call me and give me another chance. I really want to see you again.

James."

I slip the note under the door, and leave.

The next morning I am back at the hotel by 7.30 am, determined to catch her as soon as she wakes up. Too impatient to wait for the lift I run up the stairs, and am soon once more outside the entrance to Room 320.

The door is ajar, so I push it gently open and call Sarah's name.

A female voice answers me coming from the toilet. A woman steps out into the bedroom. The maid.

"I am sorry sir," she replies in a Spanish accent. "The lady left. She checked out already."

"What?"

"She eez not here. She gone."

Sitting in a café in Richmond, I ponder the course of events that has taken me from one of the highs of my life, yesterday afternoon, to how I feel now. Without doubt, one of the worst feelings I can ever recall.

Yesterday afternoon I had a choice of two futures to look forward to. Each one with its own merits.

But now I have none.

Sarah is gone, and I have no way of contacting her. Stupidly, *stupidly*, I never got a contact address for her in the UK, and the hotel refused to give me her details when I asked for them. Unless she calls me, I will not be able to contact her until she goes back to Spain. I've blown it.

As for the 'jump'? What fucking 'jump'? I missed the last opportunity to get home. Now I'm stuck here. Stuck. And without Sarah, there is no life for me here!

CHAPTER 50
How green is my grass now?

I don't make it into the office that day. By lunch time I am slightly drunk.

By three o'clock in the afternoon I am very drunk. Too drunk to remember the Professor's number, so that I can call him and shout at him over the phone, and definitely too drunk to try and spell his last name to the patient operator in Directory Enquiries, who hangs up on me after offering the telephone number for Alcoholics Anonymous.

By nine o'clock I am in the cells of Richmond Police Station. A comfortable cell, so comfortable, in fact, that I sleep through the evening without stirring, oblivious to my cell mate, a down-and-out - much like myself, really - who wakes before me and is staring keenly at my face when I eventually begin to come round.

The smell hits me first. A combination of the tramp's unwashed clothes and the stench of the vomit in the corner of the cell, vomit that must have appeared from my stomach at some time during the night, the clues to the fact that it was my stomach contents and not the tramp's being that the rest of the vomit seems to have made a trail down the front of my suit, down my trousers, and across my shoes.

The next thing to hit me is the pain. Not only does it feel as if the sky has fallen on my head, but the rest of the universe too. Talk about hangovers.

But don't talk too loud.

By eight o'clock in the morning, I am back out on the streets, thrown out of the cells with a caution, a warning, and an Alka-Seltzer, kindly provided courtesy of Her Majesty's constabulary.

Thankfully, my cellmate had resisted the urge to steal the rest of the change in my pocket, and I have enough to catch a cab home.

When I get home I shower, and make myself the strongest cup of coffee I have had in a long, long time. I sit in the front room and absorb the caffeine into my system, and slowly I begin to feel the lift. Mercifully.

I look at my watch. It's 9.15 am.

I consider calling the Professor, but decide against it. For two reasons: firstly, I'm very angry with him. He raised my expectations, led me to believe that last night was the night...that I was going home...and he was wrong. And because of him I spent last night fucking around on the underground whilst I should have been with Sarah. And now I've lost Sarah in this world too… I've lost everything.

And secondly, I'm just not in the mood to talk to anyone.

So, instead, I sit by myself, quietly, staring into space, hardly able to think, let alone move, nursing the hangover from hell.

As the hours pass, the devastating feeling of loss intensifies, and I find myself feeling scared and very alone. So alone. Alone because I have lost Sarah, for a second time.

And alone because of another loss. Another loss that I can no longer run away from. Another loss that I have been running away from for far too many years now and that I no longer have the strength to ignore.

A loss that is intrinsically linked to Sarah, and why I lost her the first time.

Weak, and with no more strength within me to fight it, or suppress the sadness from somewhere deep inside of me, a long, guttural moan begins to emerge, working its way up from my stomach, through my chest, and out through a wall of tears into the world beyond. Dropping the empty coffee cup onto the floor before me, I slip from the edge of the sofa to my knees, my shoulders shaking uncontrollably, my body racked with grief.

Tears flow freely as I cry louder and more intensely that I have ever cried in my life before.

At last, after all these years, the healing has begun.

The phone rings. I blink and reach slowly for the phone, but it stops before I make it.

I look at my watch. It is 12 noon.

Reaching up, I wipe both my hands over my face, and then wring them through my hair.

I was crying for over an hour. Then afterwards, when there was no more emotion left within me, I simply lay with my back on the floor. Quietly. Empty. Completely alone. But more at peace with myself than I have been for a long, long time.

I have begun to accept his loss.

The phone rings again.

Jane?

I pick it up, almost dreading the voice at the other end of the phone.

"James?" A man's voice.

"Professor Kasparek?" I ask.

"Yes, it's me. Oh no. You're still there then. I was hoping that since I had not heard from you, that the theory had worked and you had made the jump. What went wrong?" he asks me.

I sit up straight, pulling the phone onto my lap. Suddenly I am brought rushing back to the present.

"What went wrong? What happened on the Jubilee Line?" he asks me again.

"You tell me," I reply, angrily. "Nothing happened, that's what! *Nothing...*"

"Understandably you are upset. But please tell me about it. Tell me everything. I need to know everything, my boy..."

So, trying to contain my anger and frustration, I tell the Professor what happened, or didn't happen, and when I come to tell him that Jane is away for the weekend and how crap I feel, he suggests that I get the afternoon shuttle and fly up to Edinburgh to talk things through.

And why not? I've got nothing else to do. No life. No wife, no kids. I'm not only *Billie-No-Mates*, I'm *Billie-No-Life*!

"So," the Professor asks as we drive out of Waverley Station in Edinburgh. "How do you feel?"

"How about knackered, fed up, pissed off, scared, heart-broken, disillusioned, angry. And thirsty. So let's go straight to the nearest bar for a belated hair of the dog," I reply.

Because of some conference or other in Edinburgh, all the flights were full, so I had caught the first train out of Kings Cross and sat in 1st Class staring out of the window for the past three hours and forty five minutes.

Not bad. That's a twenty minute improvement in this world, over the fastest I've ever done the train trip from London to Edinburgh before. At least, now that I'm stuck in this world I can take solace in that fact. That the trains are faster. How fucking wonderful.

"Listen, I'm in a bad mood, so I apologise in advance for anything that I may say. I'm really short tempered, so go easy on me," I warn the Professor.

We drive in silence out of the station and park in the basement of the Caledonian Hotel at the end of Princes Street, where, a few minutes later, I check into my hotel room. I'm not carrying any luggage so we head straight out onto the street in search of alcohol and solace.

"Where are you taking me?" I ask.

"Somewhere quiet where we can talk. One of the pubs that only locals go to, which the tourists can never find."

We cross the square, walk along George Street, a large, broad, neo-classical road that runs parallel to Princes Street, then turn left at the first corner and walk down Castle Street. As I follow the Professor towards Queen Street, I find that there is a tiny cobbled road that acts as a service street between George Street and Queen Street. We turn into the little cobbled road, Thistle Street, and soon we are walking in through the doors of a very old, quaint, 'hostelry' that looks like it has come straight out of the nineteen twenties.

The pub is tiny. The Oxford. Two rooms, one where a large wooden bar props up a motley crew of locals who stare at us as we walk in, and another off to the side, where two wooden tables lurk beneath mustard nicotine caked walls. The words 'redecorate' or 'modernise' have obviously never crossed the threshold of the bar.

Truth be told, the bar is a treasure. It's amazing that none of the tour companies have promoted it or advertised it on television.

The Professor orders two pints of Caledonian 80 shillings, a delicious Scottish ale that I used to drink copiously during my student days, and we take a seat in the corner of the second room. The rest of the bar is relatively empty, save for a couple in the corner interested in nobody else save each other, and another man in the opposite corner, sitting alone with a pint of beer, and a 'nip' of whisky in a separate glass. His face is vaguely familiar. Where have I seen him before?

"Cheers!" the Professor raises his glass. "To the world we live in. Whichever one it is."

We take a much welcome sip from the beers, the frothy head leaving a moustache on both our lips. I wipe mine away, exclaiming "*Aahhhhh.* Good stuff."

"Tell me about it then. What happened?" he asks me.

"Nothing happened. And I mean nothing. I was on the tube from almost six-thirty till eleven at night. Almost two hours on either side of 8.12 pm. When it got to eleven, I couldn't stand it any longer. I felt sick, and I just had to get out of there. It's all right travelling on the tube for half an hour or something, but I can't believe that people actually work down there for hours on end. It's like working in a mine."

"So, you not only didn't see anything, but you didn't feel anything either? No dizziness, no sensations of time altering at all. Nothing?"

"No. Nothing. Honestly. If it happened whilst I was down there I would have seen it. It must have happened just before I got there, or after I left. The fact is, I'm trapped here now. I can't get home."

"No. No. I told you before. The time-space intersect cannot happen without you being there. You are the main event. Which means that it didn't happen! The question is why?"

"What do you mean? That I might still have a chance?" I ask, hope surging afresh.

"Yes. Yes. You must do. Our latest theoretical model predicted the other events so well, I can't believe we got it wrong. There has to be something else that we haven't considered. Something else…"

My pint is already almost empty, and I get up to go and buy another round. I leave the Professor lost in his thoughts, pulling out some paper from his jacket pocket and starting to scribble down some equations.

I'm standing at the bar when the man from the corner with the familiar face comes up and stands beside me. I look at his face again. I am sure I know him. I have seen his face before, often. But where?

"Anything else?" the barman asks, as he hands me over the two pints of 80-Shillings.

"Yes, two packets of crisps and some peanuts please," I reply.

The barman reaches underneath the counter for the crisps. "That'll be twelve euros please," he says, then turning to the man beside me whilst he takes my money. "And you Ian, another pint of the same?"

Ian? Ian *who*? I'm sure I know him.

I walk back and hand the professor his pint, watching as he scribbles down some more calculations. From memory I recognise a few of the equations and symbols as being some advanced form of quantum wave mechanics, mixed with a couple of Hamiltonian operators, none of which I can understand anymore. Four years of studying, all forgotten. What a waste of time.

"Fancy some crisps?" I ask. "I'm starving."

The Professor shakes his head, not answering me verbally. He scribbles some more notes, lost in his thoughts. I look around me, but end up focussing on the man 'Ian' who has now returned to his seat.

And then it hits me. It's Ian Rankin. The famous writer, creator of the Inspector Rebus novels. Of course, he is from Edinburgh! Wow, I love his books; I've read them all.

I get up and walk over to him, leaving the Professor , who probably doesn't notice me leave anyway.

"Mr Rankin? Do you mind if I join you for a second? I'm a big fan of your work," I ask.

He looks up at me, his eyebrows going up to form a question with his face.

"What work? Do I know you?" he asks.

"No. No, you don't. But I've read most of your books. I'm a big fan."

"What books? What are you talking about?" he asks, the question and his surprise seeming completely genuine.

I'm standing over him, not yet seated, just about to open my mouth to tell him how much I loved his latest book when it dawns on me. Perhaps Ian Rankin hasn't had any books published in this world. At least, not yet!

I sit down opposite him.

"Mr Rankin, my name is James. We haven't met but, and don't ask me how I know because honestly I couldn't explain it, but correct me if I'm wrong: are you writing, or have you ever written any books?"

He stares at me, then leans forward, almost whispering.

"Yes, yes, I have. I've written three. But I've never had any of them published. *How do you know?*"

"Why not?" I ask. "Why haven't you had any of them published?"

"Because everyone I send them to just sends them straight back, unread. Without any personal contacts in the literary world, I don't stand a chance of getting published, *and I don't know anyone.* Are you a writer?"

"No. I'm not. Listen, Mr Rankin…what are your books about? Have you ever written about a character called Inspector Rebus?"

"Yes. Yes I have? *How do you know?*" he asks, raising his voice. "What's going on? How do you know about him? I haven't told anyone about Rebus. I've given up on writing about him. I haven't written anything for years. Waste of bloody time. Doesn't pay the rent."

"So what do you do now?"

"I work for Scottish and Newcastle, the breweries, in alcohol research," he says, lifting the glass in front of me and looking at the dark beer inside.

"Listen, it may be none of my business, but if I were you, I would go back to writing, and try again. Don't give up. Whatever you do, don't give up. I had a dream about you, Mr Rankin. And in my dream I dreamt that your books were being published all over the world, and that the Inspector Rebus series of novels was one of the most successful series of crime thrillers ever written."

"You dreamt it?" he asks.

"Yes. Listen, I've never met you before, but I dreamt all about you and your character Inspector Rebus. If that part was true, the rest of the dream must be true too. Honestly, don't give up. You have to try again, and again. And then once more after that. I can promise you that you've got what it takes, and that one day, if you persevere, you will be very famous. And I mean, very famous."

"You honestly dreamt all of this?" he asks again.

"Yes."

"Wow…Thanks pal. Thanks."

He picks up the glass of beer and takes another look at it, then smiles at me, puts down the half-finished pint, gets up, shakes my hand, and walks out of the pub.

In the words of Clint Eastwood, I think that I've just made his day.

I walk back over to the Professor and sit down beside him.

"Peanuts?" I ask.

"What?"

"Do you want some peanuts?"

"No. No thanks," he replies without looking up. He continues scribbling. I am just about to take another drink from my glass when he turns to me, "What? *What did you just say?*" he asks.

"I said, *'Do you want some peanuts?'*"

"James. How heavy are you now?"

"What?"

"How heavy are you?"

"I don't know. I haven't weighed myself in ages."

"Are you heavier *now* than you were when we met last time?"

"Yes. I would say I am. I've noticed that I have been putting on weight in the past few months. Quite a lot actually. It's all that good food from eating out at fancy meals with clients, and drinking so much Guinness. That and the lack of exercise."

"Eureka!" he shouts. Standing up, and banging the table hard with his fist. The couple in the corner break off from kissing and look across at us, before bursting into laughter. "That's it, my boy! The calculations I made were based upon your body mass from the last time I saw you. But if you have been putting on more weight, I will have to adjust the numbers in the calculation to reflect your increased body mass. When I run the numbers again, the predicted date for the next event will be different. That's why it didn't happen last night. You've been eating too much. You've got fat!"

Ten minutes later we are both back in my hotel bedroom, staring down at the scales in my bathroom.

85kg.

That's 5kg heavier than I was the last time I weighed myself.

The Professor is excited, and he can't wait to get back to his office to run the new calculation on the university computer.

"I'll call you as soon as I can. I'll go over my numbers once again, then start running the calculation again on 'Henry', and the results should come back within a few days. A week at the most."

"Who's Henry?"

"He's a DAP, a digital array of processors, or more accurately a massive parallel array of the latest super-computing Cray computers. There's nothing else like it in the country. The Edinburgh Observatory shares it with the Physics department. Calculations that would take most other universities months to do, we can do in a day."

"Well, say 'Hi' to Henry for me. And tell him I just want to go home. Soon…"

"I will. And that may be sooner than you think, my boy. Sooner than you think…"

"Professor, don't hurry the calculations. Take your time and just get it right this time, okay? I don't think I could stand another false alarm. Just call me when you're sure. Not before…"

CHAPTER 51
Sunday

White horses ride the crests of the waves on the North Sea and sea-gulls circle high above the grey rugged cliffs which pass by the outside of the train window. The sea looks a cold and inhospitable place today, and I am happy to be sitting inside the warm train compartment, looking out, protected from the world outside.

I am leaving Edinburgh behind me, the train to London speeding back towards my future, whichever one it will be.

According to the Professor, my time in this life, *this version of my life*, may shortly come to an end. Soon I will get the chance to 'jump' again. Soon I will be able to be with my family, my real family. And soon I will be happy...

Happy.

Perhaps. Maybe. But before I can rejoin my family, I first need to heal myself.

I have come a long way in the past few weeks. I have discovered that the path back to my life with Sarah crosses many rough and bumpy tracks, and ultimately will only lead me to my destination when I take a dangerous and painful detour into my own self. A journey inside my heart and soul to discover who I have become. I know now that before I can go home, I have to find out where the old me has gone. Not only do I have to find Sarah,...I have to find myself.

Thankfully, I am now much closer to understanding where that person went.

Except now, of course, there is also that one, single added complication. Or blessing. Depending upon how fate should have me view it all. For now, I have not only the possibility of a route back to Sarah, my old Sarah, but now I have also the memory of a meeting with a new Sarah. An invigorating, fresh, mesmerising Sarah. But Sarah, just the same.

As I start this new train of thought, I start to vividly remember the night I spent with her in Richmond.

If only it were possible to see her once again before I go back, to spend some more time with her...to make love to her like we did before one last time? To apologise to her in person for the other night, for letting her down, for standing her up...

Did she get my note? Why hasn't she contacted me?

As the train hurtles south, I can't stop thinking about her. Now that I've made up my mind that I *will* make the jump back to my old life, and to the other Sarah, I can't help wondering if it would be wrong to want to see the new Sarah again in this world. Is it wrong to want to make love to her one more time? Is it possible that I can be unfaithful to my own wife, *with* my own wife?

Then I think of her in bed with me last week, the taste of her lips, and the touch of her skin against mine.

By the time the train reaches North Berwick, an hour-and-a-half after leaving Edinburgh, I am thinking of little else apart from having her naked body next to mine again, and I am doing an excellent job of trying to persuade myself that there would be no harm in sleeping with her again. No harm either for Sarah, or for me.

But as the train pulls into Newcastle almost an hour later, my conscience has got the better of me, and I know it would be wrong.

Wrong. *Perhaps*. Maybe. Well, maybe not *that* wrong…When the train stops at Doncaster, I finally manage to persuade myself that it would be okay. I will not *harm* Sarah…in fact, I am sure that I will make her happy…

Selfish lies.

By the time the train finally pulls into London, my mind is successfully made up.

I have to see her again. I must.

Only one question remains. How can I contact her?

The answer is obvious. Mary.

I have to call her. Ask her to speak to Sarah for me again. Even beg her if necessary. And soon…because I may not have much time.

Tonight. I'll call her tonight.

It's ten past eight by the time I get back to my house. True to her word, Jane and the kids are still nowhere to be seen. I pour myself a whisky, and relax into the white sofa in the front room. A little nervous I pick up the phone and dial the number for Mary, which the operator for Director Enquiries so willingly provides.

The phone at the other end rings. No one picks up. I let it ring some more. Still no one. I begin to count the number of times it rings…I'll hang up when it gets to ten.

Ten.

Blast!

I hang up.

Maybe I dialled a wrong number?

I dial it again. Nothing. I let it ring.

Shit. What do I do now…

"Hello?" a voice says, obviously out of breath.

"Mary?" I ask.

"Yes, it's me. Sorry, I just ran up the garden path. I heard the phone ringing. Who's there?"

"It's James again. I'm sorry."

Silence at the other end.

"Mary? Listen, I'm sorry. I had to speak to you…Can you give me a few minutes please?"

A moment, then her voice.

"James. This is not fair. I'm stuck in the middle here. It's between you and Sarah, not me. Whatever she wants…"

"Please Mary. I met her. Did she tell you?"

"Yes. She did."

"Did she tell you that we got on really well…that there was a real connection between us and that something wonderful happened?"

"Yes."

"Mary, Sarah means a lot to me. A lot... I can't explain it, but she means more to me than any other person on this planet. I love her…"

"But you only just met her James. Be realistic. How can you love her already?"

"It's not that simple. It's more complicated than you can possibly imagine. Anyway, things got messed up, and I think she left London. I was meant to meet her for dinner in her hotel room, but I got stuck in a lift, and didn't make it. She waited for me all evening, but by the time I got to her room, she had gone to sleep. The next day I went to the hotel first thing in the morning, but she had already gone. Vanished. I never got a chance to speak to her again. Mary, I need to call her, to speak to her. To apologise. But stupidly, I never got a contact number from her…and now I don't know how to reach her. Listen, please Mary, *please* can you give me her number. I *have* to call her!"

Another moment's silence.

"No. James, I won't give you her number. I'll speak to her myself. If she calls you back, then fine. But if she doesn't, please don't call me again. I hate being the pig-in-the-middle. This is between you and her, and I'm her friend, not yours. Okay?"

"Yes, just this one last time. I promise."

"But let me just say one thing to you, James."

"What?"

"Go easy on her. She hasn't felt anything for any man for years. Then suddenly you turn up, bewitch her, *god knows how, but you did*, and now she's like a bloody nervous teenager again. I know she likes you James. She does. But you scared her James, and then you let her down…"

"What do you mean, I *'scared her'*?"

"I mean, you scared her…you said some things that really shook her. Things that you shouldn't know about her, but did. Have you been following her or something?"

"No. No I haven't." Quick. Change the subject. "When will you call her?"

"I'll speak to her as soon as you get off the phone."

"I'll hang up now then. Mary, please, tell her I miss her. I want to see her again soon…I have to…and tell her I'm sorry I was late. But that doesn't mean I don't respect her time...It's important she knows that I rushed to the hotel as soon as I could."

"I'll tell her. *Bye* James."

"Bye…"

And a moment later, I am sitting in the room staring aimlessly at the white, marble fireplace, the phone on my lap, and the big, empty house, echoing all around me. I am suddenly very, very alone.

Please Sarah. Please call me.

Monday passes quickly in the office, and in spite of everything that is happening to me, I actually quite enjoy the day. In the morning, Claire and her partners come into the office to talk about "Find-a-Friend" and we present to them some of the ideas that the creative team have come up with. They like them. Claire is pleased, and afterwards, her partners rush off to another meeting and she buys me lunch. When she leaves, she kisses me on the cheek, and squeezes my hand. I squeeze her hand back, perhaps a mistake, for before I know what is happening she leans forward and kisses me quickly on the lips.

"For old times' sake," she says. "And don't worry, I won't be doing that every time I see you."

"Which is perhaps for the best. We've both moved on, Claire."

"True. But I couldn't resist, and now you can't sack me for trying. You know James, I was watching you during the meeting. You're such a different person now than the person you used to be. Ever since you got mugged."

"Better, or worse?" I can't resist asking.

"Hard to say. Perhaps I'm biased. I mean, I'm definitely biased. You and I were good. The old you. The devilish you. The one that was charming and sophisticated and bad. "

"You mean, I'm not charming anymore?" I push.

"Of course you are. Maybe even more so than before. But nowadays you've got a conscience, and care more about people. You do the right thing for others, not just what is right for you. I saw how you sat back in the meeting and gave Mat the chance to talk and present his ideas. You encouraged him, and then gave him all the credit. You've matured James."

"So which one do you prefer?" I ask.

"Honestly?"

"Yes…"

"Then I prefer the old you. The one that seduced me, the one that took me to a hotel room after work, and spent the night doing everything to me that he knew he shouldn't. The bad you. The naughty you. The dangerous you. I preferred Hyde. And you're Dr Jekyll."

Dr Jekyll?

I think about her words that evening on the way back home on the train. I think about who I am now, and who I used to be, in this world and my real world, or at least, the world I used to come from.

And there it is again. A moment of doubt. An instant of confusion about which is the real world, this one now, or the one 'I used to come from'?.

I realise then that if I don't go home soon, home to Sarah and Keira and Nicole, then it may soon be too late. The distinction between the *present* world and my *real* world is beginning to blur.

Which is which?

On Tuesday, I attend the launch of the television campaign for Scotia Telecom. At long last, it has all come together. After months of searching, we eventually chose a little known actor called Orlando Bloom to be the star of the campaign. "Honestly," I tell the rest of the team, "I know this is the right choice. This man's going to go a long way… and the ladies will absolutely love him." And a few of the girls in the team giggle. Which just proves my point.

The television ads will run for several months, and initially we will make several versions which will be filmed in different cities throughout Europe, dubbing his voice into French, Italian and German to play in the other countries.

We hire the Dome, and lay on a big party, all watching the very first airing of the advert on national television on a massive screen suspended from the ceiling. Everyone is there, Richard, all the gang from Cohen's, and half of Scotia Telecom's management team. We invite the Mayor of London, a bunch of actors, one of whom Orlando Bloom invites along and turns out to be Ewan Mcgregor. A potentially exciting moment, except that it turns out that no else has ever heard of him. "He was in *Star Wars*" I remind him. "No…that was Brad Pitt who played the part, not him. Who is he anyway?" Richard argues with me, over a glass of champagne.

The master stroke of the evening, was to invite the British Olympic athletes to the event, and persuade Scotia Telecom to present the Olympic squad with a very large cheque for sponsorship. Along with a brand new

Tangerine mobile phone for every member of the squad, and branded sportswear and clothing to be worn throughout the Olympics. Not cheap. But considering how many millions of people will be watching the Olympics when they come, worth every single penny, sorry, cent.

It's a good evening. An excellent evening. And a great evening for Cohen's. Before the first Tangerine advert airs live across the nation, I make a brief speech on the stage in front of the assembled crowd. Everyone cheers me, and I hand over to the Chairman of Scotia Telecom, and then in turn to Richard. A few minutes later, an expectant hush falls across the audience and the TV screen bursts into life.

And there he is, the man of the moment: Orlando Bloom.

Two minutes and twenty four seconds. Prime time TV. The advert runs, everyone cheers wildly, and the stock of Scotia Telecom begins its upward rise to staggering heights of wealth and market domination. The mobile telecommunications market is born.

I should be enjoying it all, and although I do a little, any pleasure or pride that I feel is heavily subdued by the feeling of betrayal that haunts me as I walk around the Dome, shaking hands, smiling, and again feeling like Judas.

All these people, many of them really, really nice people, some of whom have become good friends, have given me their trust, their faith, placed their careers in my hands. I have taken their money, promised them my time, my energy, my support.

Judas. Judas. Judas....

I am Judas. That is my name.

Judas, because as Stu Roberts, my new best friend, pats me on the back at the end of the evening, and tells what a wonderful job I am doing, and how pleased he is that he went with his gut instinct and gave me the campaign, I can think only of Sarah, and how much I want to walk through those tube doors, back from this world to my own.

Judas.

As Stu walks over to the bar to get us both another beer, I sneak out the back entrance. Enough is enough. It's time to leave.

The rest of the week passes in a turbulent war of emotions bubbling away inside me. I find it difficult to concentrate at work, no matter how hard I try. I find my thoughts drifting from Sarah to Jane, to my children, combined with anxiety about what I will find when I do finally make it back to my 'other' life; tinged with a little worry that I may be about to make the wrong decision, and even fear that perhaps the Professor is not going to call me back; or that when he does, he will be telling me that his calculations were wrong and that, no, there are no more opportunities for me to go home. That I am stuck here for good. Forever.

And with these thoughts I realise that I want to go home more than ever. Back to Sarah. Back to Keira and Nicole. My two little girls. My own flesh and blood.

I want to go home.

I stare at the phones on my desk for hours on end, my mobile phone lying beside the red phone, waiting, willing, praying for one of them to ring.

"Come on, Sarah, Professor,... *call me...*" I chant to myself, over and over again.

On the Thursday afternoon, I look up from my desk, interrupting my now daily routine of phone staring, suddenly acutely aware of another person in the room, and find Alice standing in my doorway, watching me, concern written all over her face.

"James," she asks before I speak. "What's the matter?"

"Nothing," I reply, sheepishly.

"Come on, I deserve better than that. I know you. Something's the matter..."

"I'll be okay," I reply.

She hovers in the doorway for a few minutes longer, her soft blue eyes glowing with warmth and affection and concern, the silent exchange between us a remnant of something deeper, something dangerous. A memory that I do not share and a place I must not go.

I turn to look out of the window, a pathetic attempt to break the intensity of the moment, and when I look back, she is gone. The doorway is empty.

Friday comes, and Friday goes. The weekend starts and still I hear nothing from the Professor. On Saturday morning I can wait no longer, and I call him at his home. No answer. So I try his office. It rings for a couple of minutes before the answer machine clicks in, and I leave a message: "Professor, it's James. Call me."

The weekend is a lonely place. The house, still empty of Jane and the children, echoes with my thoughts, and makes me feel uncomfortable. I sit in the garden for hours, clutching my mobile phone. I carry it with me when I go to the bathroom, when I have a bath, and put it beside my pillow when I fall asleep at night.

When I wake up on Sunday morning, I can't stand being in the house any more, and I drive down to the Riverside, where I have one too many to drink in '*Charlie's Corner*', hoping that somehow my dad will be able to help me one more time.

Finding no real solace in Charlie's Corner, I take my beer outside and walk over to the spot where Dad and I used to fish together, and where he first introduced me to Old Ralph. Who was then just 'Young Ralph.'

Sitting down on the soft grass I stare soullessly into the water, and cast my mind back. Soon I am with my dad again, him and me, side by side. Him thirty years old and me six, just a little boy. Him talking, me staring at him in awe, listening, absorbing, taking in every single word the man said.

Father and son.

Since those halcyon days of special time spent with my dad, away from my mother, I have always dreamt of having my own son. Always.

A million times I have dreamt of how I would come with him here to the edge of the river, and sit with him, talking man to boy, teaching him about life, and telling him tales, ---some true, most just made up--- and helping him learn how to fish.

But it was never to be…

The call came late in the afternoon. I was still at work at Kitte-Kat, finishing up a presentation and getting ready for an important meeting the next day: Sarah's waters had broken early, she was on her way to hospital.

The rest of the day was lost in a swirling cloud of dark, oppressive terror and grief, which, to this day, I have been unable to come to grips with. Better, far better, to bury it, to forget…That way, yes, that way, the pain is not so intense.

By the time I got to the hospital it was all over. The baby had been born. A boy. But as I rushed to be by Sarah's side, the doctors, their faces serious and tired, had restrained me and taken me to a private room, covered with green Venetian blinds, and sterile white walls. As they closed the door behind them and sat me down, a nurse standing on my right side with a hand on my shoulder, the words '*premature*' and '*still-born*' were whispered softly into the air before me.

And there were other words that floated in behind them: 'complications'…'haemorrhaging', 'damaged womb'…'infertile'…and then, oh yes, and then…"*I'm so sorry*…"

When I left the room, it was to go to Sarah's side. She was just waking up from a general anaesthetic. She was in need of me, she needed my strength.

She would be okay, but she would need rest, and lots of rest…But first I had to break the news to her… she didn't know yet…our son was dead.

The post-natal depression nearly killed 'us'. For her, I know now, it was a way of blocking the reality, of building her own private little cocoon into which she could retreat and regroup, and once again find the will to live.

I helped her. In any way I could. I tried to understand how post-natal depression worked. I learned everything I could about it, I took advice from the doctors, and I fought hard to win her back. And she recovered.

At first she refused to talk about the baby. The boy. She would scream whenever I tried to discuss him: "We have to talk about him…we must…we have to mourn our loss!" But she never heard. Her screaming was louder.

Only I attended the funeral. Sarah was heavily sedated and at home, being cared for by Martha, her mother.

Only I whispered goodbye to our little son as they cremated his little, empty body.

And only I said aloud in the church the name that Sarah and I had chosen for him months before.

Peter.

In hindsight, sitting here on the river bank now, so many years later, and in another world completely, I realise that while Sarah recovered and came to terms with her loss. I never did.

And for me, that one loss led to another, and then another.

First I lost Peter. Then I lost Sarah. And then I lost myself.

Not until these last few days have I managed to face facts and start the journey back to emotional health. To finding myself.

A fish leaps clear of the water somewhere in the dark shadows underneath the trees on the other side of the river, and I stir from my thoughts. I blink and look up at the sky.

Of course, I was blessed. I had, no, *we had*, two beautiful children. Keira and Nicole.

Two girls. Two beautiful girls. Whom I love and adore, and thank God for every single second of every single day.

But although I never ever mentioned it to Sarah again, I continued to long for a son. To *yearn* for a *son*.

A deep longing. A source of continued discontentment. A frustration with what life had given me, and what I had become.

And then, in a moment of enlightenment, I find the answer to the question I have been asking myself for the past year. In a single second of time, my subconscious delivers to me the answer to the question of why I started to look away from Sarah. And the answer shocks me in its simplicity: a basic, primeval instinct that controls all life. The need to procreate...

...Sarah could no longer have children. She could not give me the son I had always wanted and needed. So I started to look elsewhere...to find someone else who would continue my sad, pathetic, lineage...

...and deep down, in some subconscious corner of the most hidden recesses of the workings of a sad, grieving mind, I ...I blamed Sarah for the death of *my* son.

Although I feel no hand on my shoulder, nor hear my father speak to me from beyond the grave, nor experience anything weird or else somehow supernatural, when I leave the Riverside later that evening, I do feel comforted. Not by the whisky, or the beer.

But by the understanding that I have gained.

For now I know.

At last I understand.

It has never been about Sarah. She has always been the same, attractive, wonderful person. No, on the contrary, it has always been about me.

Me.

This past year, the whole journey from one world to another, all the months of searching...it has never really been about finding Sarah. All this time it has been about finding me. A long, drawn-out, desperate, search for myself.

And now I understand, at last, *at long, long last*, I am ready to go home.

It's seven o'clock that Monday evening, when the phone finally does ring and I pick it up to hear the excited voice of the Professor booming down the line.

"James? Fantastic news. *Fantastic news*, my boy! Are you sitting down? Ready for this?" he asks, although so obviously going to tell me whether I am ready or not.

I am standing in the hallway of my house, at the bottom of the stairs, the summer evening light streaming through the stained glass panel in the front door and casting coloured patterns on the floor of the entrance hall. I can smell smoke in the air, probably from a neighbour having a barbeque in the back garden. At the top of the stairs I can hear the clock ticking loudly and steadily, one second at a time, and as the Professor speaks, his voice anchors all the information my senses are picking up to that single moment in time. The moment I finally hear, when I will really be going home.

"The DAP array just coughed up the final answer to our calculations…we ran the programme three times, just to be sure, and all the answers came back the same." The Professor carries on. "And it's good news. As soon as I put in your new weight, and took into account the fact that you've been putting on weight in the months since you arrived in this world, we were able to confirm the other events that have already happened. In fact, even more accurately than before, this time to within thirty minutes of each event."

"And?" I ask, impatiently.

"And, the model predicts that the final viable intersection between your world and this, will occur tomorrow evening. Tuesday night."

"Tomorrow night? So soon?"

"What did you expect? Next year? You've not put on that much weight!"

"Okay, so when will it happen? What time?"

"About twenty to eight. Give or take thirty minutes. Twenty to eight! And I'm going to be there with you. I'm coming down to watch it happen. I don't know why I didn't think of it last time…the most important scientific discovery of all time, and I almost missed it."

"You're coming to watch?"

"Why not? I'm going to film it. Imagine, one minute you're there, and the next you're gone. I'll record it. Proof, my boy. Get it all on film. Then show everyone else afterwards what they missed. I tell you my boy, tomorrow night will be the making of both of us. You get to go home, and I'll get the Nobel Prize!"

The Professor continues to speak, but as he waffles on incessantly at the other end of the phone, my mind is already lost in the significance of what he has just said. Tomorrow night? It's too soon!...I need to find Sarah, to meet with her one last time. To explain to her… To hold her in my arms and to make love to her again. And in the same thought I realise that tomorrow night is also the night I am meant to go with Jane to the marriage guidance counsellor to fix our marriage.

"James, *James…*" I hear the Professor demanding attention.

"Yes?"

"So, is that okay then?"

"What? Is '*what*' okay?"

"Are you listening to me? I said, I'll meet you tomorrow night at 6 pm at Waterloo station."

"Where?"

"I don't know. You tell me."

"6 pm. Just outside the 'Bonaparte Pub', on the main concourse. Do you know where it is?"

"No. I don't, but don't worry. I'll find it..."

"Good...I'll see you there then..." I answer vaguely, not paying attention properly as the Professor winds up the conversation and hangs up. Not paying attention because an uneasy feeling is beginning to take over my mind. A feeling that leaves me confused and worried.

For the first time I *seriously* ask myself the question, "*Do I want to go home?*"

Do I?

I mean, *really?*

Then, just as before, I think of Keira and Nicole, and I know the answer is still yes.

I am sitting in the dark in the 'music room', listening to the music from the film "City of Angels", the CD of which I found in HMV last week.

I am relaxed, and my mind begins to race, thinking about tomorrow, and wondering where I will be tomorrow night. What house will I be sleeping in? And with whom?

Then I start to think of Jane, and Allison and poor little Elspeth. Innocent bystanders, the true victims of this whole weird fiasco, who ask for nothing more than to be loved by their father. Something that I cannot do, no matter how much I try. Which is the point, really. Love is given freely. I shouldn't *have* to try.

Jane. What will happen to her? I think about this for a while.

Over the past few months, she has grown a lot stronger, a lot more independent. Whoever I used to be, whoever the person I was before the new me came along, that person, that bastard that I must have been, had a negative effect on Jane. Sucked her dry, made her scared and insecure. Took away her self-confidence and turned her into a mouse.

Now the lioness is back. And if I stay it won't be long before she bites my head off and spits me out. Jane is almost back to the Jane she was. Beautiful, sexy. Someone who will make some man a very lucky husband. But not me.

I don't love Jane. I never will.

Fancy her? Yes, I know I still do. But as Track Nine on the CD begins to play, it is clear to me that the combination of such superficial sexual attraction and guilt is no reason to continue to prolong such a pointless union. The marriage is wrong. It must have worked for a while when we first got married, but then we lost something. Something important.

Now?

The best thing for Jane is to end the marriage. Not to go to marriage counselling. Not to try to save it.

Just to kill it.

She might not see that now, but she will. And she will be grateful for it. So, tomorrow, if I just walk away, take one step through the doors of an underground train, from one world to another, never to come back, it will be one small step for mankind, but one hell of a step for our marriage. A step in the right direction.

And then there's the financial aspect of it all. If I were to never come back at all, perhaps they would be able to claim that I had committed suicide, and my life insurance policy would pay out. Pay off the mortgage, set the kids up for life.

Why do all things always come down to money?

The thought of money makes me think of Pink Floyd and the '*Money*' track on *Dark Side of the Moon*, another good CD for thinking to. I walk over to the CDs stored in the recess beside the fireplace, flick through the CD cases until I find it, and then swap it over on the CD player.

Moving over to the desk by the window, I slide open one of the drawers and take out some paper and a pen.

As I start to write, I realise that I am reaching a point of no return. For a moment I look around the room, and breathe in deeply, gathering my resolve.

There's no going back now.

Tomorrow morning I am going to leave this house. I am not coming back. Even if, for some reason, the Professor is wrong, and there is no final opportunity to cross back to my real life. Even if I am stuck in this life forever. I am going to walk out of here tomorrow and not return. Anyway, this house has never really been mine. More like a guest house, or a hotel. But never my real home. I've never belonged here.

As '*Another Brick in the Wall*' begins to sing out, and with memories of dancing in nightclubs when I was younger surfacing from way-back-when, I put pen to paper.

"*Dear Jane,*

Call me a coward, because maybe that's what I am, but I couldn't face the marriage counsellor tonight. And when you come home this afternoon and find this note, I will have taken a few things and gone away for a while. I need to think, and I need more time. Please don't try to contact me. If you haven't heard from me by the weekend, perhaps it would be good if you start divorce proceedings against me. The house, and everything in it, ...it's yours. And let this note, in my handwriting, as per holograph, constitute a legal testament to that.

Don't be angry with me, Jane. Even you know that the spark has gone, and that it's only a matter of time before you leave me. So, perhaps, I'm just saving us both some time.

You know how much we have meant to each other in the past. I loved you. That will always remain. Always. But people grow, and people change. And who I am now, is not the same person you married, and I know now that I can never be the person you want me to be. And you deserve better.

James."

Short but sweet. I don't know what to say about Elspeth or Allison, so I don't. Which confirms just how much of a coward I really am.

My mobile phone rings. I look at my watch. It's five minutes past midnight.

"Hello?"

A moment's pause, then "…*James*?"

"*Sarah?*" I reply, almost urgently.

"Yes…it's me...I'm sorry for calling so late…I…James, I got the message from Mary. Thanks."

"Sarah, are you okay? Please, *please* forgive me. I had no intention of …"

"James, it's ...it's fine.... I understand. And I got your note. The one you left when I didn't answer the door…"

"Sarah, why did you run away? I came to see you the next day first thing in the morning. I wanted to explain everything to you…"

"You scared me. You *scared* me James. I knew you would probably come the next day, and I had to get away before you got there. I couldn't face you."

"*Why?* Why were you scared? That's the last thing I would want. I love you!"

"Because of what you said, and what happened between us. If you really knew me James, you would know that I'm an independent person. I don't need a man. I don't *want* a man. I've only ever loved one person before, and that was years ago. I get by better without love. I'm just not looking for it. And then one day, WHAM! You appear. From out of the blue. And WHAM again! I fall in love with you…One minute you're not there, and I'm fine, and then a moment later my whole life is different. Upside down. I can't think straight and I start to feel things again. No thanks to you, I've started to come out from under whatever rock I've been hiding myself under for the past five years. I've started to see life again, to touch, and let myself be touched. To let someone get close to me. And the strangest thing of all is that I feel like I've known you for years. *How can that be?*"

"I don't know. Maybe we're just made for each other."

"And then when you speak, you know so much about me. So many things. Too much… And some of the things you know, there's just no way you could know them…no way…" I hear her breathing, fast, excitedly. For a moment I fear that she's going to hang up. Then she speaks again. "In your letter, the one you slipped under the door, you said that you knew how important punctuality was to me, that you knew that I split up with my third boyfriend at university because he stood me up one night. How did you know that? *How*? James, I never told my mother about that? So who told you? I can't remember telling anyone else about it either? James, how do you know me so well? And how do you know where and how and when to kiss me? How do you know what I like and what I hate? How did you know how to turn me on like that? *How?*"

"Sarah. I can't explain. I just do."

"Bullshit James. *Bullshit*! You know. Somehow. And from somewhere. When I think about it, I realise there are only two possibilities: Either you are a weirdo, some mad stalker that I've somehow picked up along the way, or you are someone very, very special, but I need to know which one you are. So tell me how you know all about me!" Another pause. Then, quietly and softly. "*Please…*"

"It's not that simple, Sarah. You wouldn't believe me."

"But I might! What makes you think I won't? What?"

"Sarah, I don't even know if I understand it all myself…"

"Tell me, James. Please."

"And what if I tell you, and then you think I'm mad, and you walk away from me, and I lose you for good?"

"James, I want to believe in you. I want to. But I'm scared, and you have to help me through this. You have to…There's something I want to tell you too. Something that I have to tell you. But something that I can't even mention until I understand what's going on here."

"What do you want to tell me?" I ask, the conversation quickly swinging around to her.

"I can't tell you yet. *Not until I know the answer to my questions!*"

"Okay. So, where are you now? In Spain?"

"No. I'm in Ironbridge. With Mary."

"Ironbridge? I thought you said you were going back to Spain…"

"No, I didn't. You assumed I was, and I let you. I didn't go to Spain. When I left Richmond, I came up here. I was here when you called the other day. Listening in the background. Wanting to speak to you, but too scared. Too insecure."

Neither of us speak. The clock ticks at the top of my stairs, and outside in the street, I can hear a fox screaming.

"James, I have to see you again."

I'm about to reply, about to tell her just how much I need to see her too, when I realise that there is no time. Tomorrow I'm going home. Tomorrow night!

"Sarah. I have to see you too, but if we are going to do this, we have to do it tomorrow afternoon. And unfortunately I can't come to you. Which means that you have to get on a train and come down here. Can you?"

"Yes. I want to. But only if you promise that you will tell me everything. And I mean *everything*. You need to be completely honest with me. About everything."

A moment, then the inevitable.

"I promise. I will. So when can you be here?"

"If I leave at lunchtime, I can be there at four. Where do you want to meet?"

"What about on the bridge crossing from the South Bank at Waterloo to the Embankment. The side nearest Big Ben?"

"Okay. At four?"

"I'll be there."

Silence. Neither of us want to hang up.

"Sarah?..."

"Yes?"

"I love you... I always have."

Silence.

"Tomorrow at four...and don't get stuck in a lift!"

Click.

For a few moments I sit in silence, an explosive bag of emotions each of which fights the other to become dominant. Excitement about going home and seeing my family again, going home to the life I used to lead, my children, my old friends. Excitement about seeing Sarah tomorrow. Sadness about what I'm just about to do to Jane, and little Elspeth and Allison. Regrets about having to leave my new life behind. And fear. Fear that it will all go wrong. Fear that what I am about to do, may in fact, be a mistake.

And with that thought, I shake myself back to reality, find an envelope into which I fold the letter for Jane, and then prop it up against a glass on the island in the kitchen.

Then I go upstairs and pack.

CHAPTER 52
D-Day

I awake to an empty, sad, house.

My two suitcases are already waiting for me in the hallway outside my bedroom, and after showering, shaving and dressing, I pick them up and walk quickly down the stairs and out of the door, not stopping to look around or give myself time to change my mind. I leave the car in the garage. My dream car. The car I have always wanted to own. But where I'm going I can't take it with me, so I might as well leave it where it is. Where I first found it.

As I stand at the bus stop, waiting for the next K3 bus, I picture the solitary white envelope addressed to Jane, now propped up in the kitchen and waiting patiently for her to come through the door. A single page of writing that for Jane will cause so much anger, confusion and heartache. As I picture her walking through the front door, the two little girls running in behind her, shouting and laughing, I imagine her looking on through to the kitchen where she sees the letter waiting. I see her walk slowly towards the island, reaching out to pick it up. I blink and swallow hard.

I did not plan it this way. To be the cause of so much hurt, so much destruction. So much pain.

A few minutes later, the *K3* swings around the corner, and I pay the two Euros and climb aboard, dragging my cases along with me. In Surbiton I catch the train into Waterloo, and find a left-luggage locker where I abandon my suitcases.

If all goes well, I will never see them again. And if not, I'll be picking them up again this evening, before I find a hotel somewhere.

Leaving the station I walk aimlessly towards the river. What should I do with the rest of the day? Should I bother going into the office? I mean, if today is the end of it all, is there really any point? On the other hand, if the Professor is wrong again, there is a lot to be done. Things I shouldn't ignore…

By ten o'clock, I'm sitting at my desk. And by 10.15 I have almost forgotten the turmoil in the rest of my life. I close the door, and lose myself in my work. And it feels good. Very good.

After lunch, though, I begin to think more practically, and I write several letters. One to Richard. And one to Tracy, my new PA who has tried so hard in the past months. And succeeded. She has been a wonder.

I put the letters inside another bigger envelope and hand them to Alice on the way out.

"Give this to Tracy tomorrow afternoon if I forget to take them back from you by lunchtime…"

She looks at me with a question in her eyes, sensing something.

Looking back at her, I finally give into the temptation that has been plaguing me for the past ten months, and I bend forward and kiss Alice softly but firmly on the lips.

She does not complain.

I smile and walk out the door. Leaving my new exciting and successful career in advertising behind me.

At least, for now…

The bridge above the Thames is thronging with tourists, and I weave my way through them looking for Sarah, my heart beating fast, my resolve weakening, the questions beginning to surface again.

She is nowhere to be seen. I look anxiously from face to face, scanning all the women as they stream past, scared that I may miss her, worried that she may miss me. Petrified that she has not come.

I stand in the centre of the bridge, checking my watch, my head playing ping-pong looking from one end of the bridge to the other. It's four thirty, and she is not here.

Turning and leaning against the fence, I look out across the river and wonder when I next see this view, where I will be and who I will be with?

"James?" I hear a voice, slightly breathless, calling my name from behind.

I turn, and Sarah is running towards me. She comes to a stop just in front of me, and we stare at each other silently, looking deep into each other. She moves towards me, then hesitates, and then suddenly she is in my arms. And there are tears. Lots of tears.

"I'm sorry, " I say, holding her hand across the table, sitting in a quiet corner tucked away at the back of the wine bar.

"And so am I." She responds. "But please, before we start to talk, James, you have to tell me what this is all about. There's something more going on here that I can't understand. Something strange. And you know what it is…Don't you?"

I look away, avoiding her gaze. This is the moment of truth.

"Come on, James. You promised. You have to tell me how you know so much about me. And *honestly*. Don't lie. How did you know about all those things?"

"Sarah, there's a lot I know about you. An awful lot. More than you could possibly ever believe." I start down the inevitable path, the path that I know I have to tread if Sarah is ever to trust me, to love me, to accept me in this life. "I know, for example, that you are allergic to wheat, that you hate snails, ever since you stood on one in the garden when you were a little girl and you broke its little shell. You carried it into your house, and showed it to your dad, crying your little heart out. Your father told you that it was dead, and that you had killed it. You locked yourself in your room, and wouldn't come out all day. Not until the ice-cream van came up the street, and you ran out of the room crying but asking for a big ice-cream cone."

I look at her face, and see the amazement in her eyes.

"I know that the first boy you kissed was called Derek. And he gave you his best glass marble for the privilege. You were only seven or eight."

"Eight", she volunteers, laughing.

"And when you went to university, you broke your leg in a skiing accident in your first year. You're also allergic to oranges, hate avocado, love Elton John etc. etc. etc. Sarah, I don't just know a lot about you, I know *everything* about you."

"But how?" she pleads, squeezing my hand with both of hers. "Tell me!"

"And if you don't believe me?"

"Why shouldn't I? I'm still here aren't I. I came. I want to be with you James. I really do. But tell me, now… please…" The 'please' almost a whisper that floats on the air, and hangs between us.

"Okay, I will. But you must promise to listen till the end, and stay calm. No matter what you think, just hang on in there. It's all true. So just think to yourself, how else would I know so much about you if it wasn't! Okay?"

She nods.

"Good. I want to tell you a story Sarah. A true story. About a man that wakes up one day, and has the weirdest day of his entire life. A man who, when he wakes up in the morning, is married to a beautiful wife, and has two wonderful children, two little girls called Keira and Nicole, and who live, together, in a small house in Surbiton…"

And so I begin.

I watch her eyes and study the expressions on her face as I tell the story.

She grimaces when I tell her about Jane, perhaps a touch of jealousy, or maybe even a show of sympathy for me, that after all the lust and the longing for her, that she turned out not to be what I expected, or perhaps it was even a grimace of anger, that I had almost been unfaithful to Sarah, her other self, and that I had effectively gone from her to Jane.

She smiles when I tell her about my decision to find her in this world, at all costs, and how my father supported me on this. I see sadness in her eyes when I tell her how I visited her father in Norwich, and found him in such a sorry state. I sense regret there, and move quickly on.

When I tell her about visiting her college and school she laughs, recalling with me her memories of the battle-axes I encountered there.

When I tell her about the visit to the Transport Museum, she looks very serious, puzzled by the explanation I give her of what I found out and my discovery that the two worlds I know share a common past, which at some point diverged and went their own separate ways following different timelines.

When I come to tell her about the death of my father, she squeezes my hand in support and sympathy, but she smiles when I explain to her how through his funeral I finally found her.

I leave the story of my encounters with the Professor until the very end, telling her first about the few times when the portal back to my world opened up again, and how I couldn't cross through even though I wanted to. Then I mention my visits to the Professor and his explanations for what was happening to me.

As I come to the end of my story, I glance at my watch, suddenly very conscious of the time. It's 5.30 pm. I have to leave soon…And then I realise I haven't told her, perhaps the most important part, that the final opportunity to cross over to my other life is only hours away. Which means that I will soon have to leave her, perhaps for good.

My story finished, her silence begins to make me very uncomfortable. Her face is now expressionless. I don't speak, choosing rather to let the next move come from her. In her own time. Which it eventually does…

"It's a good story, James. But how does it relate to us?" she asks, quietly.

"It's not a story, Sarah. It's the truth. That's how I know so much about you. How I came to find you. How we ended up here today."

Slowly, I notice a red colour beginning to fill her face, from the neck upwards, her features beginning to flush.

This doesn't look good…

"James, you can't seriously believe this happened to you?"

"Yes, Sarah, it did. It is true. Unbelievable as though it may seem…"

"Come on, you can't be serious…I mean,…you don't *really* expect me to believe this do you?"

"Sarah, I told you it was hard to swallow. But if you can't believe me, please just accept the reasons why I had to try so hard to find you, and why I know so much about you. I'm not some madman, or some crazed psychotic stalker. I'm your husband, Sarah. *Your husband!*"

She pulls her hand away from me, and gives a shallow laugh.

"That's a bit hard to swallow. My husband? Please, don't push this James. I can accept the fact that maybe you are still suffering from concussion, that you might need some help, or that..."

"Sarah," I say to stop her, reaching out across the table, encircling one of her hands with both of mine, "Sarah. It *is* true. I swear to you... And it's really important to me for you to realise that I have been completely honest with you. I haven't told Jane anything about this. Only you. Apart from my dad, and the Professor, you're the only other person I've mentioned this to. I needed you to know before I make the final crossing tonight. I had to tell you before I go back to my world..."

"WHAT!?" she shouts, standing up in front of me and causing a few people around us to look over. "Going home tonight? *Leaving me*? What the hell are you talking about James? I've come all the way here to see you and you tell me all this, which, incidentally, just sounds like some pathetic excuse to cover your ass so that you don't have to see me anymore!"

"Sarah...it's true! God knows it's true. I promise you. And it's not an excuse. I'm meeting the Professor here in London in thirty minutes from now. According to his computer, tonight will be the last time for me to cross back to my real life. Which means that sometime tonight, down there on the Jubilee Line, time is going to slow down, the world is going to stop, and I'm going to step from this world back to mine. It's my last chance to be with you and the kids. To get back our life together. To be happy with you for the rest of my life... For the rest of *our* lives!"

"STOP IT JAMES! Just STOP IT!" she screams, pulling back from me, both hands flying to the top of her head and tugging at the roots of her hair. "You're talking rubbish! What about me? I'm *here*! Not there, somewhere else, or wherever the hell else I'm meant to be. I'm here James, in *this* world. Here with you. *Your* world, James. *This* is your world! Not in some dream or fantasy elsewhere... Why do you want to run away from me?" She starts to cry. "It's rubbish, all rubbish..."

I look up at her, studying her face and I realise that I have no choice now but to break a solemn promise I made to Sarah a long time ago. The promise not to ever repeat now, what I'm just about to say.

Still sitting, I speak calmly and quietly, so that the other people in the restaurant can't hear me.

"Sarah, it's not rubbish, and I'll prove it. In the other world, my world, you told me something that you have never told another human being in your life. Something that you never even told your parents. Something that you told me one night when we were lying in bed together, and just after you had told me that you were pregnant with Keira. You told me then, that when you were at university, you fell pregnant to your second boyfriend. That's why Mike really split up with you. He wasn't ready to become a father. Then after four weeks you had a miscarriage. Mike knew, but, apart from him, I'm the only other person..."

Her face has turned an ashen white, her eyes now lifeless and devoid of all emotion. Her lips begin to quiver, and for a second I think that perhaps she is going to speak.

Then, without warning, she turns, walks away, and leaves through the nearest door.

In the blink of an eye, she is gone.

For a few moments I seem to lose all power of thought. I am dumb with confusion. I remain seated, just sitting there, unable to think or act. Just staring at the door she just walked through.

So what should I do? Chase after her?

What for? I have to leave now. In fact, I'm already late, and I have to be in Waterloo in five minutes time.

Or maybe I should go after her to explain.

But explain what?

And if I do manage to calm her down, what then?

Even if I do, I will have to leave her straight afterwards if I'm not going to miss the Professor, and then in less than thirty minutes, I will probably be riding around on the Jubilee Line, watching, and waiting, ready to leave this world for ever.

No. Now she knows the truth, perhaps it's better this way.

So I let her go.

The Professor waves at me as I walk towards him, a large camera bag hanging from one shoulder, and a very large video camera clasped tightly in his other hand.

"Excited, my boy?" He asks me as he grabs my outstretched hand and shakes it wildly. "Must admit, I've not been this excited since old Higgs received his Nobel Prize! This is going to be incredible, my boy. Incredible!"

Except I don't feel excited. Instead, I feel strangely disappointed, a little lost, and quite sad. The thought of how much I have just upset Sarah, and the memory of her walking out on me, never for me to see her again, at least, never to see this version of her again, has brought me right down. I feel hollow...

As we turn to walk into Bonaparte's for a quick drink, he pats me on the back and I feel like a schoolboy just about to run a race, with my coach urging me to go on and show the rest of them just what I'm really made of.

What he doesn't know though is that I'm actually a schoolboy who is having doubts about whether or not he wants to run the race at all.

When the Professor asks me what I want to drink, and I reply "A London Pride please", I answer automatically, and my voice is distant and detached.

"Come, my boy. Let's sit down." The old man ushers me into the corner at the back of the pub.

"So what is it?" he asks. "What's the matter? Nervous? Worried? Are you scared?"

"What makes you think there's something wrong?" I ask, avoiding the answer.

"It's written all over your face. All over your face…Something is the matter, no?" he asks, his own enthusiasm beginning to quieten a little.

"I've just seen Sarah. She came back to London to meet me."

"And?"

"And I told her everything."

"So, that is good, no?"

"Not it is not. She's thinks that I'm a madman. She got really upset and stormed out. She walked out on me. Gone."

"So, I am sorry. But in a few hours you will be back with her, for good. Together again, with both of your little children. *What are their names*?"

"Keira and Nicole. I know, you're right, and don't get me wrong, I *am* excited about going home, but…"

"But what, my boy. But what?"

I turn and look past the people in the bar, outside onto the busy concourse of Waterloo. So many busy people living their own little lives. Just like in my other world, so many people, running around like ants. Each with their own set of individual problems. Everyone with a different story. Each person different, but everyone the same.

"To tell you the truth, Professor, I don't know. I just don't know. For the past week I've actually begun to ask myself *where* my real life is now. Here or there? Where do I really belong? Where?"

"Listen, James. You miss Sarah. You want to be with her. You are confused because you just saw her, and she was upset, and being a little sad just now is understandable, because instead of running to hold her in your arms and telling her that everything is going to be just fine, you have just walked away from each other. But only because, you *know* that soon you will be back with her *permanently*. And don't forget the children! They are waiting for you to come home, James. They need you. Your life is there, not here."

"I hope you are right. I mean, I *know* you are right, it's just that…"

"A few hours, James." He interrupts me. "A few hours and this will all be over. I promise you."

"I suppose you're right." I say. Not completely convinced. "So, what's the plan then?" I shake my head and smile, trying to sound a little more upbeat.

"Well," he replies. "It's six thirty now. According to *Henry*, the predicted time for intersect is seven-forty pm but the anomaly could really happen any time between seven fifteen and about ten past eight. So, to be sure I think we should finish up here, and then make our way down to the tube. We should find a place, probably on the last carriage, where it's not busy, and then we should ride back and forward between here and Hyde Park, maybe even go south a little, as far as the station you originally stepped out onto, on your first day here?"

"Lewisham North."

"Yes, Lewisham North. I remember now. The important thing is we must ensure a clear exit path for you, with no one in our way at any time, so that you can get clear access to the doors when it happens, and so that I can film it all happening."

"But Professor, don't forget that when it starts, time starts to slow down and you will become immobile, like everyone else. You won't be able to film me at all. I might not even get a chance to warn you when I see it begin to happen. Once it really starts, as far as you are concerned, one moment I'll be there, and the next I will be gone!"

"I know, my boy, I know. And I have thought of that. So long as I have the film running at each station and the camera pointed at the doors at all times, then everything will be okay. The camera I have here is a very special one. I borrowed it from the Biology department. It takes two hundred frames a second, and if anything happens, no matter how fast it is relative to myself, the camera will pick up something. So, whatever you do, just wave to the camera before you go, will you? I'll see it later, when I play it back in the lab."

Gathering our things together, we get up and leave the pub, making our way down to the Jubilee Line. We're just about to get on the escalator when my phone rings.

I reach inside my jacket, pulling it out quickly and automatically hitting the little green phone button. Please, god, please let it be Sarah!

"Hello?" I blurt out.

"James…? Oh, James, thank God I got you!! *Please*, it's Jane, I *need* to talk to you. I got your letter. *Please come home*, please? Don't just walk out this way. It won't solve anything…"

Shit.

I pull the phone away from my ear and look at it, as if it will somehow tell me the answer I need to know. And then, without saying another word, I switch the phone off, and put it back into my pocket.

The Professor looks at me, quizzically.

"That was Jane."

He grimaces, then looks away. He knows not to ask.

Wonderful. In the past hour I have managed to completely alienate and destroy two of the most important women in my life. How fantastic. I have *truly* excelled in my ability to become a *complete* and *utter* bastard. I am officially a git. A wonderful, selfish, git.

"Let's do this thing," I say, hurrying past the Professor on the escalator. "I've got nothing left in this world to stay for now anyway. I might as well go home."

CHAPTER 53
Time waits for no man.

The first train comes, and we climb aboard the last carriage. It's almost empty, and we sit down beside the last set of doors on the train, the Professor sitting opposite me.

The Professor gets out the video camera, and attaches it to a portable tripod he pulls out of his bag, adjusting its position and training it on me and the doorway. He tightens up the legs, and tests it for rigidity. It's good.

By the time we get to Marble Arch, we are all ready. I get up out of my seat and stand beside the door.

"So," the Professor says, his voice now serious and all scientific,"...the moment you begin to feel anything happening, you must let me know immediately. Now, every time the train starts to slow down as we come into a station, I will switch the camera on, and when we leave I will switch it off. That way I will save film. We could be here for a long time, and this camera eats up film. I only have four spare cassettes with me."

"No problem," I reply, looking at the doors.

We ride the train all the way up to five stations past Green Park, and nothing has happened. So the Professor lifts up the camera and its stand, and we get off the train and walk across the platform, getting onto the train opposite which is waiting to begin its run back down southwards underneath London.

All the time my mind is flooding full of thoughts, and my body is awash with emotions. I can't stop thinking about Sarah, and her face fills my mind. I think of the last year I have spent working at Cohen's, and the achievements I have made there. I think of the people I will let down, and the projects that may fail when I leave. The face of Stu Roberts fills my mind. A friend to whom I made a personal promise. A promise which will become a lie.

"*Judas*". A voice inside shouts to myself again.

I blink and shake my head, and my thoughts turn instead to my father, now dead, and then to the mother I will leave behind. And then I think of my children, my wife, and my old job at *Kitte-Kat.* What will I do for a living when I get home? It's one thing to decide to switch career, but how will I actually go about starting to get a job in advertising? It dawns on me then, just how difficult it will be for us all when I get back. I know that there's no way I'm going to return to my old job. Not now. But to get a start in the world of advertising I will have to start at the bottom, and realistically what chance will I have of getting a decent opening at my age? And then that horrible thought again, where I wonder what I will do, if after going to so much trouble to get home, I find that Sarah has got over me, or never wants to talk to me again. After all, I did just vanish without a trace for a year. And what if she's now married to someone else?

What happens if I get back to my old life, and I find that I have no life there at all?

Of course, all of these are *'what if's?'*. A man can worry himself to death by always going, "*What if this?*" or "*What if that?*". The proper response to all of them, is "*What if none of them happens at all? What if there are no 'What if's?'*

What if it is just Sarah, and Nicole, and Keira, and they are all waiting for me, needing me, desperate to see me again?

As we approach Green Park, I start to get nervous. The moment of truth could be near. At any second, I could have that feeling on my neck, that weird sensation in my mind as the wheels of time come to a grinding halt, and the doors back to my world open up.

Any moment now.

Yet in spite of the anticipation, nothing happens.

So we ride the train down to the end of the southbound line, get off and head back again.

"What time do you make it?" I ask the Professor, looking at my own watch.

"Twenty five to eight. It's almost time James. Almost time. Are you ready?"

"I don't know. I think so." I reply, unconvincingly.

"And what if it doesn't happen? What if..." but when I hear myself starting with the *'what if's'* again, I shut up, and turn back to the door.

"Relax, my boy. It will happen. And soon." The Professor says as he gets up from his seat and crosses over to me, holding out his hand. "James, if Old Henry is right, it's going to be any moment now. Any moment. We might not get a chance to say much more to each other, so I just wanted to say 'Thank you,' and 'Good luck' to you!"

I take his hand and shake it warmly, but pull my hand quickly free again, remembering the experience with Jane when time stopped with her hands wrapped around me, and me being unable to break free.

"What have you got to thank me for?" I ask, facing the doors again, and watching the signs on the tunnel wall appear as we begin to pull into Waterloo.

"For all of this. It's been fun. Exciting. And if it happens, I will at last have made the discovery of a lifetime. You will have given me something which I can spend the rest of my life working on. To theorise about and try to understand. Can you imagine how jealous all the other old eggheads are going to be?"

I can't help but smile back. At least there will have been some purpose to all this misery.

We ride in silence now, the stations outside, whooshing past, arriving, and whooshing away again. Anticipation, nervousness, disappointment, relief, regret, a cycle of circling emotions that spins around within me as we shoot along the deep underground tunnels, from light, to blackness, and back into the light again.

Quarter to eight.

Tunnels, stations, tunnels, stations.

Five to eight.

Tunnels, doors open, doors close, move, stop, doors open, doors close, accelerate, decelerate, tunnels, blackness, people getting on, getting off.

Eight o'clock.

Nothing.

Two stations past Marble Arch, we get off and head south again.

Both the Professor and I are looking worriedly at our watches. It's ten past eight. It's not looking good.

Neither of us speaks.

Green Park. Charing Cross. Then Waterloo arrives.

Then Lambeth East. Alworth Street. Then New Cross Gate North.

New Cross Gate North. The sign conjures up the sudden memory of the first time I saw those words, that sign, almost a year ago. I remember the feeling of rising panic that I experienced as I realised for the first time that something very wrong had happened. And then, in a moment of surprising clarity, I remember, clear as day, the vision of Keira and Nicole waving to me as I walked out of our house that morning for the last time. The last time I saw them...

A tear runs slowly down my cheek, and I step up closer to the door.

Suddenly I begin to feel something…It's going to happen soon. I can sense it. At the next station. And in an odd way, it makes perfect sense. This is where it began, and this is where it will end. At Lewisham North.

The doors close and the train begins to pull away into the next tunnel.

"*James! James!*" I hear a voice. It's Sarah, calling to me from my memory. Reaching out to me. Encouraging me to do what I have to do. To take that one step towards her.

A funny tingling sensation begins to work its way up my back, and I recognise the beginning of the feelings that I have been awaiting for so long. My heart starts to beat even faster and I take a step closer towards the doors.

"James!" The voice again. This time louder. Now closer. I close my eyes, trying to conjure her up in my mind.

"James...*Stop,* wait!" she shouts. "DON'T DO IT!"

I open my eyes. The voice is not coming from within inside my head. It's here. Close by, beside me, ...inside the train carriage.

I turn to see Sarah running down the carriage towards me, the door connecting the other carriage from where she has just come swinging shut behind her, tears streaming down her red, sad, face. She is about ten metres away from me now, hurrying towards me, dodging in and out of the few people who are between her and me, separating us.

"I believe you!" She shouts. "I BELIEVE YOU! I've been looking for you for hours. Searching every train on the Jubilee Line, one train after another, carriage by carriage,... trying to find you. *I have to tell you something...*"

The tingling sensation on my back has now reached my head, and I am beginning to feel a little bit light headed. I sway to my right, and nod to the Professor just as the train begins to slow down, light flooding into the carriages again from the new station outside.

Lewisham North.

The doors are opening now, and Sarah is beside me, grabbing hold of me. Kissing me.

"JAMES, DON'T DO IT! PLEASE..."

Dizzy. I am dizzy. This is it. It's going to happen. I can feel it. Stronger this time than any of the times before.

...It's starting...

I look up at the sign on the wall, and push myself gently but firmly away from Sarah.

"Sarah, please. Don't hold on to me..."

"James, don't go. Don't go. Jamesssss, III'mmmmmmm..."

But already it has begun to happen, and the 'Lewisham North' sign on the wall has begun to shimmer, to fade and blink in and out, and dimly I hear Sarah's speech beginning to slur, the word '*I'm*' getting deeper and deeper as time begins to slow, and like the Doppler effect, her beautiful female voice becomes more like a man's.

I step away from her, the tube doors immediately in front of me, open, ready, clear, the final word in Sarah's sentence grinding to a halt, the last letters stretching out, incoherently, the meaning of the word almost frozen into the air between us.

"...*ppprrrrreeeeeegggggggggnnnnnnnnnnnnnnnnnnnnnnnnnnnnnnnnnnnnnn*........"

.

And then, in an instant there is perfect quiet around me. Time has stopped, and Sarah is lifeless, a wax dummy, her eyes glazed and dull, her lips, solid and motionless...and perfect..., her hands reaching out to me, a single, solitary tear caught frozen on the side of her cheek and sparkling brightly in the light.

Now. *Now* is the time. I must go. I must make the jump. My final chance to go home is here, just as the Professor promised. I must do it NOW!

I step towards the open door, the sign on the tunnel wall beyond, now reading Canary Wharf.

Canary Wharf!

I lift my foot to make the step, to step off the train, to cross from this world back to my own, from this life back to my real life. To my real family.

"*James, I'm pregnant!*"

Sarah's final words come rushing together in my mind, my subconscious speeding up the long drawn out syllables and sounds, and replaying them back inside my brain at normal speed.

"James, I'm pregnant!"

My body freezes halfway through the door, paralysed by the revelation, and I am left standing at the crossroads between my two lives.

Sarah is pregnant!

PREGNANT!

Ohhhh, ...sssssssshiiiiiitttttttt!

At the threshold between my two worlds, between the two women that I love, ...I hesitate.

What to do? *What to do?*

Quick man, move. Don't stop. Don't wait. Go now! Go. NOW!

GO. GO. GOOOO!!!!!!!

Another moment of hesitation. And then the voice within me again, shouting at me, my heart pounding in my chest, my eardrums pulsing with the blood pumping in my head.

Go MAN, GO! *Before it's too late...*

I turn a little, glancing quickly at Sarah, my eyes running from her face down her body to her stomach. Her *womb.* The womb where she will nurture the third child she will bear for me. My *third* child!

A realisation dawns on me now, a sudden understanding, and my heart quickens…

Sarah will bear for me in this life, the child that she could not give me in the other! Our third child together.

And then another thought. One that shakes me to the core…

What if it's a son?

A son!

What if he's the boy I have always yearned for?

What if he's my son… Peter!?

And then another: *What if something happens during the pregnancy, …like before…? Can I go through all that pain again? ...What if I stay in this world, and then the baby does not survive...?*

But what if he *does* survive?...

What if…?

How do I make a decision? How do I balance one life against another? My family in the other world, versus my future family in this one... How do I chose?

I look back through the doorway and glance into the other world beyond.

I see a woman walking along the station platform, away from me, her back turned, two little girls in tow. Two little girls, beautiful girls, just like Keira and Nicole. Laughing. Happy. Their father nowhere in sight.

The elder one…*Keira? ...Is it truly Keira???*…looks over her shoulder and for a moment our eyes meet. We stare at each other for a second in time that seems to stretch itself out and stop, and in that instant something is exchanged between us.

Then she smiles.

And in this moment of absolute clarity, I know what to do.

I close my eyes, block out the *'What If's?'* that have brought me to the brink of destruction and taken me from one world to another, and take one simple step.

I take a step away from one world, towards the other. Into my future.

And when the doors close a few seconds later, I am home.

In the world I belong.

The End

QUESTIONS FOR YOUR BOOK CLUB

'London 2012: What If?' is an ideal novel for book clubs to debate and discuss: it touches upon many themes, and raises many questions. Readers are affected by the story in many different ways, depending upon their individual life experiences.

If you have enjoyed 'London 2012: What If?' the following are a list of questions or themes that you might want to debate or discuss within your book club. There are no correct or incorrect answers, but if you do come to any conclusions and would like to share them with the author, please email him your thoughts and book club's conclusions at **iancpirvine@hotmail.co.uk**.

Q1: What happened at the end of the book? -"I take a step away from one world, towards the other."- In which direction did James step?

Q2: By the end of the story, which world was James's real world?

Q3: Where should James's priorities lie: with his existing family and two daughters, or with his as yet unborn son?

Q4: Given that the scenario of London 2012 is possible, does sleeping with Sarah in the new world constitute being unfaithful to Sarah in the other world?

Q5: What should James have done? Should he have stayed, or should he have made 'the Jump?'

Q6: What would you have done, if you had been in his shoes and you had to make that choice?

Q7: We all dream of other lives. Is that healthy?

Q8: Both worlds shared a common past. What year did the two worlds diverge in? Can you work it out?

Q9: What do you think happened to the James in the old world? Where did he go...?

Q10: If you were Sarah, in the old world, and James disappeared for a year, and then suddenly turned up again, would you take him back?

Q11: Do you think that parallel worlds exist?

ABOUT THE AUTHOR

Ian Irvine was brought up in Scotland, and studied Physics for far too many years, before travelling the world working for high-technology companies. Ian has spent a career helping build the internet and delivering its benefits to users throughout the world,...as well as helping to bring up a family. Ian enjoys writing, painting and composing in his spare time. His particular joy is found in taking scientific fact and creating a thrilling story around it in such a way that readers learn science whilst enjoying the thrill of the ride. It is Ian's hope that everyone who reads an Ian C.P. Irvine novel will come away learning something interesting that they would never otherwise have found an interest in. Never Science fiction. Always science fact. With a twist.

Other Books by Ian C.P. Irvine

The Crown of Thorns : a student at Oxford University has an idea for his doctor's thesis which fulfils not only the criteria for 'originality', but goes far beyond it. For if Jason Dyke is right, his idea will soon change the world and shift the delicate balance of power from one nation to another.

Jason's idea is simple: In the genetics laboratory at Oxford University, he will clone Jesus Christ.

But when the CIA finds out about his plan, the President of America realises that if the UK succeeds, the balance of power will shift from the USA to Europe. And he realises that the only way to stop this happening is for America to create its very own clone of Jesus Christ.

The race is on...

Whoever reads this book will never forget it. And they will ask one of two questions:-

1: Is it really possible?

2: When will it happen?

The Orlando File is a fast paced thriller, based upon the latest state-of-the-art discoveries in genetics and stem-cell research. The result is a truly scientific adventure but with a thrilling twist.

When Kerrin Graham, a retired cop and now an investigative journalist with the Washington Post, receives a call in the middle of the night, his life is about to be turned upside down.

Six of the world's leading geneticists have all 'committed suicide' in the past seven days, his brother-in-law being the latest to die. Establishing that those who died were all employees of the Gen8tyx Company, a secretive research company based in Orlando, Kerrin sets out to discover the truth behind their deaths.

Discovering that those who died were killed to stop them unveiling the results of their revolutionary stem-cell research, a discovery that could usher in a new age of hope and health for all humanity, Kerrin vows to find who was responsible for their deaths and to uncover the powerful secret they were killed to protect.

On a trail that takes him around the world and back, Kerrin uncovers a sinister organisation that will stop at nothing to protect the secret behind the mysterious 'Orlando Treatment'.

When those around him start to die, and his wife disappears, it becomes a race against time to find the missing 'Orlando File', the only hope of saving his crippled wife and proving to an unsuspecting world, the truth behind the sinister Chymera Corporation of America.

And yet, when Kerrin eventually understands just what the Orlando File contains, he is faced with a choice no man should ever have to make, and everyone who reads this book must ask the same question:
"What would I do, if I were him?"

As with both 'The Crown of Thorns' and 'London 2012 : What If?', at the end of the book the reader is left thinking...and different readers may take away different views on how the novels did, or should have ended... It is hoped that in this way, the novels will make themselves ideal subjects for reading clubs or book clubs.

'Marrying Slovakia' is a romantic medical thriller that takes place in London, UK in the year 2005. Marrying Slovakia is a story about relationships, and how without trust, love cannot survive. Perhaps one of the first novels to tell this story from the eyes of a man, it will make you laugh, cry, and stop and think.

For men and women alike, it is a tale of the heart, in the form of a romantic thriller that is set against the backdrop of the terrorist attacks in London in 2005. It is a tale of our time. A tale of love between West and East. Unlike the other very fast paced thrillers Ian has written, Marrying Slovakia deliberately starts more slowly, builds steadily, then speeds on to an unexpected conclusion.

Ian hopes that if you honour him by spending your time reading one his novels, that you will find it a positive experience, and enjoy it. He also invites you to email him and let him know if you did or did not enjoy the novel. And if you did, what were your favourite parts?

iancpirvine@hotmail.co.uk

To keep up to date with other news, events and ebook releases, please visit the website at:

www.iancpirvine.com.

To connect with Ian C.P.Irvine on Twitter, connect with Ian at

@IanCPIrvine

21881495R00197

Printed in Great Britain
by Amazon